# JOHN
## DICKSON
# CARR

## FELL AND FOUL PLAY

# THE BOOKS OF JOHN DICKSON CARR

It Walks by Night, 1930
The Lost Gallows, 1931
Castle Skull, 1931
The Corpse in the Waxworks, 1932
Poison in Jest, 1932
Hag's Nook, 1933
The Mad Hatter Mystery, 1933
The Eight of Swords, 1934
The Blind Barber, 1934
Death-Watch, 1935
The Three Coffins, 1935
The Arabian Nights Murder, 1936
The Murder of Sir Edmund Godfrey, 1936
The Burning Court, 1937
The Four False Weapons, 1937
To Wake the Dead, 1937
The Crooked Hinge, 1938
The Problem of the Green Capsule, 1939
The Problem of the Wire Cage, 1939
The Man Who Could Not Shudder, 1940
The Case of the Constant Suicides, 1941
Death Turns the Tables, 1941
The Emperor's Snuff-Box, 1942
Till Death Do Us Part, 1944
He Who Whispers, 1946
The Sleeping Sphinx, 1947
The Life of Sir Arthur Conan Doyle, 1949
Below Suspicion, 1949
The Bride of Newgate, 1950
The Devil in Velvet, 1951
The 9 Wrong Answers, 1952
Captain Cut-Throat, 1955
Patrick Butler for the Defence, 1956
Fire, Burn!, 1957
The Dead Man's Knock, 1958
Scandal at High Chimneys, 1959
In Spite of Thunder, 1960
The Witch of the Low-Tide, 1961
The Demoniacs, 1962

The Grandest Game in the World, 1963 (limited-edition
pamphlet)
Most Secret, 1964
The House at Satan's Elbow, 1965
Panic in Box C, 1966
Dark of the Moon, 1967
Papa La-Bas, 1968
The Ghosts' High Noon, 1969
Deadly Hall, 1971
The Hungry Goblin, 1972
Crime on the Coast, 1984 (by Carr and others)

## WRITING AS CARTER DICKSON
The Plague Court Murders, 1934
The White Priory Murders, 1934
The Red Widow Murders, 1935
The Unicorn Murders, 1935
The Punch and Judy Murders, 1936
The Peacock Feather Murders, 1937
The Third Bullet, 1937
The Judas Window, 1938
Death in Five Boxes, 1938
The Reader Is Warned, 1939
Fatal Descent, 1939 (with John Rhode)
And So to Murder, 1940
Nine—and Death Makes Ten, 1940
Seeing Is Believing, 1941
The Gilded Man, 1942
She Died a Lady, 1943
He Wouldn't Kill Patience, 1944
The Curse of the Bronze Lamp, 1945
My Late Wives, 1946
The Skeleton in the Clock, 1948
A Graveyard to Let, 1949
Night at the Mocking Widow, 1950
Behind the Crimson Blind, 1952
The Cavalier's Cup, 1953
Fear Is the Same, 1956

## WRITING AS CARR DICKSON
The Bowstring Murders, 1933

WRITING AS ROGER FAIRBAIRN
Devil Kinsmere, 1934


SHORT-STORY AND RADIO-PLAY COLLECTIONS
The Department of Queer Complaints, 1940 (as by Carter
Dickson)
Dr. Fell, Detective, and Other Stories, 1947
The Exploits of Sherlock Holmes, 1954 (with Adrian
Conan Doyle)
The Third Bullet and Other Stories, 1954
The Men Who Explained Miracles, 1963
The Door to Doom and Other Detections, 1980
The Dead Sleep Lightly, 1983
Fell and Foul Play, 1990

# JOHN DICKSON CARR

## FELL AND FOUL PLAY

EDITED WITH AN INTRODUCTION BY DOUGLAS G. GREENE

LIBRARY OF CRIME CLASSICS®

MISTER E'S™

INTERNATIONAL POLYGONICS, LTD.
NEW YORK CITY

**FELL AND FOUL PLAY**

Copyright © 1991 by Clarice M. Carr, Bonita Cron, Julia McNiven, and Mary B. Howes.
Introductions copyright © 1991 by Douglas G. Greene

**Library of Congress Cataloging-in-Publication Data**

Carr, John Dickson, 1906–1977.
    Fell and foul play / John Dickson Carr; foreword by Isaac Asimov;
    preface by D.R. Bensen.
      p.  cm.
    ISBN 1-55882-071-X
    1. Detective and mystery stories. American.  I. Title.
  PS3505.A763A6   1990
  813′.52—dc20                                90-55854
                                                       CIP

Library of Congress Card Catalog No. 90-55854
ISBN 1-55882-071-X

Printed and manufactured in the United States of America.
First IPL printing January 1991.
10 9 8 7 6 5 4 3 2 1

# CONTENTS

Introduction by Douglas G. Greene                           1

The Casebook of Dr. Gideon Fell                             5
  The Wrong Problem                                7
  Who Killed Matthew Corbin?                       21
    Episode 1                             23
    Episode 2                             37
    Episode 3                             51
  The Proverbial Murder                            69
  The Black Minute                                 87
  The Locked Room                                  105
  The Devil in the Summer-House                    121
  The Incautious Burglar                           145
  The Dead Sleep Lightly                           161
  Invisible Hands                                  185

Historical Mystery and Romance                             203
  The Dim Queen                                    205
  The Other Hangman                                219
  Persons or Things Unknown                        233
  The Gentleman from Paris                         249
  The Black Cabinet                                273

A Locked-Room Novella                                      291
  The Third Bullet                                 293

# INTRODUCTION

The detective fiction of John Dickson Carr (1906–1977) has a special flavor. His books do not describe the ordered world of Agatha Christie with its countryhouses and gossipy villagers; Christie's world seems so safe and unchanging that her fans happily describe her books as "cozy." There is nothing cozy about a John Dickson Carr murder. Dr. Gideon Fell and his other detectives investigate cases involving modern witch-cults and spiritualism and tarot cards and people stabbed with clock-hands. Carr was the master of the "impossible crime." Bodies are found in locked or guarded rooms, and in houses surrounded by unmarked snow or sand, and at seances where all the suspects are grasping one another's hands. In all these instances and more, Carr suggests that only the powers of darkness can be responsible, until the detective reveals that the crimes were committed by humans for human motives. But some-times the human solution is more terrifying than the supernatural—see "The Wrong Problem," the first story in *Fell and Foul Play.*

During the past five years, a new generation of readers has discovered Carr's books; most of his novels, whether published under his own name or his non-secret alter ego "Carter Dickson," have recently reappeared in inexpensive paperback editions. *Fell and Foul Play* will introduce those same readers to Carr's mastery of the mystery short story. Detective fiction began with short stories by Edgar Allan Poe, and in many ways the short story remains the best way to present a tale of investigation and deduction. G. K. Chesterton, Carr's favorite writer, remarked that "the superiority of the Poe pattern . . . in artistry and abstract logic is obvi-ous enough. . . . The advantage of the short story is this: that any such riddle must really revolve on one idea; and in a short story we can sharply realize if it is a new or unique idea." Chesterton wrote these words as a preface to an anthology called *A Century of Detective Stories* (1935), which contains one of the John Dickson Carr stories reprinted in *Fell and Foul Play,* and though Chesterton could not have been thinking solely of Carr's contribution, his comments summarize Carr's strengths as a writer of short fiction. His works are filled with new or unique ideas. In novel and novel, story after story, Carr's fertility of invention was unchallenged, and he had a special strength in the short tale, where (again to quote Chesterton) "the idea would stand out in all its simple truth and beauty."

Carr's first published work was a short story, "The Ruby of Rameses," written when he was sixteen years old. Many years later, in an introduc-tion to a book containing the earliest published stories of mystery writers, he said that "when we first scribbled or blundered at a typewriter, the short story is probably what most of us wrote at the beginning. We did not want merely to 'write.' When a person says that, he often means only that he wants to dream. No; we were more practical; we wanted to write a story. Since it would have been too big an undertaking to write a long story, we simply had a go at what we considered a short story. . . . Perhaps," he continued, "we landed in such a muddle that nobody could have hauled us out." That's a fair judgment of "The Ruby of Rameses," an odd combination of pseudo-Egyptian occultism and rational detection. But even though it has all the clumsiness—and enthusiasm—of youth, the story was based on an idea that would dominate Carr's writing for more than fifty years, the impossible murder in a locked room.

Carr's grasp on the fundamentals of short-story construction became more and more sure as he wrote tales at the Hill Preparatory School and at Haverford College. Some of his detective stories at Haverford are of such maturity that they were reprinted in the posthumous collection, *The Door to Doom and Other Detections* (1980). Readers of *Fell and Foul Play* will be able to make their own judgment about Carr's apprentice work with "The Dim Queen," which was written in 1926 and is reprinted for the first time in this volume. Carr's career as a professional writer began when he expanded his locked-room novella, "Grand Guignol," which had been published in *The Haverfordian,* into his first full-length novel, *It Walks By Night* (1930).

One of Carr's closest friends during the early 1930s was John Murray Reynolds, who though working fulltime for a steamship company, was an active writer for the pulp magazines; he created the once-famous character, Ki-Gor of the Jungle. Murray explained to Carr that writing pulp stories was not time-consuming—he himself wrote while standing on subway cars on his way home from work—and he introduced Carr to his magazine editor. Carr did not follow through immediately on this contact, but after moving to England, he submitted three stories to the pulps. Published in 1935 in *Horror Stories, Dime Mystery,* and *Detective Tales,* these ingenious and highly colored tales were Carr's first professional publications in the short form. They were never reprinted during his lifetime, but like some of his college stories they were revived for modern fans in *The Door to Doom.* Soon Carr's tales began to appear in the British glossy magazines; he published Christmas ghost tales in *The Illustrated London News* and *The Sketch,* and the editor of *The Strand* purchased thirteen of Carr's stories between 1938 and 1941. After this prolific period, Carr produced short stories at irregular intervals. As a writer for the BBC and for CBS during the 1940s, he used in his radio dramas many of the ideas that might normally have appeared as short stories. Later in his life, when his productivity decreased from four books a year to only one or two, his writing of short fiction also lessened, but he continued to write an occasional tale for *Ellery Queen's Mystery Magazine* and for a British magazine or two.

Dr. Gideon Fell appeared in five short stories published between 1936 and 1957, as well as in several radio-plays from the late 1930s and early 1940s. Carr based Dr. Fell on the appearance and public personality of his literary idol, G. K. Chesterton. Fell usually enters a case with a sort of fiery goodwill: "Filling the stairs in grandeur, he leaned on an ash cane with one hand and flourished another cane with the other. It was like meeting Father Christmas or Old King Cole. . . . There are people before whom you instantly unbend. Dr. Fell was one of them. No constraint could exist before him; he blew it away with a superb puff; and, if you had any affectations, you forgot them immediately." He weighs twenty stone, and his chins roll down his collar. He has a mop of unruly hair under a shovel hat, small eyes that twinkle behind glasses that are often slightly askew, and his language is an unexpected combination of Samuel Johnsonian formality and modern slang: his favorite expressions range from "Archons of Athens" and "by Bacchus" to "wow." He is an omnivorous reader of all forms of sensational fiction, and an expert on locked rooms and other tricks and impossibilities. Indeed, it's hard to find a subject on which he is not an expert. At a dinner described in one novel, he discusses "the origin of the Christmas cracker, Sir Richard Steele, merry-go-rounds—on which he particularly enjoyed riding—Beowulf, Buddhism, Thomas Henry Huxley, and Miss Greta Garbo." He is warmhearted, scatterbrained and, in his words, "a childish old fool." Like a child watching a magician, he is seldom fooled by the trappings of a trick. His speech is full of non sequiturs and cryptic remarks that are natural to his woolgathering mind and that allow Carr to mystify the reader.

Except for some pastiches of Sherlock Holmes, which Carr wrote with Adrian Conan Doyle, *Fell and Foul Play* and its successor, *Merrivale, March and Murder,* which will be published in 1991, contain all of John Dickson Carr's short stories that were collected in various volumes during his lifetime, as well as some previously uncollected pieces. This first volume is divided into three sections: the short cases of Dr. Gideon Fell; historical mystery and detection; and a locked-room (or, to be precise, a locked-and-watched-room) novella. Prefacing each story is a note on its early publication as well as some general comments.

G. K. Chesterton described writers of short detective stories as "cutthroats . . . who, realizing that the murder story must cut short the life, decide also to cut the story short. It is their pride as artists to deal in daggers; and startle the . . . reader with the stab of the short story." The fifteen stories that follow will certainly startle, and occasionally stab, readers who revel in atmosphere, mayhem, ingenuity, and the unique idea.

—*Douglas G. Greene*
Norfolk, Virginia
July 1990

I am grateful to Tony Medawar, whose research into the lives and writings of British mystery writers continues to produce extraordinary discoveries. For this volume, Tony located the Dr. Fell version of "The Devil in the Summer-House" and the final page, which for many years had seemed irretrievably lost, of "Who Killed Matthew Corbin?"

# THE CASEBOOK
# OF DR. GIDEON FELL

# The Wrong Problem

The first short story about Dr. Gideon Fell was written at the request of Dorothy L. Sayers, the creator of Lord Peter Wimsey and one of the leading lights of London's Detection Club. The club was made up of the most important writers of the "Golden Age" of the detective story. They represented the fair-play school, which demanded not only that the story be literate but also that all the clues be given to the reader at the same time that the sleuth had them. Thus the club strove to raise the genre above the level of the average thrillers. In 1936, the London *Evening Standard* arranged with Sayers to publish a series of short stories by Detection Club members, including John Dickson Carr, who had been elected the first American member earlier that year. Carr's story was published in August 14, 1936; the earliest American printing was in *Ellery Queen's Mystery Magazine,* July 1942. It begins with a graceful reference—under a slightly different name—to the Detection Club, and the character of Dr. Fell himself is a tribute to G. K. Chesterton, the club's first president. Dr. Fell's physical appearance and many of his mannerisms are based on Chesterton; and "The Wrong Problem" is Chestertonian in atmosphere and, as you will see, in title.

# The Wrong Problem

At the Detectives' Club it is still told how Dr. Fell went down into the valley in Somerset that evening and of the man with whom he talked in the twilight by the lake, and of murder that came up as though from the lake itself. The truth about the crime has long been known, but one question must always be asked at the end of it.

The village of Grayling Dene lay a mile away toward the sunset. And the rear windows of the house looked out toward it. This was a long gabled house of red brick, lying in a hollow of the shaggy hills, and its bricks had darkened like an old painting. No lights showed inside, although the lawns were in good order and the hedges trimmed.

Behind the house there was a long gleam of water in the sunset, for the ornamental lake—some fifty yards across—stretched almost to the windows. In the middle of the lake, on an artificial island, stood a summerhouse. A faint breeze had begun to stir, despite the heat, and the valley was alive with a conference of leaves.

The last light showed that all the windows of the house, except one, had little lozenge-shaped panes. The one exception was a window high up in a gable, the highest in the house, looking out over the road to Grayling Dene. It was barred.

Dusk had almost become darkness when two men came down over the crest of the hill. One was large and lean. The other, who wore a shovel hat, was large and immensely stout, and he loomed even more vast against the sky line by reason of the great dark cloak billowing out behind him. Even at that distance you might hear the chuckles that animated his several chins and ran down the ridges of his waistcoat. The two travelers were engaged (as usual) in a violent argument. At intervals the larger one would stop and hold forth oratorically for some minutes, flourishing his cane. But, as they came down past the lake and the blind house, both of them stopped.

"There's an example," said Superintendent Hadley. "Say what you like, it's a bit too lonely for me. Give me the town—"

"We are not alone," said Dr. Fell.

The whole place had seemed so deserted that Hadley felt a slight start when he saw a man standing at the edge of the lake. Against the reddish glow on the water they could make out that it was a small man in neat dark clothes and a white linen hat. He seemed to be stooping forward, peering out across the water. The wind went rustling again, and the man turned round.

"I don't see any swans," he said. "Can you see any swans?" The quiet water was empty.

"No," said Dr. Fell, with the same gravity. "Should there be any?"

"There should be one," answered the little man, nodding. "Dead. With blood on its neck. Floating there."

"Killed?" asked Dr. Fell, after a pause. He has said afterward that it seemed a foolish thing to say; but that it seemed appropriate to that time between the lights of the day and the brain.

"Oh, yes," replied the little man, nodding again. "Killed, like others—human beings. Eye, ear and throat. Or perhaps I should say ear, eye and throat, to get them in order."

Hadley spoke with some sharpness.

"I hope we're not trespassing. We knew the land was enclosed, of course, but they told us that the owners were away and wouldn't mind if we took a short cut. Fell, don't you think we'd better—?"

"I beg your pardon," said the little man, in a voice of such cool sanity that Hadley turned round again. From what they could see in the gloom, he had a good face, a quiet face, a somewhat ascetic face; and he was smiling. "I beg your pardon," he repeated in a curiously apologetic tone. "I should not have said that. You see, I have been far too long with it. I have been trying to find the real answer for thirty years. As for the trespassing, myself, I do not own this land, although I lived here once. There is, or used to be, a bench here somewhere. Can I detain you for a little while?"

Hadley never quite realized afterward how it came about. But such was the spell of the hour, or of the place, or the sincere, serious little man in the white linen hat, that it seemed no time at all before the little man was sitting on a rusty iron chair beside the darkening lake, speaking as though to his fingers.

"I am Joseph Lessing," he said in the same apologetic tone. "If you have not heard of me, I don't suppose you will have heard of my stepfather. But at one time he was rather famous as an eye, ear and throat specialist. Dr. Harvey Lessing, his name was.

"In those days we—I mean the family—always came down here to spend our summer holidays. It is rather difficult to make biographical details clear. Perhaps I had better do it with dates, as though the matter were really important, like a history book. There were four children. Three of them were Dr. Lessing's children by his first wife, who died in 1899. I was the stepson. He married my mother when I was seventeen, in 1901. I regret to say that *she* died three years later. Dr. Lessing was a kindly man, but he was very unfortunate in the choice of his wives."

The little man appeared to be smiling sadly.

"We were an ordinary, contented and happy group, in spite of Brownrigg's cynicism. Brownrigg was the eldest. Eye, ear and throat pursued us: he was a dentist. I think he is dead now. He was a stout man, smiling a good deal, and his face had a shine like pale butter. He was an athlete run to seed; he used to claim that he could draw teeth with his fingers. By the way, he was very fond of walnuts. I always seem to remember him sitting between two silver candlesticks at the table, smiling, with a heap of shells in front of him and a little sharp nutpick in his hand.

"Harvey Junior was the next. They were right to call him Junior; he was of the striding sort, brisk and high-colored and likable. He never sat down in a chair without first turning it the wrong way round. He always said 'Ho, my lads!' when he came into a room, and he never went out of it without leaving the door open so that he could come back in again. Above everything, he was nearly always on the water. We had a skiff and a punt for our little lake—would you believe that it is ten feet deep? Junior always dressed for the part as solemnly as though he had been on the Thames, wearing a red-and-white-striped blazer and a straw hat of the sort that used to be called a boater. I say he was nearly always on the water: but not, of course, after tea. That was when Dr. Lessing went to take his afternoon nap in the summer-house."

The summer-house, in its sheath of vines, was almost invisible now. But they all looked at it, very suggestive in the middle of the lake.

"The third child was the girl, Martha. She was almost my own age, and I was very fond of her."

Joseph Lessing pressed his hands together.

"I am not going to introduce an unnecessary love story, gentlemen," he said. "As a matter of fact, Martha was engaged to a young man who had a commission in a line regiment, and she was expecting him down here any day when—the things happened. Arthur Somers, his name was. I knew him well; I was his confidant in the family.

"I want to emphasize what a hot, pleasant summer it was. The place looked then much as it does now, except that I think it was greener then. I was glad to get away from the city. In accordance with Dr. Lessing's passion for 'useful employment,' I had been put to work in the optical department of a jeweler's. I was always skillful with my hands. I dare say I was a spindly, snappish, suspicious lad, but they were all very good to me after my mother died: except butter-faced Brownrigg, perhaps. But for me that summer centers round Martha, with her brown hair piled up on the top of her head, in a white dress with puffed shoulders, playing croquet on a green lawn and laughing. I told you it was a long while ago.

"On the afternoon of the fifteenth of August we had all intended to be out. Even Brownrigg had intended to go out after a sort of lunch-tea that we had at two o'clock in the afternoon. Look to your right, gentlemen. You see that bow window in the middle of the house, overhanging the lake? There was where the table was set.

"Dr. Lessing was the first to leave the table. He was going out early for his nap in the summer-house. It was a very hot afternoon, as drowsy as the sound of a lawn mower. The sun baked the old bricks and made a flat blaze on the water. Junior had knocked together a sort of miniature landing stage at the side of the lake—it was just about where we are sitting now—and the punt and the rowboat were lying there.

"From the open windows we could all see Dr. Lessing going down to the landing stage with the sun on his bald spot. He had a pillow in one hand and a book in the other. He took the rowboat; he could never manage the punt properly, and it irritated a man of his dignity to try.

"Martha was the next to leave. She laughed and ran away, as she always did. Then Junior said, 'Cheerio, chaps'—or whatever the expression was then—and strode out leaving the door open. I went shortly afterward. Junior had asked Brownrigg whether he intended to go out, and Brownrigg had said yes. But he remained, being lazy, with a pile of walnut shells in front of him. Though he moved back from the table to get out of the glare, he lounged there all afternoon in view of the lake.

"Of course, what Brownrigg said or thought might not have been important. But it happened that a gardener named Robinson had taken it into his head to trim some hedges on this side of the house. He had a full view of the lake. And all that afternoon nothing stirred. The summer-house, as you can see, has two doors: one facing toward the house, the other in the opposite direction. These openings were closed by sun-blinds, striped red and white like Junior's blazer, so that you could not see inside. But all the afternoon the summer-house remained dead, showing up against the fiery water and that clump of trees at the far side of the lake. No boat put out. No one went in to swim. There was not so much as a ripple, any more than might have been caused by the swans (we had two of them), or by the spring that fed the lake.

"By six o'clock we were all back in the house. When there began to be a few shadows, I think something in the *emptiness* of the afternoon alarmed us. Dr. Lessing should have been there, demanding something. He was not there. We hallooed for him, but he did not answer. The rowboat remained tied up by the summer-house. Then Brownrigg, in his cool fetch-and-run fashion, told me to go out and wake up the old party. I pointed out that there was only the punt, and that I was a rotten hand at punting, and that whenever I tried it I only went round in circles or upset the boat. But Junior said, 'Come-along-old-chap-you-shall-im-prove-your-punting-I'll-give-you-a-hand.'

"I have never forgotten how long it took us to get out there while I staggered at the punt pole, and Junior lent a hand.

"Dr. Lessing lay easily on his left side, almost on his stomach, on a long wicker settee. His face was very nearly into the pillow, so that you could not see much except a wisp of sandy side whisker. His right hand hung down to the floor, the fingers trailing into the pages of *Three Men in a Boat.*

"We first noticed that there seemed to be some—that is, something that had come out of his ear. More we did not know, except that he was dead, and in fact the weapon has never been found. He died in his sleep. The doctor later told us that the wound had been made by some round sharp-pointed instrument, thicker than a hatpin but not so thick as a lead pencil, which had been driven through the right ear into the brain."

Joseph Lessing paused. A mighty swish of wind uprose in the trees beyond the lake, and their tops ruffled under clear starlight. The little man sat nodding to himself in the iron chair. They could see his white hat move.

"Yes?" prompted Dr. Fell in an almost casual tone. Dr. Fell was sitting back, a great bandit shape in cloak and shovel hat. He seemed to be blinking curiously at Lessing over his eyeglasses. "And whom did they suspect?"

"They suspected me," said the little man.

"You see," he went on, in the same apologetic tone, "I was the only one in the group who could swim. It was my one accomplishment. It is too dark to show you now but I won a little medal by it, and I have kept it on my watch chain ever since I received it as a boy."

"But you said," cried Hadley, "that nobody . . ."

"I will explain," said the other, "if you do not interrupt me. Of course, the police believed that the motive must have been money. Dr. Lessing was a wealthy man, and his money was divided almost equally among us. I told you he was always very good to me.

"First they tried to find out where every one had been in the afternoon. Brownrigg had been sitting, or said he had been sitting, in the dining room. But there was the gardener to prove that not he or anyone else had gone out on the lake. Martha (it was foolish, of course, but they investigated even Martha) had been with a friend of hers—I forget her name now—who came for her in the phaeton and took her away to play croquet. Junior had no alibi, since he had been for a country walk. But," said Lessing, quite simply, "everybody knew *he* would never do a thing like that. I was the changeling, or perhaps I mean ugly duckling, and I admit I was an unpleasant, sarcastic lad.

"This is how Inspector Deering thought I had committed the murder. First, he thought, I had made sure everybody would be away from the house that afternoon. Thus, later, when the crime was discovered, it would be assumed by everyone that the murderer had simply gone out in the punt and come back again. Everybody knew that I could not possibly manage a punt alone. You see?

"Next, the inspector thought, I had come down to the clump of trees across the lake, in line with the summer-house and the dining-room windows. It is shallow there, and there are reeds. He thought that I had taken off my clothes over a bathing suit. He thought that I had crept into the water under cover of the reeds, and that I had simply swum out to the summer-house under water.

"Twenty odd yards under water, I admit, are not much to a good swimmer. They thought that Brownrigg could not see me come up out of the water, because the thickness of the summer-house was between. Robinson had a full view of the lake, but he could not see that one part at the back of the summer-house. Nor, on the other hand, could I see them. They thought that I had crawled under the sun-blind with the weapon in the breast of my bathing suit. Any wetness I might have left would soon be dried by the intense heat. That, I think, was how they believed I had killed the old man who befriended me."

The little man's voice grew petulant and dazed.

"I told them I did not do it," he said with a hopeful air. "Over and over again I told them I did not do it. But I do not think they believed me. That is why for all these years I have wondered—

"It was Brownrigg's idea. They had me before a sort of family council in the library, as though I had stolen jam. Martha was weeping, but I think she was weeping with plain fear. She never stood up well in a crisis, Martha didn't; she turned pettish and even looked softer. All the same, it is not pleasant to think of a murderer coming up to you as you doze in the afternoon heat. Junior, the good fellow, attempted to take my side and call for fair play; but I could see the idea in his face. Brownrigg presided, silkily, and smiled down his nose.

" 'We have either got to believe you killed him,' Brownrigg said, 'or believe in the supernatural. Is the lake haunted? No; I think we may safely discard that.' He pointed his finger at me. 'You damned young snake, you are lazy and wanted that money.'

"But, you see, I had one very strong hold over them—and I used it. I admit it was unscrupulous, but I was trying to demonstrate my innocence and we are told that the devil must be fought with fire. At mention of this hold, even Brownrigg's jowls shook. Brownrigg was a dentist, Harvey was studying medicine. What hold? That is the whole point. Nevertheless, it was not what the family thought I had to fear: it was what Inspector Deering thought.

"They did not arrest me yet, because there was not enough evidence, but every night I feared it would come the next day. Those days after the funeral were too warm; and suspicion acted like woolen underwear under the heat. Martha's tantrums got on even Junior's nerves. Once I thought Brownrigg was going to hit her. She very badly needed her fiancé, Arthur

Somers; but, though he wrote that he might be there any day, he still could not get leave of absence from his colonel.

"And then the lake got more food.

"Look at the house, gentlemen. I wonder if the light is strong enough for you to see it from here? Look at the house—the highest window there —under the gable. You see?"

There was a pause, filled with the tumult of the leaves.

"It's got bars," said Hadley.

"Yes," assented the little man. "I must describe the room. It is a little square room. It has one door and one window. At the time I speak of, there was no furniture at all in it. The furniture had been taken out some years before, because it was rather a special kind of furniture. Since then it had been locked up. The key was kept in a box in Dr. Lessing's room; but, of course, nobody ever went up there. One of Dr. Lessing's wives had died there in a certain condition. I told you he had bad luck with his wives. They had not even dared to have a glass window."

Sharply, the little man struck a match. The brief flame seemed to bring his face up toward them out of the dark. They saw that he had a pipe in his left hand. But the flame showed little except the gentle upward turn of his eyes, and the fact that his whitish hair (of such coarse texture that it seemed whitewashed) was worn rather long.

"On the afternoon of the twenty-second of August, we had an unexpected visit from the family solicitor. There was no one to receive him except myself. Brownrigg had locked himself up in his room at the front with a bottle of whisky; he was drunk or said he was drunk. Junior was out. We had been trying to occupy our minds for the past week, but Junior could not have his boating or I my workshop; this was thought not decent. I believe it was thought that the most decent thing was to get drunk. For some days Martha had been ailing. She was not ill enough to go to bed, but she was lying on a long chair in her bedroom.

"I looked into the room just before I went downstairs to see the solicitor. The room was muffled up with shutters and velvet curtains, as all the rooms decently were. You may imagine that it was very hot in there. Martha was lying back in the chair with a smelling bottle, and there was a white-globed lamp burning on a little round table beside her. I remember that her white dress looked starchy; her hair was piled up on top of her head and she wore a little gold watch on her breast. Also, her eyelids were so puffed that they seemed almost oriental. When I asked her how she was, she began to cry and concluded by throwing a book at me.

"So I went on downstairs. I was talking to the solicitor when it took place. We were in the library, which is at the front of the house, and in consequence we could not hear distinctly. But we heard something. That was why we went upstairs—and even the solicitor ran. Martha was not in her own bedroom. We found out where she was from the fact that the door to the garret stairs was open.

"It was even more intolerably hot up under the roof. The door to the barred room stood halfway open. Just outside stood a housemaid (her name, I think, was Jane Dawson) leaning against the jamb and shaking like the ribbons on her cap. All sound had dried up in her throat, but she pointed inside.

"I told you it was a little, bare, dirty-brown room. The low sun made a blaze through the window, and made shadows of the bars across Martha's white dress. Martha lay nearly in the middle of the room, with her heel twisted under her as though she had turned round before she fell. I lifted her up and tried to talk to her; but a rounded sharp-pointed thing, somewhat thicker than a hatpin, had been driven through the right eye into the brain.

"Yet there was nobody else in the room.

"The maid told a straight story. She had seen Martha come out of Dr. Lessing's bedroom downstairs. Martha was running, running as well as she could in those skirts; once she stumbled, and the maid thought that she was sobbing. Jane Dawson said that Martha made for the garret door as though the devil were after her. Jane Dawson, wishing anything rather than to be alone in the dark hall, followed her. She saw Martha come up here and unlock the door of the little brown room. When Martha ran inside, the maid thought that she did not attempt to close the door; but that it appeared to swing shut after her. You see?

"Whatever had frightened Martha, Jane Dawson did not dare follow her in—for a few seconds, at least, and afterward it was too late. The maid could never afterward describe exactly the sort of sound Martha made. It was something that startled the birds out of the vines and set the swans flapping on the lake. But the maid presently saw straight enough to push the door with one finger and peep round the edge.

"Except for Martha, the room was empty.

"Hence the three of us now looked at each other. The maid's story was not to be shaken in any way, and we all knew she was a truthful witness. Even the police did not doubt her. She said she had seen Martha go into that room, but that she had seen nobody come out of it. She never took her eyes off the door—it was not likely that she would. But when she peeped in to see what had happened, there was nobody except Martha in the room. That was easily established, because there was no place where any one could have been. Could she have been blinded by the light? No. Could any one have slipped past her? No. She almost shook her hair loose by her vehemence on this point.

"The window, I need scarcely tell you, was inaccessible. Its bars were firmly set, no farther apart than the breadth of your hand, and in any case the window could not have been reached. There was no way out of the room except the door or the window; and no—what is the word I want?—no mechanical device in it. Our friend Inspector Deering made certain of that. One thing I suppose I should mention. Despite the condition of the walls and ceiling, the floor of the room was swept clean. Martha's white dress with the puffed shoulders had scarcely any dirt when she lay there; it was as white as her face.

"This murder was incredible. I do not mean merely that it was incredible with regard to its physical circumstances, but also that there was Martha dead—on a holiday. Possibly she seemed all the more dead because we had never known her well when she was alive. She was (to me, at least) a laugh, a few coquetries, a pair of brown eyes. You felt her absence more than you would have felt that of a more vital person. And —on a holiday with that warm sun, and the tennis net ready to be put up.

"That evening I walked with Junior here in the dusk by the lake. He was trying to express some of this. He appeared dazed. He did not know why Martha had gone up to that little brown room, and he kept endlessly asking why. He could not even seem to accustom himself to the idea that our holidays were interrupted, much less interrupted by the murders of his father and his sister.

"There was a reddish light on the lake; the trees stood up against it like black lace, and we were walking near that clump by the reeds. The thing I remember most vividly is Junior's face. He had his hat on the back of his head, as he usually did. He was staring down past the reeds, where the water lapped faintly, as though the lake itself were the evil genius and kept its secret. When he spoke I hardly recognized his voice.

" 'God,' he said, 'but it's in the air!'

"There was something white floating by the reeds, very slowly turning round with a snaky discolored talon coming out from it along the water, the talon was the head of a swan, and the swan was dead of a gash across the neck that had very nearly severed it.

"We fished it out with a boat hook," explained the little man as though with an afterthought. And then he was silent.

On the long iron bench Dr. Fell's cape shifted a little; Hadley could hear him wheezing with quiet anger, like a boiling kettle.

"I thought so," rumbled Dr. Fell. He added more sharply: "Look here, this tomfoolery has got to stop."

"I beg your pardon?" said Joseph Lessing, evidently startled.

"With your kind permission," said Dr. Fell, and Hadley has later said that he was never more glad to see that cane flourished or hear that common-sense voice grow fiery with controversy: "with your kind permission, I should like to ask you a question. Will you swear to me by anything you hold sacred (if you have anything, which I rather doubt) that you do not know the real answer?"

"Yes," replied the other seriously, and nodded.

For a little space, Dr. Fell was silent. Then he spoke argumentatively. "I will ask you another question, then. Did you ever shoot an arrow into the air?"

Hadley turned round. "I hear the call of Mumbo-Jumbo," said Hadley with grim feeling. "Hold on, now! You don't think that girl was killed by somebody shooting an arrow into the air, do you?"

"Oh, no," said Dr. Fell in a more meditative tone. He looked at Lessing. "I mean it figuratively—like the boy in the verse. Did you ever throw a stone when you were a boy? Did you ever throw a stone, not to hit anything, but for the sheer joy of firing it? Did you ever climb trees? Did you ever like to play pirate and dress up and wave a sword? I don't think so. That's why you live in a dreary, rarefied light; that's why you dislike romance and sentiment and good whisky and all the noblest things of this world; and it is also why you do not see the unreasonableness of several things in this case.

"To begin with, birds do not commonly rise up in a great cloud from the vines because some one cries out. With the hopping and always-whooping Junior about the premises, I should imagine the birds were used to it. Still less do swans leap up out of the water and flap their wings because of a cry from far away; swans are not so sensitive. But did you ever see a boy throw a stone at a wall? Did you ever see a boy throw a stone at the water? Birds and swans would have been outraged only if something had *struck* both the wall and the water: something, in short, which fell from the barred window.

"Now, frightened women do not in their terror rush up to a garret, especially a garret with such associations. They go downstairs, where there is protection. Martha Lessing was not frightened. She went up to that room for some purpose. What purpose? She could not have been going to get anything, for there was nothing in the room to be got. What could have been on her mind? The only thing we know to have been on her mind was a frantic wish for her fiancé to get there. She had been expecting him for weeks. It is a singular thing about that room: but its window is the highest in the house, and commands the only clear view of the road to the village.

"Now suppose someone had told her that he thought, he rather *thought,* he had glimpsed Arthur Somers coming up the road from the village. It was a long way off, of course, and the someone admitted he might have been mistaken in thinking so. . . .

"H'm, yes. The trap was all set, you see. Martha Lessing waited only long enough to get the key out of the box in her father's room, and she sobbed with relief. But, when she got to the room, there was a strong sun pouring through the bars straight into her face: and the road to the village is a long way off. That, I believe, was the trap. For on the window ledge of that room (which nobody ever used, and which someone had swept so that there should be no footprints) this someone conveniently placed a pair of—eh, Hadley?"

"Field glasses," said Hadley, and got up in the gloom.

"Still," argued Dr. Fell, wheezing argumentatively, "there would be one nuisance. Take a pair of field glasses, and try to use them in a window where the bars are set more closely than the breadth of your hand. The bars get in the way: wherever you turn you bump into them; they confuse sight and irritate you; and, in addition, there is a strong sun to complicate matters. In your impatience, I think you would turn the glasses sideways and pass them out through the bars. Then, holding them firmly against one bar with your hands through the bars on either side, you would look through the eyepieces.

"But," said Dr. Fell, with a ferocious geniality, "those were no ordinary glasses. Martha Lessing had noticed before that the lenses were blurred. Now that they were in position, she tried to adjust the focus by turning the little wheel in the middle. And as she turned the wheel, like the trigger of a pistol it released the spring mechanism and a sharp steel point shot out from the right-hand lens into her eye. She dropped the glasses, which were outside the window. The weight of them tore the point from her eye; and it was this object, falling, which gashed and broke the neck of the swan just before it disappeared into the water below."

He paused. He had taken out a cigar, but he did not light it.

"Busy solicitors do not usually come to a house 'unexpectedly.' They are summoned. Brownrigg was drunk and Junior absent; there was no one at the back of the house to see the glasses fall. For this time the murderer had to have a respectable alibi. Young Martha, the only one who could have been gulled into such a trap, had to be sacrificed—to avert the arrest which had been threatening someone ever since the police found out how Dr. Lessing really had been murdered.

"There was only one man who admittedly did speak with Martha Lessing only a few minutes before she was murdered. There was only one man who was employed as optician at a jeweler's, and admits he had his 'workshop' here. There was only one man skilful enough with his hands —" Dr. Fell paused, wheezing, and turned to Lessing. "I wonder they didn't arrest you."

"They did," said the little man, nodding. "You see, I was released from Broadmoor only a month ago."

There was a sudden rasp and crackle as he struck another match.

"You—" bellowed Hadley, and stopped. "So it was your mother who died in that room? Then what the hell do you mean by keeping us here with this pack of nightmares?"

"No," said the other peevishly. "You do not understand. I never wanted to know who killed Dr. Lessing or poor Martha. You have got hold of the wrong problem. And yet I tried to tell you what the problem was.

"You see, it was not *my* mother who died mad. It was theirs— Brownrigg's and Harvey's and Martha's. That was why they were so desperately anxious to think I was guilty, for they could not face the alternative. Didn't I tell you I had a hold over them, a hold that made even Brownrigg shake, and that I used it? Do you think they wouldn't have had me clapped into jail straightaway if it had been *my* mother who was mad? Eh?

"Of course," he explained apologetically, "at the trial they had to swear it was my mother who was mad; for I threatened to tell the truth in open court if they didn't. Otherwise I should have been hanged, you see. Only Brownrigg and Junior were left. Brownrigg was a dentist, Junior was to be a doctor, and if it had been known—But that is not the point. That is not the problem. Their mother was mad, but they were harmless. I killed Dr. Lessing. I killed Martha. Yes, I am quite sane. Why did I do it, all those years ago? Why? Is there no rational pattern in the scheme of things, and no answer to the bedeviled of the earth?"

The match curled to a red ember, winked and went out. Clearest of all they remembered the coarse hair that was like whitewash on the black, the eyes, and the curiously suggestive hands. Then Joseph Lessing got up from the chair. The last they saw of him was his white hat bobbing and flickering across the lawn under the blowing trees.

# Who Killed Matthew Corbin?

"Who Killed Matthew Corbin?" is a previously unpublished radio-script, broadcast on the BBC in three parts on December 7, 1939, January 7, 1940, and January 14, 1940. A few months earlier, Carr had met Val Gielgud, the dominant force behind British radio drama, and he invited Gielgud to be his guest at a Detection Club meeting. An actor had sent the BBC an idea for a radio-play to be called "Consider Your Verdict." The idea wasn't usable as it stood, but Gielgud suggested that Carr turn it into a drama. Surviving letters between Carr and Gielgud do not indicate whether the final gimmick in "Who Killed Matthew Corbin?" was supplied by the actor, or whether his idea (as the original title implies) was to make the play into a contest in which listeners would send in their solutions; this idea was later dropped as too cumbersome. Various additional titles were considered, including "What Say Ye?" and "Whodunnit," before the final one was chosen, and Carr tried several different ways of handling the trial scene in Episode 2 and of masking the final solution. He was in Bristol when the first installment was broadcast, "where I had about eighteen people listening in various houses and pubs." He gleefully wrote to Gielgud that almost all of them tumbled into a trap he had set by giving some misleading clues pointing to an innocent suspect. More than fifty years later, most readers will probably fall into the same trap.

# Who Killed Matthew Corbin?

## The Characters:

| | |
|---|---|
| Dr. Gideon Fell | The detective |
| Interviewer | From the BBC |
| Superintendent David Hadley | Of Scotland Yard |
| Matthew Corbin | The victim |
| John Corbin | His brother |
| Arnold Corbin | Also his brother |
| Helen Gates | Their cousin |
| Mary Stevenson | John's fiancée |
| Mr. Raeburn, K.C. | The prosecutor |
| Sir Charles Wolfe | The counsel for the defense |
| The judge | |
| Clerk of Court | |
| Usher | |
| Warder | |
| Foreman of the jury | |
| First wardress | |
| Second wardress | |
| Governor of the prison | |
| The Lord Chief Justice | |
| Policeman | |

*Setting:* London, 1932 (the murder), 1933 (the trial), and 1939–1940 (the solution)

## EPISODE 1

ANNOUNCER: Murder mysteries, old and new. Problems of crime in which the real truth has never come to light. Presented to you by Dr. Gideon Fell. We take you now to Dr. Fell's study, somewhere in London. BBC-Radio is here to interview him.
*(Flourish of music, strong and harsh)*
INTERVIEWER: Well, if you insist—just a spot, thanks. *(Sound of liquid being poured into a glass)* Whoa! Steady!
DR. FELL: A strange moderation. However. *(He has a huge, rich, Dr. Johnsonesque kind of voice. You picture him as rearing up like Dr. Johnson with immense dignity each time he speaks. There is a further and longer sound of liquid being poured into a glass.)*
INTERVIEWER *(to the microphone):* Ladies and gentlemen, to those of you who know Dr. Fell's reputation for solving criminal cases, I don't

have to explain who he is. Tonight he is going to tell us the real truth about the murder of Matthew Corbin. Is that correct, Doctor?

DR. FELL:   No, sir, it is not.

INTERVIEWER:   I beg your pardon?

DR. FELL:   I should like to tell you what I believe to be the truth. I have the Christian humility to imagine that I may be wrong, though the possibility is so slight that it need not trouble us. And I can tell you in three words what I think about the Corbin case. *(Impressively)* Everybody was wrong.

INTERVIEWER:   I don't think I understand.

DR. FELL:   The judge was wrong. The jury was wrong. The prosecution was wrong. The defense was wrong.

INTERVIEWER:   But, Doctor, *everybody* couldn't be wrong.

DR. FELL:   Sir, you do not know your own countrymen.

INTERVIEWER *(amusedly):*   Well, I'm willing to be convinced. But if I remember correctly . . .

DR. FELL:   It was a long time ago. Do you remember the case? Personally, I mean?

INTERVIEWER:   I remember the trial.

DR. FELL *(with ghoulish satisfaction):*   Aha! Then you also remember the facts. On the night of Friday, October 13th, Matthew Corbin was shot dead in the back room of his house in Hampstead.

INTERVIEWER:   Yes?

DR. FELL:   This murder must have been committed by one of four persons.

INTERVIEWER:   Do you agree with that?

DR. FELL:   Most profoundly. But which one? *(Slight pause)* Let us look first at the testimony of John Corbin. John Corbin—do you remember? —was the younger brother of the murdered man. John Corbin had just returned from abroad, and was bringing his new fiancée to meet the family. John Corbin said . . .

*(Another flourish of music, strong and harsh, to mark the changeover. At the end of a few bars John Corbin's voice is heard. It is light, distinct, the voice of a jeune premier; at times inclined to be querulous.)*

JOHN CORBIN:   You see, I'd been away from England for two years. In South Africa, as I've told you. My ship docked that afternoon, and I was going to burst in on old Matt and surprise him. On the ship coming home I met Miss Stevenson—Mary—the young lady who's here with me. And we—well, we got engaged to be married.

*(Mary Stevenson speaks. It is a light, pleasant voice, of a girl in her middle twenties.)*

MARY STEVENSON *(rather defiantly):*   We *are* going to be married.

JOHN:   I did the thing up in style. I bought a car—just like that. *(He

*snaps his fingers.)* We had supper in style, and then started out to Hampstead. Only it was raining like the devil, and . . .
*(Another and longer flourish of music, which becomes a long peal of thunder, followed by a pattering of rain forming a background. The noise of a motor-car is added, over which John's voice continues.)*

JOHN *(with rising querulousness):*   That's done it. Now the windscreen-wiper won't work.

MARY *(half-laughing):*   John, please don't be so impatient.

JOHN:   I'm not impatient. But look at this thing. You can't even . . .
*(There is a hideous and continued crashing of gears as he tries to shift.)* See?

MARY:   Could it be that you're not used to driving?

JOHN:   Nonsense.

MARY:   Why not move over and let me drive?

JOHN:   Definitely not. *(The gears still grind.)*

MARY:   But why not?

JOHN:   I don't know. It looks funny. *(After a last crash the gears mesh, and he speaks triumphantly.)* Got the swine!

MARY:   All right, darling. Just as you like.

JOHN *(in a different tone):*   Look here, Mary; I'm sorry, I'm acting like a fool, and we both know it.

MARY *(quickly):*   You're not in the least!

JOHN:   Only I had imagined us dashing up in my new car. And now we're likely to arrive like a couple of drowned rabbits, if we get there at all.

MARY:   This homecoming means a lot to you, doesn't it?

JOHN:   It does. For the first time in my life I've got money in the bank and a good flourishing business to back me up. In other words, I've succeeded.

MARY:   And your brother always said you wouldn't?

JOHN:   No. Matt always said I would. He staked me, you know. But—

MARY:   But what?

JOHN *(after a hesitation, gloomily):*   Well, I've always been the fool of a brilliant family. No, don't sit there making faces; it's true. Matt is a professor. Arnold, my other brother, is a professor. Even our good cousin Helen is too clever for me.

MARY *(coolly):*   Helen Gates? That's the girl who's in love with you, isn't it? *(In a sharper tone)* Look out for that lorry!
*(There is a sharp grind of gears, which seems to reflect the astonished indignation in John's voice when he speaks.)*

JOHN:   Good Lord, no! What gave you that idea?

MARY:   I've drawn my own conclusions.

JOHN *(urgently):*    Well, don't. Look here, Mary. I hope you haven't got any funny ideas—from anything I've said—

MARY:    About Helen being in love with you?

JOHN:    Yes. Because there's nothing it it. There never was.

MARY:    On your side?

JOHN:    On anybody's side. *(Emphatically)* Besides, you don't know Helen. Helen is one of these clever people; not like you.

MARY *(amused):*    Thanks.

JOHN:    No, no; you know what I mean. Helen gives a kind of Mona Lisa effect. I'd as soon think of making advances to a quadratic equation.

MARY *(broodingly):*    You do make them sound a depressing lot. John, I hope you realize the position I'm in. You meet me for the first time aboard ship. You know absolutely nothing about me. You go bursting in on your family with an unexpected fiancée . . .

JOHN:    You don't mind, do you?

MARY:    Well, darling, I'm not going to be awfully popular.

JOHN:    Nonsense. Matt will fall for you as soon as he sees you.

MARY:    I hope so.

JOHN:    I'll tell you something. Matt is the kindest-hearted person alive. In fact, he's too kind-hearted. That's why he gave up being a barrister. *(A peal of thunder is heard over the rain.)*

MARY *(sharply):*    Barrister? You said he was a professor of law.

JOHN:    He is. But he started as a barrister. *(Amusedly)* He gave it up after his first brief. The court appointed him to defend some woman who was accused of murder. It was a poisoning case; nasty business. He . . . *(Breaks off)* There we are, Mary. *(Excitedly)* There's the house down there. If we don't skid on this hill, we'll be home in two minutes.

MARY:    What were you saying about your brother's first case?

JOHN:    Eh?

MARY:    Your brother's first case.

JOHN *(chuckles):*    Poor old Matt. He was full of fire. He went all out to get the woman acquitted—and did. Afterwards she smiled sweetly, and thanked him, and admitted she was guilty after all.

MARY:    That must have been pleasant.

JOHN:    It was. Matt says that whenever he thinks of that woman's face even now, it still makes him sick. *(Another long peal of thunder is heard.)* That's home, Mary. Behind those trees.

MARY:    What happened to the girl?

JOHN:    What girl?

MARY:    I mean the woman who poisoned those people. What happened to her?

JOHN:  Oh, I don't know. She went abroad or something. . . . You'll see the place in a minute. It's a white house with long windows. It's—

MARY *(with sharp alarm)*:  John! *Look out!*

JOHN *(with desperate coolness)*:  It's quite all right now. I've got her under perfect control. She won't skid badly enough to—

MARY:  No, don't touch your hand-brake! Keep your hand off—

JOHN:  Duck your head! Duck!

*(Throughout the last speeches, there has grown a hissing of tires on wet concrete; and the speakers' voices are jerky. The hissing is followed during the last speech by a series of heavy bumps growing louder; then a metallic crash, and the smashing of glass. Afterwards there is dead silence while we hear the rain drumming on the roof of the car.)*

JOHN *(with a long-drawn, rather dazed breath)*:  Uuuh!

MARY:  John! Are you hurt!

JOHN:  Are *you* hurt?

MARY:  No, no, I'm all right. But what about you? You're as white as a ghost.

JOHN:  I caught my head a crack on the roof. I'm a bit woozy, that's all. *(Pause, and then in a kind of frenzied bitterness)* Oh, this is fine! I come back after two years, and the first thing I do is pile up a car against the family gatepost. They'll say I was drunk.

MARY:  Or me.

JOHN:  Anyway, this is where we get out. Will the door open on your side? *(There is a sound of a car door opening.)*

MARY:  Yes, it's all right.

JOHN:  Jump out and run for it. Straight up the driveway. *(Two car doors slam, one after the other. The noise of the rain goes sharper and harsher.)* Crikey, look at this car! She's squashed up as flat as an opera-hat. Three hundred quid gone to glory in one night.

MARY:  Come *on!* *(There is a sound of running feet on gravel; and, after two or three seconds, Mary continues breathlessly.)* There isn't a light in the whole house! They've all gone to bed.

JOHN *(also rather breathlessly)*:  No. Matt will be up.

MARY:  But why are you so sure?

JOHN *(simply)*:  He always is. Eleven o'clock to midnight. In his study. Reading an improving book. *(In a different tone)* There's a kind of portico over the front door. Run for it! *(The sound of running feet continues, ending in a kind of stamp as on stones.)* That's better. Now the key— *(We hear heavy breathing, and the jingle of keys on a ring. After a pause John speaks in a startled voice.)* Mary, I'm going mad. I'm going stark, staring mad.

MARY:  What's wrong?

JOHN:  My key is gone.

MARY *(hesitantly):*    Are you sure? After two years . . .

JOHN:    Two years! *(Jingles the keys sharply)* It was on this ring this afternoon. I looked to make sure. And now it's gone. Stop a bit. Match. *(There is the sound of a match being struck.)* No, there's no doubt of it. It's *gone.*

MARY *(half-laughing):*    Well, you don't think I stole it, do you? What does it matter. Ring the bell.

JOHN *(worried):*    It does matter, though. I'm beginning to think that crack on the head has turned my brain. No, don't ring the bell. I'll go round and rout out old Matt.

MARY:    How?

JOHN:    His study is on the ground floor at the back of the house. Just round by that path there. It's a fine old house, isn't it?

MARY:    It's a bit lonely for me.

JOHN *(with musing enthusiasm):*    I know exactly what old Matt will be doing. He'll be sitting by the fire with his back to me. I'll rap on the window, and open it, and walk in. I'll say, "Hello, Matt . . ." *(A dim mutter of thunder)*

MARY:    John, I don't want to hurry you, but if you would *please* . . .

JOHN:    Right you are. You stay here where there's shelter. I'll let you in in two seconds. *(We hear footsteps on a gravelled path, quick and swinging under the rain. These continue for several seconds, while John speaks as though to himself.)* Old Matt! . . . Ow! *(A scratching sound of thorns in bushes.)* Same old rose-bushes. *(Ruffling and jerking noise as pulls himself free.)* Not a thing changed . . . Yes. He's still up. Light in the window; curtains not quite drawn . . . Matt! *(Knuckles knock on glass. There is a slight creak as of the catch of a French window being tried. John's voice is not quite so loud.)* Matt, what have you got your hands up for? What are you looking at over there? Turn round, Matt! *(With rising terror)* Turn . . .

*(A roll of thunder merges into a loud flourish of music. As this fades, we heard Dr. Fell's voice again, slow and heavy.)*

DR. FELL:    . . . and so, you see, we have John Corbin standing outside one of the French windows, looking in.

INTERVIEWER:    Looking at his brother's murder?

DR. FELL:    Yes. So we must put ourselves in his place, and see what he saw. *(Slight pause)* We are looking into a big, square book-lined room, where only one light is burning. The fireplace is in the wall opposite us. An armchair has been drawn up to the fire—a little sideways, so that we can see the face of the man sitting there.

INTERVIEWER:    Matthew Corbin.

DR. FELL:    Yes. Matthew is reading. The single light comes from a bridge-lamp beside his chair. We can hear nothing, because of the rain.

But we watch him. *(Slight pause)* He seems to hear a noise. He looks up. He looks—not towards us, but towards a door at the other side of the room. That door is opening. *(We begin to hear the slow, heavy ticking of a grandfather-clock.)* It is the door to the main hall. Someone is standing there, in the dark hall, just out of sight. Still we can hear nothing, because of the rain on the windows. But Matthew Corbin hears a command. He is still facing the door. He rises to his feet, dropping the book. He raises his hands in the air—high above his head. We see the waxy line of his cheek-bone, and the frightened jaw. We see one of his knees jerk as the bullet strikes him.

*(Loudly and clearly, the noise of a pistol-shot. The ticking of the clock becomes a long, heavy roll of thunder; after which we hear the pouring noise of the rain and John's voice.)*

JOHN *(loud and frenzied):*  Matt! Matt! *(We hear the catch of a door being violently twisted, and the noise of knuckles hammering on glass. John speaks breathlessly.)* Stone. Rock. Something. Got it! *(Glass smashes. There is a fumbling sound with the window-catch, and the click of the handle as it turns. The rain-sound fades away, to be replaced by the ticking of the clock.)* Matt, it's John! Are you hurt? Don't bend over like that! Here. . . . *(He is answered by a loud noise like a long sob and moan. The noise deepens as though in pain. Feet stamp on the floor.)* Steady . . . stand up. . . . *(A heavy thud of a body falling to the floor, and the clock continues to tick loudly in the silence. After a second or two, a door is heard to open and close sharply.)* Who's that? Arnold!

*(Arnold Corbin speaks. He has a slow strong, very clear-speaking voice, with every syllable accentuated; pleasant, but always satiric.)*

ARNOLD:  My name is certainly Arnold Corbin. But I don't think I have the honor of your acquaintance. *(Grimly)* Get over in that corner.

JOHN:  What's the matter with you? Don't you recognize your own brother?

ARNOLD:  My . . . ?

JOHN:  It's John, you ass!

ARNOLD:  J— *(with a long-drawn inflection)* I believe it is.

JOHN:  Don't you see what's happened? *(Wildly)* He's been shot. Help me up with him. He . . .

*(A convulsive sound as of a sob and rattle of breath, followed by a lighter thud as of a hand dropping)*

ARNOLD:  No. I rather think he is no longer with us. *(The clock begins to strike midnight. It has given three measured strokes when Arnold speaks again.)* I should not have known you, John. The mustache changes you. So does that impressive coat of tan.

JOHN *(quietly):*  What's that you've got in your hand?

ARNOLD:    This, my lad, is a firearm. To be exact, it is a Browning .22 automatic. *(The clock continues to strike.)* No, you needn't jump up. *I* didn't kill him. I picked up this gun from the floor just outside that door there, where somebody dropped it.

JOHN:    Is it . . . ?

ARNOLD:    Yes. Smell the barrel. *(Flatly)* A small weapon, isn't it, to have done so much damage?
*(The clock finishes striking.)*

JOHN:    You mean you saw who did it?

ARNOLD *(as though giving this his consideration):*    I regret to say, no.

JOHN:    But the murderer must have passed you!

ARNOLD:    It is quite possible. I was in the front room, answering the telephone. When I heard that *(hesitation)* noise, I came out to investigate. The hall was dark. I saw nobody.

JOHN:    But—

ARNOLD:    I saw nobody.

JOHN:    Look here, Arnold, you don't seem to understand. *(With desperate clarity)* There's a burglar in the house. He stood in that doorway and shot Matt. Then he ran away into the hall. He must be hiding somewhere. We've got to search the house.

ARNOLD:    Perhaps.

JOHN:    There's no "perhaps" about it! I saw it happen.

ARNOLD:    *You* saw the burglar?

JOHN:    No, it was too dark. I only saw . . .

ARNOLD *(thoughtfully):*    An evil spirit?

JOHN *(desperately):*    I don't know anything about evil spirits. All I know is that somebody stood at the door and ordered Matt to put up his hands. When he did put up his hands, somebody shot him through the chest.

ARNOLD:    Yes. That is what I meant.

JOHN:    Sh-h!
*(A dim and muffled voice is heard from some distance away, calling Arnold's name not quite distinctly. It grows closer.)*

ARNOLD:    We seem to have waked up Helen. *(With sudden fierceness and bitterness, his first sign of emotion)* She mustn't see this. Get a rug and throw it over him. Poor old . . .
*(The latch of the door clicks as it opens, and we hear Helen Gates's voice. It is a full contralto, quiet, firm, and with a quality of awareness; it suggests a poised woman of thirty or so.)*

HELEN:    Arnold . . .

ARNOLD:    Stand in front of him, quick!
*(The door is heard to close.)*

HELEN *(She draws in her breath sharply. She makes a statement rather than a question):*   Matt's hurt.

ARNOLD:   He is dead, Helen. You may as well look.

*(In the ensuing silence we hear distinctly the ticking of the grandfather-clock.)*

HELEN *(in an incredulous voice):*   This isn't true. I don't believe it. Matt!

ARNOLD:   Let him alone, my dear. He will not get up again.

HELEN:   But his eyes are open. He's looking at us.

ARNOLD:   Quite possibly.

HELEN:   You needn't be alarmed. I am not going to have hysterics.

ARNOLD *(dryly):*   My dear, the possibility of your having hysterics had never entered my head. By the way—John is back again.

HELEN:   I know.

ARNOLD:   You know?

HELEN:   I heard his voice from my window. My room is just above this one. *(With a certain constraint)* Hullo, John. *(With still more constraint)* It's awfully good to see you again, even at a time like this.

JOHN *(matching Helen's tone):*   It's good to see you, Helen.

ARNOLD *(chuckling):*   You know, Helen, you interest me.

HELEN:   That is flattering.

ARNOLD:   I mean that your inhibitions interest me. After all, he is your cousin. Why don't you give him—shall we say a sisterly embrace? You two stand there shaking hands as though it would break your backs to get any closer. You might be giving him the Freedom of the City. *(Musingly)* But then he always had that, hadn't he?

JOHN *(exploding):*   Oh, for God's sake be quiet!

ARNOLD:   And you seem uncomfortable too, my lad.

HELEN *(quietly):*   Aren't you just a little bit uncomfortable yourself, Arnold? Don't you realize that Matt is dead? *(Spacing her words)* Matt —is—dead. Look at him.

ARNOLD:   I am looking at him.

HELEN:   He was the decentest, kindest . . .

ARNOLD:   Yes. That's why one of us shot him. *(A sharp metallic clang and crash)* You mustn't upset the fire-irons, Helen. It's not dignified.

HELEN *(sharply):*   Do you know what you're saying?

ARNOLD:   I do. Take a look at this pistol.

JOHN:   You're talking rot.

ARNOLD:   Go on; take a good look at the gun; I've got my handkerchief around it. Don't you recognize it?

HELEN:   I do not.

ARNOLD:   John does, though. This little toy is a relic of the nineties. It belonged to our grandfather. For the last fifteen years, so far as I know, it's been packed away in a trunk in the attic—along with a box of old but still serviceable cartridges.

HELEN *(crying out):*   No!

*(A thud as of something tossed down on wood)*

ARNOLD:   There's your evidence on the table. What becomes of your burglar now?

JOHN:   I don't believe it.

ARNOLD *(quietly):*   And yet you're looking very oddly at that gun. Why? Did you take it to South Africa with you?

JOHN:   No! That is—no, of course not! *(His tone is heavy and bewildered, but he speaks quickly.)* Only . . .

ARNOLD:   Only—what?

JOHN:   Nothing at all.

ARNOLD:   One of us killed Matt. You see, Matt had all the money.

HELEN *(quietly, but with intensity):*   Arnold, don't ever ask us to believe anything like that. Don't. It's indecent. Matt was the gentlest, kindest . . .

ARNOLD:   So you said. But haven't you ever observed that that is the sort of person in this world who does get killed? People seem to feel less compunction about it.

JOHN:   Come here, Helen. Don't listen to him.

ARNOLD:   Ah, so you don't dare hear the devil's advocate? But you must. I am not only the devil's advocate. I am the policeman who is going to come ringing at the door in a few minutes, asking questions. *(The noise of the doorbell, a long, steady, whirring buzz, begins to clamor incessantly. Arnold breaks off. He speaks next in a startled tone.)* And there's the doorbell now. *(The bell goes on.)*

HELEN:   But it can't be the police as soon as this. Did you ring up, Arnold?

ARNOLD:   I did not.

JOHN *(startled, remembering):*   Good Lord! I forgot.

ARNOLD *(satirically):*   Is this some of your work, my lad?

JOHN:   I forgot all about . . . *(Pause)* It's somebody I brought along with me. Somebody I want you to meet.

ARNOLD:   Splendid. We are just in the mood for it. . . . Go out and send him away; make any excuse you like.

*(The bell begins again.)*

JOHN:   But you don't understand. It's . . .

ARNOLD:   I don't care who it is. Go and send him away.

JOHN *(in a curious tone, between sarcasm and triumph):*   Of course I've got to obey you, haven't I? *(The triumph emerging)* Just one moment! *(The door opens and closes as John leaves. The bell goes on insistently and loudly.)*

HELEN:   I can't stand that much longer.

ARNOLD:   Steady, my dear. Keep your nerve. I wanted to talk to you.

HELEN:   About what?

ARNOLD *(calmly):*   Well, are you still in love with him?

HELEN:   With whom?

ARNOLD *(as though surprised):*   With John, of course. *(Fiercely)* Why do you think I torture you, and torture myself, every time I see you? Very well; you've seen him again after two years. Are you still in love with him? Or could you possibly pull yourself out of this *idée fixe* and take some interest in me?

HELEN:   Matt—is—dead.

ARNOLD:   So I notice. Let's have a look at him. *(Slight pause)* Yes. Through the heart. Clean wound, too. Straight through the coat, waistcoat, shirt, and—beyond. You could put a pencil through it.

HELEN:   Does this give you any pleasure?

ARNOLD:   It's got to be taken seriously, Helen. Somebody did it. *(Changing his tone)* Motive? Matt's estate is divided among you and John and me. John is the bad penny of the family. He's never kept a job in his life. Even if he happened to love you, he couldn't hope to marry without money. You didn't—speed things up for him, did you?

HELEN:   So you're asking me whether I killed Matt.

ARNOLD:   Somebody did, you know.

HELEN *(vacantly):*   It's no good flying off the handle. We're going to face worse than this before we've finished. But *(articulating the words stiffly)* —no, I did not kill Matt.

ARNOLD:   Where were you when it happened? *(Urgently)* Quick; John will be back any minute!

HELEN:   I was in my room.

ARNOLD:   In bed?

HELEN:   Going to bed.

ARNOLD:   Then it wasn't you I saw in the hall just after Matt was shot?

HELEN:   Arnold!

ARNOLD:   Was it?

HELEN:   You mean the downstairs hall? Here?

ARNOLD:   I do.

HELEN *(sweetly):*   Then you can't have it all your own way, Arnold. *You* were in the hall just after Matt was shot?

ARNOLD:   Of course. To be exact, I was answering the telephone in the front room.

HELEN *(in the same tone of cool and detatched skepticism):*   The telephone? I didn't hear it ring.

ARNOLD *(silkily):*   You wouldn't, my dear, at the back of the house. But I heard it.

HELEN:    And so you ran downstairs and answered it?

ARNOLD:    Of course.

HELEN:    In the dark?

ARNOLD:    In the dark. Haven't you ever done that?

HELEN:    No.

ARNOLD:    I hate ringing telephones. They should be silenced as soon as possible. Let me tell you more about it. *(In a different tone)* Do you know who was speaking on that phone?

HELEN:    I'm beginning to guess *what* it was. You mean . . .

ARNOLD:    It was Jimmy Parradine, very much upset for fear the rain would put off our golf tomorrow. *(Pause)* I talked on the phone to him from five minutes to midnight until the time Matt was shot. Jimmy will be willing to verify that. In fact, he heard the noise of the shot over the wire. *(Pause. Speaks slowly and grimly)* In other words, my dear, I have an alibi.

HELEN *(coolly):*    Please don't come near me.

ARNOLD:    I therefore want to know—was it you I saw in the hall just after Matt was shot?

HELEN *(as though curiously):*    You must be very jealous of John.

ARNOLD:    Please answer my question.

HELEN *(as though she had not heard):*    And so in your eyes John is the bad penny of the family? You're usually more charitable.

ARNOLD *(through his teeth):*    Charitable!

HELEN:    Even if you think he is not clever . . .

ARNOLD:    I never said he was not clever. I said he couldn't hold a job.

HELEN:    He's held this one.

ARNOLD:    In South Africa? So he says.

HELEN *(temper showing):*    And even if he does happen to be the bad penny of the family . . .

ARNOLD:    That term seems to bother you. We'll be generous. Let us say that his value is anything between two bob and a half a crown. *(The sharp, ringing sound of a slap across the face)* I beg your pardon. Any gentleman begs a lady's pardon after she has slapped his face.

HELEN:    *I'm* sorry, Arnold.

ARNOLD:    Not at all. *(Drawing a deep breath)* That cured me, I think. You don't know what it is to be jealous, do you?

HELEN:    I hope not.

ARNOLD:    Never? Sssh!

*(The door opens—this time with a bang when it is thrown back against the wall. John's voice speaks loudly and firmly.)*

JOHN:    Arnold! Will you and Helen come out in the hall for a moment?

ARNOLD:    Look here . . .

JOHN *(firmly):*    I'm afraid you've got to. This is important. *(Trium-*

*phantly)* I want you to meet Mary—Miss Stevenson. Mary, this is my cousin Helen and my brother Arnold. Mary and I are going to be married.

*(For three seconds we hear only the ticking of the grandfather-clock.)*

HELEN *(without inflection):*    How do you do, Miss Stevenson.

MARY *(flustered, but determined):*    I'm terribly sorry. I wouldn't have rung that bell for worlds if I'd known. John has just told me.

ARNOLD *(out of the corner of his mouth):*    Not bad-looking, Helen. In a blonde way, of course.

HELEN:    I think we'd better wake up the servants. John, will you take Miss Stevenson into the front room and make her comfortable?

MARY:    Thank you, no. I'd better go. If I could just ring for a taxi . . .

JOHN *(doggedly):*    I tell you, we're going to be married.

ARNOLD:    So you said. *(Politely)* But not tonight, I hope?

JOHN:    What?

ARNOLD:    Frankly, John, this is an awkward situation which you're not making any better. Miss Stevenson, I apologize for my brother and I am sorry we had to meet under these conditions. You understand, don't you?

MARY:    Of course I do, Dr. Corbin.

ARNOLD *(vaguely puzzled):*    Haven't I met you somewhere before?

MARY:    I don't think so.

ARNOLD *(still puzzled):*    You and John met aboard ship, did you?

MARY:    Yes, we . . .

HELEN *(crying out):*    Oh, *must* we go into all this?

MARY:    I know. It sounds horrible standing here talking like this. You will excuse me, won't you? If you'll just let me ring up a taxi. I think I saw a telephone in the front room.

HELEN *(in a curious tone):*    Just a moment. You say you *saw* a telephone in the front room?

MARY:    Yes, of course.

HELEN:    But how could you have, if you were outside? You haven't been in the house, have you?

MARY *(quickly):*    No! No!

HELEN:    Then . . . ?

MARY:    I was standing just outside, on the doorstep. I looked in through the window. It was dark, but the curtains weren't drawn and the phone was on a little table drawn up against the window. *(Curtly)* I'm sorry if it's bad manners to notice telephones.

HELEN *(with a sort of cold excitement):*    Please, Miss Stevenson. You don't understand at all. Don't think I'm completely mad, but . . . how long were you out there on the doorstep?

MARY:    Ever since John left me there.

HELEN *(insistently and softly):*   And, of course, during that time you noticed someone using the telephone?

MARY:   I beg your pardon?

HELEN *(still softly):*   You noticed someone using the telephone?

MARY *(slowly and wonderingly):*   No. Nobody used the telephone while I was there.

*(A long flourish of music as we return to the present)*

DR. FELL:   Four persons gave testimony in the murder of Matthew Corbin—John Corbin, Arnold Corbin, Helen Gates, and Mary Stevenson. One of these persons was telling a pack of lies. Don't you see the most significant bit of evidence there?

INTERVIEWER:   You mean the point about the telephone?

DR. FELL:   Great Scott, no!

INTERVIEWER:   Isn't that the whole point?

DR. FELL:   Not at all. The most significant bit of evidence is the fact that the dead man was wearing a waistcoat.

INTERVIEWER:   What?

DR. FELL *(fiery with earnestness):*   I repeat, sir. The most important clue is the fact that the dead man was wearing a waistcoat.

INTERVIEWER:   Dr. Fell, I may be very dense. But I'm hanged if I see what the corpse's waistcoat has to do with this.

DR. FELL:   You remember, however, that Arnold Corbin called special attention to it. "A clean wound. Straight through the coat, waistcoat, shirt, and beyond. You could put a pencil through it."

INTERVIEWER:   Yes. Well?

DR. FELL *(chuckles):*   I leave the point for your consideration. If you will return in a week or so, my boy, I shall try to expound it to you. In the meantime—what say ye? Who killed Matthew Corbin?

# Who Killed Matthew Corbin?

## EPISODE 2

ANNOUNCER: What say ye? Presenting the second episode in the murder of Matthew Corbin, reconstructed for us by Dr. Gideon Fell. We take you now to Dr. Fell's study, where again a representative of the BBC is waiting to interview him.

*(Flourish of music, strong and harsh)*

DR. FELL *(with a chuckle):* You are on time, I see.

INTERVIEWER: I certainly am, Doctor.

DR. FELL: And prepared?

INTERVIEWER: For what?

DR. FELL: Oh, for anything. But in particular to hear about the trial.

INTERVIEWER: Yes.

DR. FELL: Good! Then let us see if you have correctly assimilated the facts I gave you a fortnight ago. Suppose you give me a brief summary, in your own words, of the events leading up to the murder.

INTERVIEWER: But—er—*I* am supposed to be doing the interviewing, Doctor.

DR. FELL: No matter, sir. Go on.

INTERVIEWER: Well! *(Hesitates)* On the night of October 13th, Matthew Corbin was shot dead in the back room of his house at Hampstead. Matthew Corbin was a middle-aged and wealthy man who had formerly been a barrister, but who had given up the practice of law after a case in which he had successfully defended his client, a woman, on a poisoning charge; and had later discovered her to be guilty.

DR. FELL: Yes?

INTERVIEWER: On October 13th, Matthew Corbin's younger brother, John, had just returned to England after two years in South Africa. On the voyage home, John Corbin had met and become engaged to be married to a girl named Mary Stevenson.

DR. FELL: Go on.

INTERVIEWER: That night John was taking Miss Stevenson home to meet his family. They arrived at the house in the middle of a thunderstorm. John discovered that he had lost—or someone had stolen—his key to the front door. So he went round to the back of the house to rout out his brother Matthew, who usually sat up late in the study there.

DR. FELL: Leaving Miss Stevenson at the front door.

INTERVIEWER: Yes. Through the French windows of the study, John saw his brother murdered. Matthew was shot by someone standing out of sight in the door to the hall. This person ordered Matthew to put up his hands. He did so, but in spite of this he was shot through the heart at a distance of about fifteen feet.

DR. FELL *(earnestly):*   Ah, yes. The point to whose tremendous importance I drew your attention.

INTERVIEWER:   Steady, sir. John Corbin smashed the French window and got in. There he met his other brother—Arnold Corbin. Arnold produced the pistol with which the crime had been committed: an old .22 automatic, which had been packed away in the attic but which nobody had seen for years. Arnold accused John of having taken the gun to South Africa with him.

DR. FELL:   Which John denied.

INTERVIEWER:   Yes. They were then joined by their cousin, Helen Gates, who had formerly been in love with John. One of those four persons must have committed the murder. The question is, which one?

DR. FELL:   Well, which one would *you* have arrested?

INTERVIEWER:   I'd rather not say.

DR. FELL:   You know, at least, which one the police arrested for the crime. They arrested—

*(Long flourish of music, fading into background sounds of Courtroom Number One of the Central Criminal Court: whisperings, throat-clearings, creakings, the shuffle of feet against a hollow background. There are three loud, hollow knocks—the signal that the judge is about to enter. There is a heavier shuffling and creaking as the whole assemblage stands up.)*

A WOMAN'S VOICE *(whispering):*   D'ye think she done it?

A MAN'S VOICE *(fiercely):*   Sh-h! Stand up! 'Ere's the judge.

USHER'S VOICE *(proclaiming):*   All persons who have anything to do before my lords the King's Justices of Oyer and Terminer, and general gaol delivery for the jurisdiction of the Central Criminal Court, draw near and give your attendance. God save the King, and my lords the King's Justices.

*(Heavy shuffling as the people in the court sit down)*

CLERK OF THE COURT:   Mary Ann Stevenson, you are indicted and the charge against you is murder: in that on the 13th day of October, 1932, in the county of Middlesex, you murdered Matthew Corbin. How say you, Mary Ann Stevenson: are you guilty or not guilty?

MARY:   Not guilty.

JUDGE:   You may swear the jury.

*(Another flourish of music)*

MR. RAEBURN, THE PROSECUTOR:   May it please your lordship, members of the jury: the charge against the prisoner, as you have heard, is murder. It is my duty to open to you the case for the prosecution. And at the outset I am faced with a task which is no less unpleasant because it is undertaken with reluctance. Members of the jury, my lord will tell you that we are not here concerned with any person's past offences at law. If (for example) a man should come to this court charged with burglary, and that same man had previously served a sentence for burglary, the Crown must not mention or in any way refer to that previous conviction, lest it unduly influence the jury. Still less are we concerned with referring to any previous charge (heaven forbid!) in which the accused has been triumphantly proved innocent. But here, I shall ask leave to submit, we are faced with a very different matter. We are faced with the very motive and mainspring of this crime. The evidence in the death of Matthew Corbin will not—*cannot*—be complete unless mention is made of a certain event in the past history of the prisoner.

JUDGE:  Mr. Raeburn.

RAEBURN:  My lord?

*(The two voices are a contrast. That of the prosecutor is full, confident, suave, and with a sound of sincere impartiality. That of the judge is slow, thin, dry, and painstaking.)*

JUDGE:  I do not like to interrupt you, Mr. Raeburn; but I feel that this is a point on which I may have to rule. What will you attempt to show?

RAEBURN:  My lord, we shall attempt to show that this is not the first time that the prisoner, Mary Ann Stevenson, has stood in a dock charged with murder. *(Sensation in court)* You will hear that four years ago, at Kingston Assizes, the prisoner stood her trial on a charge of poisoning her former employer, an elderly lady to whom she had been nurse-companion.

JUDGE:  And was, I presume, acquitted?

RAEBURN:  Yes, my lord.

JUDGE:  Then I still do not understand you, Mr. Raeburn. Are you suggesting that the prisoner is guilty of this crime because she was innocent of another one?

RAEBURN:  My lord, the Crown seeks to show motive. You will hear that counsel for the defense in that other trial was the deceased, Matthew Corbin. You will hear evidence to prove whether Matthew Corbin did, or did not, cherish a violent dislike towards the prisoner. You will hear evidence to prove whether he might, or might not, have been a stumbling-block in the prisoner's projected marriage to Mr. John Corbin. You will hear—

MARY *(in a whisper):*  God help me. God help me!

*(Another long flourish of music, merging again into the background of court noises. The prosecutor's voice goes on as though after an interval.)*

RAEBURN:  Thank you, Chief Inspector. That is all. *(Pause)* Call Helen Gates.

*(Shuffling, and the sharp rap of footsteps as though along an aisle.)*

HELEN *(low and rapidly):*    I swear by Almighty God that the evidence I shall give be the truth, the whole truth, and nothing but the truth.

RAEBURN:    What is your full name?

HELEN:    Helen Ainslie Gates.

RAEBURN:    Where do you live?

HELEN:    The White House, Hampstead. *(Her voice is now clear, strong, and firm. She is collected and very determined.)*

RAEBURN:    I believe, Miss Gates, that you are a cousin of the deceased?

HELEN:    That is so.

RAEBURN:    And have lived at his house for some years?

HELEN:    Eight years.

RAEBURN:    Eight years. Thank you. Miss Gates, did you ever hear the deceased mention the case of a woman then known as Mary Ann White?

HELEN *(through her teeth):*    Yes.

RAEBURN:    I believe the deceased acted as counsel for the defense at the trial of Mary Ann White in 1928.

HELEN:    Yes.

RAEBURN:    Did you ever hear the deceased pass any comment on this case?

HELEN:    Yes. Frequently.

RAEBURN:    Frequently: I see. What in particular did he say?

HELEN *(showing her hesitation for the first time):*    Well, he . . .

RAEBURN:    Yes? Speak up, please.

HELEN *(clearly):*    He said he felt sorry for her. He said it was a—I think you call it a "legal aid" case. She had no money, and the court appointed him to defend her. He said she seemed in a stupor most of the time; that she never seemed even to know what his name was, or what he was saying to her.

RAEBURN *(swiftly):*    I see. So that when she first made the acquaintance of Mr. John Corbin, she would not necessarily have connected him with the Matthew Corbin who defended her three years before?

JUDGE *(sharply):*    Mr. Raeburn, I cannot allow that. The witness is not qualified to say what the prisoner may or may not have been thinking.

RAEBURN:    Beg-ludship's-pardon. Miss Gates, did you ever hear Mr. Matthew Corbin pass any other comment on this case?

HELEN *(grimly):*    Yes, I did.

RAEBURN:    And what was that?

HELEN:    He said that after it was all over she had admitted to him she was guilty.

MARY *(in a barely audible whisper):*    It's not true. Oh, God, it's not true!

RAEBURN:    Anything else, Miss Gates?

HELEN *(clearly and heavily):*    He said that the very thought of her made him sick. He hoped that not he or any member of his family ever set eyes on her again.

*(Flourish of music, again fading into the prosecutor's voice)*

RAEBURN:    What is your full name?

JOHN *(clearing his throat):*    John Rutherford Corbin.

RAEBURN:    Your age?

JOHN:    Twenty-two.

RAEBURN:    Where do you live?

JOHN:    I don't live anywhere now; I mean, I have a service flat in town. Raglan Mansions, Sloane Street.

RAEBURN:    How long have you known the prisoner, Mary Ann Stevenson?

JOHN:    About four months. *(He is obviously very nervous. He clears his throat again, speaking rapidly, so that the last few words are little more than a rapid and indistinguishable mumble.)*

JUDGE *(gently but insistently):*    You will have to speak up. I cannot hear a word you are saying.

JOHN:    My lord, I said about four months.

RAEBURN:    You first met the prisoner aboard *S. S. Berkeley Castle,* between Capetown and Southampton?

JOHN:    Yes.

RAEBURN:    Where you became engaged to be married?

JOHN:    Yes.

RAEBURN:    Did she ever tell you anything of her past life?

JOHN:    No.

RAEBURN:    And you never asked her for any details?

JOHN *(fiercely):*    Why should I?

RAEBURN:    Now, Mr. Corbin, please cast your mind back to the day of your arrival in England. You had not warned your brother or any of your family that you were returning?

JOHN:    No. I wanted to surprise them.

RAEBURN:    You wanted to surprise them. Quite so. I believe that on that same day you bought a motor-car? Yes. And, at shortly before midnight on the night of the 13th, you and the prisoner drove out to your brother's home?

JOHN:    Yes. It was raining. We—

RAEBURN:    Just one moment, if you please. We shall come to that in good time. On your way to your brother's house, what did you and the prisoner talk about?

JOHN:    Nothing important.

RAEBURN:    Oh, come, Mr. Corbin! Did you not tell the prisoner that your brother was a barrister who had retired from practice because of a poisoning case in which he later had reason to believe his client guilty? *(Gently, but with powerful slowness and impressiveness)* Did you not, in fact, outline the whole case of Mary Ann White?

JOHN *(snarling):* I don't remember.

RAEBURN *(with gentle incredulity):* You don't remember? *(More curtly)* Mr. Corbin, I must remind you that you are under oath.

JOHN: We talked about something. I don't know what. Besides, I was confused. We had a wreck. The car skidded. I got a crack on the head . . .

RAEBURN *(pouncing):* Ah, yes. The car skidded, you say?

JOHN: Yes, and hit the gatepost in front of the house.

RAEBURN: You say that you *(handling the words delicately)* "got a crack on the head"? You mean that you were knocked unconscious?

JOHN: Something like that, for a minute or two. Yes.

RAEBURN: For a minute or two?

JOHN: Yes.

RAEBURN: You swear to that, Mr. Corbin?

JOHN *(wildly):* Yes, I do. So how could I remember what I might have been saying when the car was wrecked? *(With triumph)* I couldn't have.

RAEBURN: I see. *(Pause)* But you were unconscious long enough for someone to have stolen the front-door key out of your pocket? *(Sensation. There is another pause.)*

JOHN *(rather shrilly):* I don't understand what you mean.

RAEBURN: Let me endeavor to make the question clearer. You had a key to the front door of your brother's house?

JOHN: I had one, yes.

RAEBURN: When did you last see this key?

JOHN: In the afternoon of that same day. It was on my keyring.

RAEBURN: Precisely. But, when you wanted to open the front door of the house immediately after your motor-smash, you discovered that the key was missing? *(Pause)* Please speak up. Is that correct?

JOHN: I must have lost it.

RAEBURN: You must have lost it. *(Out of patience)* Mr. Corbin, I put it to you that it would have been a simple matter for the prisoner to have removed this key from your pocket while you were unconscious.

JOHN *(wildly):* I don't know.

*(To indicate that several intermediate questions have been asked, the voices fade and then return.)*

RAEBURN: Again let me see if I understand you. You left the prisoner standing alone by the front door—*alone, by the front door*—while you went round to the back.

JOHN: That's right, near enough.

RAEBURN:  You told the prisoner that your brother Matthew always sat up late in his study there, and that the rest of the household would have retired?

JOHN:  Yes.

RAEBURN:  In other words, leaving a clear way open for the prisoner to walk into the house and shoot your brother through the heart?

JOHN:  I don't understand. You're twisting it all up. Everything I say, you—

RAEBURN:  Be good enough to continue, Mr. Corbin. What happened then?

JOHN *(jerkily):*  I walked round to the back. It was raining. I looked through one of the French windows in the study, and saw Matt. He was sitting by the fire, reading. He looked just the same as ever.

RAEBURN:  Go on.

JOHN:  There was thunder, and everything. I couldn't hear. But all of a sudden Matt seemed to hear something. He looked up.

RAEBURN:  Towards you?

JOHN:  No. Towards a door across the room. It leads to the hall.

RAEBURN:  That is the door shown in photograph number six? Please hand the booklet up to the witness. Thank you.

JOHN:  Yes, that's it. There was somebody standing outside the door. I couldn't tell who it was. The window was smeared with rain and there was only one light in the room. But whoever it was seemed to be ordering Matt to put up his hands—high over his head. Then the murderer shot him.

RAEBURN:  What did you do?

JOHN:  The window was locked. But I had my driving gloves on, so I smashed it with a stone. I couldn't do anything for him. He looked scared and hurt. I tried to hold him up; but he put his hands over his stomach, and moaned and fell down on the floor.

RAEBURN *(more gently):*  What did he say to you?

JOHN:  He didn't say anything. He just died.

RAEBURN:  And then?

JOHN:  Then the door to the hall opened. And my other brother—Arnold—came in. I thought at first Arnold had shot Matt himself, because Arnold was carrying that little automatic pistol. But Arnold told me he had picked up the pistol from the floor just outside the room. Arnold said . . .

*(John's voice fades slowly into a flourish of music, and is taken up by Arnold's slow, deep, satirical voice.)*

ARNOLD:  Yes. I found the .22 automatic lying just outside the door.

RAEBURN:  You found it there how long after the shot was fired?

ARNOLD:   I cannot be precise as to that. I should say perhaps two minutes, perhaps less.

RAEBURN:   You heard the shot fired?

ARNOLD:   I did.

RAEBURN:   And where were you then?

ARNOLD:   I was speaking on the telephone in the front room.

RAEBURN:   Yes. We have had police testimony to that effect. But please be a little more explicit.

ARNOLD:   Some minutes before the firing of the shot, I heard the telephone ring in the front room downstairs. I was then in my own room, upstairs. I hurried down—without bothering to turn on any lights, I may add—and answered the phone. The call was for me. It was from a Mr. Parradine, a friend of mine. I was still speaking with him, at close on midnight, when both of us heard the shot.

RAEBURN:   What did you do then?

ARNOLD:   I said a few more words to Mr. Parradine, and rang off. Then I went out into the hall.

RAEBURN:   Was the hall dark?

ARNOLD:   Almost dark. There was a very faint light from the partly open door of my brother Matthew's study.

RAEBURN:   Did you see anyone in the hall at this time?

ARNOLD:   I did.

RAEBURN:   Whom did you see?

ARNOLD:   I regret to say that it was the accused, Miss Stevenson.
   *(There is the sound of the scrape of a chair being pushed back, sharply, on the polished floor of the dock. Then the sound of someone pounding on the rail of the dock. Mary Stevenson speaks. She is not hysterical, but her voice has a trapped and battered anguish.)*

MARY:   I can't stand this. It isn't true. Can't anyone of you *see* that it isn't true?

A WARDER'S VOICE *(in an urgent whisper):*   Ss-t, now, miss! Sit down! Easy!

MARY:   But you don't know what it feels like. I never poisoned Mrs. Frobisher. I never told Mr. Corbin I did. He never thought I did. He—

JUDGE *(sharply, but not unkindly):*   Are you unwell?

MARY:   No, but—

JUDGE:   If you are unwell, I shall be glad to grant a recess. Otherwise I must tell you that I cannot allow these interruptions. You are not upon trial for a crime of which you have already been acquitted. I shall make that sufficiently clear to the jury.

MARY:   But what difference does that make? They've heard it, haven't they?

JUDGE *(in a soft, deadly voice):*  For the last time, I must tell you that I cannot hear you now. You may proceed, Mr. Raeburn.

RAEBURN:  Now, Mr. Corbin: you tell us that you saw the accused in the hall shortly after the shot was fired?

ARNOLD:  I did.

RAEBURN:  But did it not surprise you to see a stranger in the hall?

ARNOLD:  No. I should explain that at first I mistook her for my cousin, Miss Helen Gates. So I paid no attention; I did not even speak.

RAEBURN:  What was the accused doing in the hall?

ARNOLD:  Standing by the staircase, I think. I cannot be positive.

RAEBURN:  No doubt. What did you do then?

ARNOLD *(with acerbity):*  I ran down toward the study. I was not unnaturally startled when I heard a shot fired in my brother's study: an event somewhat rare in our household.

RAEBURN:  No doubt. And you found?

ARNOLD:  I found the automatic pistol lying by the door. I also found my brother Matthew dead; and my other brother, John, standing over him.

RAEBURN:  Go on.

ARNOLD:  There was no doubt as to Matthew's being dead. It was a good clean wound. You could have run a pencil in a dead straight line through jacket, waistcoat, shirt, and heart.

RAEBURN:  Thank you, Mr. Corbin. We have already heard the medical evidence. Now—this automatic pistol, exhibit number eight. Can you identify the pistol?

ARNOLD:  I can.

RAEBURN:  It was the property of your grandfather, and has been in the possession of your family for some years?

ARNOLD:  It has.

RAEBURN:  When did you last see this pistol?

ARNOLD *(in a loud, firm voice):*  To the best of my knowledge, when my brother John took it with him to South Africa two years ago.

*(Another flourish of music, fading into Dr. Fell's voice)*

DR. FELL:  Hm'f. And on that point, it appeared, rested the whole crux of the trial. Sir, I was present. I heard the girl crying out for her life. I saw the noose tighten and heard the perjured testimony. And even then—I say this to my shame and sorrow—even then I did not see the point which seems so painfully obvious now.

INTERVIEWER *(uneasily):*  Well, Dr. Fell, I don't know what you think. But it seems a fairly strong case to me.

DR. FELL:  Ah, but then you have heard only one side of the evidence. You haven't heard the cross-examinations, which were potent and damaging. Mary Stevenson (do you remember?) was defended by Sir

Charles Wolfe, that red-haired ferret. He gave every witness for the prosecution a bad time—over certain points which will have occurred to you. He ridiculed and trampled on their evidence. In particular he manhandled Arnold's evidence about the gun. *(Chuckles)* I am not likely to forget the moment when Sir Charles Wolfe rose to open the case for the defense.

*(Dr. Fell's voice fades away into courtroom noises, and is replaced by the voice of Sir Charles Wolfe. He has a very distinctive voice: sharp, worrying and pouncing, as though each word had a bad smell and he sniffed before uttering it. It suggests the voice of Javert in* Les Miserables.*)*

SIR CHARLES:  Me lord. *(Sniff)* Members of the jury. My learned friend presents his case against this girl on three counts. *(Pause and slight sniff)* A murder she did not commit. *(Longer pause and deeper sniff)* A key. *(Still longer pause and sniff)* And a pistol. Members of the jury, before calling this girl into the witness box, I want to call your attention to a few things—just a few—in the tissue of improbabilities my learned friend asks you to swallow.

Now either this crime was premeditated, or else it was done on the spur of the moment. What do the prosecution say? They say it was done on the spur of the moment. When did this girl decide to commit murder? Not five minutes, they tell you, before she arrived at the house! They are in this car . . . John Corbin tells her about the case of Mary Ann White . . . they are in sight of the house . . . and then (only *then*) she makes up her mind to kill Matthew Corbin. Yes. And how does she go about it? She takes advantage of a motor-smash to steal a key off his keyring. Just think of that! Here's a keyring . . . John Corbin's keyring . . . with nine or ten keys on it: as he tells it. Unerringly, and by some miracle of mind-reading, she picks out the right key to the front door, and detaches it. Mr. John Corbin has told you he never mentioned the subject of keys to her. She did not even know he had a key to the house. Yes, by this miracle of my learned friend's, she finds the right key to the front door. *(A jingle of keys)* Would any of you ladies and gentlemen like to take this keyring of mine and try to perform the same feat?

WOMAN'S VOICE *(whispering):*  Sarcastic old beggar, ain't 'e?

MAN'S VOICE:  Sh-h!

SIR CHARLES:  And *why* does she do this? Why? Here my learned friend's argument is even more difficult to follow. Does this girl know in advance that she is going to be left alone for some minutes outside the front door? Is she mind-reading again? Has she foretold not only the right key, but all the circumstances that are going to happen in the next ten minutes? Apparently. For she walks into the house—a casual treatment of murder, my friends!—and kills this man—*(sinking his voice)* with what? With a pistol which, so far as anybody except Mr. Arnold Corbin knows, has not been out of the Corbins' house in twenty years. A pistol which is a family relic. A pistol firing ammunition which, I shall call evidence to show, has not even been manufactured since the year 1900.

Where did she get this pistol? Did she get *that* out of John Corbin's pocket too? Or, in this minute during which he is unconscious, did she search through his suitcases in the hope of finding a lethal weapon there? You've heard John Corbin flatly deny that he ever took the gun to South Africa. You can judge of his sincerity. And why should he have taken it? Why? A blunderbuss or a crossbow would have been more convenient, since the only ammunition he can get for it is in his home six thousand miles away. Yet he takes it. He brings it back. And Mary Stevenson mysteriously finds it—in his pocket, or in his luggage *(sniff)*—just as soon as she decides to commit a murder.

HELEN *(in a low whisper):*    Arnold, don't fidget so. He's only doing his duty, after all.

ARNOLD:    My dear Helen, it is all very well to expect me to be the iron man on all occasions. But have you quite realized what Sir Charles is suggesting? He's suggesting—

A VOICE:    Sh-h!

SIR CHARLES:    And this pistol. What does *Mr Arnold Corbin* say about it? He "thinks." He "cannot be positive." To a dozen questions he "cannot be positive." Does he say, "I *saw* my brother John remove this gun from the house"? I saw it in his hand"? I saw it in his suitcase"? No. This is merely his "impression." *(Sternly)* Members of the jury, this girl has not been so well-treated by the world that she deserves to be judged by "impressions" now. She has not had so happy a life that she should be hanged by the neck because someone "cannot be positive." That is all I need to say here, since I propose to let the accused and the evidence speak for themselves, in order to prove the case against her to be a tissue of malicious nonsense from end to end. I call the prisoner.

*(Shiftings, throat-clearings, release of breath in court, which fade into Mary's voice)*

MARY:    . . . and that was why, you see. I couldn't tell John. I couldn't!

SIR CHARLES:    Now, Miss Stevenson, you have never denied that you were accused of having killed a certain Mrs. Frobisher in the year 1928?

MARY:    No. It's true.

SIR CHARLES:    But did you ever tell Mr. Matthew Corbin, after the trial, that you were guilty?

MARY *(desperately):*   No, of course not. I never even saw him after the trial.

SIR CHARLES *(powerfully enlightened):*   Oh? You never even spoke to him, then?

MARY:   No, except when he offered congratulations after the verdict, and there were dozens of people with us. I went straight from the courtroom to Eastbourne, and sailed for Africa two days later. I never exchanged a word with him.

SIR CHARLES *(softly):*   Yes. I shall call witnesses to that fact, Miss Stevenson. . . . So Matthew Corbin always knew you were innocent?

MARY:   Of course. He was terribly nice.

SIR CHARLES:   He always knew you were innocent. But you have heard Miss Helen Gates's suggestion to the contrary?

MARY:   Yes. I—

SIR CHARLES:   What do you think of that suggestion?

MARY:   It's a lie! *(Checking herself, confused)* I—I mean: that is—Miss Gates must have misunderstood.

HELEN *(in an implacable whisper):*   Snivelling little devil. Trying to wind men around her little finger again. I wish *I* were on the jury.

ARNOLD:   Not the most admirable state of mind for a witness, my dear Helen. Where does the shoe pinch now?

SIR CHARLES:   So, so. At the end of the trial, you went to South Africa?

MARY:   Yes, to Port Elizabeth. I have a sister there.

SIR CHARLES:   And didn't return for four years?

MARY:   No, not until—*(She stops)*

SIR CHARLES *(soothingly):*   Quite, quite. Now, when you met Mr. John Corbin aboard ship, did you connect him with the barrister who had defended you at the Frobisher trial?

MARY:   No, I didn't. Not once. You see, I—thought the barrister's name was Coburn. C-o-b-u-r-n. I hardly saw him at all. I didn't know.

SIR CHARLES:   When did you begin to suspect who he really was?

MARY:   That part of what they say is true. I *did* begin to suspect when John told me about—you know—the woman accused of poisoning. It was horrible. But I only suspected. I didn't know for sure.

SIR CHARLES *(wearily):*   And these other suggestions of my learned friend. When the car struck the gatepost, and Mr. Corbin was knocked out, did you take a key from him?

MARY:   No!

SIR CHARLES:   Or a pistol?

MARY:   No, no, no!

SIR CHARLES:   But one more thing. When Mr. Corbin left you alone in the rain outside the front door, did you go inside?

MARY *(in a low voice, after a pause):*   Yes, I did.

*(Mild sensation)*

SIR CHARLES:   Hardly a sinister circumstance. Let's see. Why did you go in?

MARY:   The front door wasn't locked. John hadn't even tried it to see. I just put out my hand, and the door opened. So I . . . well, it was raining, and I . . . I just walked in.

SIR CHARLES:   Quite naturally.

MARY:   Please. I admit I didn't tell the truth about it afterwards, but I was afraid to. I just—walked in. The hall was dark. I didn't know what to do. Whether to call out, or turn on a light, or what. *(Swallows hard)* And then—

SIR CHARLES:   Go on.

MARY:   I heard a shot. *(The muttering in the court, which has been going on under this testimony for a short while, stops in dead silence. There is a pause.)* I thought I saw somebody moving down at the end of the hall, where there was a tiny little light from a door. But I was too frightened to go and see. I don't know who fired the shot. I don't know *anything.*

*(Long flourish of music, fading into Dr. Fell's voice)*

DR. FELL:   —and so, d'ye see, the witness passed in review. Sir Charles Wolfe made his final speech for the defense, and Mr. Raeburn for the Crown. The judge summed up. The jury retired. And we waited for the verdict. I have since spoken to someone who was sitting very close to Arnold Corbin and Helen Gates when that thin little line of jurymen came. I have sometimes fancied I could see their faces then. I have even fancied that I could hear Helen Gates's voice. . . .

HELEN:   Arnold, I think you had better hold my hand. Do you *really* think they'll convict her?

ARNOLD:   They are not looking at her. That's a bad sign. Or a good sign —from your point of view.

HELEN:   Arnold—

ARNOLD:   Sh-h!

CLERK OF THE COURT:   Members of the jury, are you agreed upon your verdict?

FOREMAN OF THE JURY:   We are.

CLERK:   What say you? Do you find the prisoner guilty, or not guilty? *(Slight pause)*

FOREMAN:   Guilty.

*(A woman screams.)*

CLERK:   Prisoner at the bar, you have been arraigned upon a charge of murder, and have placed yourself upon your country. Have you anything to say why judgment of death should not be pronounced upon you, and why you should not die according to law?

MARY:   I am not guilty. Oh, God, I am not guilty!

HELEN *(in a whisper):*   Arnold! What is it? What's that little dark patch of a thing that the judge is putting on his wig?

ARNOLD:   You should know, my dear. That is the black cap. She's going to be hanged.

# Who Killed Matthew Corbin?

## EPISODE 3

ANNOUNCER: What happened next? Presenting the third and final episode in the murder of Matthew Corbin, narrated for us by Dr. Gideon Fell. We take you now to Dr. Fell's study where the Gargantuan doctor is waiting to tell us what happened.

*(Flourish of music, out of which we hear Dr. Fell speaking. He is addressing a third party.)*

DR. FELL: My dear Hadley, it is impossible to tell. A slip may be made even yet. *(Breaks off)* Ah! *(With thunderous joviality)* Good evening, my friend.

INTERVIEWER: Good evening, Dr. Fell. I hope I'm not late?

DR. FELL: Not at all. Sit down.

INTERVIEWER: We—er—have another guest with us tonight?

DR. FELL: Ah, yes. Forgive me. This is my friend, Superintendent Hadley, of the Criminal Investigation Department. Hadley, this is the young man from the BBC who asks all the inconvenient questions.

INTERVIEWER *(laughing):* For my sins.

HADLEY *(in a curt, rather gruff, noncommittal voice):* How do you do?

INTERVIEWER: Two notable authorities on crime in front of one microphone! This is a bit of luck. Are you interested in this case, Superintendent?

HADLEY: The police are always interested in murder. It's one of our failings. But in this case . . .

INTERVIEWER: You mean failures, don't you? Dr. Fell, you know, just says sweepingly that everybody was wrong. The judge was wrong; the jury was wrong; the prosecution was wrong; even the defense was wrong.

HADLEY: He would.

DR. FELL *(rearing up):* Sir, I said that, and I repeat it.

HADLEY *(querulously):* Well, you needn't look at me like that. I wasn't in charge of the case. *(Thoughtfully)* All the same, it was a queer business.

DR. FELL *(with evil glee):* Aha! Were you satisfied with the evidence?

HADLEY: No. But if you've got anything to say, get on and say it.

DR. FELL *(after a slight pause, as though settling himself):* Mary Stevenson was sentenced to death on January 25th, 1933. They took her back to Holloway Prison; and the clock began to tick off another week, another day, another hour of the short time she would have even in the condemned cell. *(Pause)*

John Corbin, her fiance, had moved heaven and earth at the trial to

get her acquitted. There was nothing more he could do. He went back
to his West End flat—and began to drink; so that he was even more
useless than ever.

We are concerned with only two other persons. Arnold Corbin, the
murdered man's other brother. And Helen Gates, the cousin. I have
been fascinated by those two. I saw them leave the court. Arnold, the
tall, heavy-faced scholar, of somber and powerful imagination. Helen
Gates, not much less tall, fashionable, a beauty in her way, as dark-
complexioned as a gypsy. They went back to the bleak house at Hampstead, which seemed all the more bleak for being called The White
House. They tried to pick up their lives again. But it was not easy.
February came in with squalls of rain. I have sometimes fancied I
could see them sitting by the fire, night after night, perhaps even in the
room where Matthew had been shot. Arnold, I know, had resumed his
habit of reading aloud.

*(Dr. Fell's voice fades, and is taken up by the slow, heavy ticking of the
grandfather-clock. It is barely audible, but continues throughout to indicate that the time grows short.)*

ARNOLD *(reading):*    Here where the world is quiet,
                      Here, where all trouble seems
                    Dead winds, and spent waves riot
                      In doubtful dreams of dreams;
                    I watch the green field growing
                      For reaping folk and sowing. . . .

HELEN *(interrupting):*    Oh, Arnold, *stop* it!

ARNOLD *(suavely):*    I beg your pardon?

HELEN:    I said, stop it. It's . . . *(groping for an idea)* it's trite. Listen,
Arnold. When are they going to . . . ? *(She hesitates.)*

ARNOLD:    You mean, when are they going to hang her?

*(A brief pause while the clock is heard distinctly)*

HELEN:    Yes, if you must make me say it.

ARNOLD *(calmly):*    I think we agreed, my dear, that the subject is taboo.
Allow me to help you to some more Swinburne. It's very soothing.
*(Reads again)*

                    I am tired of tears and laughter,
                      And men that laugh and weep;
                    Of what may come hereafter
                      For men that sow to reap;
                    I . . .

HELEN *(interrupting fiercely):*    Yes, I know you are. What's come over
you? What's got into you? Aren't you even human anymore?

ARNOLD:    I?

HELEN:    Yes, you. Can't you put that book down?

ARNOLD:    Just as you like. *(Noise of book striking wood)* I might more properly ask: what's come over *you?* My brother, and your cousin, was shot dead in this room four months ago. At the trial you were implacable. You said that you would willingly hang Mary Stevenson with your own hands. Have you changed your mind?

HELEN:    No, it isn't that at all. Only—I wish you wouldn't sit there and look at me like that. I wish you'd *say* something.

ARNOLD:    Very well. I'll tell you what you want to know. *(Curtly)* Mary's appeal against the verdict will be heard tomorrow. That is a formality: the appeal will be dismissed. They will hang her three days later.

HELEN    *(gives a sort of sobbing gasp, as though of protest. The noise of the clock is again heard loudly.)*

ARNOLD:    You spoke?

HELEN:    No.

ARNOLD:    And now, my handsome Amazon, question for question. Are you still in love with John?

HELEN *(wearily):*    Oh, Arnold, didn't we have all that out on the night Matt died?

ARNOLD *(suavely but sharply):*    I think not. Murder is a most damnable interrupter of conversations. You've been to John's flat recently, haven't you?

HELEN:    Yes. He was drunk.

ARNOLD    *(Snorts)*

HELEN *(coldly):*    I should prefer, Arnold, that you didn't sneer at John —or at me. You are perfect, of course. You have no human weaknesses.

ARNOLD:    I have the human weakness to be in love with you. And, by gad, that's weakness enough! *(Checking himself, coolly)* However, forget that. John is yours for the plucking now.

HELEN *(harshly):*    What do you mean by that?

ARNOLD:    What I say. Yours for the plucking. Consider the change this has made for us. You are wealthy now. John is wealthy. Even I am wealthy, now that Matt is dead. How well it has turned out for all of us!—except, of course, Mary. *(Slowly and softly)* What a pity she is innocent.

HELEN *(crying out):*    Innocent?

ARNOLD:    Oh, quite innocent. You had guessed that, hadn't you?

HELEN:    Don't say that! Don't even think it! She's guilty, and you know it. The jury—

ARNOLD *(with concentrated contempt):*    The jury! Twelve good fools and true, who should not have been permitted the powers of life and death over a garter-snake. Did they listen to the judge? Oh, no. The judge practically directed them to find a verdict of not guilty. But did it have any effect? Oh, no. Didn't you see those three women? Didn't you see their virtuous lips tighten and their virtuous hats wag? They found her guilty solely and simply because she had been on trial once before. Can't you imagine the platitudes that flowed? *(Mimicking)* "Where's there's smoke there must be fire, my dear." "She wouldn't have been tried before if there hadn't been something in it." *(Fiercely)* That's why a human being was sentenced to death. That, Helen, is justice. Justice!

HELEN:   You seem to feel strongly about it.

ARNOLD:   Strongly!

HELEN:   And it was all talk, wasn't it?

ARNOLD:   What was?

HELEN:   Your saying she was innocent. *(Insistently)* You said that just to torture me—didn't you?

ARNOLD *(quietly):*   I happen to know she is innocent.

*(The ticking of the clock is heard during a pause.)*

HELEN *(in a harsh whisper):*   Arnold . . . you killed . . . Matt . . . yourself.

ARNOLD *(amusedly):*   Oh, no, my dear. No, no. Consider my alibi. I have the strongest alibi in the world. Let's reconstruct the crime, and I'll show you.

HELEN *(in sudden horror):*   Go away!

ARNOLD:   Let's reconstruct the crime, as they say the French police do. Come, now! We are back on the night of October 13th. You are sitting —just where Matt was sitting then. In front of the fire, with a book in your lap. It is midnight, and raining.

HELEN:   Are you completely mad? Where are you going?

ARNOLD *(grimly but enjoying himself):*   Not far, my dear. Only out into the hall. I open the door  . . . so. Now we reconstruct. John and Mary arrive at the front door of this house. They can't get in, or think they can't get in. John leaves Mary at the front door and comes round to the back of the house. *(Slight pause)* He looks in through the French windows of this room. What does he see? He sees Matt sitting where you are sitting. *(In a lower voice)* John does not see the murderer. The murderer, presumably, is standing where I am standing—just outside the door to the hall. The murderer orders Matt to put up his hands. Matt does put up his hands—high above his head—so. Then the murderer pulls the trigger. Like this.

HELEN *(sharply, but a little frightened):*   Arnold Corbin, would you be good enough to stop this nonsense and come in here?—What's that you've got in your hand?

ARNOLD:   Only a pipe, my dear. Nothing more lethal than a pipe. *(Satirically)* But where was I during this time? I was at the telephone in the front room. All that time I was talking to Jimmy Parradine. I have proved it. No, Helen: you can't connect me with this crime. My alibi shines before all men.

HELEN *(steadily):* Arnold, listen . . .

ARNOLD: Yes?

HELEN *(significantly):* If you have anything to tell me about this crime —tell me. It will be safe with me. I won't betray you. Do you understand?

ARNOLD: I wonder.

HELEN: *Do you understand?*

ARNOLD: I have nothing to tell you except to call your attention, for the hundredth time, to the wound in Matt's body. A clean wound, in a dead straight line. *(Softly)* That's all.

HELEN: Damn your subtleties. Do you understand?

ARNOLD: In other words, I should tell you that I killed Matt?

HELEN *(swiftly):* Did you?

ARNOLD: You mean, my dear, that even if you knew this girl was innocent you wouldn't lift a finger to save her?

HELEN *(coolly):* Are you lifting a finger to save her? You say you know she's innocent. Then why didn't you tell the police? Why didn't you tell the court? Why do you only sit and torture *me,* night after night? *(Pause)* You see, you don't answer. It's all words.

ARNOLD: Can't you guess why I didn't tell?

HELEN: No, I can't. She's guilty, and you know it. That snivelling little devil shot Matt so that she could marry John. That's all there is to it. If it isn't on the jury's conscience, it certainly isn't on mine. Will you please sit down?

ARNOLD *(drawing a deep breath):* Just as you like.

HELEN: I can't stand this waiting. Do something. Go on reading. Only for heaven's sake, no more Swinburne.

ARNOLD: No? Then perhaps this would suit the case better. *(Pauses, and then begins to read)*

>With sudden shock the prison clock
>    Smote on the shivering air,
>And from all the gaol rose up a wail
>    Of impotent dispair,
>Like the sound the frightened marshes hear. . . .

*(The voice fades into a long flourish of music, which is presently taken up by the boom of the clock striking eight. It has just finished when we hear the first voice. But throughout the next scene a clock also continues to tick. It is slightly louder than during the scene between Helen and Arnold—it grows progressively louder to the end of the episode, when it stops at a place which will be indicated.)*

MARY *(in a slow, dull and dead-sounding voice):*  Did you count it?

FIRST WARDRESS *(in a comfortable, mothering, wheedling voice):*  Eight, I made it, dearie.

MARY:  Yes. Eight.

SECOND WARDRESS *(significantly, in a crisp, competent voice):*  Eight at *night,* Mrs. Blair.

FIRST WARDRESS:  Yes, of course. Lord 'a' mercy, I didn't think it was eight in the . . . *(Breaks off, coughs, and goes on with immense heartiness)* Almost time for your supper, dearie. Now, whatsay? Shall you and me and Miss Ray have a game of three-handed bridge?

MARY    *(Laughs. There is a touch of hysteria in it.)*

SECOND WARDRESS *(gently):*  Please don't, Miss Stevenson. We don't like it either, you know.

MARY:  I'm sorry. It's because you're so decent to me. That makes it worse.

FIRST WARDRESS *(soothingly):*  Now, dearie . . .

MARY:  And this is the condemned cell. *(Laboriously, as though trying to explain a doubtful and fuddled point)* You see, it isn't like anything I'd expected. Wallpaper and pictures and a fire. Like—*(laughs a little but still puzzled)*—like being at home: you know? And all so that at the end of it they can take me out in the morning for what's going to be done.

FIRST WARDRESS:  Easy, dearie. Somebody's coming.

*(There is the rattle of a key being turned, and a door opens.)*

THE GOVERNOR OF THE PRISON *(gruffly but heartily):*  Got a visitor here to see you, Miss Stevenson.

MARY *(stung out of apathy):*  John!

GOVERNOR:  Well—no. It's your counsel, Sir Charles Wolfe. With good news, I hope. And now, by your leave, I won't waste any more of your time.

*(Sir Charles Wolfe is also hearty, though on a more subdued note: bustling, but a trifle uneasy.)*

SIR CHARLES *(in a low voice):*  Good evening, my dear.

MARY:  Good evening, Sir Charles.

FIRST WARDRESS:  Give Sir Charles the rocking chair, Miss Ray.

MARY *(starts to laugh again, but manages to check herself. Sir Charles breaks in heartily.)*

SIR CHARLES:  Now, my dear, it's most unprofessional of me to come here. *(Laughs unconvincingly)* Your solicitor would have a fit if he knew. But I wanted to tell you—you mustn't lose heart. Your appeal is to be heard tomorrow morning.

MARY:  Appeal? You mean I must go back to that court again?

SIR CHARLES:   Only for a short time. I must plead the case before the judges.

MARY:   What chance have I got?

SIR CHARLES:   Well . . .

MARY *(interrupting):*   No, wait! Would you call yourself a cruel person?

SIR CHARLES:   Cruel? I don't think so, my dear. Why?

MARY:   Then tell me: what chance have I got? You needn't be afraid. I'm not going to break down, or anything like that. Tell me just as you'd tell one of your own clerks. Tell me as though you were reading about it in a newspaper. What chance have I got?

SIR CHARLES *(slowly):*   Miss Stevenson.

MARY:   That means you think I have none.

SIR CHARLES *(in his worrying, bulldog manner):*   Miss Stevenson, the verdict of the jury was not supported by the evidence. Nothing is clearer than that. It was an infamous verdict. But—I don't want to give you any false hopes. You mustn't hope for too much. *(Cheerfully)* But at the same time you mustn't lose heart.

MARY *(reflectively):*   I mustn't hope for too much, but at the same time I mustn't lose heart. You know, if I had heard that said to anybody else, I should have thought it was funny.

SIR CHARLES:   No, my dear—

MARY:   John always said I hadn't much sense of humor. Perhaps I haven't. Have you seen John?

SIR CHARLES *(hesitates):*   Yes.

MARY:   He hasn't been to see me. Did he send any message?

SIR CHARLES *(hesitates, uncomfortably):*   I didn't exactly talk to him. He was—indisposed.

MARY *(quickly):*   You mean he's ill?

SIR CHARLES:   Well, yes, in a way. *(Hastily)* But it's nothing serious; nothing at all. You'll see him tomorrow.

MARY *(slowly):*   Tomorrow.

*(Flourish of music fading into the striking of a clock, which this time strikes eleven. We hear the ticking a little louder. Then there is a sound of a woman's footsteps on a stone floor. For some seconds, they pace back and forth.)*

MARY *(barely above a whisper):*   This can't go on. It mustn't.

FIRST WARDRESS:   Easy, dearie. You've been wonderful up to now. Don't spoil it.

MARY:   But it's so long. So long. Why do they keep me waiting down here for so long?

FIRST WARDRESS:   The judges are at it, dearie; considering your case. *(Reassuringly)* The longer they take at it, the better for you. Don't fret yourself. *I* know.

MARY:   Yes, I suppose you do. *(Quickly)* What's that you've got there?

FIRST WARDRESS *(innocently):*   Where, dearie?

MARY:   There! Behind you. You're hiding it from me. What is it?

FIRST WARDRESS:   It's only your hat, dearie.

MARY:   My hat?

FIRST WARDRESS:   Of course, dearie. To put on when they turn you loose. Lord 'a' mercy, you couldn't go out in the street without your hat; now could you?

MARY *(after a pause):*   You know, I never thought a thing like that could mean so much. A hat. Out on the street. People. Life. *(Quickly)* Give it to me. I know what I'll do. I'll put it on.

FIRST WARDRESS *(encouragingly):*   That's right, dearie. And what about a little lipstick, now? Eh?

MARY *(feverishly):*   Yes, that's right. They *are* going to turn me loose, aren't they? *(She pauses, and there is a definite note of coldness in her voice.)* Did you see the people in court today?

FIRST WARDRESS:   You mean your young man? *(Offhandedly)* Looked as though he hadn't shaved for a couple of days.

MARY:   Yes. He did look like that, didn't he?

FIRST WARDRESS *(heartily):*   Well, dearie, we'll hope you'll be seeing him in a very few minutes.

MARY *(fiercely):*   We will hope *not.*

FIRST WARDRESS *(shocked):*   Now, now! 'Ere, what on earth's got into you? What do you mean?

MARY:   What I say. I . . .

*(Throughout the foregoing few speeches, a moving and shuffling of feet has been heard, as though overhead. A man's voice, seeming to come from a distance, speaks. It is a full, clear voice.)*

THE VOICE:   Put up the prisoner.

FIRST WARDRESS *(softly):*   There it is, dearie. That's us.

MARY:   You mean they've decided?

FIRST WARDRESS:   Yes. Up those stairs now. What are you doing?

MARY *(with desperate quiet):*   I can't wear this hat. Take it. Take it, please! It's no good. They're not going to let me go.

FIRST WARDRESS:   Listen, miss. Are you going to be ever so brave right up until the last minute, and break down then? Up you go, now! Don't think about anything. Just look straight across at the Lord Chief Justice, and don't think about anything. Say the multiplication-table to yourself, and don't think.

MARY:   But—

FIRST WARDRESS:   Up you go. Mind the grating.

*(Footsteps, slowly, on an iron stair and then across wood—the floor of the dock. We hear the noises of the courtroom: coughings, shufflings of*

*feet. The Lord Chief Justice speaks. He has a deep, slow, powerful voice. The ticking of the clock is heard clearly.)*

LORD CHIEF JUSTICE:   The prisoner will remain standing.

FIRST WARDRESS:   Easy, dearie. Stand away from me.

LORD CHIEF JUSTICE:   The appellant, Mary Ann Stevenson, was charged at the Central Criminal Court with the murder of Matthew Grey Corbin on October 13th, last. In the result she was convicted, and on January 25th she was sentenced to death. She now appeals against that conviction. *(Clears his throat)* Three facts are obvious. The first is that at the conclusion of the case for the Crown, no submission was made on behalf of the appellant that there was no case to go to the jury. The second fact which seems to be obvious is that the evidence was summed up by the learned judge with complete fairness and accuracy. The third obvious fact is that the case is eminently one of difficulty and doubt.

MARY *(in a barely audible whisper):*   Mrs. Blair! Mrs. Blair!

FIRST WARDRESS:   Sh-h.

MARY *(still whispering):*   But I can't hear him. I don't know what he's saying.

LORD CHIEF JUSTICE:   Now, the whole of the material evidence has been closely and critically examined before us, and it does not appear to me to be necessary to discuss it again. Suffice it to say that we are not concerned here with suspicion, however grave; or with theories, however ingenious. Section 4 of the Criminal Appeal Act of 1907 provides that the Court of Criminal Appeal shall allow appeal if they think that the verdict of the jury should be set aside on the ground that it cannot be supported by the evidence.

A MAN'S VOICE *(whispering):*   My God, I believe he's going to—

LORD CHIEF JUSTICE:   The conclusion at which we have arrived is that the case against the appellant, which we have carefully and anxiously considered, was not proved with that certainty which is necessary in order to justify a verdict of guilty. Therefore, it is our duty to take the course indicated by the section of the statute to which I have referred. This appeal will be allowed, and the conviction will be quashed. *(The clock stops ticking.)*

*(A stir in court, followed by the beginning of a cheer. There is the sound of a key being turned in the lock of the glass door of the dock.)*

A WARDER *(almost bored):*   This way out, miss.

MARY *(piteously):*   I don't understand. What did he say? What are they? What are they going to do to me?

FIRST WARDRESS:   That's the way out, dearie. You're free.

MARY *(not understanding):*   Free?

FIRST WARDRESS:   Don't you see the judge motioning to you? *(With heavy relief and cheerfulness)* Go on: get out before they lock you up again. Now put your 'at on nice and straight. There! Here's Sir Charles Wolfe coming to shake hands.

MARY:    Free? *(She is still dazed.)* Free? *(It begins to dawn on her.)* Free? *(She realizes at last)*
*(A long flourish of music, fading into the sound of footsteps along a corridor. A door opens and closes.)*

A POLICEMAN:    Just you wait in here for a minute, miss. There's a big crowd out in front, and I thought maybe you'd rather go another way. I'll have a taxi round in half a tick.

MARY:    Thank you.

POLICEMAN:    Not at all, miss. If . . . *(He breaks off as the door is again heard to open and close.)* Sorry, sir: you can't come in here.

ARNOLD:    My name is Arnold Corbin. I must have a word with Miss Stevenson.

POLICEMAN:    Sorry, sir . . .

MARY:    Let him come in.

POLICEMAN:    Just as you like, miss. Back in a moment.
*(The door opens and closes.)*

ARNOLD *(heavily constrained, after a pause):*    I wanted to—congratulate you. I am glad. *(She does not reply. He evidently sees what she thinks, for he goes on with desperate insistence.)* Yes, glad. I don't expect you to believe that. But there is one thing I do earnestly want you to believe. If this appeal had gone against you, I should have spoken.

MARY *(dully, without much interest):*    You would have spoken?

ARNOLD:    I hope I should have had that much courage left.

MARY:    Courage . . . what of it? What do you want with me now?

ARNOLD:    I am trying to tell you that I knew, or guessed, something which would have saved you.

MARY:    Please. Before you go. I'm very tired. What I want to do most is lie down, where nobody can see me. But I don't understand. Why do you come and tell me this now? Do you think it interests me? *(Wonderingly)* Do you even expect me to be grateful to you? *(She has been speaking in a monotone, which now grows a little louder.)* A month ago, a week ago, even a few days ago I might have been interested. Lying there in that room, watching the cracks in the ceiling. Wondering why it had happened to me. Wondering whether they mightn't be fooling me; wondering whether they mightn't have set the date of the execution for the next morning, without telling me; so that, when I woke up in the morning, the door would open and in would come the . . . *(She stops.)*

   If you had come to me *then,* and said that, I'd have been interested. I think I could have cried. But I don't feel anything now. Do you expect me to be grateful to you? Do you expect me to press your hand, and say how chivalrous you are? I'm sorry: I don't feel like that. I'm not even interested. You only seem to be rather hateful and slightly silly.

ARNOLD:   Yes. That is how humiliation feels.

MARY:   Is it? *You* know about humiliation?

ARNOLD *(in a low voice):*   By God, I do. Listen. Open your eyes and look at me. There's something I've got to tell you.

*(Sharply, the door opens. Helen Gates speaks.)*

HELEN:   Arnold, I . . . *(She breaks off, evidently seeing Mary.)* Oh!

MARY:   That's Helen, isn't it? Our Helen. I don't want to open my eyes and look.

HELEN *(with cold formality):*   Many congratulations.

MARY *(dully):*   Thank you so much. Where is John?

HELEN:   He's coming. He tried to get near you after the verdict, but the crush of your admirers was too great. John! Here they are.

*(Noise of hurrying footsteps)*

JOHN *(breathing the word):*   Mary.

MARY:   Hello.

JOHN *(checked):*   Mary, what's wrong with you? Aren't you glad it's all over? Aren't you glad to see me?

MARY:   Yes.

JOHN *(baffled):*   Well, it's . . . it's *(struggling for something to say)*— anyway it's all over now. *(With forced cheerfulness)* And we can forget about it, and be together again. Come along. I've got a car outside. We're going off to celebrate.

ARNOLD:   Haven't you been celebrating already?

JOHN *(rather shrilly):*   Are you telling me I'm drunk?

ARNOLD:   No. But you might take a look at yourself in a mirror.

JOHN:   I've been worried. Who wouldn't be? *(Abruptly)* Come along, Mary.

MARY:   Thanks. I can't go with you. I've already ordered a taxi.

JOHN *(incredulously):*   Ordered a . . . Nonsense! Look here, what's wrong with you? What's wrong with all of us? We're standing here like a lot of stuffed dummies—except Helen, and she's shaking. What's wrong with us?

HELEN:   You know what's wrong with us, John. Murder.

JOHN:   Which Mary did not commit.

POLICEMAN *(interposing):*   Taxi's here, miss. This way, and look sharp.

JOHN *(frantically):*   I'm not going to allow this. Mary, look at me. Have you gone out of your mind? You'll be saying next you're not going to marry me.

MARY:   I'm not. Please! *(She still speaks listlessly, but her tone sharpens to keep him from interrupting.)* I don't want to talk about it now. I'm tired, tired, tired. Above all I'm tired of noble gestures. Did you ever once come to see me while I was in there? Did you ever write me a line, or so much as send me a message?

JOHN:   I was busy.

MARY *(gently):*   I'm not blaming you. But you still think I killed your brother. Even if I didn't kill your brother, you still think I poisoned that woman at Kingston. Don't deny it. I saw your eyes in court. You can't face it, my dear. You're not in love with me, and I haven't been in love with you for as much as a month. Goodbye.

JOHN:   You don't mean that. You can't mean that. You're hysterical.

MARY:   Perhaps I am. Goodbye.

*(The door closes.)*

JOHN:   Mary. Mary!

*(The door opens, and slams hard.)*

*(Longer flourish of music, taking us back to Dr. Fell and his companions. There is a rattling of glasses, and the sound of liquid poured into a tumbler.)*

DR. FELL:   . . . and that, gentlemen, is the end of the official record in the case of Matthew Corbin. An old story, Mr. Interviewer. An old story, Hadley. Soda?

HADLEY:   Plenty of soda. *(The siphon hisses.)* Is that all?

INTERVIEWER:   I hope not, Superintendent. It may be an old story, Dr. Fell; but it's not a very complete one.

HADLEY:   The girl had guts. Nobody's ever denied that. And she seems to be happy enough nowadays.

INTERVIEWER *(laughing):*   Hold on! Are you going to tell us that Mary and John made it up, and lived happily ever afterwards?

DR. FELL *(richly):*   You forget, my dear sir, that this is a true story. True stories seldom end on a note of drama. Truth has to keep on happening; whereas drama exists only for a moment. *(Chuckles)* I believe Mary Stevenson later married a journalist named Breckenridge. She has two children, and remains very happy to this day. *(With sudden grimness)* Is your romantic soul disappointed?

INTERVIEWER:   I don't understand you, Doctor. If Mary Stevenson didn't murder him, who did?

DR. FELL:   You can't guess?

INTERVIEWER:   No, certainly not.

DR. FELL:   And you would really like to know who the murderer was?

INTERVIEWER *(with a forced sort of amusement):*   Dr. Fell . . . and you too, Superintendent . . .

DR. FELL:   Soda?

INTERVIEWER *(absently):*   Thanks. *(The siphon hisses.)* Look here, something seems to be wrong with both of you. *(Laughs uneasily)* If I didn't want to be polite about it, I should say you looked like a pair of maniacs. Who really killed Matthew Corbin?

DR. FELL *(with ponderous patience):*   You are sure you would like me to answer that question?

INTERVIEWER:   Yes, of course.

DR. FELL:   Sir, I ask you to consider very carefully. Thousands of people are listening to every word we say. It is neither safe nor easy to pronounce a human being guilty of murder. Shall I take that risk, and answer your question?

INTERVIEWER:   I don't see why you should back down now. . . . What's the Superintendent doing?

DR. FELL:   He is locking the door. Are you sure you want me to go on?

INTERVIEWER *(almost screaming):*   Dr. Fell, who really killed Matthew Corbin?

DR. FELL:   As a matter of fact, you did.

*(A crash of glass as a tumbler drops and smashes.)*

INTERVIEWER:   *I* did?

DR. FELL:   Yes. Your real name is John Corbin, isn't it?

*(Short, harsh, quick flourish of music, out of which the Interviewer, speaking clearly in John Corbin's voice, is heard above the rattling of a door handle)*

INTERVIEWER (JOHN CORBIN):   Open this door! *(Hysterically)* I don't understand what you're talking about. I don't know what kind of cat-and-mouse game you think you're playing.

DR. FELL:   Listen to his voice, Hadley. Don't you hear John Corbin now?

JOHN:   My name is my own affair. I've been brought here under false pretenses. I demand to be let out.

HADLEY *(slowly and heavily):*   Sit down, Mr. Corbin.

JOHN:   I tell you, my name is not Corbin!

HADLEY:   Then sit down anyway. If you're not John Corbin, there's no harm done—is there?

JOHN:   I mean, I won't be treated like this. You can't say I did it. You've got nothing on me.

DR. FELL *(calmly):*   Now there speaks the true murderer's vanity. The old sweet song: "You can't say I did it. You've got nothing on me." *(More grimly)* My dear fellow, you couldn't let well enough alone, could you? You couldn't be content with committing what you thought was the perfect crime, could you? No. You had to tickle your own vanity a little further. You had to hear about your own cleverness, or die. *(With sudden fierceness)* And now, by thunder, you *shall* hear about it. Sit down.

*(The rattlings at the door knob are now followed by the noise of fists beating at the door.)*

DR. FELL:    I said, sit down. *(The noises stop.)* Your brother Arnold guessed, of course. He spotted the one flat, thumping, obvious lie which is going to hang you. Over and over again, with such persistence that it became monotonous, he kept on mentioning a certain bit of evidence which nobody else seems to have understood. . . . Do *you* understand, even now, what your mistake was?

JOHN *(through his teeth):*    I made no mistakes.

DR. FELL:    That, my dear sir, is open to question. But, before I tell you what the mistake was, let me feed your vanity still further by telling you a little more about your own crime. *(Pause)* You planned to kill your brother Matthew for the money you knew you would inherit. You planned it with loving care. You planned it even before you went to South Africa. That was why you took away with you that little pistol, loaded with ancient ammunition. . . . Just as your brother Arnold said you did. *(Another pause)* Your plan was simple. You intended to kill Matthew on the very night of your return from abroad. That was the cleverness of your scheme. Nobody would believe that, after two years' absence, your first act would be to walk into the study and kill your brother. I repeat: nobody would believe that. The very daring of it would cover you up. Shall I mix you another drink?

JOHN *(coolly):*    Thank you, no. If you insist on talking, I can't stop you. But try to prove it. *Try* to prove it.

DR. FELL:    But you did more than that. Aboard ship coming home, you met Mary Stevenson. And you did the thing which shall not be forgiven you. You recognized her. You deliberately selected that girl to be the scapegoat for your own crime. You never were in love with her. You never cared a rap for her. You brought her home with you so that you could fit her into your plan, and leave her on the doorstep to be accused of your brother's murder. *(Reflectively)* You're a cold-hearted young swine, you know.

HADLEY:    Steady, my lad. If you don't want to see trouble, stay where you are.

JOHN:    So you're both in this, are you?

HADLEY *(sharply):*    Put down that poker, I warn you.

DR. FELL:    Shall I go on?

JOHN *(half-screaming):*    You can do as you damn well like. *I* don't mind.

DR. FELL:    Let us return to your scapegoat—Mary Stevenson. On the night of October 13th, you drove her out to Hampstead in a new car. You took care to arrive very late, so that your brother Matthew should be alone. You deliberately smashed up your car against the front gatepost. Why? So that you could pretend to be unconscious for a few minutes, and later explain the absence of the front-door key from your keyring. Of course, you took that front-door key yourself. Mary Stevenson's counsel at the trial showed that only you could have taken that key off your own keyring; though he did not realize what it meant. You stole your own key for two reasons. First, to incriminate Mary Stevenson. Second, to get an excuse for leaving her alone at the front door . . . while *you* walked around to the back. And there you killed your brother.

JOHN: I suppose you can tell me how I did it?

DR. FELL: With pleasure.

JOHN: Well?

DR. FELL: You looked in through the French window, which was closed but not locked. You saw your brother sitting alone in front of the fire. You had gloves on, as you yourself have admitted.

JOHN: Well?

DR. FELL: You went in through the French window. You walked straight across the room to the door . . . turned around . . . and shot your brother as he jumped to his feet. Then you tossed the pistol outside the door, and ran back to the French window.

JOHN: That's a dirty lie, and you know it.

DR. FELL: The whole thing took only ten seconds. Once outside the window again, you pretended to find it locked. You set up a tumult of shouting . . . smashed the window with a stone and ran in. You pretended you had seen your brother standing there, with his hands raised in the air. That was a lie. Matthew Corbin never raised his hands at all. There was nobody threatening him from the door to the hall. But you had to tell that lie, in case someone asked you how you knew he was being threatened when you saw nobody else in the room.

JOHN (with desperate coolness): Superintendent Hadley, I appeal to you. Is there one bit of evidence in anything this man has said? Is there?

HADLEY: Well, sir, if you're not Mr. John Corbin, that doesn't matter, does it?

JOHN (desperately): All right: if you can prove anything by that, I *am* John Corbin.

DR. FELL: Oh?

JOHN: Yes, and what of it? I'm not ashamed of it. I've done nothing to be ashamed of.

DR. FELL (suavely): Then you would not mind answering a question or two?

JOHN: You ask what you please, and I'll answer if I choose. There's nobody on earth who can prove I shot Matt; and you can't either.

DR. FELL: Then let's see. You still say your brother was being threatened by someone standing at the door to the hall?

JOHN *(snarling):* Yes!

DR. FELL *(still suavely):* Then perhaps you will be good enough to watch while Superintendent Hadley and I try a little experiment. Hadley, stand up. *(Slight pause)* Fasten one button of your jacket. Good. *Now I am threatening you with a pistol. Put up your hands.*

JOHN: What is it? *(Hysterically)* What are you doing?

DR. FELL *(softly):* Watch the coat, my young friend. Watch his coat.

JOHN: What about the coat?

DR. FELL: It's rising, man! Don't you see that as he puts up his hands —high, like that—the coat rises at least three inches?

JOHN: Well?

DR. FELL: The coat rises. But the waistcoat, which is buttoned tightly round the body, does not move at all. Don't you see that? If I were to fire a bullet at him now, the bullet-hole in the coat would be at least three inches above the corresponding bullet-hole in the waistcoat. You see? *(Very softly)* And yet over and over again we have heard the description of the wound in your brother's body. The bullet entered in a dead straight line through coat, waistcoat, shirt—and heart. You could never have put a pencil through it, as Arnold Corbin never tired of telling us. My dear fellow, look for yourself. That would have been absolutely impossible if Matthew Corbin's hands had been raised at all. His hands were never raised. They were still at his sides when you shot him.

JOHN *(still more hysterically):* Let go my arm! What are you doing?

DR. FELL: And so you lied. You deliberately described a whole set of circumstances which could not possibly have been true. Your brother Matthew's sudden start . . . his looking toward the door . . . his getting up . . . his slowly raising his hands . . . all that long story of the intruder was no error of observation, but a careful piece of invention. The person who told such a string of impossibilities was the murderer, and I take great pleasure in handing you over to the law. Look out, Hadley!

*(A stamp of running feet; a door unlocked, opened, and slammed; and more sounds of running merging into the blasts of a police-whistle)*

Well, did you get him?

HADLEY: Got him on the second flight down. *(Bitterly)* Of course you had to be melodramatic about it.

DR. FELL: You must allow me these small pleasures, Hadley. I'm not so spry as I once was.

HADLEY: You couldn't have come out flat and told him we can produce a witness who swears he took that pistol to South Africa and brought it back?

DR. FELL *(agitated):*    Sh-h!

HADLEY *(bitterly):*    You couldn't have told him it was sheer, plodding, commonplace police work that caught up with him; and that your brilliant inspiration about the hole in the coat wouldn't have come near convicting him by itself? By George, you're a wonder!

*(Throughout this, Dr. Fell is chuckling.)*

You disrupt the police force; you pour scorn on the courts; you accuse the barristers of not knowing their business; and now you've even managed to mess up broadcasting. We've seen some equally queer endings. But what are you going to call *this* one?

DR. FELL *(happily):*    I should call it the BBC Home Service.

*(He is still chuckling as the play ends.)*

## The Proverbial Murder

During the First World War, Dr. Fell acted as a spycatcher. According to *The Mad Hatter Mystery,* he seems to have specialized in uncovering secret means of communication; he caught a University of Chicago professor who had recorded information on the lens of his spectacles, and a naturalist whose drawings of butterflies contained the plans for British minefields. It was thus natural that he became involved in the espionage surrounding "The Proverbial Murder." This story is a source of frustration for Carrian bibliographers. Its earliest *known* publication was in *Ellery Queen's Mystery Magazine,* July 1943. The editor's preface says that it is "here published for the first time in the United States," and it seems likely that it was previously published in Britain. Repeated searches, however, have failed to find it, and all that can be said is that the story probably takes place shortly before the declaration of war in 1939 or during the so-called Phony War between October 1939 and Spring 1940 when Hitler was digesting his conquests in Poland and at least publicly paying little attention to Britain and France. In any event, it is one of Carr's best short stories.

# The Proverbial Murder

The timbered cottage, which belonged to Herr Dr. Ludwig Meyer and which was receiving attention from the man with the field glasses, stood some distance down in the valley.

In clear moonlight, the valley was washed clean of color except at one point, where a light showed in a window to the right of Dr. Meyer's door. It was a diamond-paned window with two leaves, now closed. The lamplight streamed out through it, touching grass and rose beds.

At a desk beside the window, Dr. Meyer sat at his endless writing. *A Dissertation on the Theory of the Atom* was its official title. The white cretonne curtains of the window were not drawn. From this angle the watchers had an awkward, sideways view of him.

Some quarter of a mile away, on the edge of the hill, the man with the field glasses lay flat on his face. His back ached and his arms felt cramped. Momentarily he lowered the glasses and peered round.

"S-ss-t!" he whispered. "What are you doing? Don't light a cigarette!"

His companion's voice sounded aggrieved. "Why not? Nobody can see it up here."

"It's orders, that's all."

"And, anyway," grumbled the other, "it's two o'clock in the morning. Our bloke's not coming tonight: that's certain. Unless he's already gone in by the back door?"

"Lewes is covering the back door and the other side. Listen!"

He held up his hand. Nothing stirred in the valley. There was no noise except, far away, the faint drag and thunder of the surf at Lynmouth.

It was mellow September weather, yet the man with the field glasses, Detective-Inspector Ballard, of the Special Branch attached to the Metropolitan Police, felt an unaccountable shiver. Lifting the glasses again, he raked the path leading up to the cottage. He looked at the lighted window. Beyond the edge of a cretonne curtain, he could just make out a part of the bony profile, the thick spectacles, the fishlike movements of the mouth, as Dr. Meyer filled page after page of neat handwriting.

"If you ask me," grumbled Sergeant Buck, "the A. C.'s barking up the wrong tree this time. This Meyer is a distinguished scientist—a real refugee—"

"No."

"But where's your evidence?"

"In cases of this kind," returned Ballard, lowering the glasses to rub his aching eyes, "you can't afford to go by the rules of legal evidence. The A. C. isn't sure; but he thinks the tip-off came from Meyer's wife."

Sergeant Buck whistled.

"A good German hausfrau tip off the English?"

"That's just it. She's not German: she's English. There are some very funny things going on in this country at the moment, my lad. If we can nab the man who's coming to see Meyer tonight, we'll catch somebody high up. We can—"

"Listen!" said Buck.

It was unnecessary to ask anyone to listen. The report of the firearm crashed and rolled in that little valley. It was an illusion, but Ballard almost imagined he could hear the wiry *whing* of the bullet.

Both men jumped to their feet. Ballard, his knee joints painful from their cramped position, whisked up the glasses again and scanned the front of the cottage. His gaze came to rest on the window.

"Poachers?" suggested Buck.

"That was no poacher," said Inspector Ballard. "That was an Army rifle. And it didn't miss either. Come on!"

The pigmy picture rose in his mind as he scrambled down the hill: the flutter of the cretonne curtain, the bald head fallen forward across the desk. Neither he nor Buck made any effort at concealment. The echoes hardly seemed to have settled in the valley when they arrived in front of the house. Holding his companion back, Ballard pointed.

The lighted window was not far up from the ground. First of all Ballard noticed the bullet hole in the glass, close to the lead joining of one of the diamond panes. It was a neatly drilled hole, with hardly any starring of the glass, such as is made by a smallish, high-velocity rifle bullet (say a .256) fired from some distance away.

Then they both saw what was inside, lying limply across the desk with a mark on the left temple; and they both hurried for the front door.

The door knocker was stiff and rusty, giving only a padded sound which Ballard had to supplement by banging his fist on the door. It seemed interminable minutes before the bar was drawn back on the inside, and the door opened.

A white-faced woman, carrying a kerosene lamp and with a dressing gown hastily pulled round her, peered out at them. She was perhaps thirty-five, some ten or fifteen years younger than Ludwig Meyer. Though not pretty, she was attractive in a pink-and-white fashion; blue-eyed, with heavy, rich-brushed fair hair over her shoulders.

"Mrs. Meyer?"

"Yes?" She moistened her lips.

"We're police officers, ma'am. I'm afraid something has happened to your husband."

Slowly Harriet Meyer held up the lamp. Just as slowly, she turned round and looked toward the door of the room on the right of the hall. The lamp wabbled in her hand, its golden light spilling and breaking among shadows.

"I—I heard it," she said. "I wondered."

Gritting her teeth, she turned round and walked toward the door of that room. With a word of apology Ballard brushed past her.

"Well," said Sergeant Buck, after a pause, "there's nothing we can do for *him,* sir."

There was not. They stood in a long, low-ceilinged room, its walls lined with improvised bookshelves. The smell of burning oil from the lamp on the desk by the window competed with a fog of rank tobacco smoke. A long china-bowled pipe lay on the desk near the dead man's hand. The fountain pen had slipped from his fingers. His face and shoulders lay against the paper-strewn desk; but, as the creaking of their footsteps jarred the floor, he slowly slid off and fell with an unnerving thump on his side. It was a grotesque mimicry of life which made Harriet Meyer cry out.

"Steady, ma'am," said Ballard.

Circling the body, he went to the window and tried to peer out. But in the dazzle between lamp and moonlight he could see nothing. The bullet hole in the glass, he noted, had tiny splinters—the little shell-shaped grooves on the edge of the opening—which showed that the bullet had been fired from outside.

Inspector Ballard drew a deep breath and turned round.

"Tell us about it, ma'am," he said.

Late on the following afternoon, Colonel Penderel sat in a wicker chair on the lawn before The Red Lodge, and looked gloomily at his shoes.

Everything about Red Lodge, like Colonel Penderel himself, was of a brushed trimness. The lawn was of that smooth green which seems to have lighter stripes in it; the house, of mellow red brick under mellow September sunshine, opened friendly doors to all the world.

But Hubert Penderel, a long lean man with big shoes, and wiry wintry-looking hair like his cropped mustache, slouched down in the chair. He clenched his big-knuckled fist, stared at it, and brought it down on the arm of the chair. Then he glanced round—and stopped guiltily as he caught sight of a brown-haired girl in a sleeveless white tennis frock, who had just come round the side of the house with a tennis racket under her arm.

The girl did not hesitate. She studied him for a moment, out of blue eyes wide-spaced above a short straight nose. A colored silk scarf was tied round her head. Then she marched across the lawn, swinging the tennis racket as though she were going to hit somebody with it.

"Daddy," she said abruptly, "what on earth *is* it?"

Colonel Penderel said nothing.

"There *is* something," she insisted. "There has been, ever since that police superintendent came here this morning. What is it? Have you been getting into trouble with your car again?"

Colonel Penderel raised his head.

"Professor Meyer's been shot," he answered with equal abruptness. "Somebody plugged him through the window last night with a .303 service rifle. —Nancy, how would you like to see your old man arrested for murder?"

He had tried to say the last words whimsically. But he was not a very good actor, and his conception of the whimsical was somewhat heavy-handed.

Nancy Penderel backed away.

"What on earth are you talking about?"

"Fact," said the Colonel, giving a slight flick to his shoulders. He peered round the lawn, hunching up his shoulders. "That superintendent (Willet, his name is) wanted to know if I owned a rifle. I said yes: the one we all used to shoot with, on our own range. He said, where was it kept? I said, in the garden shed. He said, could he see it? I said, certainly."

Nancy was having difficulty in adjusting her wits to this.

"He said, can I borrow this?" the Colonel concluded, hunching up his shoulders still further, and avoiding her eye. "He took it away with him. It can't be the rifle that killed Meyer. But if by any chance it should happen to be—?"

"Dr. Meyer?" Nancy breathed. "Dr. Meyer *dead?*"

Colonel Penderel jumped to his feet.

"I didn't like the blighter." His tone was querulous. "Everybody knows it. We had a rare old row only three days ago. Not because he was a German, mind. After all, I've got a German staying here as my guest, haven't I? But—well, there it is. And another thing. That garden shed has a Yale lock. *I've* got the only key."

There was another wicker chair near her father's. Nancy groped across to it, and sat down.

She felt no sense of danger or tragedy. It was merely that she could not understand. It was as though, in the midst of a dinner, the cloth were suddenly twitched off and all the dishes with their contents overturned.

It was a pleasant afternoon. She had just finished playing three sets of tennis with Carl Kuhn. There couldn't, she assured herself, be anything really wrong: nothing that could blacken the daylight or spoil her week. Yet she watched her father tramping up and down the lawn, in his old checkered brown-and-black sports coat, more disturbed than she had ever seen him.

"But it's absurd!" Nancy cried. "We can't take it seriously. Everybody knows you. The local police know you."

"Ah," said Colonel Penderel. "Yes. The local police know me. But the fellows who've taken this over aren't local. They're down here from Scotland Yard."

"Scotland Yard?"

"Special Branch. Look here, mouse." He approached closer, and lowered his voice. "Keep this under your hat. Don't mention it to your mother, whatever you do. But this fellow Meyer was a wrong 'un. A spy."

"Impossible! That doddery little man?"

"Fact. Willet wouldn't say much, naturally. But I did gather they've got the goods on him, and his papers prove it. Damn it, you can't trust anybody nowadays, can you?"

Colonel Penderel's face darkened. He rubbed his hands together with a dry, rustling sound.

"If that's what he was—I say, good luck to the man who plugged him! But I didn't do it. Can you imagine me sneaking up on a man (that's what worries me, mouse) and letting drive at him when he wasn't looking?"

"No, of course not." Nancy was beginning to reflect. "If anybody killed him, I'm betting it was that simpering blonde wife of his."

"Harriet Meyer? Great Scott, no!"

"Why not? She's fifteen years younger than he is. And they live all alone in that house, without even a maid to help with the work."

Colonel Penderel was honest enough not to pursue this. He shook his head.

"There are reasons why not, mouse. Which you might understand, or you might not. . . ."

"Daddy, stop treating me like a child! Why couldn't she have done it?"

"First, because the bullet that killed Meyer came from outside. Second, because there were Special Branch men watching every side of the house, and nobody went out or in at any time—certainly not Harriet Meyer. Third, they made an immediate search of the house, and there was no weapon in it except an old 16-bore shotgun which couldn't possibly have fired a rifle bullet."

"S-ss-t!" said Nancy warningly.

Colonel Penderel whirled round.

The latch of the front gate was being lifted. Detective-Inspector Ballard, nondescript and fortyish, might have been any business man; but to the two watchers he had policeman written all over him. He came up the brick path smiling pleasantly, and raised his hat.

And, at the same time, Carl Kuhn strolled out of the open front door.

Carl Kuhn, in his late twenties, was one of those Teutonic types which seem all the more Nordic for being dark instead of fair. He was a middle-sized, stockily built, amiable young man with a ruddy complexion and a vast fund of chuckles. His heavy black hair grew low on his forehead; a narrow mustache followed the line of his wide mouth. Wearing white flannels, a sports coat, and a silk scarf, he came sauntering across the lawn to put his hands on the back of Nancy's chair.

But nobody looked at him.

"Good afternoon," Ballard said pleasantly. "Colonel Penderel?"

"I am Colonel Penderel," said the owner of that name, looking very hard at him. "This is my daughter. And Mr. Kuhn."

Ballard gave them a brief glance.

"Colonel Penderel, I am a police officer investigating the murder of Dr. Ludwig Meyer," continued Ballard; and Kuhn, who had started to light a cigarette, flicked up his head and blew two jets of smoke through his nostrils like an amiable dragon. "I wonder if I could have a word with you in private, sir?"

"Say it," said the Colonel.

"Pardon?"

"If you've got anything to say to me," pursued the Colonel, sitting down deliberately and taking tight hold of the arms of the chair, "say it. Here. Now. In front of these people."

"You're sure that's what you'd prefer, sir?"

"Yes."

Ballard's own deliberate gaze moved round the group. He took a notebook out of his pocket.

"Well, sir, you own a rifle. This morning you loaned that rifle to Superintendent Willet."

"Yes?"

"Certain tests," said Ballard, "were made with this .303 rifle by the ballistics consultant to the Devonshire County Constabulary." He looked at his notebook. " 'Number of grooves: five and a half. Direction of twist: right-hand. Individual markings—' Never mind the technicalities, though." His manner remained expressionless, almost kindly. "The fact is, sir, that the bullet which killed Dr. Meyer was fired from your rifle."

From behind the house came the drowsy whir of a lawn mower.

Not even yet had Nancy Penderel a full sense of danger or even death. The sheer incredibility of the thing flooded her mind. She thought of the garden shed by the tennis-court; and of the miniature rifle range, sandbags backed by sheet iron, which her father had constructed at the end of the meadow.

"I see," observed Colonel Penderel. His manner was stiff and impassive. He lifted one hand as though to whack it down on the arm of the chair, but he lowered it gently instead. "Someone stole it, then. Or—am I by any chance under arrest?"

Ballard smiled, though his eyes did not move.

"Hardly that, sir. All we know is that your rifle was used."

Throughout this, Carl Kuhn had been shifting from one foot to the other as though in a hopping agony of indecision. He took short, quick puffs at his cigarette.

"You are not saying," he exploded, in English not far from perfect, "that this man Meyer was shot yesterday afternoon?"

Ballard glanced at him quickly.

"Yesterday afternoon? What makes you say that?"

"Because," returned Kuhn, "yesterday afternoon I took a walk in the direction of that house. It iss not more than a quarter of a mile from here. And I heard a rifle shot. I looked over the edge of the hill, and saw this Meyer standing in front of the house. He seemed very angry. But he wass not dead then. No, no, no!"

He illustrated this story by cupping his hands over his eyes, and other elaborate gestures. Ballard stared at him.

"But what did you do, sir? Didn't you go closer to see what had happened?"

"No."

"Why not?"

"His blood," said Kuhn, holding himself very stiffly, "wass not my blood. His race wass not my race. I would have nothing to do with him. But there!" Kuhn's tension relaxed, and he smiled. "Not to talk politics in this house we have agreed. Is it not so, Colonel Penderel?"

"Yes, it's so," admitted the Colonel, shifting. "I didn't care anything about the fellow's race or politics. I just didn't like him." He eyed Ballard. "I suppose you've heard all about that?"

Ballard was silent for a moment.

"Knowledge hereabouts is pretty general, sir. Is it true that on Tuesday you threatened to kill him?"

The colonel went rather white.

"I threatened to wring his neck, if that's what you mean."

"Why?"

"I didn't like his manners. He browbeat the tradespeople and threw his weight about wherever he went. He was supposed to have come out of Germany penniless, but he had everything he wanted. At a garden party here on Tuesday—when my wife was trying to conciliate him—he said calmly that the English had no taste, no education, no manners, and no knowledge of science."

"Ach, so?" murmured Kuhn.

"I didn't say anything at the time. I just walked part of the way home with him, and told him a few things. There was a hell of a row, yes."

"Oh, this is absurd!" Nancy protested; but Ballard very gently and persuasively silenced her.

"Dr. Meyer," Ballard said without comment, "was shot at about two o'clock in the morning, with a rifle taken from the garden shed here. . . ."

"Which was locked," said the Colonel stonily, "and to which I've got the only key."

"Daddy!" cried Nancy.

"And," persisted the Colonel, "at two o'clock in the morning I was asleep. I don't sleep in the same room as my wife; and I can't produce an alibi. Furthermore, the rifle was in that shed as late as nine o'clock in the evening; I know, because I put away the garden sprinkler then. The window won't open and there's no way into the shed except by the door. Now you know everything. But I didn't kill Meyer."

Ballard was about to speak when there was an interruption.

Round the side of the house, at a blundering and near-sighted gait, lumbered a twenty-stone man in a white linen suit. He wore eyeglasses on a broad black ribbon, carried a crutch-handled stick, and seemed to be muttering down the slope of his several chins.

Colonel Penderel jumped up.

"Fell!" he shouted. "Gideon Fell! What in the name of sanity are you doing here?"

Dr. Fell woke up. He beamed all over his face like Old King Cole. He swept off his broad-brimmed white hat and ducked them a sort of bow. Then, wheezing gently after the exertion of this, he scowled.

"I trust," he said, "you will forgive my informal entrance by way of the back garden. I was—ahem—examining your miniature rifle range."

Inspector Ballard intervened quickly.

"You're acquainted with Dr. Fell, Colonel?"

"Lord, yes! One of my oldest . . . Here, sit down! Have a drink. Have something. You don't happen to have heard what's going on here, do you?"

Dr. Fell seemed uncomfortable.

"Not to put too fine a point on it," he answered, "yes. I came down here to discuss a point of practical science, the use of thermite in a safe-breaking case, with Dr. Meyer. My second visit. I find him—" He spread out his hand, widening the fingers. "Sir Herbert Armstrong wired to ask if I would—um—lend a little consulting assistance."

"Glad of any help, sir," smiled Ballard.

"Not as glad as I am," said the Colonel. "You see, Fell, they think I did it."

"Nonsense!" roared Dr. Fell.

"Well, what do you think?"

A mulish expression overspread Dr. Fell's face.

"Proverbs," he said. "Proverbs! I don't know. Before I express my opinion, there are two things about which I must have some information. I must know all about the wildcat and the moss."

They stared at him.

"The what, sir?" demanded Inspector Ballard.

"The wildcat," said Dr. Fell, "and the moss."

Grunting acceptance of the chair which Colonel Penderel set out for him, he lowered his vast bulk into it. He got out a red bandanna handkerchief and mopped his face.

"When I last visited Dr. Meyer," he went on, "I noticed on the mantelpiece in his study a big figure of a stuffed wildcat."

"That's right," agreed the Colonel.

"But when I went there today, the wildcat was gone. I asked Mrs. Meyer about this, and she informed me that three days ago he took the stuffed wildcat out into the garden and burned it."

"Burned it? Why should he do that?"

"Precisely," said Dr. Fell, flourishing the handkerchief, "the shrewd, crafty question I asked myself. Why? Then there is the question of the moss. Somebody has been pulling up large quantities of moss from the vicinity of that house."

It was Nancy Penderel's first sight of the man about whom she had heard so much from her father. Her first impulse, on seeing Dr. Fell, was to laugh. She looked again, and was not so sure.

"Mark you," the doctor went on suddenly, "it was always *dry* moss. Very dry moss. The picker would have no traffic with anything damp. Archons of Athens! If only—"

He shook his head, sunk deep in mazy meditations. Inspector Ballard hesitated.

"Are you sure either of those two things has any bearing on the matter, sir?"

"Not at all. But we must look for some clue or retire to Bedlam. My first thought, of course, was that the stuffed wildcat might have been used as a kind of safe: a receptacle for papers. Since our evidence proves that Dr. Meyer was a German espionage-agent . . ."

"S-ss-t!" warned Inspector Ballard.

But Dr. Fell merely blinked at him.

"My good sir,"—he spoke with some testiness,—"you can't keep it dark. Everybody in North Devon knows about it. At the pub, where I had the pleasure of lowering several pints before coming on here, the talk was of nothing else. Somebody has been industriously spreading it."

He looked thoughtful.

"But observe! Dr. Meyer burns the safe, but leaves the papers. A version (I suppose) of locking the stable door after the horse is stolen. And a rolling stone gathers no moss. And—" He blinked at Carl Kuhn. "You, sir. You are the other German I've heard so much about?"

Kuhn had been shifting excitedly from one foot to the other. His color was higher. His surprise seemed deep and genuine. Once he made a gesture like one who removes an invisible hat and stands to attention.

"At your service, Doctor," he said.

Dr. Fell scowled. "You're not providing us with still another proverb, I hope?"

"Another proverb?"

"That birds of a feather flock together?"

Kuhn was very serious. "No. I regret what has happened. I deeply regret it. But—do not judge too harshly. Such tasks are often glorious. I misjudged him."

Colonel Penderel stared at him. So did Nancy. She had a confused idea that her ordered world was crumpling round her.

"Glorious!" she repeated. "That little worm was a spy, doing heaven knows what, and you say 'such things are often glorious'?"

Kuhn's color was still higher.

"Perhaps I express myself badly in English."

"No, you don't, either! You've spent half your life in England. I've known you since you were ten years old. You're more English than German anyway."

"I regret, no," said Kuhn. "I *am* a German." He drew himself up, but his anxious eyes regarded first Nancy and then the Colonel. "This does not interfere with our long friendship?"

"Hanged if I know *what* it does," muttered Colonel Penderel, after a pause. "It seems to me we've got a parable here instead of a proverb; but never mind. What I do know is that we're in an unholy mess." He frowned. "You didn't happen to kill Meyer yourself, did you?"

"Is it likely?" Kuhn asked simply.

"Don't you think," said Nancy, "you've got rather a nerve?"

"Little one, you do not understand!" Kuhn seemed in agony. "Ach, now, let us forget this! It is no business of ours. Instead they should inquire who was firing at Herr Meyer yesterday afternoon—"

Dr. Fell spoke in such a sharp voice that they all swung round.

"What's that? Who was firing at him yesterday afternoon?"

Kuhn repeated his story. As he did so, Inspector Ballard's expression was one of growing suspicion; but Dr. Fell, with a sort of half-witted enlightenment dawning in his eyes, merely shaded those eyes with his hand.

"How did you happen to be there, Mr. Kuhn?" asked Ballard.

"I was going for a walk. That is all."

"In the direction of Professor Meyer's house?"

"No, no, that was quite by chance. Man must go somewhere when he walks."

"A point," observed Dr. Fell, "which is sometimes open to dispute. And last night?"

"Now that is very odd." Suddenly Kuhn knocked his knuckles against his forehead. "I had forgotten. Excuse. You say that Herr Meyer was shot at two o'clock in the morning?"

"Yes."

"Towser!" said Kuhn with powerful relief. "The dog! He was restless! He kept barking!"

"That's true," breathed Nancy.

"So! Listen to me. I was disturbed. I could not sleep. Finally I rise to my feet and put my head out of the window. I saw McCabe, the gardener, going along the path in his dressing gown. I called and asked if he could quiet the dog, and he said he was going to do it. The stable clock, I heard, was just striking two."

There was a silence. Kuhn's anxious eyes turned toward the Inspector.

"I see," said Ballard, making a note. "Alibi, eh?"

"If you wish to call it so, yes. The man McCabe will tell you what I say is true. It was bright moonlight: I saw him and he saw me."

"Inspector," remarked Dr. Fell, without taking his hand away from his eyes, "I think you'd better accept that."

"Accept the alibi?"

"Yes," said Dr. Fell. With infinite labor he propelled himself to his feet on his crutch-handled stick. "Because it isn't necessary. I know how Professor Meyer really died. As a matter of fact, you told me."

"*I* told you?" repeated Ballard.

"And if you'd care to come with me to the house," pursued Dr. Fell, "I think I can show you." He looked curiously at Colonel Penderel. "If I remember correctly, my lad, you used to be something of an authority on firearms. You'd better come along too."

"Is the answer," asked Colonel Penderel, "as easy as that?"

"The answer," said Dr. Fell, "is another proverb."

In late afternoon light, the timbered cottage in the valley stood deserted and rather sinister. The bullet hole in the diamond-paned glass looked itself like a scar on a body.

Repeated knockings on the door roused nobody. Dr. Fell tried the knob, and found that it was open. He beckoned Inspector Ballard inside for a short whispered conference, after which the Inspector disappeared. Then Dr. Fell, his face very red, invited the other three in.

Colonel Penderel walked in boldly. Nancy and Carl Kuhn followed with more hesitation. The German was obviously upset, and muttered something to himself as he crossed the threshold.

In the long, low-ceilinged study there was still a smell of stale tobacco smoke. Ludwig Meyer's body had been removed. Of his murder there now remained no trace except a spot of brown, dried blood on the papers which littered his desk. They were the sheets of his latest scientific treatise, which he would not now complete.

Dr. Fell, his underlip drawn up over his bandit's mustache, stood in the doorway. His eyes moved left toward the mantelpiece in the narrower wall of the oblong, and right toward the window in the wall facing it. He lumbered across to the desk, where he turned round.

"Here," he said, tapping the desk, "is where Meyer was sitting. Here," —he picked up a few sheets of manuscript, and dropped them,—"is Meyer's last book. Here,"—he drew open a drawer of the desk,—"was the evidence which proved, so very obviously, that Meyer was an espionage agent. By thunder, but wasn't it obvious!"

He closed the drawer with a bang. Only the sun entered. The bang of the drawer shook and disturbed dust motes against the sunlight. Dr. Fell reached across and fingered the cretonne curtain. It was very warm in here, so warm that Nancy Penderel's head swam.

"I have a particular question to ask," continued Dr. Fell. He looked at the Colonel. "Why is everybody so sure that the bullet which killed Meyer was fired from your rifle?"

Colonel Penderel put a hand to his forehead.

"See here, Fell," he began querulously, but checked himself. "It was fired from my rifle, wasn't it?"

"Oh, yes. I merely ask the question. Why is everyone so sure of that?"

"Because of the distinctive marks of rifling left on the bullet," returned the other.

"True. Palpably and painfully true. Harrumph. Now, then: you've built a miniature rifle range in the meadow behind your house, haven't you?"

"You ought to know," retorted the Colonel, regarding him with some exasperation. "You said you'd been looking at it."

"And what do you use to catch the bullets there?"

"Soft sand."

"So that," said Dr. Fell, "the many rounds fired into that sand would be lying about all over the place?"

"Yes."

"Yes. And each bullet, though keeping exactly its original shape, would bear the distinctive marking of your rifle. Wouldn't it?"

The door of the study banged open, making them all jump. Inspector Ballard entered and gave Dr. Fell a significant glance, and nodded.

Dr. Fell drew a deep breath, shutting his eyes for a moment before he went on.

"You see," he said, "this crime is very much more ingenious than it looks. A certain person who is listening to me now has created something of an artistic masterpiece.

"Those bullets, for instance. A bullet, selected for its most distinctive markings, could be fished out of that soft sand. It could easily be fitted into a loaded cartridge case and fired again. Couldn't it?"

"Not without . . ." Colonel Penderel began, but Dr. Fell stopped him.

"Then there is this question of the window curtain." The doctor leaned across and flicked it with his thumb and forefinger. But he was not looking at it; he was looking at Inspector Ballard.

"You, Inspector, were watching this house last night with a pair of field glasses. On the second the shot was fired, you jumped up and focused your glasses on this window. At least, so you told me this morning?"

"Yes, sir. That's right."

"And, when the shot was fired, you saw this curtain flutter. Is that correct too?"

In Ballard's mind the picture returned with sharp clearness of light and shadow. He nodded.

"It is a flat impossibility," said Dr. Fell, "for any shot fired from some distance away outside a closed window to agitate a curtain *inside* that window. There is only one thing which could have caused it: the expansion of gases from the muzzle of a firearm when the shot was fired in this room."

Supporting himself on his stick, he lumbered across to the door, which was an inch or two open. He opened it fully into the little hall.

Just outside, her fingers pressed to her cheeks, stood Harriet Meyer. Her startled expression, with the upper lip slightly lifted to expose the teeth, was caught as though by a camera.

"Come in, Mrs. Meyer," said Dr. Fell. "Will you tell us how you killed your husband, or shall I?"

She struck out at him with a slap like a cat's. When he tried to catch her arm, she backed away swiftly to the other side of the room. There she stood against the bookshelves: her blue eyes as shallow as a doll's, but her breast rising and falling heavily.

Again Dr. Fell drew a weary breath.

"Colonel Penderel," he continued, "will tell you that a .303 bullet can be fired from a 16-bore shotgun, such as the one in this house. When you say it 'can't possibly' be done, you don't really mean that. What you mean is that it can't be fired without leaving traces, and it can't be fired with accuracy.

"But accuracy, at more or less point-blank range, isn't necessary. And there is one way of firing it, out of a smooth-barreled shotgun, so that it leaves no traces. You'll find that method fully outlined in Gross's *Criminal Investigation.*"

Colonel Penderel's eyes opened wide, and then narrowed.

"Moss!" he said. "By the Lord Harry, dry moss! I must have been half-witted. Wrap the bullet in dry moss. It doesn't touch the inside of the gun, and no marks are left. The combustion ignites and destroys the moss: so that there's nothing left except a fouled barrel. When I was musketry instructor . . ."

Nancy was pointing wordlessly to the window.

Dr. Fell nodded again.

"Oh, yes," he agreed, contemplating the bullet hole. "Made yesterday afternoon, as you've guessed. Made by a bullet out of a real rifle, probably a .256. Made, of course, to set the stage.

"While her husband was occupied elsewhere, this lady calculated all angles, stood back some distance, and fired a clean hole through the window—lodging the bullet in a stuffed wildcat on the mantelpiece. If you will just note the line of fire, here, you'll see what happened.

"She could explain to Professor Meyer that she had been practicing, and made a wild shot. We can't blame him for being 'enraged.' But it was an accident. Later she could burn the stuffed figure and hide the rifle outside the house. Then she was ready for real business that night.

"She and her husband lived alone here. There was nobody to notice that inconspicuous hole in the window—until the time came for it to be noticed. There would be (as she had arranged) police officers round the house, to trap a mythical spy-head who was supposed to be calling on Dr. Meyer. They would not come close until they heard a shot. But when they heard a shot, it would be too late."

Still Harriet Meyer had not spoken. Her eyes, with the poised look of one who cannot decide whether to fight or run, moved round the room.

"She had only," said Dr. Fell, "to walk in here. Meyer would turn round (you note the position of the door) so that his left temple would be exposed. Any aftersmell of smokeless powder, which is very slight, would go unnoticed in the fog of rank tobacco smoke.

"The crime was all outlined for her, of course. In any good German scientist's house you are likely to find a copy of Hans Gross's *System der Kriminalistik.* There's one, I think, in the shelf just over her head now."

They heard Harriet Meyer's fingernails scratch against the books. Two voices spoke almost together.

"Frau Meyer—" began Kuhn.

"But she's English!" cried Nancy.

"Of course she is," said Dr. Fell, and rapped the ferrule of his stick sharply against the floor. "Confound it, don't you realize that's what makes her so dangerous?"

Harriet Meyer threw back her head and laughed.

"Don't you see," thundered Dr. Fell, "that poor old Meyer, objectionable as he was, wasn't a spy at all? That he was just what he pretended to be? That this charming lady here, a convert to what some call the modern ideology, was the real spy?

"The Special Branch thought they were hot on Meyer's track, because all trails led to his house. They were getting too close. So she had to sacrifice him. She tipped off the police and planned Meyer's murder, leaving incriminating evidence which was far too incriminating to be true, and bringing the police themselves as witnesses to her innocence. By thunder, I rather admire her!"

Harriet Meyer was still laughing. But it was a choked, vicious sort of laughter which turned her listeners cold. And it stopped, with a whistling inhalation of breath, as Inspector Ballard walked slowly across toward her.

Her eyes searched him. Then she seemed to make up her mind. She straightened up, her heels together. Her hand flashed outwards, palm uppermost, in salute. Then, striking at him with the same hand, she lowered her head and ran for the door.

Dr. Fell seized Ballard's arm.

"Let her go," he said quietly. "The house is surrounded. She won't get far. You have that shotgun safely locked up?"

"Yes; but—"

"The traces of burned moss in the barrel should be good enough. These clever people usually overlook something."

The room was very hot. Again Dr. Fell got out his bandanna handkerchief and mopped his face. Carl Kuhn hurried across to the window and peered out.

"You would not," said Dr. Fell softly, "you would not like her to get away?"

"I cannot say," said Kuhn, whose face had lost its color. "I do not know. She is a compatriot of yours, not mine. It is none of my affair."

Dr. Fell stowed away his handkerchief.

"Sir," he said gravely, "I know nothing against you. I believe you to be an honest man."

Kuhn ducked his head, and his heels came together.

"Even if you were not, you fly your own colors and present yourself for what you are. But there,"—he pointed his stick in the direction Harriet Meyer had taken,—"there goes a portent and a warning. The alien we can deal with. But the hypnotized zealot among ourselves, the bat and the owl and the mole who would ruin us with the best intentions, is another thing. It has happened before. It may happen again. It is what we have to fear; and, by the grace of God, *all* we have to fear!"

In silence he put on his broad-brimmed white hat.

"And now you must excuse me," he added, "I have no relish for cases such as this."

"I said it was Harriet," Nancy told him, in a voice hardly above a whisper. "I always thought she was queerer than he was. And yet, you know, I didn't *really* think so either. What did you mean when you told us the answer to this whole business was a proverb?"

Dr. Fell made a hideous face.

"Oh, that?" he said. "I wondered if she might be our quarry when I heard about her denouncing her husband to the police. Haven't I heard somewhere that people who live in glass houses shouldn't throw stones?"

# *The Black Minute*

"The Black Minute" is John Dickson Carr's second radio-play, broadcast by the BBC on February 14, 1940, but not printed until 1983 when it appeared in a posthumous collection of his radio scripts called *The Dead Sleep Lightly*. Carr had been reading Harry Houdini's *A Magician Among the Spirits* (1924), and one of the gimmicks in this play was taken from that book, but Carr used it in a way that Houdini had not predicted. The radio announcer asked listeners to turn out their lights as they joined Dr. Fell at a seance. We can't ask readers to do the same, but in all fairness we should warn you to pay attention to the very fact of darkness.

# The Black Minute

## The Characters:

| | |
|---|---|
| Dr. Gideon Fell | The detective |
| Sir Francis Church | An elderly scientist |
| Margery Grey | His niece |
| Mr. Riven | Student of psychical research |
| Anna | His housekeeper |
| Harry Brewster | In the rubber tire business |
| Taxi driver | |

*Setting:* London, 1940

*(The sound of a high wind, thin and shrill, continues throughout the following conversation. A taxi approaches and stops.)*

TAXI DRIVER *(hoarse and confidential):* This the 'ouse, miss? Can't see any numbers in this blackout.

MARGERY GREY: Yes, this is the house. I think. *(The voice is that of a girl in her middle twenties: very pleasant, and palpably worried.)*
*(A car door opens and slams. The wind blows shrilly.)*

MARGERY: Here you are.

TAXI DRIVER *(gratefully):* Thank *you,* miss. Like me to 'old a light on the steps while you go up?

MARGERY *(shivering):* No, thanks. I can manage. Good night.

TAXI DRIVER: Good night, miss.
*(The gears grind and the car drives away. Footsteps rasp on stone steps. Then—dull and hollow, giving the impression of depths in the house— the thud of an iron knocker.)*

MARGERY *(to herself, determined but nervous):* So this is the ogre's den! This is—
*(Front door opens. Anna, the housekeeper, speaks. She has a middle-aged, hard, thick, expressionless voice; the voice of a woman who sees much and says little.)*

ANNA *(coldly):* Yes?

MARGERY: I want to see Mr. Riven, please.

ANNA: I'm sorry, Miss. Mr. Riven isn't at home.

MARGERY *(afraid but insistent):* My name is Margery Grey. I'm Sir Francis Church's niece. We're all coming here for the séance tonight. I'm just a bit early, that's all; and I've got to see Mr. Riven.

ANNA *(enlightened):* Oh. You'd better come in, then.

MARGERY: Thank you. *(Crying out, startled)* Oh!

ANNA: Be careful, miss. Don't stumble. We've got no lights in the house for a minute or two. The fuses blew. Here, take my hand. *(Slight pause; then sardonically)* What's the matter? Not afraid, are you?

MARGERY: Why should I be afraid?

ANNA *(grimly):*  That's right, miss. We'll just lock up. . . .
*(The door closes, and a heavy bar is shot into place. This shuts out the noise of the wind, though it can still be heard blowing faintly from time to time.)*
ANNA:  Now over here to the stairs. You can feel the stair carpet with your foot. Now up . . . up . . . straight on up . . .
*(Faintly at first, far away and growing a bit louder, but never very loud, we hear the music of a violin playing "Humoresque.")*
MARGERY *(quickly):*  What's that?
ANNA *(noncommittally):*  It's him. . . . You see that door? Where there's firelight? Go in there and wait. I'll tell him you're here.
*(A door closes, shutting out the sound of the violin.)*
MARGERY *(to herself, bitterly):*  Wouldn't you know it? All the stage trappings. Deep carpet and firelight. Suit of Japanese armor with devil mask. Globe and books . . . Drat him! (In a lower voice, daringly but with conviction) Damn him!
*(The door opens and closes. Riven speaks. He has a slow, heavy, deliberate voice, not without amusement underneath; the voice of one who knows how to use words and is aware of their power.)*
RIVEN:  Were you calling down curses on *my* head, Miss Grey?
MARGERY *(startled and incredulous):*  Are you Mr. Riven?
RIVEN:  I am.
MARGERY *(impulsively):*  But you don't . . . I mean, you don't look anything like what I'd expected!
RIVEN *(gravely):*  My dear young lady, did you expect me to come in wearing a conical hat and a robe covered with signs of the zodiac? *(Laughs)* I am an ordinary person like yourself. Though far from being beautiful like yourself, if you'll allow me to say so.
MARGERY *(still rather incredulous):*  You're the medium?
RIVEN:  I am a student of psychical research.
MARGERY *(girding up her courage and flinging out at him):*  I'll tell you what you are. You're a fake.
*(In the ensuing pause, the wind is heard blowing thinly. Riven's voice is still thoughtful, but it is not pleasant.)*
RIVEN:  There is no need to back away, Miss Grey. I won't hurt you. Shall we forget what you just said?
MARGERY *(fiercely):*  No, we won't! *(Changing her tone)* Please, Mr. Riven, I didn't mean to offend you. I didn't. But I want you to let my uncle alone.
RIVEN *(slowly):*  Sir Francis Church is a very distinguished scientist.
MARGERY:  Yes, but he's an old man; an old, old man. And I won't have them laughing at him. That's what they're all doing, and you know it.

RIVEN: Indeed?

MARGERY *(desperately):* It's true, and you know it! I shouldn't mind if you were honest and sincere about it. Maybe there is an afterlife. I don't know. Maybe we can get into communication with the dead. I don't know. But you're not like that. Do you know Sir Barton MacNeile?

RIVEN: I have that honor. He is head of the Psychical Research Society.

MARGERY: Well, *he* says you're a fake. He says no honest spiritualist will have anything to do with you. He says . . . *(She breaks off)* Oh, I know I'm doing this badly! I'm only offending you, and all I wanted to do was to appeal to you. Will you let my uncle alone? It's impossible to live with him any more. And it's an awful thing to say, but sometimes I wish he'd—die. *(Slight pause)* Ever since you told him his wife had died of being poisoned . . .

RIVEN *(authoritatively):* Just one moment, Miss Grey. Please understand that, whatever the entities may say when they speak through my mouth, I know nothing of it. . . . Er—I believe you nursed the late Lady Church before she died?

MARGERY: What do you mean by that?

RIVEN *(surprised):* Nothing. I stated a fact.

MARGERY: I don't know what you mean, and I don't care. All I know is that my uncle can't think of anything but trying to get in touch with her. He even thinks he hears her tapping at the window at night, trying to get in. *(Three sharp, quick raps are heard on a pane of glass.)* What was that?

*(Short pause, with the sound of the wind blowing thinly)*

RIVEN: I heard nothing.

MARGERY *(in a low, steady voice):* Yes, you did. You're trying to scare me. I want to go.

RIVEN: But, my dear young lady, aren't you going to stay for the séance? Sir Francis will be here in a moment. So will young Mr. Harry Brewster *(complacently),* whom I hope to make our latest convert.

MARGERY *(pouncing):* Yes. And so will Dr. Fell.

RIVEN *(sharply):* Who?

MARGERY *(with underlying triumph):* Dr. Gideon Fell. I thought that would make you jump.

RIVEN: You invited this Dr. Fell to my house?

MARGERY: Yes, I did. He's coming with my uncle. Are you afraid to have him here?

RIVEN: I shall welcome him. Believe me, Miss Grey, you misjudge me. I am much maligned. I have no devils concealed up my sleeve. I cannot whistle the dead out of their graves at my will. Of course, if they choose to come to me, that is another matter. *(Three more sharp, quick raps on a pane of glass)* Give me your hand!

MARGERY:  Why?

RIVEN:  For the last time, I will not hurt you! Give me your hand!

MARGERY *(crying out):*  Uncle! Uncle! *Uncle!*

*(Her voice trails off and is lost in the loud whistling of the wind. Again we hear a motorcar draw up and stop.)*

TAXI DRIVER *(confidently):*  This is the 'ouse, gentlemen. I brought a young lady 'ere not fifteen minutes ago.

*(Sir Francis Church speaks. His voice is that of an old man—inclined at times to be fretful and querulous, but still strong and far from being senile. It is also that of a man used to commanding and dominating: probably in his earlier years a Tartar. It remains full of suspicion. But he has dignity; and, if you do not like him, you are bound to give him respect.)*

SIR FRANCIS *(suspiciously):*  A young lady, you say? That must be my niece.

TAXI DRIVER:  Dunno about that, guv'nor. *(Casually)* Tipped 'and-some, though.

SIR FRANCIS:  We'll get out here.

*(Car door opens.)*

TAXI DRIVER *(doubtfully):*  Excuse me, sir. But can the other gentleman—the stout gentleman—manage to get out of the cab?

DR. FELL *(thunderously intervening):*  Sir, that is an implication I resent. *(Warmly)* To be stuck forever in a taxicab . . . to spend the rest of my life in a taxicab . . . to bore holes for my feet and walk about clad in a taxicab . . . is a prospect to make any man shudder. I *can* get out of here. I WILL get out of here. *(Heavy grunt)*

TAXI DRIVER:  Thank you, sir. Good night.

*(As the cab goes off, Sir Francis speaks doggedly as though continuing an argument.)*

SIR FRANCIS:  So you won't be persuaded to believe in the cause, Dr. Fell?

DR. FELL:  Sir, I neither believe nor disbelieve.

SIR FRANCIS:  Then you're nothing. *(Bitterly)* Hate the cause; sneer at the cause; fight the cause. But don't be indifferent to the cause. *(Changing his tone)* Oh, I know! I was a sceptic myself. I prided myself on being . . . *(still more bitterly)* . . . the cold man of science. I once wrote, "The term 'afterlife' sounds rather like 'anticlimax,' and must, I imagine, amount to much the same thing."

DR. FELL:  And you don't believe that any longer?

SIR FRANCIS *(simply):*  I am reborn. Elsie talks to me.

DR. FELL:  Elsie?

SIR FRANCIS:   My wife. She died four years ago.

DR. FELL *(quietly):*   Just a moment, Sir Francis, before you lift that knocker. *(Slight pause)* Frankly, you puzzle me.

SIR FRANCIS:   Oh? How?

DR. FELL:   I have had some slight acquaintance with you, now, for a good many years. You're a fighter. You are also an intelligent man. It would take a very superior brand of tomfoolery to deceive you. *(Sir Francis snorts, but Dr. Fell goes on.)* Before coming here, I obtained some information about this Mr. Riven of yours.

SIR FRANCIS:   From Lord Senlac? I had Riven at Senlac House the other night.

DR. FELL:   No. From Scotland Yard.

SIR FRANCIS *(sharply):*   Scotland Yard?

DR. FELL:   Yes. Now you know my state of mind. Shall we go in?
*(The wind whistles thinly.)*

SIR FRANCIS *(with concentrated bitterness):*   That, eh? I see. The police persecute Riven. Even the spiritualists persecute him. And therefore I am to turn away from the pioneer. I'm to get down on my knees like another scientist and deny that the earth moves. Well, I won't do it. I know what I know. I've never been afraid of ridicule in my life, and I'm not afraid of it now. *(This seems to have exhausted him. His voice grows fretful.)* Things are hard sometimes. Very hard on a man. We must have a creed, Fell. Even you must have a creed. What do you affirm?

DR. FELL:   I affirm—

SIR FRANCIS:   Yes?

DR. FELL *(in a sharper, clearer tone):*   I affirm that I just heard somebody scream.
*(The whistle of the wind is mingled with the heavy banging of the iron knocker. This fades away into Margery's voice.)*

MARGERY *(frightened but triumphant):*   There, you see! That's my uncle downstairs now. I can hear his voice.

RIVEN *(mildly protesting):*   But, my dear young lady, you act as though you thought I were trying to molest you.

MARGERY:   Aren't you?

RIVEN:   Hardly . . . *(significantly)* . . . at this moment. Excuse me.
*(A door opens, and Riven raises his voice.)* Sir Francis? This way.
*(A soft but heavy bump, as of someone falling on carpeted stairs. An exclamation of pain. Sir Francis's voice, angry and querulous, comes closer.)*

SIR FRANCIS:   Riven! Where the devil are you, Riven? What do you mean, keeping all the lights out in this house? *(Still more querulously)* Tripped and nearly broke my knee on those stairs of yours. *(In pain)*

Ffff! No, I won't shake hands. Got my hand all over dirt. *(Breaking off)* What are you doing here, girl?

MARGERY:   You promised I could attend the séance, Uncle Francis.

SIR FRANCIS:   Went out without your dinner, didn't you? All right! Sit down there and be quiet. *(Pauses)* Riven, this is Dr. Gideon Fell.

DR. FELL:   How do you do?

RIVEN:   I am honored.

MARGERY *(under her breath):*   You're a bad-tempered old man, that's what you are. *I* won't try to help you.

SIR FRANCIS *(sharply):*   What did you say, Margery?

MARGERY *(submissively):*   Nothing, Uncle Francis.

RIVEN:   I am sorry about the lights, Sir Francis. The fuses will be mended in a moment. In the meantime, we are waiting for Mr. Harry Brewster.

MARGERY:   Listen: There's someone else at the front door now.
   *(Distantly a heavy door is heard to open and close.)*

VOICE:   Hullo, hullo, hullo! Anybody at home?

MARGERY *(half-laughing):*   That's Harry Brewster, all right.
   *(Harry talks himself up into the room. He is a brisk, breezy, bouncing young man in his late twenties; likeable but loud, confident, and rather credulous.)*

HARRY:   Nice of you to let me in, Anna. Anna, you get older and prettier every day . . . *(Imitating a bus conductor)* Mind the step, madam! *(Bursting in) Hel* -lo, everybody! Where's the Grand Goblin and Rainmaker?

RIVEN:   Good evening, Mr. Brewster.

HARRY *(with breezy heartiness):*   Wot-cher, old cock? Hello, Margery. Evening, Sir Francis. Who's this?

RIVEN:   Mr. Brewster, Dr. Gideon Fell.

HARRY *(breaking off, impressed):*   I say! Is it? Hel-lo, Doctor. Going to catch another murderer for us?
   *(Again there are three sharp, vicious raps on the pane of glass.)*

HARRY *(surprised):*   Hullo! Something seems to be trying to get in.

SIR FRANCIS *(rasping):*   Don't talk like that, you young fool! Do you want to attract evil forces?

HARRY *(hurt):*   No offence, Sir Francis; no-o-o offence. Just trying to keep the party merry and bright. *(Amused)* The last time they turned Dr. Fell loose to catch a murderer, he nailed a BBC announcer. When that happens, nobody's safe. *(Confidentially)* What do you think about all this, Doctor? Spooks, I mean. Are you a spook-fancier?

DR. FELL *(amused):*   At least, Mr. Brewster, I gather that you are a sceptic?

HARRY:   Me? *(With sudden intense solemnity)* No, no, no!

DR. FELL:  No?

HARRY:  Not a bit of it. What I say is, these things can't be taken too seriously. Now, I'm a modern man. A practical man. *(Breaking off to explain)* I'm in the rubber tire business, Doctor. Here's my card. Dear old Lady Church set me up in business, bless her. *(Returns to his theme)* Well, what I say is, how do we know about these things? I believe in an afterlife. And what's believing in an afterlife *but* believing in ghosts, if you see what I mean? Or, if it's not ghosts, it's something. Maybe a scientific force. Maybe we'll discover it. No, indeed. *(Proudly)* I'm a practical man; I can believe anything.

RIVEN *(drily):*  Very aptly put. Then shall we proceed to the test?

SIR FRANCIS *(vacantly):*  Yes. I feel that there will be visitors tonight.

RIVEN:  First, let us see if the lights work. *(A sharp click)* Yes, they're on now. And I have a word to say in all humility to all of you. *(But he does not sound humble.)* I have been accused of being a fraud and a charlatan. *(Arrogantly, as there is a slight murmur of protest)* Oh, yes, I have! That charge has not been made against me in any of the great houses into which Sir Francis has introduced me. But it has been made here. *(Hypnotically)* Now please understand one thing. When I am in my trance, I know nothing of what goes on. If you waked me, you might kill me. I therefore propose to answer the scoffers in their own language. I propose to submit to a test in which any fraud would be impossible. You see that door over there?

DR. FELL:  We see it.

RIVEN:  That door leads to a small room, without windows. It has plaster walls and a bare board-floor. In the way of furniture, it contains only some chairs, a table, and a gramophone.

SIR FRANCIS:  *She* will be there.

RIVEN:  We shall bolt the door on the inside. I shall ask to be tied with cords to one of the chairs. We will take one further precaution which will make it absolutely impossible for me to move. Are you ready?

*(The following three voices speak swiftly on the heels of each other.)*

SIR FRANCIS:  *I* am ready, by heaven.

HARRY *(through his teeth):*  Carry on, old son.

MARGERY:  No! . . . Yes! All right.

*(A door opens.)*

RIVEN *(with smiling courtesy):*  Then—will you walk into my parlor?

*(The sound of the wind rises and falls strongly.)*

MARGERY:  It's awfully cold in here.

RIVEN:  Are you now convinced, Mr. Brewster, that I am tied to this chair in such a way that I cannot possibly move?

HARRY:  Ho! *Am* I! *(In an aside)* Margery, if he can get out of that, he's a ghost himself. I've even got his fingers tied together with thread.

RIVEN: If you please! We will take one further precaution. Miss Grey, will you reach into the upper right-hand pocket of my waistcoat? Don't be afraid. You will find there a small bottle of luminous paint. Have you got it?

MARGERY: Yes.

RIVEN: Please take the brush and make a plain mark in luminous paint on each side of my collar—just beside the necktie. I must apologize for these absurdities, gentlemen. But I want you to be sure. Even if I could dislodge any of these cords, I could scarcely move without being seen. You agree? *(Three voices almost simultaneously say "yes." Dr. Fell does not speak.)* Good! Then will the four of you sit down round the table? My chair will be a little way back from you all. *(Scraping of chairs on a bare board-floor.)* One moment! Mr. Brewster, will you go and start the gramophone? It will stop itself. When you hear my command, turn out the lights and come back to the group round the table.

MARGERY: Do you want us to clasp hands?

RIVEN: That will not be necessary.

SIR FRANCIS: I think it will be. Listen to me. *(With the ring of authority)* I've sat quietly by. I've heard you called a charlatan and myself an old fool. There are forces tonight, and they're bad. I want a chain of linked hands round this table. Margery, give me your hand.

MARGERY: You got your hand awfully dirty on those stairs, Uncle Francis.

SIR FRANCIS: Never mind that. Give me your hand. Now you, Fell, on my other side. Harry, attend to those lights and complete the circle. Quickly!

*(Faintly, at some distance away, three more raps are followed by the noise of glass shattering.)*

HARRY: It seems to have got in.

RIVEN *(rather drowsily):* That was the other room. There are no windows here. Start the gramophone, Mr. Brewster. *(A sound of footsteps on the bare board-floor. Then the scratch of a gramophone needle as the disk starts to turn, but it does not yet play.)*

RIVEN: Now. Turn . . . out . . . the . . . lights . . . please.

*(More footsteps and a click. The footsteps return to the table.)*

HARRY: Your hand, Margery. Your other hand, Dr. Fell. I felt—

SIR FRANCIS *(dully):* Be quiet. Be quiet.

*(After a pause, the music swells out, but not at all loudly.)*

RIVEN *(drowsily):* I shall be leaving you soon. Do not attempt to speak to me afterwards.

*(The music still plays for some seconds.)*

MARGERY *(in a whisper):* I felt something.

SIR FRANCIS *(fiercely):* Sh-h!

MARGERY:  Those luminous-paint spots. They look like eyes. I can't stand—

RIVEN *(still more drowsily):*  Do not attempt to speak to me after—
*(The speech ends in a kind of bubbling screech, rising to a cry of agony, but choked thickly as though by liquid in mouth and throat.)*

HARRY *(breathing):*  For God's sake, what was it?

DR. FELL:  I think we had better have the lights on.

SIR FRANCIS:  Don't break the circle! Don't break—

DR. FELL *(grimly):*  At the same time, I think we had better have the lights on. Mr. Riven!
*(No reply.)*

HARRY *(struck with superstitious terror in spite of himself):*  I say, sir, shall I—?

DR. FELL:  Yes.
*(Scraping of chairs and blundering footsteps. A chair is knocked over.)*

DR. FELL:  Hurry!

HARRY:  Got it!
*(A switch clicks sharply. Silence except for the music. Then Margery screams. The gramophone slows down, scratching hollowly, and stops.)*

HARRY *(after a pause; and in a low incredulous voice; almost guilty):*  I don't . . . believe it.

MARGERY *(not loudly; too tense to be hysterical):*  That . . . isn't blood, is it? All over Mr. Riven's neck?

SIR FRANCIS:  He's holding his head in an uncommonly queer way.

DR. FELL:  That, my friend, is not part of his head. That's the handle of the knife. He's been stabbed through the throat.

MARGERY:  He's falling sideways.

DR. FELL:  He can't fall. Not held up by all those cords.

HARRY *(with heavy and hollow incredulity):*  I don't believe it. He's playing a joke on us. *(Tentatively)* And a poor joke too. Rotten bad form, if you ask me. *(Insistently)* Come on, old chap! Say something.

MARGERY:  Don't touch him!

HARRY:  But it can't be. You mean somebody came in here, and . . . ?

DR. FELL:  The door is bolted on the inside.
*(Quick footsteps on the floor. Noise of a bolt being shot back, and into its socket again.)*

HARRY:  It's true. *(Blustering scepticism is fighting with superstitious terror.)* Go on! It's a joke. I still don't believe it. I'm not going to let you say that one of us . . .

MARGERY:  Harry, that can't be. *(Slowly reflecting)* I had Uncle Francis's hand in my left hand, and Harry's hand in my right. I was holding tight.

DR. FELL:    That, Miss Grey, is quite true. I can testify that I had Sir
Francis's hand on my right and Mr. Brewster's hand on my left.

HARRY *(startled):*    And I had you on my right and Margery on my left.
Neither of you let go.

SIR FRANCIS *(very tired):*    If it's any satisfaction to your *(bitterly)* practical minds, I can tell you that the circle was complete. I held my niece's
hand at the right and Dr. Fell's at the left. We formed a closed chain.

HARRY:    But—

DR. FELL *(sternly and heavily, quieting possible panic):*    One moment.
*(Murmurs subside)* We shall all have questions to answer shortly. Let's
be quite clear about one thing from the start . . . Did anyone let go
another hand at any time? Even for a second?

HARRY:    No, definitely not!

MARGERY:    Never!

SIR FRANCIS:    Not for a tenth of a second.

HARRY *(stupidly):*    Then there's nothing for it. He didn't stab himself;
not trussed up like that. And where did the knife come from? Someone
must have sneaked in—

DR. FELL:    Need I remind you, sir, that the door is bolted on the inside?
*(Pause)*

SIR FRANCIS:    My dear friends. My good foolish friends. *(Wearily)* Do
you need to be told who killed him? Fell, come here and look at this
knife.

DR. FELL:    Be careful. I advise you not to touch him either.

SIR FRANCIS:    What does it matter? A little dirt. A little blood. A little
span of life composed of the two . . . Here's a man you thought was a
charlatan. He's dead.

HARRY:    Well, you needn't look at me like that. I didn't kill him.

MARGERY:    Then who did?

HARRY:    I don't know. But I mean to find out. I'm a practical man, and
I'm not going to be put upon. *(Almost pleading, as though urging
someone to give up a tedious joke)* Come on, now? Who let go somebody's hand? Did you, Margery?

MARGERY:    No, I tell you.

HARRY:    Dr. Fell?

DR. FELL *(sternly):*    For the second time, young man, no. Besides, you
don't seem to see the difficulties in the way of that. If one of us did
such a thing, he would require two accomplices—one on each side of
him. I'm afraid it won't do.

HARRY:    But the thing's impossible.

SIR FRANCIS:    By ordinary standards, yes.

HARRY:    Ordinary standards?

SIR FRANCIS:    Yes. And if you want to see how impossible . . . what

*you* call impossible . . . come closer and look at the knife. *(Fiercely)*
Oh, come, man! Will you let an old fool look where you daren't? . . .
That's right. . . . The handle of that knife is made of polished steel,
as bright as new silver. If you don't mind getting close to him, bend
down and breathe on the handle. Yes, I said breathe on it! . . . You
see?

HARRY:   What about it?

SIR FRANCIS:   There are no fingerprints on the handle.

HARRY *(after confused thought):*   But look here! Gloves . . . or a
handkerchief . . .

SIR FRANCIS:   A handkerchief, or even gloves, would have left smudges.
There are no smudges. *(Vacantly)* No human hand held that knife.

HARRY:   You're not trying to tell us he was murdered by a . . .
*(A sharp, heavy knocking at the door interrupts him.)*

MARGERY *(now near hysteria):*   Is it coming for the rest of us?

HARRY *(in a commonsense voice):*   Nonsense, old girl. It's only Anna.
The housekeeper or maid or whatever she is.

MARGERY:   Then why don't you open the door?

HARRY:   I will. I—
*(The knocking begins again. We hear hesitant footsteps, the sound of a
bolt shot back, and the door sharply opened.)*

HARRY *(with a quick breath, as though he half expected someone
else):*   It's Anna. *(Angrily)* What did I tell you?

ANNA:   Excuse me, sir. I heard a kind of sound I shouldn't have heard.
Is anything . . .
*(She breaks off, evidently catching sight of Riven. The exclamation she
gives is not loud, nor anything like a scream; it is more like that of
someone being hurt, but it is very definite.)*

DR. FELL:   Yes. Someone has killed Mr. Riven. You had better go for
the police.

ANNA:   I'll dial 999. I've always wanted to dial 999.

DR. FELL:   You don't seem very surprised.

ANNA:   Me? Naow. I'm not surprised. *(Thoughtfully, without pity)*
Through the throat, eh? He always was one for talking.
*(The door closes.)*

SIR FRANCIS:   I must get out of here.

DR. FELL:   Steady, my lad. Take it easy.

SIR FRANCIS *(brusquely):*   I'm quite all right. Just a bit queasy, that's
all. *(Shivers a little)* I want to get out of this room! It must be deadly
cold in here, even for you young people. Can't we at least go into
Riven's study?

DR. FELL:   Why not? But I don't think any of us had better go further
than the study.

SIR FRANCIS *(snapping at him):*    Still materialistic, eh?

DR. FELL:    I don't think you quite understand my attitude towards these matters. I am very sympathetic towards supernatural happenings . . . when they are genuine supernatural happenings.

HARRY:    When they are—

DR. FELL:    Let me make it clearer. Suppose you tell me that the ghost of Julius Caesar appeared to Brutus before the Battle of Philippi and warned him of approaching death. All I can say is that I know nothing about it. But suppose you tell me that the ghost of Julius Caesar walked into the cutlery department at Selfridge's, bought a stainless-steel knife, paid for it with spectral banknotes, and then stabbed Brutus in the middle of Oxford Street. All I shall beg leave to murmur, gently, is: rubbish. You cannot mix the two worlds like that. *(More sternly)* This was a human crime, planned by a human being. Don't you see that those two luminous points on Riven's collar showed the murderer . . . or murderess . . . exactly where to strike?

MARGERY *(in a low voice):*    In the dark?

DR. FELL:    In the dark.

HARRY:    But, hang it, Riven himself suggested using the luminous paint!

DR. FELL:    Yes. After careful prompting by somebody before we arrived. How else did he happen to have that bottle so conveniently in his pocket?

HARRY:    Prompted by . . . ?

DR. FELL:    The murderer.

MARGERY:    But, Dr. Fell, there was nobody here before the rest of you arrived. *(Laughs)* Except me, of course.

SIR FRANCIS *(curtly):*    Be good enough, Margery, not to speak until you're spoken to. . . . Are you telling us, my friend, that you know how this crime was managed?

DR. FELL:    I rather think so.

SIR FRANCIS:    Are you saying that somebody got in through that bolted door after all?

DR. FELL:    No.

SIR FRANCIS *(with increasing shrillness):*    Do you mean that one of us got a hand loose in order to stab Riven?

DR. FELL:    No.

*(The wind is heard thinly.)*

HARRY *(not loudly):*    In just about one minute, I'm going to give a yell and go mad. If you don't want to see me rolling on the hearth rug, say what you mean. . . . I suppose it wasn't suicide?

DR. FELL:    No. *(Sincerely)* Believe me, I am not making mysteries. You have made the mysteries. Your minds work like the minds of . . .

shall we say? . . . modern dictators. The old-time dictator first started wars and then won medals. The modern dictator first puts on medals and then starts wars. That is your trouble. You have got the crime turned the wrong way round.

MARGERY *(helplessly):*   No, Harry, don't look at me. *I* don't know what he's talking about. When we heard Riven utter that horrible cry . .

DR. FELL *(abruptly):*   One moment. How do you know it was Riven who uttered the cry?

HARRY:   *What?*

DR. FELL *(in a louder, slower voice):*   I said, what reason have you for supposing that it was Riven who uttered the cry?
*(Pause)*

HARRY *(dazed):*   But . . . wasn't it?

DR. FELL:   You see, that was what the murderer wanted you to think. You heard a terrible kind of screech, which seemed to have death in it. Presently we turned on the lights and found a man with a knife in his neck. So we assumed what was not true. The murderer knew that the source of sound cannot be located in the dark. It was the murderer who let out that appalling cry. Riven, who was supposed to be in a trance, could not speak and ask what had happened. And we . . . including that poor, blind fool, myself . . . we fell straight into the trap. We broke up the circle. It was at least eight seconds before the lights could be turned on. And during that interval, the murderer merely leaned across and stabbed Riven through the neck. The luminous marks on the collar showed him exactly where to strike.

HARRY *(hollowly):*   I don't believe that. You can't prove it. *(Breaking off)* Who did that?

DR. FELL:   Before I answer that question .

SIR FRANCIS *(very coolly):*   Yes?

DR. FELL:   Before I answer that question, I should like to look at Margery's hand.

MARGERY:   No, you don't. Why do you want to look at it? That's the second time tonight somebody's asked. Riven wanted to. Why? There's nothing on them—either of them. Look! They're perfectly clean.

DR. FELL *(heavily):*   They are . . . Mr. Brewster, you tell me that you are in the rubber tire business. I think I have your card here. Then you would know something about liquid rubber?

HARRY *(harshly):*   Yes, I do. What about it?

MARGERY *(reflecting):*   Harry, he was sitting just behind *you.*

DR. FELL *(sharply):*   One moment. Now, Mr. Brewster, suppose a murderer, after the fashion of many continental criminals, were to paint his fingers and a part of his hand with liquid rubber? He would leave no fingerprints, I think. Not even fabric-mark traces. It would form a thin coating, not even discernible to the touch. The one thing the murderer could not disguise would be its color. What is the color of liquid rubber?

HARRY *(blankly):* Why it's . . . smudgy kind of stuff. Medium or dark grey in color, rather like . . . *(As the meaning of this flashes over him, he hesitates and then brings out the word with a jerk of inspiration.)* . . . dirt!

MARGERY *(crying out):* No!

DR. FELL: Exactly. Then the murderer is the man who staged that unnecessary fall on the stairs, to account for the large amount of "dirt" on his right hand. He is the man who . . . though he was tightly holding Miss Grey's hand for some time during the séance . . . transferred no trace of that "dirt" to her left hand. See for yourself. He is the man who refused to wash his hands before the crime, but wanted to get out of the room afterwards. To wash his hands! He is the man who has that betraying stuff on his fingers now. *(Wearily, without triumph)* In short, Sir Francis Church.

*(Below and distantly, the iron knocker on the front door begins to pound.)*

MARGERY: Uncle Francis! Look at me! Look round!

SIR FRANCIS *(calmly):* Yes, my dear?

MARGERY: Aren't you going to say anything? Don't just sit there and nod at the fire. Aren't you going to tell him it's not true?

SIR FRANCIS: Why, my dear, what he says *is* true.

MARGERY: I don't believe it.

SIR FRANCIS *(with a cynicism so deep that it sounds almost careless):* A little dirt. A little blood. A little span of life composed of the two. I've nothing much to lose there. But for a man to be forced to lose the one thing in life he knows to be of any value, his intellectual self-respect . . . *(Breaking off)* Margery, you're over twenty-one. It's time you faced at least some of the facts. *(Bluntly)* I killed my wife. And that swine in there knew it.

MARGERY *(wildly):* Don't say anything more! Keep your voice down. I can hear Anna coming now. She's . . .

ANNA *(interrupting, with subdued triumph):* That's the police at the door. They said they were sending the inspector from the divisional station. Shall I bring 'em up?

*(The door knocker pounds again.)*

SIR FRANCIS *(almost affably):* Bring them up, Anna. Bring them up! This is quite a triumph for you, Dr. Fell.

DR. FELL: No. Believe me; I don't want triumphs like this. *(Bitterly)* So it was blackmail, then? That's what they said about him at Scotland Yard.

SIR FRANCIS *(almost surprised):*    Blackmail? *(Contemptuously)* If it had been the ordinary kind of blackmail, do you think I should have minded? Oh, no. I should have paid. But do you know what that man wanted? He wanted to be known as a great medium. He wanted the world to think he had made a convert of me. He wanted me to introduce him into the houses of my friends as a great medium. *(With rising intensity)* He wanted a man of science to babble the degrading nonsense he put into my mouth. He even compelled *me* . . . the one person whose honesty everyone trusted; yes, trusted . . . to play his paltry little parlor tricks while he sat tied in a chair. If you can think of any way for Frank Church to sink lower than that, just tell me what it is.

MARGERY *(murmuring):*    Then that was why . . .

SIR FRANCIS:    That was why. It surprised him very much when I insisted on our linking hands round the table tonight. But he learned the reason presently. *(Reflectively)* I don't mind what they do now. Even when I stand in a dock . . .

DR. FELL:    Need you stand in a dock?

SIR FRANCIS:    What do you mean by that?

DR. FELL:    If you killed your wife, you deserve to be hanged. But you don't deserve this. You have been a great man, and I will not see you shamed.

*(The loud banging at the front door begins again. Anna's voice is heard distantly, calling angrily.)*

ANNA:    All right, not so fast! I'm coming.

DR. FELL:    There is still time if you hurry. Get out of here quickly. Scrub that stuff off your hands. Then come back here and tell what story you like. I am no policeman. Let them find out who killed Riven if they can.

SIR FRANCIS *(incredulously):*    You . . . mean . . . that?

MARGERY *(frantically):*    Of course he means it! So do all of us. Only hurry, hurry, hurry! They're . . .

*(The bar is drawn back on the big door below, and we hear it creak open.)*

ANNA *(distantly):*    You'd better come in, the lot of you. Straight upstairs.

SIR FRANCIS *(with growing incredulity):*    Do you support this too, Harry?

*(No reply. Sir Francis's voice grows harsh.)*

SIR FRANCIS:    Well, what is it? Do you support this or don't you?

HARRY:    I don't like it, sir, and that's flat. But, if Margery says so, I'll stand by you. *(Hastily)* Only for Lord's sake clear out of here quickly, before they catch you with that stuff on your hands.

MARGERY:   Sh-h! Hurry!

SIR FRANCIS *(with maddening deliberation):*   What about Anna?

DR. FELL:   The good Anna is undoubtedly an old accomplice of
Riven's. Also, it was undoubtedly Anna who made all those very crude
and clumsy rappings on the window—with the aid of another window,
an air-well, and a broomstick. Let her take her broomstick and fly
away on it.

MARGERY *(screaming):*   They're nearly at the door.

SIR FRANCIS *(calmly):*   You're wrong, my dear. They're in the room.
. . . *(Breaking off)* Good evening, gentlemen. Come in. *(Blandly)*
Whichever of you is the inspector, I wish to give myself up for murder.
The question is, will you be able to prove it in court? I have just one
small request to make before we go. Do you mind if I wash a pair of
exceedingly dirty hands?

*(We hear no reply, but Sir Francis's voice takes on a curious inflection
which we do not quite interpret, and are not intended to interpret.)*

SIR FRANCIS:   You don't mind? Thank you. Thank you *so* much.

# *The Locked Room*

"The Locked Room" was published in *The Strand Magazine,* July 1940 —the same magazine that had published the Sherlock Holmes stories fifty years earlier. The first American printing of Carr's story was in *Ellery Queen's Mystery Magazine,* November 1943. In addition to its original solution to the locked-room problem, what is most interesting to Carr fans is the character of the victim, Francis Seton. Carr had been on the high seas on his way from England to the United States when war was declared. Almost immediately, he returned to England: "A gallant and quite uncalled-for gesture on his part," wrote Val Gielgud in his diary, "to see the war through in a country he is fond of." Seton's reaction to the war is quite different.

# The Locked Room

You may have read the facts. Francis Seton was found lying on the floor behind his desk, near death from a fractured skull. He had been struck three times across the back of the head with a piece of lead-loaded broom handle. His safe had been robbed. His body was found by his secretary-typist, Iris Lane, and his librarian, Harold Mills, who were, in the polite newspaper phrase, "being questioned."

So far, it seems commonplace. Nothing in that account shows why Superintendent Hadley of the C.I.D. nearly went mad, or why ten o'clock of a fine June morning found him punching at the doorbell of Dr. Gideon Fell's house in Chelsea.

Summer touched the old houses with grace. There was a smoky sparkle on the river, and on the flower-veined green of the Embankment gardens. Upstairs, in the library, with its long windows, Superintendent Hadley found the learned doctor smoking a cigar and reading a magazine.

Dr. Fell's bulk overflowed from a chair nearly large enough to accommodate him. A chuckle animated his several chins, and ran down over the ridges of his waistcoat. He peered up at Hadley over his eyeglasses; his cheeks shone, pinkly transparent, with warmth of welcome. But at Hadley's first words a disconsolate expression drew down the corners of his mustache.

"Seton's conscious," said Hadley. "I've just been talking to him."

Dr. Fell grunted. Reluctantly he put aside the magazine.

"Ah," he said. "And Seton denies the story told by the secretary and the librarian?"

"No. He confirms it."

"In every detail?"

"In every detail."

Dr. Fell puffed out his cheeks. He also took several violent puffs at the cigar, staring at it in a somewhat cross-eyed fashion. His big voice was subdued.

"Do you know, Hadley," he muttered, "I rather expected that."

"I didn't," snapped Hadley. "I didn't; and I don't. But that's why I'm here. You must have some theory about this impossible burglar who nearly bashed a man's head off and then disappeared like smoke. My forthright theory is that Iris Lane and Harold Mills are lying. If . . . hullo!"

Standing by the window, he broke off and glanced down into the street. His gesture was so urgent that Dr. Fell, with much labor, hoisted himself up wheezily from the chair and lumbered over to the window.

Clear in the strong sunshine, a girl in a white frock was standing on the opposite pavement, by the railings, and peering up at the window. As Dr. Fell threw back the curtains, she looked straight into their eyes.

She was what is called an outdoor girl, with a sturdy and well-shaped body, and a square but very attractive face. Her dark-brown hair hung in a long bob. She had light-hazel eyes in a tanned, earnest face. Her mouth might have been too broad, but she showed fine teeth when she laughed. If she was not exactly pretty, health and vigor gave her a strong attractiveness which was better than that.

"Iris Lane," said Hadley ventriloquially.

Dr. Fell, in an absent-minded way, was startled. He would have expected Francis Seton's typist to be either prim or mousy.

When she saw the two men at the window, Iris Lane's expressive face showed many things. Disappointment, surprise, even fear. Her knee moved as though she were about to stamp angrily on the pavement. For a second they thought she would turn and hurry away. Then she seemed to come to a decision. She almost ran across the street toward the house.

"Now what do you suppose—?" Hadley was speculating when the doctor cut him short.

"She wants to see me, confound you," he roared. "Or she did want to see me, until you nearly scared her off."

And the girl herself confirmed it a moment later. She was making an attempt to be calm and even jaunty, but her eyes always moved back to Hadley.

"It seems," she said, after a quick look round the room, "that I'm always trailing the Superintendent. Or he's always trailing me. I don't know which."

Hadley nodded. He was noncommittal.

"It does seem like that, Miss Lane. Anything in particular on your mind now?"

"Yes. I—I wanted to talk to Dr. Fell. Alone."

"Oh? Why?"

"Because it's my last hope," answered the girl, raising her head. "Because they say nobody, not even a stray dog, is ever turned away from here."

"Nonsense!" said Dr. Fell, hugely delighted nevertheless. He covered this with deprecating noises which shook the chandelier, and an offer of refreshment. Hadley saw that the old man was half hooked already, and Hadley despaired.

Yet it seemed impossible to doubt this girl's sincerity. She sat bolt upright in the chair, opening and shutting the catch of a white handbag.

"It's quite simple," she explained, and hunched her shoulders. "Harold Mills and I were alone in the house with Mr. Seton. There was nearly three thousand pounds in the safe in his study."

Dr. Fell frowned.

"So? As much money as that?"

"Mr. Seton was leaving," said Iris Lane, with an effort. "He was going abroad, to spend a year in California. He always made his decisions suddenly—just like that." She snapped her fingers. "We didn't know anything about it, Harold and I, until he broke the news that morning. The man from the bank brought the money round; Mr. Seton put it into the safe, and told us why he had sent for it. That meant we were out of our jobs."

And she began to tell the story.

Of course (Iris admitted to herself), her nerves had been on edge that night. It was caused partly by losing a good job at a moment's notice, partly by the thick and thundery weather round the old house in Kensington, and partly by the personality of Francis Seton himself.

Francis Seton was a book collector. When Iris had first answered his advertisement for a secretary-typist, she had expected to find someone thin and ancient, with double-lensed spectacles. Instead she found a thickset bull of a man, with sandy hair and a blue guileless eye. His energy was prodigious. He animated the old house like a humming top. He had the genuine collector's passion; he was generous, and considerate when it did not inconvenience him.

But he whirled off at a new tangent that morning, a hot overcast day, when he called Iris Lane and Harold Mills into his study. They had been working in the long library on the first floor. The study, which opened out of it, was a large room with two windows overlooking a tangled back garden.

Seton stood by the big flat-topped desk in the middle of the study. Out of a canvas bag he was emptying thick packets of banknotes, one of which fell into the waste-paper basket.

"Look here," he said, with the confiding candor of a child. "I'm off to America. For a year at least."

(He seemed pleased at the way his hearers jumped.)

"But, sir—" began Harold Mills.

"Crisis!" said Seton, pointing to a newspaper. "Crisis!" he added, pointing to another. "I'm sick of crises. California's the place for me. Orange groves and sea breezes: at least, that's what the booklets say. Besides, I want to make old Isaacson sick with my 1593 *Venus and Adonis* and the 1623 folio."

His forehead grew lowering and embarrassed.

"I've got to let you both go," he growled. "I'd like to take you both with me. Can't afford it. Sorry; but there it is. I'll give you a month's salary in place of notice. Damn it, I'll give you two months' salary in place of notice. How's that?"

Beaming with relief now that this was off his chest, he dismissed the subject briskly. He gathered up the packets of banknotes, fishing the dropped one out of the waste-paper basket. It made his face crimson to bend over, since Dr. Woodhall had warned him about high blood pressure; but he was all energy again.

A little iron safe stood against one wall. Seton opened it with his key, poured the money into a tin box, closed the safe, and locked it. In a vague way Iris noted the denominations on the paper bands round the packets of notes: £1, £5, £10, £20. A little treasure-trove. Almost a little fortune.

Perhaps because of the heat of the day, there was perspiration on Harold Mills's forehead.

"And when do you want to leave, sir?" he asked.

"Leave? Oh, ah." Seton considered. "Day after tomorrow," he decided.

"Day after tomorrow!"

"Saturday," Seton explained. "Always a good ship leaving. Yes, make it Saturday."

"But your passport—" protested Iris.

"That's completely in order," said Seton coolly.

The word which flashed through Iris Lane's mind just then was "robbed." She could not help it. There are times with everyone when the sight of so much money, all in a lump, makes the fingers itch and brings fantastic dreams of what might be.

She didn't mean it—as she was later to explain to the police. But there was a tantalizing quality in what had happened. Only yesterday she had been safe. Only a week ago she had returned from a holiday in Cornwall, where there had been little to do except lie on lemon-colored sands in a lemon-colored bathing suit; or feel the contrast between sun on baking shoulders and salt water foaming and slipping past her body, in the cold invigoration of the sea. The future would take care of itself.

And more. There was a pleasant-looking man, just on the right side of middle age, who came to do sketches at the beach. They were such intolerably bad sketches that Iris was relieved to discover he was a doctor from London.

By coincidence, a breeze blew one of the sketches past her, and she retrieved it. So they fell into conversation. By coincidence, it developed that the man's name was Charles Woodhall; and that he was Francis Seton's doctor. It astounded Iris, who saw in this a good omen of summer magic. She liked Dr. Woodhall. He was as good a talker as Seton himself, without Seton's untiring bounce. And he knew when to be comfortably silent.

Dr. Woodhall would sit on a campstool, attired in ancient flannels, tennis shoes, and shirt, and draw endless sketches of Iris. A cigarette would hang from the corner of his mouth. He would blink as smoke got into one eye, and amusement wrinkles deepened from the corners of his eyes almost back to temples that were slightly gray. Meantime, he talked, he talked happily of all things in earth and sky and sea. He also offered a profound apology for the bad sketches. But Iris, though she secretly agreed with him, kept them all; and so passed the fortnight.

They would meet again in London.

And she had a good job to go back to there.

All the future looked pleasant—until Francis Seton exploded everything that morning.

The thunderstorm, which had been imminent all day, broke late in the afternoon.

It brought little relief to Iris. She and Harold Mills went on with their work and were still working long after dinner, in the library under the shaded lamps and the rows of books behind their wire cages. It was a rich room, deep-carpeted like every other room in the house; but it was tainted with damp. Iris's head ached. She had sent off two dozen letters, and arranged every detail of Seton's trip: all he had to do now was pack his bag. Seton himself was in the study, with the door closed between, cleaning out the litter in his desk.

Harold Mills put down his pen.

"Iris," he said softly.

"Yes?"

Mills glanced toward the closed door of the study, and spoke still more softly.

"I want to ask you something."

"Of course."

She was surprised at his tone. He was sitting at his own writing table, some distance away from her, with a table lamp burning at his left. The light of the lamp shone on his flat fair hair, brushed with great precision round his head, on his waxy-colored face, and on his pince-nez. Since he was very young, it was only this pince-nez which gave him the sedate and donnish appearance; this, or the occasional slight fidgeting of his hands.

He almost blurted out the next words.

"What I mean is: are you all right? Financially, I mean?"

"Oh, yes."

She didn't know. She was not even thinking of this now. Dr. Woodhall had promised to drop in that evening, to see Seton. It was nearly eleven now. Seton, who always swore that his immense vitality was due to the regularity of his habits, was as regular as that clock over the mantelpiece.

At eleven o'clock he would smoke the last of the ten cigarettes allowed him a day, drink his one whisky and soda, and be in bed by eleven-thirty sharp. If Dr. Woodhall didn't hurry . . .

Iris's head ached still more. Mills kept on talking, but she did not hear him. She awoke to this with a start.

"I'm sorry. I'm afraid I didn't catch—?"

"I said," repeated the other, somewhat jerkily, "that I'm sorry for more reasons than one that we're leaving."

"So am I, Harold."

"You don't understand. Mine is rather a specialized job. I'll not get another in a hurry." Color came up under his pince-nez. "No, no, that isn't what I mean. I'm not complaining. It's very decent of Seton to provide two months' salary. But I'd hoped that this job would be more or less permanent. If it turned out to be that, there was something I wanted to do."

"What was that?"

"I wanted to ask you to marry me," said Mills.

There was a silence.

She stared back at him. She had never thought of him as awkward or tongue-tied, or anything like the man who now sat and cracked the joints of his knuckles as though he could not sit still. In fact, she had hardly ever thought of him at all. And his face showed that he knew it.

"Please don't say anything." He got to his feet. "I don't want you to feel you've got to say anything." He began to pace the room with little short steps. "I haven't been exactly—attentive."

"You never even . . ."

He gestured.

"Yes, I know. I'm not like that. I can't be. I wish I could." He stopped his pacing. "This fellow Woodhall, now."

"What about Dr. Woodhall?"

He never got the opportunity to say. This was the point at which they heard, very distinctly, the noise from the next room.

When they tried to describe it afterward, neither could be sure whether it was a yell, or a groan, or the beginning of incoherent words. It might have been a combination of all three. Then there were several soft little thuds, like the sound of a butcher's cleaver across meat on the chopping block. Then silence, except for the distant whisper of the rain.

That was the story which Iris Lane began to tell at Dr. Fell's flat. Both Dr. Fell and Superintendent Hadley listened with the closest attention, though they had heard it several times before.

"We didn't know what had happened," said Iris, moving her shoulders. "We called out to Mr. Seton, but he didn't answer. We tried the door, but it wouldn't open."

"Was it locked?"

"No; it was warped. The damp from the rain had swollen and warped the wood. Harold tried to get it open, but it wouldn't work until he finally took a run and jumped at it."

"There was nobody in the study except Mr. Seton," she went on. "I know, because I was afraid we should see someone. The place was brilliantly lighted. There's a big bronze chandelier, with electric candles, hanging over the flat-topped desk in the middle. And there was even a light burning in the cloakroom—it's hardly more than a cupboard for a washbasin, really—which opens out of the study. You could see everything at a glance. And there wasn't anybody hiding in the room."

She paused, visualizing the scene.

Francis Seton lay on the far side of the desk, between the desk and the windows. He was unconscious, with blood coming out of his nostrils.

His cigarette, put down on the edge of the desk, was now scorching the mahogany with an acrid smell. The desk chair and a little table had been overturned. There was a stain on the thick gray carpet where his glass had been upset, together with a stoppered decanter which had not spilt, and a siphon enclosed in metal crossbands. Seton was moaning. When they turned him over on his side, they found the weapon.

"It was that hollow wooden thing with lead inside," said Iris. She saw it as vividly as though it lay on the carpet now. "Only six or seven inches long, but it weighed nearly a pound. Harold, who'd started to study medicine once, put his fingers down and felt round the back of Mr. Seton's head. Then he said I'd better hurry and phone for a proper doctor.

"I had backed away against the windows—I remember that. The curtains weren't quite drawn. I could hear the rain hitting the window behind me. I looked round, because I was afraid there might be somebody hiding in the curtains. We pulled the curtains back on both windows. Then we saw the edge of the ladder. It had been propped up against the right-hand window, from the garden below. And I noticed something else that I'll swear to, and swear to, and go on swearing to until you believe me. But never mind what it was, for a minute.

"I ran out to phone for Dr. Woodhall, but it wasn't necessary. I met him coming up the stairs in the front hall."

There were several things she did not tell here.

She did not say how heartening it was to see Dr. Woodhall's shrewd, humorous face looking at her from under the brim of a sodden hat. He wore a dripping mackintosh with the collar turned up, and carried his medicine case.

"I don't know how he got in," Iris went on. "Mr. Seton had dismissed the servants after dinner. The front door must have been unlocked. Anyway, he said, 'Hullo; is anything wrong?' I think I said, 'Come up quickly; something terrible has happened.' He didn't make any comment. But when he had examined Mr. Seton he said it was concussion of the brain all right, from several powerful blows. I asked whether I should phone for an ambulance. He said Mr. Seton wasn't in shape to be moved, and that we should have to get him to bed in the house.

"When we were carrying him in to his bedroom, things started to fall out of his pockets. The key to the safe wasn't there: it had been torn loose from the other end of his watch chain. And he kept on moaning.

"You know the rest. The safe had been robbed, not only of the money, but two valuable folios. Apparently it was all plain sailing. There was the ladder propped against the window sill outside. There were scuffed footprints in a flower bed below. It was a burglar. It must have been a burglar. Only—" She paused, clearing her throat. "Only," she went on, *"both those windows were locked on the inside."*

Dr. Fell grunted.

Something in this recital had interested him very much. He drew in several of his chins, and exchanged a glance with Superintendent Hadley.

"Both the windows," he rumbled, "were locked on the inside. You're quite sure of that? Hey?"

"I'm absolutely positive."

"You couldn't have been mistaken?"

"I only wish I could have," said Iris helplessly. "And you know what they think, don't you? They think Harold and I caught him and beat his head in.

"It's so awfully easy to think that. Harold and I were alone in the house. We were sitting outside the only door to the study. There was no intruder anywhere. Both the study windows were locked on the inside. It —well, it just couldn't have been anybody else but us. Only it wasn't. That's all I can tell you."

Dr. Fell opened his eyes.

"But, my dear young lady," he protested, blowing sparks from his cigar like the Spirit of the Volcano, "whatever else they think about you, I presume they don't think you are raving mad? Suppose you had faked this burglary? Suppose you had planted the ladder against the window? Would you and Mills then go about swearing the windows were locked in order to prove that your story couldn't be true?"

"Just a moment," said Superintendent Hadley sharply.

Hadley was beaten, and he knew it. But he was fair.

"I'll be frank with you, Miss Lane," he went on. "Before you came in,

I was telling Dr. Fell that Mr. Seton is conscious. He's talked to me.
And—"

"And?"

"Mr. Seton," said Hadley, "confirms your story in every detail. He
clears you and Mills of any complicity in the crime."

Iris said nothing. All the same, they saw her face grow white under its
tan.

"He says," pursued Hadley, in the midst of a vast silence, "that he was
sitting at his desk, facing the door to the library. He swears he could hear
you and Mills talking in the library. His back, of course, was toward the
windows. He agrees that the windows were locked, since he had just
locked them himself. At a few minutes past eleven, he heard a footstep
behind him. A 'shuffling' footstep. Just as he started to get up, something
smashed him across the head, and that's all he remembers. So it seems
you were telling the truth."

"H'mf," said Dr. Fell.

Iris stared at Hadley. "Then I'm not—you're not going to arrest me?"

"Frankly," snapped the Superintendent, "no. I'm sorry to say I don't
see how we can arrest anybody. The windows were locked. The door was
watched. There was nobody hidden in the room. Yet someone, by the
victim's own testimony, did get in and cosh Seton. We've got a blooming
miracle, that's what we've got; and, if you don't believe me, come along
and talk to Seton for yourself."

Francis Seton lived, and nearly died, in the grand manner. His bedroom was furnished in the heavy, dark and florid style of the Second
French Empire, with a four-poster bed. He lay propped up with his neck
above the pillows, glowering out of a helmet of bandages.

"Time's nearly up," warned Dr. Charles Woodhall, who stood at one
side of the bed. His fingers were on Seton's wrist, but Seton snatched the
wrist away.

Superintendent Hadley was patient.

"What I'm trying to get at, Mr. Seton, is this. When did you lock those
two windows?"

"Told you that already," said Seton. "About ten minutes before that
fellow sneaked up and hit me."

"But you didn't catch a glimpse of the person who hit you?"

"No, worse luck. Or I'd have—"

"Yes. But *why* did you lock the windows?"

"Because I'd noticed the ladder outside. Couldn't have burglars getting
in, could I?"

"You didn't try to find out who put the ladder there?"

"No. I couldn't be bothered."

"At the same time, you were a little nervous?"

For some time Iris Lane had the impression that Seton, if it were not for his injury, would have rolled over on his side, buried his face in the pillows, and groaned with impatience. But the last question stung him to wrath.

"Who says I was nervous? Nervous! I'm the last man in the world to be nervous. I haven't got a nerve in my body." He appealed to Dr. Woodhall and to Harold Mills. "Have I?"

"You've got an exceptionally strong constitution," replied Dr. Woodhall blandly.

Seton appeared to scent evasion here. His bloodshot eyes rolled, without a turn of his neck, from Woodhall to Mills; but they came back to Hadley.

"Well? Anything else you want to know?"

"Just one more question, Mr. Seton. Are you sure there was nobody hidden in the study or the cloakroom before you were attacked?"

"Dead certain."

Hadley shut up his notebook.

"Then that's all, sir. Nobody hidden, before or after. Windows locked, before and after. I don't believe in ghosts, and so the thing's impossible." He spoke quietly. "Excuse me, Mr. Seton, but are you sure you were attacked after all?"

"And excuse *me,*" interrupted a new voice, thunderous but apologetic.

Dr. Fell, whose presence was somewhat less conspicuous than a captive balloon, had not removed his disreputable slouch hat: a breach of good manners which ordinarily he would have deplored. But his manner had a vast eagerness, like Old King Cole in a hurry. Iris Lane could not remember having seen him for some minutes. He lumbered in at the doorway, with one hand holding an object wrapped in newspaper and the other supporting himself on his crutch-handled stick.

"Sir," he intoned, addressing Seton, "I should regret it very much if my friend Hadley gave you an apoplectic stroke. It is therefore only fair to tell you that you were attacked, and very thoroughly battered about the head, by one of the persons in this room. I am also glad the police have kept your study locked up since then."

There was a silence as sudden as that which follows a loud noise.

From the newspaper Dr. Fell took out a soda-water siphon, and put it down with a thump on the center table. It was a large siphon, bound round with metal bands in a diamond design.

And Dr. Fell reared up.

"Dash it, Hadley," he complained, "why couldn't you have told me about the siphon? Ten days in a spiritual abyss; and all because you couldn't tell me about the siphon! It took the young lady to do that."

"But I did tell you about a siphon," said Hadley. "I've told you about it a dozen times!"

"No, no, no," insisted Dr. Fell dismally. "You said 'a' siphon. Presumably an ordinary siphon, the unending white bulwark of the English pub. You didn't say it was this particular kind of siphon."

"But what the devil has the siphon got to do with it anyway?" demanded Hadley. "Mr. Seton wasn't knocked out with a siphon."

"Oh, yes, he was," said Dr. Fell.

It was so quiet that they could hear a fly buzzing against one half-open window.

"You see," continued Dr. Fell, fiery with earnestness, "the ordinary siphon is of plain glass. It doesn't have these crisscross metal bands, or that nickeled cap at the other side of the nozzle. In short, this is a 'Fountain-fill' siphon; the sort which you fill yourself with plain water, and turn into soda water by means of compressed-air capsules."

Enlightenment came to Superintendent Hadley.

"Ah!" chortled Dr. Fell. "Got it, have you? The police, as a matter of ordinary routine, would closely examine the dregs of a whisky glass or any decanter found at the scene of a crime. But they would never think twice about a siphon, because the ordinary soda-water siphon can't possibly be tampered with. And yet, by thunder, *this* one could be tampered with!"

Dr. Fell sniffed. He lumbered over to the bedside table, and picked up a tumbler. Returning with it to the center table, he squirted some of the soda into the glass. He touched his tongue to it.

"I think, Mr. Harold Mills," he said, "you had better give yourself up for theft and attempted murder."

Dr. Fell chuckled as he sat again in his own library at Chelsea.

"And you still don't see it?" he demanded.

"Yes," said Dr. Woodhall.

"No," cried Iris Lane.

"The whole trick," their host went on, "turns on the fact that the 'Mickey Finn' variety of knockout drops produces on the victim exactly the same sensation as being struck over the head: the sudden bursting explosion of pain, the roaring in the ears, and almost instant unconsciousness.

"Mills had a dozen opportunities that day to load the 'Fountain-fill' siphon with the drug. He knew, as you all knew, exactly when Francis Seton would drink his one whisky and soda of the day. Mills had already removed what he wanted from the safe. Finally, he had propped up a ladder outside the study window to make the crime seem the work of a burglar. All he had to do then was to wait for eleven o'clock.

"At eleven o'clock Seton drank the hocused mixture, cried out and fell, knocking over a number of objects on the carpet. Since the whole effect of this drug depends on a violent cerebral rush of blood, a man already suffering from high blood pressure would be likely and even certain to bleed from the nostrils. It provided the last realistic touch."

Dr. Fell growled to himself, no longer seeming quite so cherubic. Then he looked at Iris.

"Mills," he went on, "deliberately fiddled with the door, pretending it was stuck: which it was not. He wanted to allow time for the imaginary burglar to loot the safe. Then he ran in with you. When he turned Seton over, he took that piece of lead-filled broom handle out of his sleeve, slipped it under the body, and dramatically called your attention to it.

"Next, you remember, he felt at the base of Seton's skull in pretended horror, and told you to go out and phone for a doctor. As a result of this, you also recall, he was for several minutes completely alone in the study."

Iris was looking at the past, examining each move she herself had made.

"You mean," she muttered, "that was when he—?" She brought up her arm in the gesture of one using a life preserver.

"Yes," said Dr. Fell. "That was when he deliberately struck several blows on the head of an unconscious man to complete his plan.

"He removed the key to the safe from Seton's watch chain. In case the police should be suspicious of any drinks found at the scene of a crime, he rinsed out the spilled whisky glass in that convenient cloakroom, and poured into the glass a few drops of harmless whisky from the decanter. He had no time to refill and recharge the siphon before you and Dr. Woodhall returned to the study; so he left it alone. A handkerchief round his hand prevented any fingerprints. Unfortunately, mischance tripped him up with a resounding wallop."

Dr. Woodhall nodded.

"You mean," he said, "that Seton noticed the ladder, and locked the windows?"

"Yes. And the unfortunate Mr. Mills never discovered the locked windows until it was too late. Miss Lane, as you have probably discovered, is a very positive young lady. She looked at the windows. She knew they were locked. She was prepared to swear it in any court. So Mills, floundering and drifting and never very determined except where it came to appropriating someone else's property, had to keep quiet. He could not even get at that betraying siphon afterward, because the police kept the room locked up.

"He had one bit of luck, though. Francis Seton, of course, never heard any footsteps behind him just before the attack. Anybody who takes one look at the thick carpet of the study cannot fail to be convinced of that. I wondered whether the good Mr. Seton might be deliberately lying. But a little talk with Seton will show you the real reason. The man's boasted vitality is killing him: it has got him into such a state of nerves that he really does need a year in California. Once he saw that ladder outside the window, once he began to think of burglars, he was ready to imagine anything."

Iris was glancing sideways at Dr. Woodhall. Woodhall, a cigarette in the corner of his mouth, was glancing sideways at her.

"I—er—I don't like to bring it up," said Iris. "But—"

"Mills's proposal?" inquired Dr. Fell affably.

"Well, yes."

"My dear young lady," intoned Dr. Fell, with all the gallantry of a load of bricks falling through a skylight, "there you mention the one point at which Mills really showed good taste. Discernment. *Raffinement.* It also probably occurred to him that a criminal who proposes marriage places the lady in a blind-eyed and sympathetic mood if the criminal should happen to make a slip in his game afterward. But can you honestly say you are sorry it was Mills they took away in the Black Maria?"

Iris and Dr. Woodhall were not even listening.

# The Devil in the Summer-House

This radio-play has not previously been printed in its Dr. Fell version. It was broadcast on the BBC on October 14, 1940. When Carr was called back to the United States in 1942 to register for military service, he shortened the script for the *Suspense* program on CBS. It was this version —without Dr. Fell, with a different murderer and set in Tarrytown, New York, rather than in England—that was printed in *Ellery Queen's Mystery Magazine,* September 1946 and in *The Door to Doom and Other Detections* (1980). Both plays are among Carr's finest radio work, but probably most readers will prefer the version that includes Dr. Fell.

# The Devil in the Summer-House

## The Characters:

| | |
|---|---|
| Dr. Gideon Fell | The detective |
| Marvin Brown | A barrister |
| Captain Richard Burnham | On leave from the Western Front |
| Isabel Burnham | His wife |
| Paul Stanfield | Her brother |
| Angela Fisk | The other woman |
| Kitty Ingram | The maid |
| Inspector Mathers | Of the local police |
| Superintendent Hadley | Of Scotland Yard |

*Setting:* An English countryhouse, 1916 (the murder) and London, 1940 (the solution)

ANNOUNCER: Again we take you to the study of Dr. Gideon Fell, somewhere in London. Again Dr. Fell will analyze one of his crime-puzzles. This time he will be interviewed by a well-known barrister—whose name, for obvious reasons, cannot be given, but whom we shall refer to as "Mr. Brown."
*(The announcer's voice fades. We hear a series of chuckles from Dr. Fell, then the sound of a bottle on a glass's rim, and beer being poured into a glass.)*

DR. FELL: Have some more beer.

MR. BROWN: Thank you very much. As a lawyer, Dr. Fell, I distrust these paradoxes of yours. What precisely do you mean?
*(Mr. Brown has the voice of a man in his middle fifties: dry but suave, careful, choosing each word; a typical barrister's voice.)*

DR. FELL *(fierily):* Only, sir, that there are cases in which the criminal's mistake has been too big to be seen. It has been too obvious to be noticed.

MR. BROWN *(coughs)*

DR. FELL: I think you spoke?

MR. BROWN *(drily):* I was hesitating to commit myself. You say—ah—that a criminal may leave a clue which is too obvious to be seen?

DR. FELL: I do.

MR. BROWN: Yes. Do you know of any such case?

DR. FELL: *You* do.

MR. BROWN: I do?

DR. FELL: I was referring to the murder of Captain Richard Burnham in 1916.
*(Slight pause)*

MR. BROWN *(drily):*    Indeed. *(Changing the subject quickly)* To go on with what we were discussing before we began this . . .

DR. FELL *(interrupting, with a chuckle):*    Oh, come, sir! Don't tighten up your mouth and look at me like that! After all, it happened over a quarter of a century ago. You were not then the eminent . . . Mr. Brown. In any event, you figured in the case not as a barrister but as a witness. *(Softly)* You were a friend of the murdered man's wife.

MR. BROWN *(guardedly):*    Yes.

DR. FELL:    Let me refresh your memory. Captain Richard Burnham, on leave from the Western Front, was shot dead in the late afternoon of August 10th. His body was found in a summer-house at the bottom of a garden behind his home. It was a deep garden, overhanging the river . . .

MR. BROWN:    And the boats went by. *(Slight pause)* He could have returned to the Western Front; and died by a cleaner bullet.

DR. FELL:    Ah! Have I refreshed your memory?

MR. BROWN *(quietly):*    God knows it needed no refreshing.

DR. FELL *(with soft insistence):*    What do you remember best about that case?

MR. BROWN *(absently):*    I remember that it was a very hot day. I remember the garden, which was all grass and trees. I remember the white-painted summer-house at the end of the garden, and the river glittering beyond.

DR. FELL:    Yes?

MR. BROWN *(as though it were forced from him):*    I remember how I went to call on Isabel Burnham—that was Captain Burnham's wife— at her own request.

DR. FELL:    Yes?

MR. BROWN *(with slightly more intensity):*    That was about four o'clock in the afternoon. *(Repeating more faintly, as though to keep the facts firmly in his own mind)* Four o'clock in the afternoon. Burnham's house was called Grey Lodge. The windows of the back sitting room and the dining room looked into the garden. Isabel Burnham received me in the back sitting room. But we could not see out into the garden, because the sun-blinds were drawn on the windows. . . .

*(The voice fades. We hear, faintly, strains of an old popular song, perhaps "Pack Up Your Troubles," fading into the voice of Kitty the maid. It is a poised, almost insolent, precocious voice, that of a girl of nineteen or twenty.)*

KITTY:    Gentleman to see you, Mrs. Burnham. Name of—Brown.

ISABEL:    Oh! Show him . . . no, wait! Where is my husband?

*(Isabel has the voice of a woman of about thirty: full, rather intense,*

*rapid, clear; yet sometimes with a quality of indecision or almost morbid introspection.)*

KITTY *(as though surprised):*    Upstairs, ma'am.

ISABEL:    And my brother?

KITTY *(insolently):*    Nobody ever knows where Mr. Paul is. Shall I raise the sun-blinds?

ISABEL *(crying out):*    No!

KITTY *(with complete insolence):*    Maybe you're right, ma'am. *(Significantly)* Not without a bit of face-powder, anyway.

*(Isabel gasps. The tension here is obvious.)*

ISABEL *(after a pause, incredulously):*    How dare! How *dare* you?

KITTY *(unimpressed):*    No offence, ma'am, I'm sure. Shall I show the gentlemen in?

ISABEL:    Yes.

*(A door closes. We hear Isabel breathing hard, with a sob. But she seems to be trying to get a grip on her nerves.)*

ISABEL *(in a whisper, as though praying):*    Pity! Pity! *Pity!* Come in.

*(The door opens, hesitates, and closes. Mr. Brown speaks. His voice is the same, hardly any younger.)*

BROWN:    Good afternoon, old friend.

ISABEL *(half-jocosely, getting a grip on herself):*    Old friend to you! Marvin Brown! You know, you're becoming terribly distinguished-looking already. Those glasses are the making of you. In another twenty years—

BROWN *(laughing slightly):*    Yes. I know. *(Formally)* You wanted to see me, Mrs. Burnham?

ISABEL:    Mrs. Burnham! Mrs. Burnham! It used to be Isabel. Now it's *(mimicking)* Mrs. Burnham! *(Intensely, but without hysteria)* Yes, I wanted to see you. Do you know why? Because I'm miserable. Nobody in hell is as miserable as I am!

BROWN *(instinctively):*    Now, now.

ISABEL *(hopefully):*    Tell me the truth. Am I so very unattractive? And so—so feeble that even the servants sneer at me? Like that girl Kitty.

BROWN:    You are a beautiful woman, Isabel.

ISABEL:    Am I? Do you remember how you used to write poetry to me?

BROWN *(correcting):*    Verse, not poetry. But I remember. Now tell me why you've been crying.

ISABEL:    Is it as obvious as all that?

BROWN:    Yes. Your husband, I suppose?

ISABEL *(quickly):*    Why do you say that?

BROWN *(calmly):*    It usually is.

ISABEL:    You know, Marvin, in that queer way of yours I never can tell when you're dead serious and when you're making fun of me. I can't tell even yet! I think that was why I . . . well, took up with Richard. I thought I could understand *him*. I understand him, all right.

BROWN:    Isabel—

ISABEL:    Wait, please. I'm not going to be hysterical and embarrass you. But I tell you, I can't stand it any longer. He's been on leave eight days and six of them he's spent with this Angela creature in town. Did you know that today is the fifth anniversary of our marriage?

BROWN:    Who is Angela?

ISABEL:    Oh, I don't know what her name is. Angela Fisk, or something of the sort. As though she were the only one! Do you know what the worst of it is? The worst of it is when they come to me and say, consolingly, "Never mind, my dear; Richard loves you; he always comes back to you." And so he does. And they think they're consoling me. What they're really telling me is that I'm not attractive enough, or stimulating enough, to hold him except when he can't find anyone else. . . . Oh, sometimes I wish I were dead.

BROWN *(sharply):*    Look here, this has got to stop.

ISABEL *(insistently):*    I do. Sometimes I want to take one of Richard's revolvers, and put it to my head, and . . .

*(We hear the sharp noise of a revolver shot.)*

BROWN *(startled):*    What was that?

ISABEL *(beginning to laugh, and growing more calm):*    It's all right, Marvin. Nobody's hurt. That was only Paul.

BROWN:    Paul?

ISABEL:    My brother Paul. Paul Stanfield. You've met him. He's practicing with a revolver.

*(Five more shots in rapid succession)*

BROWN:    But those shots sound as though they were in the house.

ISABEL:    They are. They're in the cellar: the range is down there. Sometimes it goes on half the day. *(Impatiently)* But never mind that. What am I going to *do?* About Richard, I mean.

BROWN:    The question is, Isabel, what do you want to do? Would you like a divorce?

ISABEL:    No.

BROWN:    I see. You still love him?

ISABEL:    Yes. Except when I think of him holding . . .

*(Three more shots)*

BROWN:    If you don't mind my saying so, Isabel, that confounded revolver practice is getting on my nerves. Now see here. The next question is, what about this girl Angela—Angela Fisk? What do you know about her?

ISABEL *(in a prim tone, as though trying to be fair):*    She's awfully pretty. She's got red hair.

BROWN *(impatiently):*   My dear Isabel, I don't want to hear about *that.* I mean—

ISABEL *(ignoring him):*   And she comes here to the house to meet him. Oh, yes, she does! She's got a motorboat . . . if you can fancy that; anyway, her people have pots of money . . . and she comes down the river to the back of the summer-house. They meet in the summer-house. Here, I'll show you. Reach over and pull the cord of that sun-blind.

BROWN:   Where?

ISABEL:   On your right. Beside my knitting-bag.

*(A long scuffling sound of a blind being raised and fastened)*

BROWN:   Hullo! Somebody is going out to the summer-house now. Judging by the uniform, may I make the brilliant deduction that it's your husband?

ISABEL *(in a low, voice, incredulously):*   You don't think . . . ?

BROWN:   Not in the middle of the afternoon, my dear. Hardly.

ISABEL:   Yes, but . . . *(Calling)* Richard! Richard!

RICHARD BURNHAM *(returning the call from a distance):*   Hullo?

ISABEL:   Richard, please! Will you come here a moment?

RICHARD *(still at a distance, with powerful weariness):*   Oh Lord, Isabel, what is it *now? (He has the strong, full voice of a man about thirty-five.)*

ISABEL:   Aren't you coming in to tea, dear? It's almost ready.

RICHARD:   I'll be along presently. You go ahead.

*(In the distance, very faintly, we hear the put-put-put of a motorboat.)*

ISABEL *(as though she realizes what it is):*   But can't you come here to the window for a minute? I want to see you.

*(Two voices are heard muttering, one after the other. The first is Isabel's, the second Richard's.)*

ISABEL:   You see, Marvin? He's wearing his cap and his Sam Browne. He's going somewhere with her.

RICHARD *(to himself):*   Lord, woman, can't you stop making my life a perfect . . . *(His mutter breaks off. He speaks in ordinary tones, now evidently close to the window, for his voice is as loud as the others.)* Oh, sorry! I didn't know there was anyone with you.

ISABEL *(eagerly):*   Richard, may I present a very old friend of mine? Mr. Brown, my husband.

*(The noise of the motorboat grows louder.)*

RICHARD *(courteously, but anxious to be off):*   How do you do? . . . Er —I'm afraid you'll have to excuse me. Just for the moment. Got to have a look at Bob Rolfe's cabin-cruiser down at the landing-stage. Promised Bob I would.

ISABEL:   Richard, where are you going?

RICHARD *(exasperated):*    I told you, old girl. Got to have a look at Bob Rolfe's cabin-cruiser down at—

ISABEL *(past endurance):*    Richard, don't lie!

RICHARD:    Oh, for God's sake!

BROWN *(quietly):*    Drop that blind.

*(A rattle as the sun-blind is lowered. This sound merges again into the tune of "Pack Up Your Troubles," which in turn fades into Brown's voice talking with Dr. Fell.)*

BROWN:    About fifteen minutes after that, Captain Burnham was murdered.

*(Slight pause.)*

DR. FELL:    In the summer-house, as we know.

BROWN *(reflectively):*    Yes. We were sitting twenty yards of that summer-house. Yet we saw nothing behind those dim, concealing blinds. The last time I saw Burnham alive, he was standing facing us in the hot, bright garden, with the open door of the summer-house beyond him. His face was red and his cap was slung on rakishly, as he always wore it. He also wore his .45 service revolver. Then—

DR. FELL:    Then?

BROWN:    I tried to calm Isabel. Presently, I think I did calm her. She wheeled the tea-wagon in from the dining room—the maid, Kitty, must have prepared the tea, though I didn't see her do it because the door was closed. Isabel and I . . . talked. Or, rather, Isabel knitted and I talked. It was nearly six o'clock when . . .

*(Brown's voice fades, and we hear Isabel.)*

ISABEL *(sighing):*    You know, you have done me good. I feel almost reconciled.

BROWN *(sharply):*    Listen! What was that?

ISABEL:    What?

BROWN:    It sounded like somebody shouting.

ISABEL *(amused):*    Probably my brother Paul. He's still quite a boy, but mad to get into the army.

BROWN:    Listen!

ISABEL *(surprised):*    It *is* Paul! And running! *(A door opens and closes with a bang.)* Paul, what on earth is the matter?

PAUL STANFIELD *(after a pause, in which he breathes hard, but speaks steadily):*    Look here, sis. I've got to tell you something. You've got to be steady, now.

*(He is eighteen or nineteen: trying to be very much the man of the world, but with some of his sister's nature occasionally showing through.)*

ISABEL:    What is it? What's wrong?

PAUL *(insistently):*    You've got to be steady now.

BROWN:   She's steadier than you are, my lad. Here, sit down. I'll get you some water.

PAUL *(offhandedly):*   You haven't got any brandy, have you?

ISABEL *(an indignant sister):*   Brandy! I should think not, at your age.

PAUL:   I'm nearly nineteen. And don't start that kind of talk again, when you hear what I've got to tell you. When did you last see Richard?

ISABEL *(quickly):*   About an hour ago. Why?

PAUL *(almost without expression):*   You won't see him again. He's shot himself.

*(During a silence, a clock slowly strikes six.)*

ISABEL *(incredulously):*   You don't know what you're saying!

PAUL:   He's lying on his back in the summer-house, with a bullet-hole through his head. I saw him. Go and look for yourself.

BROWN *(sharply):*   Isabel! Wait!

*(A door opens and slams.)*

PAUL:   Let her go. She won't rest till she knows.

BROWN:   Nor afterwards either, I imagine. Now before this gets any further, sit down and tell me what happened. Have a cigarette?

PAUL *(surprised):*   Thanks! They don't like me to. . . . Thanks very much.

BROWN:   Light?

PAUL:   Thanks. *(Stopping to reflect)* I say, sir; who are you?

BROWN:   I'm an old friend of your sister. I'm also a lawyer, if that will help us. *(Impressively)* We've got to have a decent story to tell the police. You realize that?

PAUL *(surprised):*   Police! Lord, yes. I hadn't thought of that. Yes, rather. Poor old Dick!

BROWN:   Well?

PAUL:   I can't tell you what happened, if that's what you mean. Up to half an hour ago, I was down in the cellar overhauling Richard's collection of guns and shooting with a .38. *(Struck by this)* I suppose that's why I didn't hear the shot. Or notice it, at least.

BROWN:   That, young man, is why none of us noticed it. And then?

PAUL *(uneasily):*   Well . . . I went upstairs, and had a bath, and changed my clothes. Then I went down to the summer-house.

BROWN:   Why to the summer-house? *(No reply)* I said, why to the summer-house?

PAUL:   Look here, sir, what have my movements got to do with poor old Richard killing himself? *(Gloomily)* Couldn't stand the gaff, I suppose. They say it's pretty hard on a fellow's nerves Out There after a few months. Though I'd like to see the bombardment that could scare *me*.

BROWN:  Why did you go the summer-house?

PAUL *(sullenly):*  If you must know, it was to meet a girl.

BROWN:  So?

PAUL:  Yes; why not? She was to push along in a motorboat, and . . . what's the matter?

BROWN:  May I ask the name of this girl?

PAUL:  Her name is Angela Fisk. *(We hear the long, pealing note of a doorbell.)* Somebody at the front door. *(Calling)* Kitty! Kitty! Why don't you answer the door? *(To Brown)* Who do you suppose that is?

BROWN *(through his teeth):*  I don't know. I don't think I particularly care. I do know that you and I had better join Isabel in the garden at once.

PAUL:  But—

BROWN:  At once.

*(Brown's voice fades, to be taken up by Paul's.)*

PAUL *(in a whisper):*  There's Isabel, standing by the door of the summer-house. Who's that with her?

BROWN *(in the same low tone):*  By the look of him, I diagnose a police officer.

ISABEL:  Here he is now. *(Calling half-hysterically):* Marvin! Marvin! Will you come here and talk to this man. He says—

*(Inspector Mathers speaks. Gruff but soothing; smooth, sliding over difficult matters with practiced ease.)*

MATHERS:  Now, ma'am, no call to get excited! Just a matter of form, you know.

ISABEL *(wildly):*  He rushed up at me as I was coming out of the summer-house. His name is—

MATHERS:  Inspector Mathers, sir. Divisional Detective Inspector. Here's my warrant-card, if you'd like to see it. You're Mr. Brown?

BROWN *(once more cold and grim):*  Yes. You got here with remarkable promptness, Inspector.

MATHERS *(rebuking him):*  Not exactly, sir. I happened to be passing in the street. Your maid here—Kitty something—ran out shouting that Captain Burnham had been murdered.

*(Sensation)*

BROWN *(quelling it):*  Indeed? I understood that Captain Burnham had committed suicide.

MATHERS:  Oh? And who told you that, sir?

BROWN:  I said I "understood" it. You don't appear to think so.

MATHERS *(noncommittally):*  That's for the inquest to say, sir. But what would *you* say, just to look at him?

BROWN:  Excuse me. Stand away, Paul. *(Sound of footsteps on a board-floor)* So!

MATHERS:   You see, sir? He's been shot through the left temple at very close range. You see the powder-burns. Captain Burnham wore his cap at what you might call a rakish angle, down over the left eye. The bullet went through the brim of the cap before it killed him. Well, sir! I doubt if a right-handed man—as they tell me Captain Burnham was— could twist his wrist round far enough to put a gun at the left temple. And it don't seem likely, does it, that a gentleman would shoot himself with his hat on?

BROWN:   Inferences, Inspector.

MATHERS *(sharply):*   Very well, sir: then I'll tell you something that's not an inference. The weapon is gone.

ISABEL:   I knew it!

MATHERS *(quickly):*   You knew what, ma'am?

ISABEL:   I knew my husband didn't kill himself. He couldn't have. He was too vital. He'd *fight* death. He'd fight it with everything in him.

BROWN:   Just one moment, Mrs. Burnham. Then, Inspector, he was not shot with that army revolver of his? The gun he's wearing?

MATHERS *(with the beginning of a heavy snort):*   No, sir. Not likely. That's a .45. Saving the lady's presence, it 'ud have blown the top of his head off. This was a little gun—maybe a .32. It's a small wound, and there's hardly any blood.

ISABEL:   So there was a devil in the summer-house. A little crawling devil.

MATHERS:   Don't know about that, ma'am. There was a murderer here, anyway. Somebody Captain Burnham trusted. Somebody who could get close enough to draw a gun, and do *that.*

ISABEL *(flatly):*   Quite.

MATHERS:   Meaning what, ma'am?

BROWN *(quickly):*   Inspector, I can tell you very briefly what you want to know. Captain Burnham was last seen alive about five o'clock.

MATHERS *(repeating, as though writing in a notebook):*   Five o'clock.

BROWN:   He was seen by Mrs. Burnham and myself. We talked to him through the window. He said he was going down to the landing-stage to look at somebody's cabin-cruiser. His body was found at shortly before six o'clock by young Mr. Paul Stanfield here.

PAUL:   You needn't look at me like that. *I* didn't have anything to do with it.

MATHERS *(with bluff and reassuring joviality):*   Now, now, sir! No call to be alarmed. Just a matter of form, that's all. You found the body?

PAUL:   I didn't "find" him. I saw him.

MATHERS *(bluffly):*   One very important thing, sir. Did you touch anything in there? Touch the body, or anything like that?

PAUL:   No! I didn't even go into the summer-house.

MATHERS:   You're sure of that, now?

PAUL:   Positive. I stopped outside. If you don't believe me, ask Kitty. She was here in the garden. There: that's Kitty coming out of the back door now. *Kitty!*

KITTY *(irascible, at a distance):*   Coming!

MATHERS:   Any special reason for your going down to the summer-house, sir?

PAUL:   Yes, there was. It was to meet the girl I'm going to marry. You may as well hear this now, Isabel: Angela's only twenty-two, and I'm nearly nineteen. This is wartime, don't you see? Things are different in wartime.

ISABEL *(heavily):*   Yes. I've discovered that.

MATHERS:   Steady, Mrs. Burnham!

ISABEL *(stolidly):*   I'm all right. It's this heat. There's going to be a storm. Inspector, you may as well hear everything. My husband didn't come down here to see anybody's cabin-cruiser. He came down here to meet a girl named Angela Fisk, with whom he'd been on—intimate terms. *(Pause)* I tell you that because you're bound to find it out for yourself. My husband never cared a scrap for me. He was just *used* to me. If I thought he had cared at all . . . if I thought he could have spared a bit of consideration for me: just one bit of real consideration . . . then I'd go and join him tonight. But he never did. He wasn't capable of it. That's all.

PAUL:   She doesn't know what she's saying, Inspector. *(Quickly)* About Angela, I mean. Do you, Isabel? *(No reply)* You don't, do you? . . . Yes, Kitty, what do *you* want?

KITTY *(huffily):*   You called me, Mr. Paul. And here's a parcel for Mrs. Burnham.

ISABEL:   A parcel for me?

KITTY:   It's this box. Flowers or something. I'm sorry, ma'am. I opened it.

ISABEL:   You opened it?

KITTY:   I thought it was for me. I'm sorry.

BROWN:   Let me hold it for you, Isabel. . . . Fold back the tissue paper . . . that's it . . .

ISABEL *(uncomprehendingly):*   Orchids . . . and a jeweler's box inside . . . a diamond wrist-watch!

BROWN:   And a card, Isabel. Don't drop the card. Here it is: read it.

ISABEL *(after a pause):*   "To my darling wife, Isabel, on the fifth anniversary of our marriage. With all my love, Richard."
*(Isabel cries out, as there is a faint and distant roll of thunder. The thunder fades away, to indicate a change of scene; but presently it returns loudly. We hear the clock strike eleven.)*

ISABEL *(vacantly):*    Five hours. Just five hours since Paul came into this same room, and told us.

BROWN:    Yes.

ISABEL:    Will you turn down the gas, Marvin? The light hurts my eyes.

BROWN:    Of course.

*(Roll of thunder)*

ISABEL *(petulantly):*    I wish the storm would break. Have they all gone?

BROWN:    Who?

ISABEL:    The police. There were six of them here: I counted. Questions, questions, questions. Have they all gone?

BROWN:    Sh-h! No. Mathers is still upstairs. Wait!—I think I hear him now. *(A door opens and closes.)* Finished, Inspector?

MATHERS *(comfortably):*    Yes, sir, I think that's all we need trouble you tonight. Sorry to make such a nuisance of myself, ma'am, but you know how these things are.

BROWN:    Would it be too much to ask, Inspector, whether you've found out anything more?

MATHERS *(meaningfully):*    Well, sir, it's only fair to tell you that there's a .32 automatic missing from Captain Burnham's collection of guns in the cellar.

BROWN:    Indeed?

MATHERS:    Also, we can't find a witness who saw a motorboat anywhere near the landing-stage here at any time this afternoon.

BROWN:    Meaning that you think the murderer came from this house?

MATHERS *(broadly):*    Not necessarily, sir. Not necessarily! What with these high garden walls, none of the neighbors can tell *who* went into the garden, or when. *(Significantly)* Still—it's very interesting, don't you think? Ve-ry interesting! You might sleep on it. Good night, ma'am. Good night, sir. Go-od night! *(The door opens.)* Oh, and one thing more, Mrs. Burnham. If I were you, I should go upstairs and have a word with Mr. Paul Stanfield. He's feeling pretty bitter, you know. Good night.

*(The door closes.)*

ISABEL:    What did he mean by that?

BROWN:    The good Inspector is playing cat-and-mouse. Don't be alarmed. All I can say is, I should like to have a word with Miss Angela Fisk.

*(A squeak, as of a warped door swinging on its hinges)*

ANGELA FISK:    Would you? Here I am then. *(A long roll of thunder)* That's right, Mrs. Burnham. You recognize me. I'm Angela Fisk.

*(She has a young, singularly sweet voice, a delicate kind of voice, in contrast to Isabel's emotionalism and Kitty's sullenness. But she is evidently a person of considerable determination.)*

ISABEL *(taken aback):* What are you doing here?

ANGELA: Silly, isn't it? I've been hiding in that cupboard for the past half hour. I should have stayed outside, only I'm afraid of thunderstorms. Silly, isn't it?

ISABEL: I asked what you were doing here.

ANGELA *(with a sort of desperate flippancy):* Dodging the police. The last little Robert has gone, hasn't he?

ISABEL *(exploding):* Really . . . of all . . . !

ANGELA: Now you're going to call me "bold-faced," or "fast" or something. This is 1916, not 1880. *(Changing her tone, pleading)* Mrs. Burnham, I've always wanted to be friends with you.

ISABEL: Have you?

ANGELA: Yes, I have!

ISABEL: How do you usually make your friends?

ANGELA: Now you're merely being nasty.

ISABEL: I'm glad you're able to see that at least.—Marvin!

BROWN: For heaven's sake, Isabel, don't make things worse!

ISABEL: You wanted a word with her. Why do you leave it to me, then? Marvin, Inspector Mathers can't be very far down the road. Will you go after him and ask to come back? I'm sure he'll have one or two questions to ask Miss Fisk.

ANGELA *(in a harder but quieter tone):* Don't do it, Mrs. Burnham. Please don't do it. I warn you.

ISABEL: Marvin!

ANGELA: *Will* you give me a chance to speak?

BROWN: Be quiet, Isabel. To speak about what, Miss Fisk?

ANGELA *(bracing herself):* You think I was interested in your husband. Don't you? Or that he was in love with me? No, don't look like that. Don't draw yourself up and say, "I wouldn't demean myself to discuss it." *Me* in love with Dick Burnham? In love with that nice, pleasant, silly, good-natured—

ISABEL *(in a cold fury):* I want you to remember that Richard is dead.

ANGELA *(flustered):* Yes. I didn't mean that, exactly. May I sit down?

ISABEL: Just as you please.

ANGELA: What I wanted to tell you is that Paul and I are going to be married, in spite of what you or anyone else can say or do. I love Paul, I tell you. Do you think I could care for Dick Burnham when I had Paul?

BROWN *(gravely):* I see. Your "honor rooted in dishonor stands." Do you want us to believe that you are all the more sincere because you were unfaithful to both of them?

ANGELA: That's not true. I was never unfaithful to Paul. Whoever says that is lying.

ISABEL:  Yes?

ANGELA:  Yes! And don't put me off by treating me like a little girl either. If I'm old enough to do what you say I did, I'm old enough to be treated decently. Don't you *see* what Dick was trying to do? He was trying to take me away from Paul. *(Flatly)* Dick thought I was a bad lot.

ISABEL:  Oh?

ANGELA:  All right. Maybe I am. But I love Paul. So your good husband, always the chivalrous gentleman, thought he'd show me up by taking me away from Paul. He didn't tell you. You always nagged his life out anyway.

ISABEL:  Haven't we had enough of this?

ANGELA:  It's true. Of course I let him take me out! What else could I do? I thought I might get on the good side of him. But I've never cared for anybody but Paul! Never for a second!

BROWN *(quietly)*:  Turn up the gas, Isabel. Let me see her face.

*(Pause, and a roll of thunder)*

ANGELA *(quickly)*:  You believe me, don't you? Even *she* believes me!

BROWN:  Yet you haven't hesitated to humiliate Mrs. Burnham by coming here after him. Today, for instance.

ANGELA:  I didn't come here today. The police can tell you that.

ISABEL:  But you were to meet Richard in the summer-house. Weren't you?

ANGELA:  No, I wasn't. I was to meet Paul at six o'clock, that's all. But my boat broke down, and I couldn't get here until late. I—

BROWN:  Sh-h!

*(The door opens and closes.)*

PAUL:  Angela!

ANGELA:  Hullo, Paul. *(Regaining her flippancy)* Do go and brush your hair, old boy. You look a sight.

PAUL:  What are you doing here?

ANGELA:  The old familiar question. I've been telling your sister a few home truths. Put your arm round me, Paul.

PAUL:  Look here. Isabel says you were Richard's mistress. Is that true?

ANGELA:  No.

PAUL *(Snorts)*

ANGELA *(tensely, almost in tears)*:  All right. I can't fight the lot of you. I seem to have tangled things up beautifully, haven't I? If you don't believe me, that's that.

PAUL:  I do believe you, old girl. I know you've gone out with him once or twice; yes, and told me why. Only whenever Isabel starts to talk, I begin imagining all sorts of things. Isabel—you didn't know Angela and I were in love with each other, did you?

ISABEL:  No.

PAUL:  Then it must have made you feel pretty sick.

ISABEL:  What?

PAUL:  When you found you'd killed poor old Richard for nothing.
*(A long peal of thunder, followed insistently by the first fall of rain. We hear it deepening, while nobody speaks.)*

ISABEL:  Paul, are you mad? Are you saying that to me? Your own sister?

PAUL:  I've been thinking, that's all. All I know is that the .32 automatic, the one that's missing, belonged to you. Richard taught you how to shoot with it.

ISABEL *(crying out):*  And you honestly think *I* would kill Richard?

PAUL:  I don't know. I'm all mixed up.

ISABEL:  But I was with Mr. Brown! I was with Mr. Brown all the time! He'll tell you that.

PAUL *(as though grasping at a straw):*  Is that true, sir?

BROWN:  Quite true. We last saw Captain Burnham alive at five o'clock. You found him dead at shortly before six. During that hour Mrs. Burnham was not ten feet away from me at any time. Whoever killed Burnham, she didn't. *(Raspingly)* Don't be an ungenerous fool, lad.

PAUL:  You wouldn't—well, you wouldn't be protecting anybody, would you?

BROWN *(with grave impressiveness):*  There are many persons I would lie to protect: Mrs. Burnham included. But in this case I am not lying. I am telling the perfect truth; as they say in court, so help me God.

PAUL:  But somebody shot him!

BROWN:  Yes. Somebody.

PAUL *(as though reflecting to himself):*  Inspector Mathers said that whoever did it didn't come by way of the river, because there was no boat seen near the landing-stage. . . .

ANGELA:  Thank you.

PAUL:  But there's no other way into the garden except through the house. Dash it all, it's . . . it's . . . *(Giving up the struggle)* Look here, Angela, where were you?

ISABEL:  Yes. The police will want to know that.

ANGELA:  I tell you, my boat broke down by the Nautilus Yacht Club. Paul and I were to go swimming at Ferryman's Pool. I had a lunch-basket aboard and everything. Only I couldn't get there. I didn't get there until past eight.

PAUL:  But somebody killed him. Who did it? *(Pause)* Who did it? *(Pause) Who did it?*
*(The voice fades. We hear for the last time a few bars of "Pack Up Your Troubles," and then the sound of chuckles from Dr. Fell.)*

BROWN:   . . . and that, Dr. Fell, is all I can tell you. You must forgive me for dwelling on old and foolish and far-off things. But I felt that case terribly, at the time. I felt every emotion of it.

DR. FELL *(expostulating):*   My dear sir, are you to be blamed for that? Tell me: did the police discover any new evidence?

BROWN:   No positive evidence.

DR. FELL:   Any evidence at all?

BROWN:   Burnham had, in fact, been killed by a bullet fired from a .32. The weapon was never found, though they dragged the river for it. The police-surgeon put the time of Burnham's death as between five o'clock and five-thirty. Nearer five, he said.

DR. FELL *(thoughtfully):*   Yes, I think we can agree on that. Say he was shot at a quarter past five. That's my view.

BROWN:   You mean you have—ah—an idea?

DR. FELL *(rearing up, powerfully):*   My dear sir, a clearer case of guilt, from what you have just told me, has seldom been outlined against anybody.

BROWN *(sharply):*   Against whom?

DR. FELL *(soothingly):*   One moment. The case, if I remember, created an enormous stir. What was the popular view of the matter? What did the man in the street think?

BROWN *(with concentrated bitterness):*   What does the man in the street ever think? He has only one answer for an unhappy marriage. The wife dies; who could have killed her but the husband? The husband dies; who could have killed him but the wife?—They blamed Isabel Burnham, of course. And this, mind you, in spite of the fact that I could swear Isabel Burnham was never away from me between five and six o'clock.

DR. FELL:   They gave you some trouble over that, I daresay?

BROWN *(grimly):*   They did. I nearly ruined my career over it. But I fought it out. And I tell you again, Isabel Burnham was not the devil in the summer-house.

DR. FELL *(as though surprised):*   Oh, that? I quite agree.

BROWN:   You agree?

DR. FELL *(chuckling):*   Damme, man! I tell you again, the truth was much too obvious to be seen. *(Argumentatively)* Now, offhand, what would you say was the most important clue in the whole case?

BROWN *(reflecting):*   I suppose . . . the presence or absence of a boat on the river.

DR. FELL:   Nonsense! No! Boat? Suppose the murderer swam? Didn't you tell me that Angela Fisk had intended to go swimming that afternoon?

BROWN *(in consternation):*   You're not saying—?

DR. FELL:  Tut, tut, now! Let me urge you: don't take the fences too fast. I repeat: what would you say, offhand, was the most important clue in the case? And, in case you should be tempted to brain me with the umbrella-stand—as, curiously enough, people have sometimes wished to do—I'll tell you. The most important clue was the dead man's cap.

BROWN:  The dead man's cap?

DR. FELL:  His army cap, you remember.

BROWN:  Well? What about it?

DR. FELL *(expansively):*  You spoke a while ago of a flower-box in which Captain Burnham sent orchids to his wife. Let me show you another box. And a very different kind of exhibit. . . . Here we are . . .

BROWN:  What is it? What's inside?

DR. FELL:  The exhibit in this box was borrowed, under protest, from the Black Museum at Scotland Yard. Let me show it to you.

BROWN *(dully):*  It's an army cap.

DR. FELL:  It's Richard Burnham's army cap. I hold it under the light —so. You observe how the insignia still glitters. You observe how the peak is still appreciably bent down on the right-hand side. You observe the powder-stains . . . the small bullet-hole . . . with almost no blood. . . . A dusty object, fit for a glass case. But it tells us the truth. You saw it years ago, and yet it was too obvious to be seen. I ask you your old question over again. *(Pause)* Who killed Captain Burnham? *(Pause. Sharp and heavy knocking at a door. Dr. Fell speaks as though out of a reverie.)* Eh? *(The knocking goes on.)* Oh! Come in! Come in! *(The door opens and closes.)* It's you, Hadley.

SUPERINTENDENT HADLEY:  Yes, it's me.

DR. FELL *(thundering at him):*  "*I,*" sir.

HADLEY *(testily):*  All right: it's I. What's the matter with you in here? Are you both asleep?

DR. FELL:  We were just looking at ghosts.

HADLEY:  Oh?

DR. FELL:  Yes. You know Mr. Marvin Brown, don't you? Superintendent Hadley of the C. I. D.

HADLEY *(chuckling):*  I've had the pleasure, if you could call it that, of encountering Mr. Brown in court. Evening, sir.

BROWN *(also vaguely rousing):*  Ah yes. Good evening. Superintendent, would you call me a fanciful man?

HADLEY *(amused):*  Not exactly.

BROWN:  Or one addicted to crystal-gazing?

HADLEY:  No.

BROWN *(in his driest, most precise tone):*  And yet I saw things that happened twenty-four years ago. I saw Captain Burnham shot to death in a summer-house by a bright river. *(Vaguely)* I saw Isabel Burnham, who has been dead these ten years. I even hoped I might see truth.

HADLEY *(with sudden explosive suspicion):*    Dr. Fell, have you been up to any more of your tricks?

DR. FELL *(immensely injured):*    Tricks? My dear fellow! Did you ever know me to indulge in any tricks?

HADLEY:    I never knew you to indulge in anything else. What's he been up to, Mr. Brown?

BROWN *(laughing):*    Nothing. Only I hoped he might be able to tell me who killed Richard Burnham.

HADLEY:    I wish he could. It's more than we've been able to do.

BROWN:    And this relic . . . this cap . . . is everything that remains?

HADLEY:    Everything. Any ideas, Doctor?

DR. FELL:    Sit down, gentlemen. It is just on midnight: let's evoke the ghosts again. Captain Burnham was shot at a quarter past five o'clock in the afternoon. His body was found in the summer-house at shortly before six. There were powder-burns on the side of his cap, showing that the weapon must have been held within an inch of his head. The summer-house was about twenty yards away from the main house. Who killed Burnham? For instance, there was his wife Isabel. . . .

ISABEL'S VOICE *(it cuts across Dr. Fell's in not much more than a whisper):*    But you know *I* didn't do it, Marvin. I was with you in the back sitting room between five and six o'clock. I never once left your side, except to wheel the tea-wagon out of the dining room, and even then I wasn't away from you. Oh, Marvin, if things had been different! If things had been different!

BROWN *(sharply):*    Did you hear anything?

DR. FELL:    It's in your imagination, my boy. Nothing more. Then there was Isabel Burnham's young brother, Paul Stanfield. . . .

PAUL'S VOICE *(faintly):*    I blame myself, in a way. I was practicing with a revolver in the cellar. I kept on firing and firing; so nobody noticed the real shot when someone killed Richard. But at a quarter past five I was in the cellar, and nobody can prove any different.

DR. FELL:    Then again, there was the young and attractive Angela Fisk. . . .

ANGELA'S VOICE:    I was a silly young fool then. But I don't regret anything. I was in love with Paul. I never cared anything for Richard Burnham, as they said I did. I didn't meet him in the summer-house, and I proved it. I was at the Yacht Club a mile down the river. . . . Paul! Paul! Can you hear me now?

PAUL'S VOICE:    Yes.

ANGELA'S VOICE:    Isabel's dead. Are you dead too?

PAUL'S VOICE:    No, my dear. Only asleep, like yourself. A middle-aged man asleep in my comfortable bed. Do you have any regrets, Angela? Are you sorry we never married?

ANGELA'S VOICE:  No. I've had a nice life, though *(petulantly)* not as nice as I thought it ought to be.

PAUL'S VOICE:  It never is. Angela!

ANGELA'S VOICE:  Yes?

PAUL'S VOICE:  I've been thinking. What ever became of that maid, Kitty? Kitty Ingram? Rather a good-looking piece, now I remember it. What ever became of her?

KITTY'S VOICE:  So very nice of you to ask what became of me, Mr. Paul! *Mr.* Paul! Cor! Didn't I think things was all plums and skittles then? I'm all right, thank you. I've got my own boarding-house, and as genteel a trade as you'll find. But the police never asked *me* what happened. They never paid any attention to me. And yet I could tell 'em a thing or two even now. I could. . . .

*(The voice fades.)*

BROWN *(crying out):*  Stop!

HADLEY:  Still daydreaming, Mr. Brown? Nothing wrong, is there?

DR. FELL:  Like myself, he was reviewing the people of the drama.

BROWN:  A little more personally than you, Doctor. I said I wanted to know what really happened. I don't. Let the past sleep; and me with it. I—will you excuse me if I leave you rather abruptly? *(In fussy haste)* It's late and the doctor has forbidden me late hours. You'll excuse me, won't you?

DR. FELL:  Of course, if you insist.

BROWN:  My hat . . . thank you, Superintendent . . . stick . . . thanks. I trust we shall talk of this again, Doctor; and I only hope I haven't bored you with my long memories. Good night, gentlemen. Good night.

*(The door opens and closes.)*

HADLEY *(wonderingly):*  What's the matter with *him?*

DR. FELL *(somberly):*  Hadley, there goes an honest man and a gentleman.

HADLEY:  Rum old bird, if you ask me. What ailed him?

DR. FELL:  I rather think he guessed. Have some beer?

HADLEY:  Thanks. Guessed what?

*(A clink of bottle against glass, and a sound of beer being poured out)*

DR. FELL *(still in deep reflection):*  When he first came here tonight, I intended to tell him. Tell him at least what I was sure had happened. But at the last moment I couldn't face it: physically couldn't. So I didn't tell him. I even had to lie to him.

HADLEY *(exasperated):*  What is all this? What couldn't you tell him?

DR. FELL:   That it was really Isabel Burnham who shot her husband, of course.

*(A crash of glass)*

HADLEY:   *What?*

DR. FELL *(still absently and argumentatively explaining):*   You see, I hadn't realized that he had been in love with the woman. He worships her memory. And I couldn't in decency smash that up for him, could I?

HADLEY *(yelling at him):*   Are you raving mad?

DR. FELL:   No. *(Surprised, roused out of his musings)* Good Lord, Hadley, you surely realized that Isabel Burnham was guilty, didn't you?

HADLEY *(with restraint):*   Not exactly. You said yourself she couldn't be guilty. She had a cast-iron alibi.

DR. FELL *(with vast contempt):*   Oh, that?

HADLEY:   Some day, my lad, you are going to get murdered yourself. And probably by me. What about the alibi? Are you saying that Brown himself wasn't telling the truth—about her being with him between five and six o'clock?

DR. FELL:   Oh, no. Brown was telling the perfect truth. As far as he knew it.

HADLEY:   Then how the devil could she have gone out to the summer-house and shot Burnham at five-fifteen?

DR. FELL *(with a gusty sigh):*   She never did go out to the summer-house, Hadley. That's the whole sad story.

HADLEY:   But—

DR. FELL *(testily):*   The cap, man! Look at the cap!

HADLEY:   Well?

DR. FELL:   Inspector Mathers found a dead body in the summer-house. He said to us, "Here is a man who has been shot through the left side of the head, the bullet passing through the cap and killing him. This man has been shot at very close range." Now, why did he say close range?

HADLEY:   Because of the powder-burns on the cap. There they are!

DR. FELL *(wearily):*   Yes. Because of the powder-burns on the cap. That's all. It never occurred to him that Burnham was shot at long range—and that this cap, perforated by another bullet and artistically decorated with powder-burns, had been placed on his head after he was dead.

HADLEY *(after a pause):*   Go on.

DR. FELL:   But it should occur to anybody who takes one look at that cap. Perhaps—hurrm! Perhaps it's because we see so many soldiers in the streets nowadays that I've fallen into the habit of noticing. Most officers wear their caps slightly on one side: usually the right side. Have you noticed? Or is it too obvious to be seen?

HADLEY:   Go on.

DR. FELL:   Burnham certainly wore his cap at a very rakish angle— pulled down on the right-hand side. If you want proof of that, look at the cap. You see how the peak is definitely bent down on the right, from long usage and habit of twitching it down on that side. Habit, my boy: habit. No man accustomed to wearing a hat ever gets out of that.

HADLEY:   Well?

DR. FELL:   Yet when Burnham's body was found, we know, his cap was pulled down at a very rakish angle over the left eye. *(Pause)* Don't you always wear your own hat tilted down on the same side, Hadley? . . . Burnham, as we know, had taught Mrs. Burnham to shoot. She had to fire only twenty yards, less than the distance of an ordinary cricket-pitch, from the dining room window through the open door of the summer-house. Even so, her aim wasn't quite true. So she had to jam down the prepared cap to fit the bullet-hole. And she put the cap over the wrong eye.

HADLEY:   You say the "prepared" cap. I still don't understand.

DR. FELL:   Look here. We've heard, haven't we, that the windows of the dining room faced the summer-house?

HADLEY:   Yes.

DR. FELL:   And that the distance between the two was only twenty yards?

HADLEY:   Yes.

DR. FELL:   We've also heard, I think, that at about five-fifteen Isabel Burnham left the sitting room to get the tea-wagon. Brown himself said that the door was always closed between the two rooms.

HADLEY:   You mean she deliberately went in there, and . . .

DR. FELL:   Yes. She excused herself for a few seconds. She closed the door behind her. Burnham was in the summer-house—keeping a wary eye on the house itself, because he expected to be summoned in to tea. All she had to do was walk to the dining room window and beckon to Burnham in the summer-house. He, of course, would look out towards her. She lifted a .32 automatic and shot him through the brain. He was then, of course, wearing his original cap. Then she coolly wheeled the tea-wagon into the other room. *(Pause)* A remarkable woman, Hadley. In some ways, a very remarkable woman.

HADLEY *(drily):*   Very.

DR. FELL:   Brown, in the next room, noticed no shot because Paul Stanfield was blazing away with a .38 below. Brown could see nothing, because the sun-blinds in the sitting room were kept down—at her request. Brown was her alibi, you see. Old friend: strong alibi. She had planned with great care. All afternoon she'd been carrying round the duplicate cap and the .32 automatic. . . .

HADLEY:    Hold on! That's where I can't follow you. You say that all afternoon she'd been carrying round an army cap and the little gun. How is that Brown never saw them? Where did she keep them?

DR. FELL:    In the knitting bag, my boy. Don't you remember the knitting bag she took with her everywhere?

*(Slight pause)*

HADLEY:    Even out to the summer-house, afterwards?

DR. FELL:    Yes. Her original plan, I suspect was to "find" Burnham's body herself, so that she could exchange the caps. Paul Stanfield forestalled her by finding the body. But—you remember?—he didn't go into the summer-house. In other words, he didn't look closely enough at the body to see there were no powder-burns. In fact, he thought it was suicide. So she knew she was not yet lost. She then—you also remember—went haring out to the summer-house as hard as she could pelt. She had some seconds alone there, time enough to change the caps. Then she turned on everyone a soulful, tearful face, and she played the martyr to the last.

*(Pause)*

HADLEY *(ruminating):*    She must have been a cold-blooded devil. And we can't do anything to her now, worse luck.

DR. FELL:    My dear Hadley, you still don't understand. She was not cold-blooded; she was just the reverse. You've guessed, haven't you, that it was really Isabel who sent a fake message purporting to come from Angela Fisk, so as to make sure Burnham was in the summer-house at five o'clock? That was a part of the plan too. She was jealous of Angela; she wanted her husband dead. And so—

HADLEY:    Then you think there *was* something serious between Burnham and the Fisk girl after all?

DR. FELL:    Well, what do *you* think?

HADLEY:    I see. And, because of a bullet-hole in a cap, you decided . . .

DR. FELL:    Oh, nonsense! I could have told you the woman was guilty, before any crime had been committed. Brown would have noticed it himself, if he hadn't been in love with her.

HADLEY:    Noticed what?

DR. FELL *(musingly):*    A stimulating woman, Hadley. Burnham himself never realized how stimulating, until it was too late. But these great actresses nearly always forget something. When Brown arrived at the house, Isabel Burnham pretended to be in a hysterical state of nerves. She shook and shivered and wept. She could not face the servants. She jumped at a shadow. Yet during the whole afternoon she never once protested, never once jumped, never once batted an eyelid, throughout a series of sudden and shattering revolver shots coming unexpectedly from the cellar. I fancied that there might be something wrong with her brain or heart or soul. But, by thunder!—I knew there was nothing wrong with her nerves.

# The Incautious Burglar

This story was first published under the title "A Guest in the House" in *The Strand Magazine,* October 1940. Its earliest American publication was in a scarce paperback, *Dr. Fell, Detective and Other Stories* (1947), edited by Ellery Queen. It was not called "The Incautious Burglar" until it was reprinted in *Ellery Queen's Mystery Magazine,* November 1956. Once again when Dr. Fell is on hand, the story is Chestertonian: his remark that the case has five possible explanations is reminiscent of Father Brown's discussion of the mysterious clues in Chesterton's "The Honour of Israel Gow." Experts in Carr's work will notice that some of the plotline of "The Incautious Burglar" reappeared in a Sir Henry Merrivale novel, published under Carr's pseudonym "Carter Dickson." I won't tell you which one.

# The Incautious Burglar

Two guests, who were not staying the night at Cranleigh Court, left at shortly past eleven o'clock. Marcus Hunt saw them to the front door. Then he returned to the dining-room, where the poker-chips were now stacked into neat piles of white, red, and blue.

"Another game?" suggested Rolfe.

"No good," said Derek Henderson. His tone, as usual, was weary. "Not with just the three of us."

Their host stood by the sideboard and watched them. The long, low house, overlooking the Weald of Kent, was so quiet that their voices rose with startling loudness. The dining-room, large and panelled, was softly lighted by electric wall-candles which brought out the sombre colours of the paintings. It is not often that anybody sees, in one room of an otherwise commonplace country house, two Rembrandts and a Van Dyck. There was a kind of defiance about those paintings.

To Arthur Rolfe—the art dealer—they represented enough money to make him shiver. To Derek Henderson—the art critic—they represented a problem. What they represented to Marcus Hunt was not apparent.

Hunt stood by the sideboard, his fists on his hips, smiling. He was a middle-sized, stocky man, with a full face and a high complexion. Equip him with a tuft of chin-whisker, and he would have looked like a Dutch burgher for a Dutch brush. His shirtfront bulged out untidily. He watched with ironical amusement while Henderson picked up a pack of cards in long fingers, cut them into two piles, and shuffled with a sharp flick of each thumb which made the cards melt together like a conjuring trick.

Henderson yawned.

"My boy," said Hunt, "you surprise me."

"That's what I try to do," answered Henderson, still wearily. He looked up. "But why do you say so, particularly?"

Henderson was young, he was long, he was lean, he was immaculate; and he wore a beard. It was a reddish beard, which moved some people to hilarity. But he wore it with an air of complete naturalness.

"I'm surprised," said Hunt, "that you enjoy anything so bourgeois—so plebeian—as poker."

"I enjoy reading people's characters," said Henderson. "Poker's the best way to do it, you know."

Hunt's eyes narrowed. "Oh? Can you read my character, for instance?"

"With pleasure," said Henderson. Absently he dealt himself a poker-hand, face up. It contained a pair of fives, and the last card was the ace of spades. Henderson remained staring at it for a few seconds before he glanced up again.

"And I can tell you," he went on, "that you surprise *me*. Do you mind if I'm frank? I had always thought of you as the Colossus of Business; the smasher; the plunger; the fellow who took the long chances. Now, you're not like that at all."

Marcus Hunt laughed. But Henderson was undisturbed.

"You're tricky, but you're cautious. I doubt if you ever took a long chance in your life. Another surprise"—he dealt himself a new hand—"is Mr. Rolfe here. He's the man who, given the proper circumstances, would take the long chances."

Arthur Rolfe considered this. He looked startled, but rather flattered. Though in height and build not unlike Hunt, there was nothing untidy about him. He had a square, dark face, with thin shells of eyeglasses, and a worried forehead.

"I doubt that," he declared, very serious about this. Then he smiled. "A person who took long chances in my business would find himself in the soup." He glanced round the room. "Anyhow, I'd be too cautious to have three pictures, with an aggregate value of thirty thousand pounds, hanging in an unprotected downstairs room with French windows giving on a terrace." An almost frenzied note came into his voice. "Great Scot! Suppose a burglar—"

"Damn!" said Henderson unexpectedly.

Even Hunt jumped.

Ever since the poker-party, an uneasy atmosphere had been growing. Hunt had picked up an apple from a silver fruit-bowl on the sideboard. He was beginning to pare it with a fruit-knife, a sharp wafer-thin blade which glittered in the light of the wall-lamps.

"You nearly made me slice my thumb off," he said, putting down the knife. "What's the matter with you?"

"It's the ace of spades," said Henderson, still languidly. "That's the second time it's turned up in five minutes."

Arthur Rolfe chose to be dense. "Well? What about it?"

"I think our young friend is being psychic," said Hunt, good-humoured again. "Are you reading characters, or only telling fortunes?"

Henderson hesitated. His eyes moved to Hunt, and then to the wall over the sideboard where Rembrandt's *Old Woman with Cap* stared back with the immobility and skin-coloring of a red Indian. Then Henderson looked towards the French windows opening on the terrace.

"None of my affair," shrugged Henderson. "It's your house and your collection and your responsibility. But this fellow Butler: what do you know about him?"

Marcus Hunt looked boisterously amused.

"Butler? He's a friend of my niece's. Harriet picked him up in London, and asked me to invite him down here. Nonsense! Butler's all right. What are you thinking, exactly?"

"Listen!" said Rolfe, holding up his hand.

The noise they heard, from the direction of the terrace, was not repeated. It was not repeated because the person who had made it, a very bewildered and uneasy young lady, had run lightly and swiftly to the far end, where she leaned against the balustrade.

Lewis Butler hesitated before going after her. The moonlight was so clear that one could see the mortar between the tiles which paved the terrace, and trace the design of the stone urns along the balustrade. Harriet Davis wore a white gown with long and filmy skirts, which she lifted clear of the ground as she ran.

Then she beckoned to him.

She was half sitting, half leaning against the rail. Her white arms were spread out, fingers gripping the stone. Dark hair and dark eyes became even more vivid by moonlight. He could see the rapid rise and fall of her breast; he could even trace the shadow of her eyelashes.

"That was a lie, anyhow," she said.

"What was?"

"What my uncle Marcus said. You heard him." Harriet Davis's fingers tightened still more on the balustrade. But she nodded her head vehemently, with fierce accusation. "About my knowing you. And inviting you here. I never saw you before this weekend. Either Uncle Marcus is going out of his mind, or . . . will you answer me just one question?"

"If I can."

"Very well. Are you by any chance a crook?"

She spoke with as much simplicity and directness as though she had asked him whether he might be a doctor or a lawyer. Lewis Butler was not unwise enough to laugh. She was in that mood where, to any woman, laughter is salt to a raw wound; she would probably have slapped his face.

"To be quite frank about it," he said, "I'm not. Will you tell me why you asked?"

"This house," said Harriet, looking at the moon, "used to be guarded with burglar alarms. If you as much as touched a window, the whole place started clanging like a fire-station. He had all the burglar alarms removed last week. Last week." She took her hands off the balustrade, and pressed them together hard. "The pictures used to be upstairs, in a locked room next to his bedroom. He had them moved downstairs—last week. It's almost as though my uncle *wanted* the house to be burgled."

Butler knew that he must use great care here.

"Perhaps he does." (Here she looked at Butler quickly, but did not comment.) "For instance," he went on idly, "suppose one of his famous Rembrandts turned out to be a fake? It might be a relief not to have to show it to his expert friends."

The girl shook her head.

"No," she said. "They're all genuine. You see, I thought of that too."

Now was the time to hit, and hit hard. To Lewis Butler, in his innocence, there seemed to be no particular problem. He took out his cigarette-case, and turned it over without opening it.

"Look here, Miss Davis, you're not going to like this. But I can tell you of cases in which people were rather anxious to have their property 'stolen.' If a picture is insured for more than its value, and then it is mysteriously 'stolen' one night—?"

"That might be all very well too," answered Harriet, still calmly. "Except that not one of those pictures has been insured."

The cigarette-case, which was of polished metal, slipped through Butler's fingers and fell with a clatter on the tiles. It spilled cigarettes, just as it spilled and confused his theories. As he bent over to pick it up, he could hear a church clock across the Weald strike the half-hour after eleven.

"You're sure of that?"

"I'm perfectly sure. He hasn't insured any of his pictures for as much as a penny. He says it's a waste of money."

"But—"

"Oh, I know! And I don't know why I'm talking to you like this. You're a stranger, aren't you?" She folded her arms, drawing her shoulders up as though she were cold. Uncertainty, fear, and plain nerves flicked at her eyelids. "But then Uncle Marcus is a stranger too. Do you know what I think? *I* think he's going mad."

"Hardly as bad as that, is it?"

"Yes, go on," the girl suddenly stormed at him. "Say it: go on and say it. That's easy enough. But you don't see him when his eyes seem to get smaller, and all that genial-country-squire look goes out of his face. He's not a fake: he hates fakes, and goes out of his way to expose them. But, if he hasn't gone clear out of his mind, what's he up to? What can he be up to?"

In something over three hours they found out.

The burglar did not attack until half-past two in the morning. First he smoked several cigarettes in the shrubbery below the rear terrace. When he heard the church clock strike, he waited a few minutes more, and then slipped up the steps to the French windows of the dining-room.

A chilly wind stirred at the turn of the night, in the hour of suicides and bad dreams. It smoothed grass and trees with a faint rustling. When the man glanced over his shoulder, the last of the moonlight distorted his face: it showed less a face than the blob of a black cloth mask under a greasy cap pulled down over his ears.

He went to work on the middle window, with the contents of a folding tool-kit not so large as a motorist's. He fastened two short strips of adhesive tape to the glass just beside the catch. Then his glass-cutter sliced out a small semi-circle inside the tape.

It was done not without noise: it crunched like a dentist's drill in a tooth, and the man stopped to listen.

There was no answering noise. No dog barked.

With the adhesive tape holding the glass so that it did not fall and smash, he slid his gloved hand through the opening and twisted the catch. The weight of his body deadened the creaking of the window when he pushed inside.

He knew exactly what he wanted. He put the tool-kit into his pocket, and drew out an electric torch. Its beam moved across to the sideboard; it touched gleaming silver, a bowl of fruit, and a wicked little knife thrust into an apple as though into someone's body; finally, it moved up the hag-face of the *Old Woman with Cap*.

This was not a large picture, and the burglar lifted it down easily. He pried out glass and frame. Though he tried to roll up the canvas with great care, the brittle paint cracked across in small stars which wounded the hag's face. The burglar was so intent on this that he never noticed the presence of another person in the room.

He was an incautious burglar: he had no sixth sense which smelt murder.

Up on the second floor of the house, Lewis Butler was awakened by a muffled crash like that of metal objects falling.

He had not fallen into more than a half doze all night. He knew with certainty what must be happening, though he had no idea of why, or how, or to whom.

Butler was out of bed, and into his slippers, as soon as he heard the first faint clatter from downstairs. His dressing-gown would, as usual, twist itself up like a rolled umbrella and defy all attempts to find the arm-holes whenever he wanted to hurry. But the little flashlight was ready in the pocket.

That noise seemed to have roused nobody else. With certain possibilities in his mind, he had never in his life moved so fast once he managed to get out of his bedroom. Not using his light, he was down two flights of deep-carpeted stairs without noise. In the lower hall he could feel a draught, which meant that a window or door had been opened somewhere. He made straight for the dining-room.

But he was too late.

Once the pencil-beam of Butler's flashlight had swept round, he switched on a whole blaze of lights. The burglar was still here, right enough. But the burglar was lying very still in front of the sideboard; and, to judge by the amount of blood on his sweater and trousers, he would never move again.

"That's done it," Butler said aloud.

A silver service, including a tea-urn, had been toppled off the sideboard. Where the fruit-bowl had fallen, the dead man lay on his back among a litter of oranges, apples, and a squashed bunch of grapes. The mask still covered the burglar's face; his greasy cap was flattened still further on his ears; his gloved hands were thrown wide.

Fragments of smashed picture-glass lay round him, together with the empty frame, and the *Old Woman with Cap* had been half crumpled up under his body. From the position of the most conspicuous bloodstains, one judged that he had been stabbed through the chest with the stained fruit-knife beside him.

*"What is it?"* said a voice almost at Butler's ear.

He could not have been more startled if the fruit-knife had pricked his ribs. He had seen nobody turning on lights in the hall, nor had he heard Harriet Davis approach. She was standing just behind him, wrapped in a Japanese kimono, with her dark hair round her shoulders. But, when he explained what had happened, she would not look into the dining-room; she backed away, shaking her head violently, like an urchin ready for flight.

"You had better wake up your uncle," Butler said briskly, with a confidence he did not feel. "And the servants. I must use your telephone." Then he looked her in the eyes. "Yes, you're quite right. I think you've guessed it already. I'm a police-officer."

She nodded.

"Yes. I guessed. Who are you? And is your name really Butler?"

"I'm a sergeant of the Criminal Investigation Department. And my name really is Butler. Your uncle brought me here."

"Why?"

"I don't know. He hasn't got round to telling me."

This girl's intelligence, even when over-shadowed by fear, was direct and disconcerting. "But, if he wouldn't say why he wanted a police-officer, how did they come to send you? He'd have to tell them, wouldn't he?"

Butler ignored it. "I must see your uncle. Will you go upstairs and wake him, please?"

"I can't," said Harriet. "Uncle Marcus isn't in his room."

"Isn't—?"

"No. I knocked at the door on my way down. He's gone."

Butler took the stairs two treads at a time. Harriet had turned on all the lights on her way down, but nothing stirred in the bleak, over-decorated passages.

Marcus Hunt's bedroom was empty. His dinner-jacket had been hung up neatly on the back of a chair, shirt laid across the seat with collar and tie on top of it. Hunt's watch ticked loudly on the dressing-table. His money and keys were there too. But he had not gone to bed, for the bedspread was undisturbed.

The suspicion which came to Lewis Butler, listening to the thin insistent ticking of that watch in the drugged hour before dawn, was so fantastic that he could not credit it.

He started downstairs again, and on the way he met Arthur Rolfe blundering out of another bedroom down the hall. The art dealer's stocky body was wrapped in a flannel dressing-gown. He was not wearing his eyeglasses, which gave his face a bleary and rather caved-in expression. He planted himself in front of Butler, and refused to budge.

"Yes," said Butler. "You don't have to ask. It's a burglar."

"I knew it," said Rolfe calmly. "Did he get anything?"

"No. He was murdered."

For a moment Rolfe said nothing, but his hand crept into the breast of his dressing-gown as though he felt pain there.

"Murdered? You don't mean the *burglar* was murdered?"

"Yes."

"But why? By an accomplice, you mean? Who is the burglar?"

"That," snarled Lewis Butler, "is what I intend to find out."

In the lower hall he found Harriet Davis, who was now standing in the doorway of the dining-room and looking steadily at the body by the sideboard. Though her face hardly moved a muscle, her eyes brimmed over.

"You're going to take off the mask, aren't you?" she asked, without turning round.

Stepping with care to avoid squashed fruit and broken glass, Butler leaned over the dead man. He pushed back the peak of the greasy cap; he lifted the black cloth mask, which was clumsily held by an elastic band; and he found what he expected to find.

The burglar was Marcus Hunt—stabbed through the heart while attempting to rob his own house.

"You see, sir," Butler explained to Dr. Gideon Fell on the following afternoon, "that's the trouble. However you look at it, the case makes no sense."

Again he went over the facts.

"Why should the man burgle his own house and steal his own property? Every one of those paintings is valuable, and not a single one is insured! Consequently, why? Was the man a simple lunatic? What did he think he was doing?"

The village of Sutton Valence, straggling like a grey-white Italian town along the very peak of the Weald, was full of hot sunshine. In the apple orchard behind the white inn of the Tabard, Dr. Gideon Fell sat at a garden table among wasps, with a pint tankard at his elbow. Dr. Fell's vast bulk was clad in a white linen suit. His pink face smoked in the heat, and his wary lookout for wasps gave him a regrettably wall-eyed appearance as he pondered.

He said:

"Superintendent Hadley suggested that I might—harrumph—look in here. The local police are in charge, aren't they?"

"Yes. I'm merely standing by."

"Hadley's exact words to me were, 'It's so crazy that nobody but you will understand it.' The man's flattery becomes more nauseating every day." Dr. Fell scowled. "I say. Does anything else strike you as queer about this business?"

"Well, why should a man burgle his own house?"

"No, no, no!" growled Dr. Fell. "Don't be obsessed with that point. Don't become hypnotized by it. For instance"—a wasp hovered near his tankard, and he distended his cheeks and blew it away with one vast puff like Father Neptune—"for instance, the young lady seems to have raised an interesting question. If Marcus Hunt wouldn't say why he wanted a detective in the house, why did the C.I.D. consent to send you?"

Butler shrugged his shoulders.

"Because," he said, "Chief Inspector Ames thought Hunt was up to funny business, and meant to stop it."

"What sort of funny business?"

"A faked burglary to steal his own pictures for the insurance. It looked like the old, old game of appealing to the police to divert suspicion. In other words, sir, exactly what this appeared to be: until I learned (and today proved) that not one of those damned pictures has ever been insured for a penny."

Butler hesitated.

"It can't have been a practical joke," he went on. "Look at the elaborateness of it! Hunt put on old clothes from which all tailors' tabs and laundry marks were removed. He put on gloves and a mask. He got hold of a torch and an up-to-date kit of burglar's tools. He went out of the house by the back door; we found it open later. He smoked a few cigarettes in the shrubbery below the terrace; we found his footprints in the soft earth. He cut a pane of glass . . . but I've told you all that."

"And then," mused Dr. Fell, "somebody killed him."

"Yes. The last and worst 'why.' Why should anybody have killed him?"

"H'm. Clues?"

"Negative." Butler took out his notebook. "According to the police surgeon, he died of a direct heart-wound from a blade (presumably that fruit-knife) so thin that the wound was difficult to find. There were a number of his fingerprints, but nobody else's. We did find one odd thing, though. A number of pieces in the silver service off the sideboard were scratched in a queer way. It looked almost as though, instead of being swept off the sideboard in a struggle, they had been piled up on top of each other like a tower; and then pushed—"

Butler paused, for Dr. Fell was shaking his big head back and forth with an expression of Gargantuan distress.

"Well, well, well," he was saying; "well, well, well. And you call that negative evidence?"

"Isn't it? It doesn't explain why a man burgles his own house."

"Look here," said the doctor mildly. "I should like to ask you just one question. What is the most important point in this affair? One moment! I did not say the most interesting; I said the most important. Surely it is the fact that a man has been murdered?"

"Yes, sir. Naturally."

"I mention the fact"—the doctor was apologetic—"because it seems in danger of being overlooked. It hardly interests you. You are concerned only with Hunt's senseless masquerade. You don't mind a throat being cut; but you can't stand a leg being pulled. Why not try working at it from the other side, and asking who killed Hunt?"

Butler was silent for a long time.

"The servants are out of it," he said at length. "They sleep in another wing on the top floor; and for some reason," he hesitated, "somebody locked them in last night." His doubts, even his dreads, were beginning to take form. "There was a fine blow-up over that when the house was roused. Of course, the murderer could have been an outsider."

"You know it wasn't," said Dr. Fell. "Would you mind taking me to Cranleigh Court?"

They came out on the terrace in the hottest part of the afternoon.

Dr. Fell sat down on a wicker settee, with a dispirited Harriet beside him. Derek Henderson, in flannels, perched his long figure on the balustrade. Arthur Rolfe alone wore a dark suit and seemed out of place. For the pale green and brown of the Kentish lands, which rarely acquired harsh color, now blazed. No air stirred, no leaf moved, in that brilliant thickness of heat; and down in the garden, towards their left, the water of the swimming-pool sparkled with hot, hard light. Butler felt it like a weight on his eyelids.

Derek Henderson's beard was at once languid and yet aggressive.

"It's no good," he said. "Don't keep on asking me why Hunt should have burgled his own house. But I'll give you a tip."

"Which is?" inquired Dr. Fell.

"Whatever the reason was," returned Henderson, sticking out his neck, "it was a good reason. Hunt was much too canny and cautious ever to do anything without a good reason. I told him so last night."

Dr. Fell spoke sharply. "Cautious? Why do you say that?"

"Well, for instance. I take three cards on the draw. Hunt takes one. I bet; he sees me and raises. I cover that, and raise again. Hunt drops out. In other words, it's fairly certain he's filled his hand, but not so certain I'm holding much more than a pair. Yet Hunt drops out. So with my three sevens I bluff him out of his straight. He played a dozen hands last night just like that."

Henderson began to chuckle. Seeing the expression on Harriet's face, he checked himself and became preternaturally solemn.

"But then, of course," Henderson added, "he had a lot on his mind last night."

Nobody could fail to notice the change of tone.

"So? And what did he have on his mind?"

"Exposing somebody he had always trusted," replied Henderson coolly. "That's why I didn't like it when the ace of spades turned up so often."

"You'd better explain that," said Harriet, after a pause. "I don't know what you're hinting at, but you'd better explain that. He told you he intended to expose somebody he had always trusted?"

"No. Like myself, he hinted at it."

It was the stolid Rolfe who stormed into the conversation then. Rolfe had the air of a man determined to hold hard to reason, but finding it difficult.

"Listen to me," snapped Rolfe. "I have heard a great deal, at one time or another, about Mr. Hunt's liking for exposing people. Very well!" He slid one hand into the breast of his coat, in a characteristic gesture. "But where in the name of sanity does that leave us? He wants to expose someone. And, to do that, he puts on outlandish clothes and masquerades as a burglar. Is that sensible? I tell you, the man was mad! There's no other explanation."

"There are five other explanations," said Dr. Fell.

Derek Henderson slowly got up from his seat on the balustrade, but he sat down again at a savage gesture from Rolfe.

Nobody spoke.

"I will not, however," pursued Dr. Fell, "waste your time with four of them. We are concerned with only one explanation: the real one."

"And you know the real one?" asked Henderson sharply.

"I rather think so."

"Since when?"

"Since I had the opportunity of looking at all of you," answered Dr. Fell.

He settled back massively in the wicker settee, so that its frame creaked and cracked like a ship's bulkhead in a heavy sea. His vast chin was outthrust, and he nodded absently as though to emphasize some point that was quite clear in his own mind.

"I've already had a word with the local inspector," he went on suddenly. "He will be here in a few minutes. And, at my suggestion, he will have a request for all of you. I sincerely hope nobody will refuse."

"Request?" said Henderson. "What request?"

"It's a very hot day," said Dr. Fell, blinking towards the swimming-pool. "He's going to suggest that you all go in for a swim."

Harriet uttered a kind of despairing mutter, and turned as though appealing to Lewis Butler.

"That," continued Dr. Fell, "will be the politest way of drawing attention to the murderer. In the meantime, let me call your attention to one point in the evidence which seems to have been generally overlooked. Mr. Henderson, do you know anything about direct heart-wounds, made by a steel blade as thin as a wafer?"

"Like Hunt's wound? No. What about them?"

"There is practically no exterior bleeding," answered Dr. Fell.

"But—!" Harriet was beginning, when Butler stopped her.

"The police surgeon, in fact, called attention to that wound which was so 'difficult to find.' The victim dies almost at once; and the edges of the wound compress. But in that case," argued Dr. Fell, "how did the late Mr. Hunt come to have so much blood on his sweater, and even splashed on his trousers?"

"Well?"

"He didn't," answered Dr. Fell simply. "Mr. Hunt's blood never got on his clothes at all."

"I can't stand this," said Harriet, jumping to her feet. "I—I'm sorry, but have you gone mad yourself? Are you telling us we didn't see him lying by that sideboard, with blood on him?"

"Oh, yes. You saw that."

"Let him go on," said Henderson, who was rather white round the nostrils. "Let him rave."

"It is, I admit, a fine point," said Dr. Fell. "But it answers your question, repeated to the point of nausea, as to why the eminently sensible

Mr. Hunt chose to dress up in burglar's clothes and play burglar. The answer is short and simple. He didn't."

"It must be plain to everybody," Dr. Fell went on, opening his eyes wide, "that Mr. Hunt was deliberately setting a trap for someone—the real burglar.

"He believed that a certain person might try to steal one or several of his pictures. He probably knew that this person had tried similar games before, in other country houses: that is, an inside job which was carefully planned to look like an outside job. So he made things easy for this thief, in order to trap him, with a police-officer in the house.

"The burglar, a sad fool, fell for it. This thief, a guest in the house, waited until well past two o'clock in the morning. He then put on his old clothes, mask, gloves, and the rest of it. He let himself out by the back door. He went through all the motions we have erroneously been attributing to Marcus Hunt. Then the trap snapped. Just as he was rolling up the Rembrandt, he heard a noise. He swung his light round. And he saw Marcus Hunt, in pyjamas and dressing-gown, looking at him.

"Yes, there was a fight. Hunt flew at him. The thief snatched up a fruit-knife and fought back. In that struggle, Marcus Hunt forced his opponent's hand back. The fruit-knife gashed the thief's chest, inflicting a superficial but badly bleeding gash. It sent the thief over the edge of insanity. He wrenched Marcus Hunt's wrist half off, caught up the knife, and stabbed Hunt to the heart.

"Then, in a quiet house, with a little beam of light streaming out from the torch on the sideboard, the murderer sees something that will hang him. He sees the blood from his own superficial wound seeping down his clothes.

"How is he to get rid of those clothes? He cannot destroy them, or get them away from the house. Inevitably the house will be searched, and they will be found. Without the blood-stains, they would seem ordinary clothes in his wardrobe. But with the bloodstains—"

"There is only one thing he can do."

Harriet Davis was standing behind the wicker settee, shading her eyes against the glare of the sun. Her hand did not tremble when she said:

"He changed clothes with my uncle."

"That's it," growled Dr. Fell. "That's the whole sad story. The murderer dressed the body in his own clothes, making a puncture with the knife in sweater, shirt, and undervest. He then slipped on Mr. Hunt's pyjamas and dressing-gown, which at a pinch he could always claim as his own. Hunt's wound had bled hardly at all. His dressing-gown, I think, had come open in the fight, so that all the thief had to trouble him was a tiny puncture in the jacket of the pyjamas.

"But, once he had done this, he had to hypnotize you all into the belief that there would have been no time for a change of clothes. He had to make it seem that the fight occurred just *then*. He had to rouse the house. So he brought down echoing thunders by pushing over a pile of silver, and slipped upstairs."

Dr. Fell paused.

"The burglar could never have been Marcus Hunt, you know," he added. "We learn that Hunt's fingerprints were all over the place. Yet the murdered man was wearing gloves."

There was a swishing of feet in the grass below the terrace, and a tread of heavy boots coming up the terrace steps. The local Inspector of police, buttoned up and steaming in his uniform, was followed by two constables.

Dr. Fell turned round a face of satisfaction.

"Ah!" he said, breathing deeply. "They've come to see about that swimming-party, I imagine. It is easy to patch up a flesh-wound with lint and cotton, or even a handkerchief. But such a wound will become infernally conspicuous in anyone who is forced to climb into bathing-trunks."

"But it couldn't have been—" cried Harriet. Her eyes moved round. Her fingers tightened on Lewis Butler's arm, an instinctive gesture which he was to remember long afterwards, when he knew her even better.

"Exactly," agreed the doctor, wheezing with pleasure. "It could not have been a long, thin, gangling fellow like Mr. Henderson. It assuredly could not have been a small and slender girl like yourself.

"There is only one person who, as we know, is just about Marcus Hunt's height and build; who could have put his own clothes on Hunt without any suspicion. That is the same person who, though he managed to staunch the wound in his chest, has been constantly running his hand inside the breast of his coat to make certain the bandage is secure. Just as Mr. Rolfe is doing now."

Arthur Rolfe sat very quiet, with his right hand still in the breast of his jacket. His face had grown smeary in the hot sunlight, but the eyes behind those thin shells of glasses remained inscrutable. He spoke only once, through dry lips, after they had cautioned him.

"I should have taken the young pup's warning," he said. "After all, he told me I would take long chances."

# The Dead Sleep Lightly

"The Dead Sleep Lightly" was broadcast on BBC Radio on August 23, 1943, and the script was printed in *The Dead Sleep Lightly* (1983). With its shuddery atmosphere, seemingly impossible events, and rational solution, it is one of Dr. Fell's greatest cases. Unlike the radio-play that follows, the version of "The Dead Sleep Lightly" later broadcast on the CBS show *Suspense* did not feature Dr. Fell, but it has a memorable opening with a clergyman at a graveyard, intoning "Ashes to ashes, dust to dust."

# The Dead Sleep Lightly

## The Characters:

| | |
|---|---|
| Dr. Gideon Fell | The detective |
| Hoskins | His manservant |
| George Pendleton | A publisher |
| Pamela Bennett | His secretary |
| Mrs. Tancred | His housekeeper |
| Wilmot | His chauffeur |
| Superintendent Hadley | Of Scotland Yard |
| Mary Ellen Kimball | A voice |
| Taxi Driver | |
| Telephone Operator | |

*Setting:* London, 1933

NARRATOR: It was dark that night too. Very dark. A gusty March evening ten years ago in London. There was peace; there was security; and no living thing could harm you. But a black wind whistled that night in the narrow streets off the Strand, and flapped at the shutters and growled in the chimneys, and penetrated even into the snug book-lined study up two flights of stairs. There in the great padded armchair before the fire, sat Dr. Gideon Fell. His face had grown even ruddier in the heat of the fire. His several chins folded out over his collar. Cigar ash was spilled down the mountainous ridges of his waistcoat. His eyeglasses, on the wide black ribbon, had become a trifle lopsided. Doubtless he was deep in thought over some difficult problem, since . . .

*(As the voice fades, there are several long and impressive snores. Door opens as Hoskins approaches.)*

HOSKINS: Dr. Fell, sir! Wake up! Dr. Fell!

DR. FELL *(at end of a snore, starting):* Eh? What's that?

HOSKINS: Begging your pardon, sir, but *will* you wake up?

DR. FELL *(with dignity):* Yes, of course; I was merely concentrating. What is it?

HOSKINS: There's a lunatic downstairs, sir.

DR. FELL: A *what?*

HOSKINS: A lunatic, sir.

DR. FELL: Then what's wrong, my good Hoskins? What ails you? Why don't you show him up?

HOSKINS: Are you sure you *want* to see him, sir?

DR. FELL: That depends. What sort of a lunatic is he?

HOSKINS: He's a big, fine-looking gent, about fifty. Got a limousine outside. But he's shaking all over, and near purple in the face. I don't like the look of him.

DR. FELL:   Did he give any name?

HOSKINS:   Well, sir, he started to take out a card case. But his fingers shook so much that he spilled the cards all over the floor. Then he scooped up the lot and put 'em back in his pocket again. I think he said "Pendleton" or something like that.

DR. FELL *(ruminating):*   Pendleton. That wouldn't be George Pendleton, the publisher?

HOSKINS:   I dunno, sir.

DR. FELL:   Mr. George Pendleton, Hoskins, is a very celebrated and successful man. What he should be doing at *my* humble door . . . Ask him to come up, will you?

HOSKINS *(rapidly, under his breath):*   Cripes, sir, I don't need to. 'Ere 'e is.

*(Door opens. Pendleton has an authoritative and pompous voice, the voice of a man used to getting his own way. Just now he has himself in hand, but he is badly frightened.)*

PENDLETON *(huskily):*   I beg your pardon. Am I addressing Dr. Gideon Fell?

DR. FELL:   At your service, sir. Mr. Pendleton?

PENDLETON:   Yes. I followed your servant up. That dark hall down-stairs . . . *(Correcting himself quickly)* I mean, I hope you'll excuse my intrusion at this time of the night. I mean . . .

DR. FELL:   Steady, man! Don't trip over anything. Here, come up to the fire. It's a cold night.

PENDLETON *(fervently):*   It is, it is!

DR. FELL:   Hoskins, take Mr. Pendleton's hat and coat. Now draw up a chair.

PENDLETON:   Tell me, Doctor: there's no clay in this house, is there?

DR. FELL:   Clay?

PENDLETON:   Clay soil. And gravel. Of the sort you often find in   . . graveyards.

HOSKINS *(under his breath):*   'Ere! Stop a bit!

DR. FELL:   That will be all, Hoskins. You may go.

HOSKINS *(unwillingly):*   Very good, sir.

*(Door closes)*

PENDLETON:   I thought I stepped on some clay and gravel as I was coming upstairs. Perhaps a trick of the imagination.

DR. FELL:   It certainly must have been, unless Hoskins is an even worse housekeeper than I think he is.

PENDLETON:   You see, Doctor . . . I went to a funeral yesterday.

DR. FELL:   You've lost someone?

PENDLETON:   No, no, no! It was only a fellow club-member. A lot of us went to the funeral in a body, as a mark of respect. *(Pompously)* I'm a busy man, Doctor, but I find it pays to keep up the little social duties like that. Business, with the right personal touch: that's how I've got on in the world, if you don't mind my saying so.

DR. FELL: I see. And on this particular social occasion . . . ?

PENDLETON *(startled):* Social occasion? Who the devil said anything about social occasions?

DR. FELL: I thought *you* did. Please go on.

PENDLETON: It was a wet day in Kensal Green cemetery. There we were, a lot of middle-aged men, standing about an open grave in the rain. Feeling liverish; nothing right; you know how it is.

DR. FELL: Unfortunately, I do.

PENDLETON: I was arranging to get away next day for a long holiday in the south of France. After that I was giving up my house in St. John's Wood, and taking a flat closer to the West End. Light! Life! *Something!* I'd taken my secretary along to that infernal funeral in case I wanted to dictate any last letters. *(Suddenly struck by this) Last letters!* Never mind! *(Fade in sounds of rain)* As we were on our way out of the cemetery, we must have got confused, because . . .

*(The voice fades into a long roll of thunder. The steady noise of rain backs the scene throughout. Pamela Bennett speaks. She is young and keeps her voice, as a rule, at a colorless level.)*

PAMELA: Mr. Pendleton, are you sure we haven't taken the wrong turning? This isn't the way to the car.

PENDLETON *(irritably):* You said it was, Miss Bennett.

PAMELA: No, sir, I said . . .

PENDLETON: Anyway, how can you expect to see anything in this rain? And all this nightmare of tombstones?

PAMELA: It looks like an older part of the cemetery.

PENDLETON: It is. It's where they bury you when you haven't much money. Always remember that, Miss Bennett.

PAMELA: I'm sorry if I got the directions mixed, Mr. Pendleton. I thought . . .

PENDLETON *(magnanimously):* Please don't mention it, Miss Bennett. It's a small matter, in fact, compared to other things. I'll pay you the compliment of saying you're the best secretary I ever had. Yet you want to leave me?

PAMELA: I want to get married, yes.

PENDLETON: That's what Mr. Fraser was telling me. *(Spitefully)* And who is this paragon of yours? What does he do? Does he make any money?

PAMELA: Frank's a radio technician. He's not very well-off, I admit.

PENDLETON: Well-off? I'll bet he doesn't make as much as I pay you, yet you want to get married!

*(Fade up rain)*

PAMELA *(bewildered):*   Is there anything so very strange about that?

PENDLETON:   Yes, if it interferes with your career. It . . .

*(Peak and fade rain to background)*

PAMELA *(as though alarmed):*   What's wrong?

PENDLETON *(in a low voice):*   Good . . . *God!*

PAMELA:   What is it? Don't lower your umbrella like that, or you'll get soaking wet. What's wrong?

PENDLETON:   Do you see that grave?

PAMELA:   Which one?

PENDLETON:   On the end. The very-much-neglected grave with the little stone cross. The name's almost effaced. Can you read it?

PAMELA *(slowly):*   "Sacred to the Memory of Mary . . . Ellen . . . Kimball."

PENDLETON *(astonished):*   So it is; so it is!

PAMELA:   "Born . . ." No, I can't read that part of it. What about her?

PENDLETON *(genuinely moved):*   Poor Mary Ellen! *(He sighs.)* Now I come to think of it, she did have an aunt or someone living at Kensal Rise. It's a girl I used to know twenty-five, thirty years ago.

PAMELA:   Did you know her well?

PENDLETON *(brooding):*   I'll tell you a deep secret, Miss Bennett. I would have married her . . . yes, so help me! . . . only . . .

PAMELA:   Only . . . what?

PENDLETON:   Do I have to explain these things? I came from small beginnings. I had my way to make in the world. And she wouldn't have helped me.

PAMELA:   I still don't think I understand.

PENDLETON *(dogmatically):*   A man of my sort owes it to himself to make a wealthy marriage or none at all. That's what I've always said, and that's what I believe. Anything else is sentimental rubbish. I was sorry to break with her, but I thought it was kinder to break cleanly. I was sorry to hear of her death . . . that was years afterwards . . . *(Fade in thunder)* But . . . well, I had other things to think about.

PAMELA *(under her breath):*   You *poisonous* . . . *(The word is almost but not quite drowned out by a roll of thunder.)*

PENDLETON *(startled, not hearing):*   What's that? Did you say something?

PAMELA *(colorless again):*   No, Mr. Pendleton. Hadn't we better get on to the car?

PENDLETON:   Yes, I suppose so. *(Wistfully)* Poor Mary Ellen, though.

PAMELA:   I'm sorry, Mr. Pendleton, but I've got suede shoes on, and this clay is ruining them. Couldn't we go on?

PENDLETON:   She was a pretty little thing, and absolutely devoted to me. *(Defensively)* I was *sorry* for her, you know.

PAMELA:   If you really feel like that, Mr. Pendleton . . .

PENDLETON:   Well?

PAMELA:   You could have her grave tidied up, and some flowers put on it. Shall I attend to it for you?

PENDLETON *(eagerly):*   By George, yes! That's a good idea. She'd have liked that. But . . . how are they going to identify her?

PAMELA:   Identify her?

PENDLETON:   There must be thousands of graves here. Look!

PAMELA:   Yes. Didn't you ever have anything to do with cemeteries, Mr. Pendleton?

PENDLETON *(shuddering):*   No! I hate the thought of death! I . . .

PAMELA:   Each grave has a number cut into the stone at one side. This one is Kensal Green 1-9-3-3.

PENDLETON *(blankly):*   Kensal Green 1-9-3-3.

PAMELA:   Sounds like a telephone number, doesn't it?

PENDLETON *(quietly):*   Yes. Doesn't it? Kensal Green 1-9-3-3. Kensal Green 1-9-3-3.

PAMELA *(pleading):*   *Couldn't* we go on now, Mr. Pendleton?

PENDLETON *(unheeding):*   Make a note of that, Miss Bennett. Attend to it first thing next week, and . . . *(Waking up)* Wait a minute! I forgot. You're leaving the office. Has it ever occurred to you, Miss Bennett, that you take the most impossible times for inconveniencing me with your personal affairs?

PAMELA *(helplessly):*   I'm sorry, Mr. Pendleton. I can't seem to do anything to please you today.

PENDLETON:   You could please me, at least, by staying on at the office.

PAMELA:   I've told you before that . . .

PENDLETON *(significantly):*   You're not a bad-looking girl. I could do a lot for you, you know, if I wanted to.

PAMELA *(unemotionally):*   As you did for Mary Ellen Kimball?

PENDLETON:   Confound your impertinence!

PAMELA:   Were *you* speaking of impertinence, Mr. Pendleton?

PENDLETON *(stiffly):*   Perhaps you're right. Yes, I'm quite sure you're right. Shall we forget I ever mentioned it?

PAMELA:   If you please.

PENDLETON *(blankly):*   Kensal Green 1-9-3-3. Kensal Green 1-9-3-3.

PAMELA:   Why do you keep on repeating that number?

PENDLETON:   Not because I regret anything, mind you!

PAMELA:   I'm sure you don't.

PENDLETON:   After all, you can't take a girl like that into society. Not when she's thrown her cap over the windmill for you, and got herself talked about. It's just that her utter devotion touched me a good deal.

PAMELA:  I'm sure it did.

PENDLETON:  She always said she'd come back if I called her. And sometimes . . .

PAMELA:  You felt like calling her?

PENDLETON:  Years ago, maybe. But there she is with the worms and clay *(arrogantly),* and here *I* am where I've always wanted to be. It's too late now, isn't it?

PAMELA:  Much too late, Mr. Pendleton. *Much too late.*
*(Swell thunder and then fade into Pendleton's voice)*

PENDLETON:  . . . and that, Dr. Fell, was all that happened at the cemetery. Little enough, you'd say. But it started preying on my mind. I couldn't forget that girl.

DR. FELL:  You mean Miss Bennett?

PENDLETON *(impatiently):*  Miss Bennett . . . No! I can't think what made me forget myself there. I mean Mary Ellen Kimball.

DR. FELL:  You've made your mental state fairly clear, I think. And then?

PENDLETON:  For some reason I began to get nervous. I lunched at my club, and couldn't eat. I went to my office, and couldn't work. That infernal number kept running through my head: Kensal Green 1-9-3-3. Then, when I went home in the evening . . . *(Abruptly)* Have you ever seen my house?

DR. FELL:  I have not had that pleasure, sir. But I believe it's one of the showplaces of St. John's Wood.

PENDLETON *(bitterly):*  Great ugly mausoleum of a place! I told you I was moving house, into a flat that'd suit me better when I came back from Europe. I knew most of the servants would be gone, of course. But I thought Mrs. Tancred—that's my housekeeper—would still be there. *(Fade in rain)* It was still raining, with thunder about. Then, when I went up the path about half-past six . . .
*(Swell rain and fade down. Distant ringing of a doorbell. A heavy door is opened. Mrs. Tancred is elderly and well-spoken.)*

MRS. TANCRED *(surprised):*  Bless me, sir; I didn't know it was you.
*(Door shuts out the rain)*

PENDLETON:  Sorry to trouble you, Mrs. Tancred. I seem to have mislaid my latchkey. And yet I could have sworn I had it on my keyring this morning.

MRS. TANCRED:  It's no trouble, Mr. Pendleton.

PENDLETON *(irritably):*  Confound it, what are all these packing-cases doing in the hall?

MRS. TANCRED *(reproachfully):* I hope you haven't forgotten you're leaving here, sir?

PENDLETON *(waking up):* Oh, yes. Yes, of course. Have you got my bags packed?

MRS. TANCRED: All ready for you, sir. Your hat and coat? Will you be dining at home tonight?

PENDLETON *(still rather dazed):* Yes. Yes, I suppose I'd better. For the last time.

MRS. TANCRED: It does seem a pity, doesn't it?

PENDLETON *(quickly):* What seems a pity?

MRS. TANCRED: Leaving here, after all these years.

PENDLETON *(hurriedly):* Now you've been a very good housekeeper, Mrs. Tancred. I've always treated *you* generously, haven't I? I've got you a good position to follow this one, haven't I?

MRS. TANCRED *(offended):* I wasn't meaning that, sir.

PENDLETON: Then what did you mean?

MRS. TANCRED: Breaking up a lovely home like this.

PENDLETON: *This?* This infernal picture gallery? Where I feel like . . . like old Scrooge every time I come home!

MRS. TANCRED *(sympathetically):* It must have been a bit lonely at times, I daresay.

PENDLETON *(fiercely):* Lonely? I am never lonely!

MRS. TANCRED *(submissively):* No, sir.

PENDLETON: There are a lot of people who envy me, Mrs. Tancred. And, what's more, I deserve their envy.

MRS. TANCRED: Yes, sir.

PENDLETON: I . . . *(giving it up)* . . . never mind. They haven't taken the furniture out of the library, have they?

MRS. TANCRED: No, sir. Only the books off the shelves.

PENDLETON: I shall be in the library, then. Dinner at seven-thirty. And . . . Mrs. Tancred!

MRS. TANCRED: Yes, sir?

PENDLETON: If I ever feel the need of any sympathy for my unhappy lot, I'll ask for it. Do I make myself quite clear?

MRS. TANCRED: Yes, sir. Just as you wish, sir.

*(Door opens and closes heavily. Slight pause. Pendleton draws a deep breath.)*

PENDLETON *(muttering):* What's a library without books? Empty mortuary kind of place . . . Confound her; she's even taken the writing paper off my desk. Nothing's right. Nothing *has* ever been right! And where's my Venetian mirror? Have they gone and stolen my Ven . . . Oh, no. No. Here we are. *(Slight pause. He changes his tone.)* George Pendleton, my lad, you might as well face the fact that you can't stick dinner alone in this house tonight. Never mind *why* you can't do it. Never mind whether it's your health *(fade in rain)*, or what it is. Rain going on forever. It'll be wet in that cemetery. And is there any reason on earth why you shouldn't go out for dinner and enjoy yourself? That's it! Ring Bill Fraser, and go out to dinner. Ring Bill Fraser. Telephone . . . here we are.

*(Noise of receiver lifted, and receiver-hook jiggled up and down.)*

PENDLETON:   Hello! Hello! Hello!

OPERATOR:   Number, please?

PENDLETON:   Hello? I want . . . *(Groping)* Bill's number. Now what's Bill's number? What the devil *is* Bill's number?

OPERATOR:   Number, please?

PENDLETON:   I want . . . I want . . . *(Blurting it out)* Kensal Green 1-9-3-3. *(Heavy crash of thunder)* Good God! What have I said?

OPERATOR *(unemotionally)*:   Kensal Green 1-9-3-3.

PENDLETON *(in consternation)*:   Operator, wait! There's some mistake! I said the wrong thing! I want . . .

OPERATOR:   Kensal Green 1-9-3-3.

*(Ringing tone. Then a woman's voice answers; it is a girlish voice, very faint and almost whispering.)*

VOICE:   Yes? Who is it?

PENDLETON *(wildly)*:   There's been some mist . . .

VOICE *(with sudden eagerness)*:   George dear, is that you?

PENDLETON *(alarmed)*:   Who is that? Who's speaking?

VOICE:   It's Mary Ellen, dear. Don't you recognize my voice?

PENDLETON:   No! No! No!

VOICE:   I knew you'd call me sooner or later, dear. But I've waited *ever* so long.

PENDLETON:   I . . .

VOICE *(eagerly)*:   And of course I'll come if you want me. I'll be there just as soon as I can.

PENDLETON:   I tell you—!

VOICE:   I'll be there by seven o'clock, truly I will. But you mustn't be frightened at how I look now.

PENDLETON:   You're not Mary Ellen! This is a trick! *Mary Ellen is dead!*

VOICE:   Yes, dear. But the dead sleep lightly. And they can be lonely too.

PENDLETON:   Don't talk to me! You can't talk to me! I won't listen to you! I . . .

VOICE:   I'll wear a veil, dear. Because I'm not very pretty now. But I won't hurt you, my darling. Truly I won't!

PENDLETON *(frantically)*:   Go away, do you hear? Go . . .

VOICE:   Goodbye, dear. Remember, when the clock strikes seven.
*(There is a click and a long pause.)*
PENDLETON *(breathing hard):*   Mrs. Tancred! *(Shouting)* Mrs. Tancred!
*(Door opens)*
MRS. TANCRED *(flustered):*   Lord 'a' mercy, sir, what's the matter?
*(Door shuts)*
PENDLETON *(levelly but hoarsely):*   Who's been playing tricks on me?
MRS. TANCRED:   Tricks, sir?
PENDLETON:   I want to know who's been playing the fool with this
telephone.
MRS. TANCRED *(surprised):*   Nobody, sir. It's only what you ordered.
*(Nervously amused)* You haven't been trying to *use* the phone, have
you?
PENDLETON:   Use it? I rang up a friend of mine. A woman's voice
answered and pretended to be somebody I used to know years
ago . . .
MRS. TANCRED *(alarmed and offended):*   Now, sir, stop your joking.
PENDLETON:   You think I'm *joking?*
MRS. TANCRED *(commiseratingly):*   You're all upset, that's what it is.
Sit down by the desk. Hang up the receiver and put the phone down.
. . . There!
PENDLETON *(desperately):*   Will you kindly tell me . . . ?
MRS. TANCRED:   You didn't use that telephone, sir. Nobody could have
used that phone.
PENDLETON:   And why not?
MRS. TANCRED:   Because it was disconnected this morning. *(After a
pause, she continues patiently.)* You're giving up the house, sir. Don't
you remember? You ordered the telephone to be removed. The man
came this morning, and disconnected all the wires, and took the metal
box off the baseboard of the wall.
PENDLETON *(not loudly):*   Are you mad, or am I?
MRS. TANCRED:   Just look for yourself, then. There's the flex of the
phone hanging halfway down to the floor. It ends in mid-air; it's not
connected with anything.
PENDLETON *(breathing it):*   That's . . . true!
MRS. TANCRED:   Of course it's true.
PENDLETON:   The phone's *not* connected. It wasn't connected when I
spoke to . . .
MRS. TANCRED:   When I saw you there with the phone in your hand,
and the receiver off the hook, and the cord not going anywhere, and
looking as though you'd really *been* talking to somebody . . . *(Doubtfully)* You *were* just pretending, weren't you, sir?
PENDLETON:   What if I said no?

MRS. TANCRED:    Really, Mr. Pendleton! Please!

PENDLETON:    I tell you, I was talking to a woman on this telephone just before you came in here!

MRS. TANCRED *(flatly):*    Indeed, sir.

PENDLETON:    You don't believe me, do you?

MRS. TANCRED:    I must ask to be excused, if you don't mind. I'm the only person here, and I've got to see to your dinner, and . . .
*(Door opens)*

PENDLETON *(hoarsely):*    Mrs. Tancred! Wait a minute!

MRS. TANCRED:    Yes, sir?

PENDLETON:    Mrs. Tancred *(pause),* how long have you been my housekeeper?

MRS. TANCRED:    Three years and eight months. Why, sir?

PENDLETON:    Sometimes, in certain lights, I get the notion we'd met before you came here.

MRS. TANCRED:    Indeed, sir.

PENDLETON *(sharply):*    Had we met before?

MRS. TANCRED:    If I'd ever met you, sir, it isn't likely I should have forgotten you. Now is it?

PENDLETON:    Mrs. Tancred! Wait! Don't go away! You're not going to leave me here alone?

MRS. TANCRED:    Leave you alone? A big, able-bodied man! Really, sir!
*(Door closes)*

PENDLETON:    Mrs. Tancred! *(Desperately)* Mrs. Tancred! What . . . time is it?

MRS. TANCRED *(coldly, through closed door):*    There's a clock on the mantel in there, sir. It must be . . .
*(Clock slowly strikes seven. Music up.)*

DR. FELL:    I see, Mr. Pendleton. I see. But surely the story doesn't end there?

PENDLETON *(huskily):*    End there . . . how do you mean?

DR. FELL:    The clock strikes. The mystic hour arrives. Well? Did the ghostly visitor appear?

PENDLETON:    I don't know.

DR. FELL:    You don't know?

PENDLETON:    I lost my head and bolted out of that house as though the devil were after me. Maybe he was.

DR. FELL:    And afterwards?

PENDLETON:    I spent the night at a hotel. Going abroad today was out of the question. I'm a practical man; I had to *know.*

DR. FELL:    You . . . investigated?

PENDLETON:    I got in touch with the telephone people. That phone was disconnected yesterday morning. Besides, I could see that for myself. I can take my living oath there was no wire leading from that phone.

DR. FELL: Yet you heard a voice speaking from the receiver?

PENDLETON: I did.

DR. FELL: Mary Ellen Kimball's voice?

PENDLETON *(after a pause):* Yes.

DR. FELL: I see. Did you find out anything else in your investigations today?

PENDLETON: There's no doubt she's dead, if that's what you mean. I couldn't find her aunt at Kensal Rise . . . the aunt's gone away as a servant or something. But I found the doctor who attended Mary Ellen. She died of pneumonia brought on by . . . *(Hesitates)*

DR. FELL: Brought on by what?

PENDLETON: Well. Brought on by undernourishment. Anyway, she died. Called herself Mrs. Kimball.

DR. FELL *(quickly):* Why did she call herself Mrs. Kimball?

PENDLETON *(just as quickly):* I don't know.

DR. FELL: I must repeat the question, my good sir. It may be the most important thing in the whole affair. Why did she call herself Mrs. Kimball?

PENDLETON: I tell you, I don't know!

DR. FELL *(persuasively):* Mr. Pendleton, I am at the service of anyone with a problem in his head or a trouble on his back. But if you won't tell me the truth about this . . .

PENDLETON: You mean you won't help me?

DR. FELL: How can I?

PENDLETON: Look here, Dr. Fell. I've been through a lot already. I don't propose to be questioned and cross-questioned about something I don't think is important.

DR. FELL: Why not let *me* be the judge of that?

PENDLETON: If you think I'm afraid to go back to that house tonight, you're mistaken. *(Blustering)* I'm not without people I pay, and pay well, to look after me. There's Wilmot, for one.

DR. FELL *(sharply):* Wilmot? Who's Wilmot?

PENDLETON: My chauffeur. He's outside in the car now.

DR. FELL: Is Wilmot by any chance a young man?

PENDLETON: Yes, fairly young. Very *(mockingly)* superior sort of chap, but reliable. Why?

DR. FELL: It may not mean anything. It probably doesn't.

PENDLETON: As a matter of fact, I'd already had a word about this with a friend of mine at Scotland Yard. Superintendent Hadley.

DR. FELL: Oh? You've mentioned this to Hadley?

PENDLETON: Unofficially, of course.

DR. FELL:   And what did *he* say?

PENDLETON:   He told me to see you. I came here, fair and square, to get advice. And do I get advice? No! I get a lot of wrangling and quibbling when I'm trying to tell my story. I can't go to the police; I can't go to you; where *can* I go?

DR. FELL:   If I were less polite, sir, I should tell you.

PENDLETON:   That's your last word?

DR. FELL:   Until you say yours.

PENDLETON *(grimly):*   All right! I'll take it as that. Where's that man-servant of yours? *(Calling) Hoy!*
*(Door opens)*

HOSKINS:   Yes, sir?

PENDLETON:   Get me my hat and coat, please.

HOSKINS:   Got 'em right 'ere, sir. *(Conversationally)* Wind's rising to-night, gentlemen.

DR. FELL:   Blowing hard, is it?

HOSKINS:   Regular gale, and black as your hat.

PENDLETON *(bursting out):*   And you want me to go home alone?

DR. FELL:   Look here, man; why not be sensible? Tell me the whole story.

PENDLETON:   I've told just as much as I'm going to tell this side of eternity. If anything happens to me, it's on your own head. Good night, and I can find my own way out.

DR. FELL *(under his breath):*   Hoskins!

HOSKINS:   Yes, sir?

DR. FELL *(in a low voice):*   When you've seen Mr. Pendleton out, bring my cloak and walking-stick. . . .

HOSKINS:   Stop a bit, sir! You're not . . .

DR. FELL:   Quiet! He's on the stairs; he'll hear you. Close the door.

HOSKINS:   Yes, sir.
*(Door closes)*

DR. FELL *(querulously):*   Now he's made me feel like a selfish hound. I suppose I've got to follow him.

HOSKINS:   You're not going out of the house tonight, sir?

DR. FELL *(with dignity):*   And why not, my good custodian?

HOSKINS:   'Cos you oughtn't to be out at any time, that's why. You haven't got the foggiest idea where you're going; you concentrate across the street against a red light; you walk off Underground platforms onto trains that ain't there . . .

DR. FELL *(with still more dignity):*   If you are implying, my good Hoskins, that I occasionally suffer from a slight . . . a very slight . . . absent-mindedness . . .

HOSKINS *(awed):*   Absent-mindedness, sir?

DR. FELL:    That was the word.

HOSKINS:    So help me, sir, when you was solving that Vickerly case, you came home cold sober and stood for twenty minutes trying to open the front door with a corkscrew.

DR. FELL:    Listen to me, Hoskins.

HOSKINS:    Yes, sir?

DR. FELL:    Our friend Pendleton is going to have a bad night. Probably the worst night of his life. He may be in real danger.

HOSKINS:    If you've got to go out, sir, let me ring Superintendent Hadley and have him meet you.

DR. FELL:    Oh, no, my lad. No. We don't want the police in this.

HOSKINS:    The man's in danger, but you *don't* want the police?

DR. FELL:    That's exactly what I mean. Wait till he's gone, and then get me a taxi. What is he going to see in that house tonight? *What* is he going to see in that house tonight?
*(Music up and down. Sounds of wind and a motorcar, which approaches and stops.)*

TAXI DRIVER:    I'm sorry about the engine trouble, governor. But I couldn't make it any sooner.
*(Car door opens. Grunt suggesting heavy body getting out. Door closes.)*

DR. FELL *(grimly resigned):*    That's all right. It can't be helped. You're sure this is where Mr. Pendleton lives?

DRIVER:    Dead sure, governor. You can't mistake those funny towers and the fir trees growing up the path. *(Breaking off)* Hullo! There's somebody standing by the gate.

DR. FELL *(calling sharply):*    Who's there? Who's there?
*(Superintendent Hadley has a military voice and a no-nonsense manner.)*

HADLEY:    *I'm* here, Fell. And wishing to blazes I'd stayed at the pub.

DR. FELL:    That's not Hadley? Superintendent Hadley?

HADLEY:    Oh, yes, it is. Waiting for twenty minutes in the perishing cold, while . . .

DR. FELL:    But how did *you* get here?

HADLEY *(surprised):*    You sent for me, didn't you?

DR. FELL:    *I* sent for you?

HADLEY:    Hoskins did, anyway. He said it was an urgent matter for the police. He said . . .

DR. FELL:    So the blighter's disobeyed my orders again. *(Breaking off)* That's all, driver. Good night.

DRIVER:    Good night, governor.
*(Taxi moves away)*

HADLEY:    Let me get things straight, Fell. This is George Pendleton's house. I was here two years ago about a little matter of a burglary, and

I know. You didn't drag me here at this hour to discuss that crazy yarn about a dead woman and a ghost telephone?

DR. FELL *(rather testily):*  My good Hadley, I didn't drag you here to discuss anything. I gather, though, you didn't believe the yarn?

HADLEY *(past comment):*  Believe it? For the love of . . . !

DR. FELL:  There's no time to argue that. The point is, did Pendleton get home safely tonight?

HADLEY:  *I* don't know. There's a light in the library, anyway. *(Wind up)* Look up the path, past the fir trees. Those two French windows to the left of the front door.

DR. FELL:  And one of these French windows, you notice, is standing part-way open.

HADLEY:  Well? What about it?

DR. FELL:  It's a fine night for that, isn't it?

HADLEY *(impatiently):*  Maybe it blew open. Maybe Pendleton likes fresh air. Maybe . . .

*(Pamela's voice cries out as though startled.)*

HADLEY:  I *beg* your pardon, miss. It's so dark here I didn't see you.

PAMELA *(tense but composed):*  That's quite all right. But would you mind letting me through the gate, please?

DR. FELL:  Do you by any chance want to go in and see Mr. Pendleton?

PAMELA *(surprised):*  Yes, of course. I . . . why do you ask that?

DR. FELL:  I ask because my friend here is Superintendent Hadley from Scotland Yard . . .

PAMELA *(startled):*  Scotland Yard?

DR. FELL:  And I am Dr. Gideon Fell, an old scatter-brain occasionally found where there's trouble.

PAMELA:  I'm Pamela Bennett. Mr. Pendleton's secretary. I came here because of Mrs. Tancred. She phoned the office today. She said Mr. Pendleton had gone rushing out last night, leaving his suitcases and everything else in the house, and hadn't been back since. He hasn't been in touch with the office, either. Mr. Fraser was worried. He asked me if I'd come round here, and . . . Mr. Pendleton *is* all right, isn't he?

DR. FELL:  I very much fear he isn't.

HADLEY:  Don't talk nonsense, Fell!

DR. FELL:  It may *be* nonsense, of course. I've talked a lot of it in my time. But let's go in and see him, Hadley. Let's face the powers of darkness in their lair. Let's open the gate . . .

*(Metallic creaking of the gate. Then Wilmot speaks: a soft, insinuating, well-bred voice. He is in his middle twenties and speaks as one trying to be agreeable.)*

WILMOT:  If I were you, gentlemen, *I* shouldn't touch that gate.

PAMELA *(crying out):* Who spoke then? *(No reply, except the whistling of the wind)* I heard somebody! Who was it?

WILMOT: You heard *me,* young lady. I'm inside the gate; you're outside. Let's leave it at that.

HADLEY *(exasperated):* Look here, young fellow, what's going on in this place? Who *are* you?

WILMOT: My name is Wilmot. I turn an electric torch round and . . . notice my chauffeur's uniform. Also notice the rifle in my other hand.

HADLEY: I'm a police officer, cocky. What's the idea of the rifle?

WILMOT: The governor's orders are to patrol these grounds and make sure nobody gets in. I'm doing it.

HADLEY: And has anybody got in?

WILMOT: No. Not a living soul.

DR. FELL: That's an interesting choice of phrase, young man. If you're Mr. Pendleton's chauffeur . . .

WILMOT: Such is my humble position, Dr. Fell.

DR. FELL *(sharply):* You know who I am?

WILMOT: As a matter of fact, I just recognized you. I drove the boss to your house tonight. *Is* this man here a police officer?

DR. FELL: Yes. And the young lady beside me is Mr. Pendleton's secretary.

WILMOT: Excuse me if I didn't recognize her. I haven't been on this job very long.

PAMELA: Mr. Pendleton *is* all right, isn't he?

WILMOT: He couldn't be in a happier state. I drove him to Dr. Fell's; I brought him back safely; I delivered him to the mercies of Mrs. Tancred; I went down the street to put the car away . . .

DR. FELL: If you went to put the car away, how can you be sure nobody's got in?

WILMOT *(sharply):* It's impossible!

DR. FELL: Why?

WILMOT: That was half an hour ago!

DR. FELL: He could have died half an hour ago.

PAMELA: Don't *say* that!

WILMOT *(quickly):* His Nibs was upset about something; I'll give you that. He went lurching up the path talking to himself, and Mrs. Tancred couldn't do anything with him.

DR. FELL: What was he talking to himself about?

WILMOT: *I* don't know. Some woman or other. He said he was going to ring her up and dare her to come back again.

DR. FELL *(quietly):* Look here, Hadley. We've *got* to go up there now.

HADLEY: But what in blazes do you think is wrong? He couldn't have been attacked without an outcry. And there hasn't been a sound. Look at this place. Only that little light from the library. Dark, silent, and peaceful as the gra— *(A woman's distant scream, very shrill)* What was that?

PAMELA:   It sounded like a woman's voice!

DR. FELL *(grimly):*   Would anybody like to bet it isn't Mrs. Tancred?

PAMELA:   Look! It *is* Mrs. Tancred! She's coming out of that open French window, and she looks . . .

MRS. TANCRED *(calling):*   Wilmot! Wilmot! Wilmot!

WILMOT *(calling):*   I'm here, Mrs. Tancred! Out by the gate!

*(Mrs. Tancred is almost hysterically frightened, but trying to be steady.)*

MRS. TANCRED:   He said he didn't want any sympathy. All right! He won't *get* any sympathy. Just as though a body didn't try to do the best she could every single day of her life, and . . . and . . . for God's sake, get a doctor!

WILMOT:   You don't mean it's the governor?

MRS. TANCRED:   "If ever I need any sympathy for my unhappy lot" . . . that's just what he said . . . "I'll ask for it." All right! Let him try to ask for it *now,* and see if anybody cares!

HADLEY:   What is it, ma'am? What's wrong?

MRS. TANCRED:   It's murder, that's what it is! He's lying on the floor in the library with the telephone beside him. His face is an awful colour, and I don't think he's breathing.

WILMOT:   There hasn't been a sound out of that house. I swear there hasn't!

MRS. TANCRED:   No, of course there wasn't a sound. All I did was go in and ask him if he wanted some coffee. And there he was in a dim little ugly light, with his face as blue as though he'd had a stroke. . . .

HADLEY:   As though he'd had a stroke, eh? Then what's all this about murder?

MRS. TANCRED:   I tell you, his face . . . ! And then there's the clay tracked across the floor, from the window to where he's lying. There's even wet clay on Mr. Pendleton, as though . . .

HADLEY:   As though . . . what?

MRS. TANCRED *(slowly):*   As though somebody covered with clay had tried to hold him.

*(Music up and down. A door opens.)*

DR. FELL *(musing):*   And this, apparently, is the famous library. This is the place where bogies walk and a telephone talks of its own accord.

PAMELA *(urgently):*   Dr. Fell! Please!

DR. FELL:   "From the hag and the hungry goblin
                That into rags would rend ye:
            And the spirit that stands by the evil lands
                In the book of moons . . . defend ye!"

*(Waking up)* Er . . . I beg your pardon. What's that?

PAMELA:    Dr. Fell, you've got to tell me. Is he . . . dead?

DR. FELL:    No, Miss Bennett. He's not dead. Hadley and Wilmot have carried him upstairs. He's had a bad heart attack. But I'm afraid he'll pull through.

PAMELA *(surprised)*:    You're *afraid* he'll pull through?

DR. FELL:    If Mr. George Pendleton has got a soul, it must be a pretty shabby one. *(Casually)* Don't you think so?

PAMELA *(hesitating)*:    I didn't exactly like him, no. But you get *used* to a person, I suppose. I shouldn't like to think he was . . .

DR. FELL:    Haunted to death?

*(Gust of wind rises strongly. Wooden noise suggesting flapping of window.)*

DR. FELL:    Don't be frightened, Miss Bennett. It's only the French window banging.

PAMELA:    I'm not frightened. At least . . . not much. What did you mean by "haunted to death"?

DR. FELL *(unheeding)*:    There's the claw-footed desk. There's the Venetian mirror where his own reflection scared him. There's the famous telephone. There's the line of clay marks. There's the whole show-piece of death and terror, my dear.

PAMELA *(more loudly)*:    What did you mean by "haunted to death"?

DR. FELL:    Just that, my dear. Literally that.

PAMELA:    You mean he's been haunted by—by a dead person?

DR. FELL:    Oh, no. Not at all. I mean he's been haunted by a very much living person.

PAMELA:    Dr. Fell!

DR. FELL *(musingly)*:    What's your opinion of Mrs. Tancred, by the way? With her demure grey hair and her great devotion?

PAMELA:    What on earth has Mrs. Tancred got to do with this? Or Wilmot or anybody here?

DR. FELL *(with lordly effect)*:    "I can call spirits from the vasty deep." "Ay, but will they come, if you do call them?" *(Changing his tone, distressed)* Especially by telephone. Oh, my eye! Surely it's plain that some person . . . one single person . . . has been trying to scare that man out of his wits? Don't you see now what happened here tonight?

PAMELA:    No, I don't think I do.

DR. FELL:    As Pendleton sat here in the dim little ugly light, a ghostly figure appeared at that French window. It wore long old-fashioned skirts and heavy black veil. It walked towards him, tracking graveyard clay. It stretched out its arms to him, like this . . .

PAMELA:    Dr. Fell, please keep away from me! You look . . .

DR. FELL:   Forgive me. I was *(clearing his throat)* carried away. *(Pause)* Would you care to hear how the whole trick was worked?

PAMELA:   Trick! What trick?

DR. FELL:   Has anyone told you about the ghost-voice on the disconnected telephone?

PAMELA:   Yes, Mrs. Tancred was gabbling something about it. But . . .

DR. FELL:   Suppose you ask, as Pendleton did, to have a telephone disconnected. They disconnect it at the Central Exchange. If you're leaving the house, they come round and collect it later. But, my dear Miss Bennett, I'll tell you what they *don't* do.

PAMELA:   Well?

DR. FELL:   They don't send a man round to yank the whole apparatus off the wall, put it on the desk, and say he'll be back for it next day. That's obvious nonsense.

PAMELA:   You mean Mrs. Tancred wasn't telling the truth when she said that?

DR. FELL:   Oh, no. She was telling the truth. But this "man from the telephone company" was an imposter.

PAMELA:   The man from the telephone company . . . who was he?

DR. FELL:   Can't you guess?

PAMELA:   No, I don't think so. What did he do?

DR. FELL:   He took away the real phone and substituted a "spirit telephone." You don't know what a "spirit telephone" is?

PAMELA:   No, of course not.

DR. FELL:   It's an old device used by fake spiritualists. You see a telephone, without wires, standing on a desk. Like that one on the floor now. You lift the receiver and talk to the dead. Of course, you never really talk into the phone at all.

PAMELA:   But if you don't really talk into the phone, then how . . . ?

DR. FELL:   Fixed underneath the desk is a tiny two-button microphone, with hidden wires leading to another room in the same house. The microphone under the desk picks up every word you think you're saying to that telephone. Am I clear?

PAMELA:   Yes, I think so.

DR. FELL:   The dummy telephone contains a low-power radio receiving unit. Somebody in another room can talk back to you, with every possible ghostly effect . . . Would you mind picking up the telephone now?

PAMELA:   You don't mean it works now?

DR. FELL:   Oh, no. It's been changed. Just pick it up.

PAMELA:   All right. There you are.

DR. FELL:   If Pendleton hadn't rung Kensal Green 1-9-3-3, then rest assured that same number would have rung *him*.

PAMELA: The scheme couldn't fail either way?

DR. FELL: Correct.

PAMELA *(tensely):* The ghost-voice, you said, came from a room in this house?

DR. FELL: Yes. I can't tell you which one, because the mechanism's been removed.

PAMELA: Then the person responsible for it must *live* in this house.

DR. FELL: Not necessarily. You see, there's one thing I guess . . . I firmly believe . . . but I can't prove.

PAMELA: Oh? And what's that?

DR. FELL: Tell me, Miss Bennett, just *why* did you work this whole trick? Why did you try to scare your father to death? *(Crash of an object dropped on the floor; Dr. Fell continues mildly.)* Don't drop the telephone, my dear. Pendleton surely *is* your father, isn't he? And the late Mary Ellen Kimball was your mother?

PAMELA *(through her teeth):* I do not like you, Doctor Fell. The reason why I cannot tell . . .

DR. FELL *(heartily):* Now I, on the other hand, admire you tremendously. *(Deprecating)* But my dear girl, hang it all, I knew you must be behind this when I heard your fiancé is a radio technician.

PAMELA: You leave Frank out of this!

DR. FELL: This fiancé, I imagine, installed the ghost-mechanism and took it away today. He probably thought it was only a joke.

PAMELA: He did! I swear he did!

DR. FELL: There was surely a reason, you see, why Mary Ellen Kimball called herself Mrs. Kimball. *You* led Pendleton to the wrong gate in the cemetery, past that neglected grave. *You* put it into his mind. *You* suggested the telephone number. *You* stole his latchkey to this house, since he had it at the office that morning. You needed that key to come and go as you liked, and impersonate the two voices on the phone. Then when you were ready for your last appearance tonight . . .

PAMELA *(fiercely):* Is there any need to go on with this? He killed her.

DR. FELL *(startled):* You mean Pendleton killed your mother?

PAMELA: Oh, not cleanly. Not with a knife or a bullet or poison. All he did was break her heart and leave her to starve.

DR. FELL: Did he know about you?

PAMELA: He knew there *was* a child; that's all.

DR. FELL: Yes, I thought he knew it.

PAMELA: But she was too proud to ask for anything. And he *(mimicking)* "had other things to think about." I think I've dreamed all my life of getting close to him, one day, when he didn't know who I was.

DR. FELL:    For the love of Mike, go easy! If somebody should come in here now . . .

PAMELA:    I've done what I wanted to do. I've torn his whole rotten life in pieces; and there he is gasping for breath upstairs; and I'm glad! I'm . . . *(Breaking down)* Oh, God, I can't go on with this! Call your superintendent and give the game away. *I'm* not sorry!

DR. FELL *(amazed):*    Just one moment. Hey! You don't think *I'm* going to tell Hadley anything?

PAMELA *(taken aback):*    Aren't you? Isn't that why you're here?

DR. FELL:    On the contrary, I've been trying to keep the police away from this house all evening.

PAMELA:    What's the good of trying to hide it, even if I wanted to? *They'll* find out!

DR. FELL:    Are you quite sure they'll find out?

PAMELA:    Look at the clay marks on the floor.

DR. FELL:    Those footprints can't be identified, you know. They're only smudges.

PAMELA:    I think I can hear somebody outside in the hall. If it's Super-intendent Hadley . . .

DR. FELL *(grimly):*    If it is, my dear, and you dare to say one word about this . . .

PAMELA:    Then who made the footprints?

DR. FELL *(blandly):*    Didn't you know? Why, Pendleton made them himself.

PAMELA:    What on earth are you talking about?

DR. FELL:    Hadley thinks the esteemed gentleman is mad. Obviously, of course, he is mad. He kept dashing to that window on the lookout for a pursuing ghost. So he tracked in clay soil from the garden, and col-lapsed here when he heard an imaginary noise.

PAMELA:    But his shoes! There'll be no clay on his shoes!

DR. FELL:    Oh, yes, there will. Please remember that the gentleman didn't come home last night or take a suitcase with him. His shoes, if I'm not mistaken, will still bear excellent traces of the clay he really did get yesterday in Kensal Green cemetery. *(Complacently)* I often think that I should have made an admirable criminal myself.

HADLEY *(from a distance):*    Dr. Fell! Dr. Fell! Where are you?

DR. FELL *(galvanized):*    There's Hadley now! If you don't keep your head and brace up, I'll come and haunt you myself. Don't turn on the tears now, when you've come through all the rest of it with a poker face. Just keep repeating after me, "I do not like you, Doctor Fell . . ."

*(Door opens.)*

HADLEY:    Look here, my fat detective; there's been no crime committed in this place. Pendleton's own shoes . . .

DR. FELL *(loudly):*    Oh, Miss Bennett, what were you saying?

PAMELA *(hysterically):*    Nothing! Nothing at . . .

DR. FELL *(reciting, still more loudly):*    I do not like you, Doctor Fell, the reason why I cannot tell . . .

PAMELA *(almost crying):*    But this I know, and know full well . . . I think *I like you,* Dr. Fell!
    *(Music up)*

# *Invisible Hands*

Twenty-four years passed between the first broadcast of "The Dead Sleep Lightly" and the publication of Dr. Fell's final short case. "Invisible Hands" was published under the title "King Arthur's Chair" in the British magazine *Lilliput,* August 1957. When it had its first American publication in *Ellery Queen's Mystery Magazine,* April 1958, it was retitled "Death By Invisible Hands." Although all other Dr. Fell novels and short stories appeared under Carr's own name, both printings of this tale were attributed to "Carter Dickson." I have no idea why. Unlike Carr's earlier stories, many of which have the relaxed storytelling mood of let's-discuss-this-over-our-port-and-cigars, "Invisible Hands" begins with emotions already near the snapping point, and we are ready for the impossible crime of a woman strangled on a beach with only her own footprints leading to the body.

# Invisible Hands

He could never understand afterward why he felt uneasiness, even to the point of fear, before he saw the beach at all.

Night and fancies? But how far can fancies go?

It was a steep track down to the beach. The road, however, was good, and he could rely on his car. And yet, halfway down, before he could even taste the sea-wind or hear the rustle of the sea, Dan Fraser felt sweat on his forehead. A nerve jerked in the calf of his leg over the foot brake.

"Look, this is damn silly!" he thought to himself. He thought it with a kind of surprise, as when he had first known fear in wartime long ago. But the fear had been real enough, no matter how well he concealed it, and they believed he never felt it.

A dazzle of lightning lifted ahead of him. The night was too hot. This enclosed road, bumping the springs of his car, seemed pressed down in an airless hollow.

After all, Dan Fraser decided, he had everything to be thankful for. He was going to see Brenda; he was the luckiest man in London. If she chose to spend weekends as far away as North Cornwall, he was glad to drag himself there—even a day late.

Brenda's image rose before him, as clearly as the flash of lightning. He always seemed to see her half laughing, half pouting, with light on her yellow hair. She was beautiful; she was desirable. It would only be disloyalty to think any trickiness underlay her intense, naïve ways.

Brenda Lestrange always got what she wanted. And she had wanted him, though God alone knew why: he was no prize package at all. Again, in imagination, he saw her against the beat and shuffle of music in a night club. Brenda's shoulders rose from a low-cut silver gown, her eyes as blue and wide-spaced as the eternal Eve's.

You'd have thought she would have preferred a dasher, a roaring bloke like Toby Curtis, who had all the women after him. But that, as Joyce had intimated, might be the trouble. Toby Curtis couldn't see Brenda for all the rest of the crowd. And so Brenda preferred—

Well, then, what was the matter with him?

He would see Brenda in a few minutes. There ought to have been joy bells in the tower, not bats in the—

*Easy!*

He was out in the open now, at sea level. Dan Fraser drove bumpingly along scrub grass, at the head of a few shallow terraces leading down to the private beach. Ahead of him, facing seaward, stood the overlarge, overdecorated bungalow which Brenda had rather grandly named "The King's House."

And there wasn't a light in it—not a light showing at only a quarter past ten.

Dan cut the engine, switched off the lights, and got out of the car. In the darkness he could hear the sea charge the beach as an army might have charged it.

Twisting open the handle of the car's trunk, he dragged out his suitcase. He closed the compartment with a slam which echoed out above the swirl of water. This part of the Cornish coast was too lonely, too desolate, but it was the first time such a thought had ever occurred to him.

He went to the house, round the side and toward the front. His footsteps clacked loudly on the crazy-paved path on the side. And even in a kind of luminous darkness from the white of the breakers ahead, he saw why the bungalow showed no lights.

All the curtains were drawn on the windows—on this side, at least.

When Dan hurried round to the front door, he was almost running. He banged the iron knocker on the door, then hammered it again. As he glanced over his shoulder, another flash of lightning paled the sky to the west.

It showed him the sweep of gray sand. It showed black water snakily edged with foam. In the middle of the beach, unearthly, stood the small natural rock formation—shaped like a low-backed armchair, eternally facing out to sea—which for centuries had been known as King Arthur's Chair.

The white eye of the lightning closed. Distantly there was a shock of thunder.

This whole bungalow couldn't be deserted! Even if Edmund Ireton and Toby Curtis were at the former's house some distance along the coast, Brenda herself must be here. And Joyce Ray. And the two maids.

Dan stopped hammering the knocker. He groped for and found the knob of the door.

The door was unlocked.

He opened it on brightness. In the hall, rather overdecorated like so many of Brenda's possessions, several lamps shone on gaudy furniture and a polished floor. But the hall was empty too.

With the wind whisking and whistling at his back Dan went in and kicked the door shut behind him. He had no time to give a hail. At the back of the hall a door opened. Joyce Ray, Brenda's cousin, walked toward him, her arms hanging limply at her sides and her enormous eyes like a sleepwalker's.

"Then you did get here," said Joyce, moistening dry lips. "You did get here, after all."

"I—"

Dan stopped. The sight of her brought a new realization. It didn't explain his uneasiness or his fear—but it did explain much.

Joyce was the quiet one, the dark one, the unobtrusive one, with her glossy black hair and her subdued elegance. But she was the poor relation, and Brenda never let her forget it. Dan merely stood and stared at her. Suddenly Joyce's eyes lost their sleepwalker's look. They were gray eyes, with very black lashes; they grew alive and vivid, as if she could read his mind.

"Joyce," he blurted, "I've just understood something. And I never understood it before. But I've got to tell—"

"Stop!" Joyce cried.

Her mouth twisted. She put up a hand as if to shade her eyes.

"I know what you want to say," she went on. "But you're not to say it! Do you hear me?"

"Joyce, I don't know why we're standing here yelling at each other. Anyway, I—I didn't mean to tell you. Not yet, anyway. I mean, I must tell Brenda—"

"You can't tell Brenda!" Joyce cried.

"What's that?"

"You can't tell her anything, ever again," said Joyce. "Brenda's dead."

There are some words which at first do not even shock or stun. You just don't believe them. They can't be true. Very carefully Dan Fraser put his suitcase down on the floor and straightened up again.

"The police," said Joyce, swallowing hard, "have been here since early this morning. They're not here now. They've taken her away to the mortuary. That's where she'll sleep tonight."

Still Dan said nothing.

"Mr. —Mr. Edmund Ireton," Joyce went on, "has been here ever since it happened. So has Toby Curtis. So, fortunately, has a man named Dr. Gideon Fell. Dr. Fell's a bumbling old duffer, a very learned man or something. He's a friend of the police; he's kind; he's helped soften things. All the same, Dan, if you'd been here last night—"

"I couldn't get away. I told Brenda so."

"Yes, I know all that talk about hard-working journalists. But if you'd only been here, Dan, it might not have happened at all."

"Joyce, for God's sake!"

Then there was a silence in the bright, quiet room. A stricken look crept into Joyce's eyes.

"Dan, I'm sorry. I'm terribly sorry. I was feeling dreadful and so, I suppose, I had to take it out on the first person handy."

"That's all right. But how did she die?" Then desperately he began to surmise. "Wait, I've got it! She went out to swim early this morning, just as usual? She's been diving off those rocks on the headland again? And—"

"No," said Joyce. "She was strangled."

*"Strangled?"*

What Joyce tried to say was "murdered." Her mouth shook and faltered round the syllables; she couldn't say them; her thoughts, it seemed, shied back and ran from the very word. But she looked at Dan steadily.

"Brenda went out to swim early this morning, yes."

"Well?"

"At least, she must have. I didn't see her. I was still asleep in that back bedroom she always gives me. Anyway, she went down there in a red swim suit and a white beach robe."

Automatically Dan's eyes moved over to an oil painting above the fireplace. Painted by a famous R.A., it showed a scene from classical antiquity; it was called *The Lovers,* and left little to the imagination. It had always been Brenda's favorite because the female figure in the picture looked so much like her.

"Well!" said Joyce, throwing out her hands. "You know what Brenda always does. She takes off her beach robe and spreads it out over King Arthur's Chair. She sits down in the chair and smokes a cigarette and looks out at the sea before she goes into the water.

"The beach robe was still in that rock chair," Joyce continued with an effort, "when I came downstairs at half-past seven. But Brenda wasn't. She hadn't even put on her bathing cap. Somebody had strangled her with that silk scarf she wore with the beach robe. It was twisted so tightly into her neck they couldn't get it out. She was lying on the sand in front of the chair, on her back, in the red swim suit, with her face black and swollen. You could see her clearly from the terrace."

Dan glanced at the flesh tints of *The Lovers,* then quickly looked away.

Joyce, the cool and competent, was holding herself under restraint.

"I can only thank my lucky stars," she burst out, "I didn't run out there. I mean, from the flagstones of the lowest terrace out across the sand. They stopped me."

" 'They' stopped you? Who?"

"Mr. Ireton and Toby. Or, rather, Mr. Ireton did; Toby wouldn't have thought of it."

"But—"

"Toby, you see, had come over here a little earlier. But he was at the back of the bungalow, practising with a .22 target rifle. I heard him once. Mr. Ireton had just got there. All three of us walked out on the terrace at once. And saw her."

"Listen, Joyce. What difference does it make whether or not you ran out across the sand? Why were you so lucky they stopped you?"

"Because if they hadn't, the police might have said I did it."

"Did it?"

"Killed Brenda," Joyce answered clearly. "In all that stretch of sand, Dan, there weren't any footprints except Brenda's own."

"Now hold on!" he protested. "She—she *was* killed with that scarf of hers?"

"Oh, yes. The police and even Dr. Fell don't doubt that."

"Then how could anybody, anybody at all, go out across the sand and come back without leaving a footprint?"

"That's just it. The police don't know and they can't guess. That's why they're in a flat spin, and Dr. Fell will be here again tonight."

In her desperate attempt to speak lightly, as if all this didn't matter, Joyce failed. Her face was white. But again the expression of the dark-fringed eyes changed, and she hesitated.

"Dan—"

"Yes?"

"You do understand, don't you, why I was so upset when you came charging in and said what you did?"

"Yes, of course."

"Whatever you had to tell me, or thought you had to tell me—"

"About—us?"

"About anything! You do see that you must forget it and not mention it again? Not ever?"

"I see why I can't mention it now. With Brenda dead, it wouldn't even be decent to think of it." He could not keep his eyes off that mocking picture. "But is the future dead too? If I happen to have been an idiot and thought I was head over heels gone on Brenda when all the time it was really—"

*"Dan!"*

There were five doors opening into the gaudy hall, which had too many mirrors. Joyce whirled round to look at every door, as if she feared an ambush behind each.

"For heaven's sake, keep your voice down," she begged. "Practically every word that's said can be heard all over the house. I said never, and I meant it. If you'd spoken a week ago, even twenty-four hours ago, it might have been different. Do you think I didn't want you to? But now it's too late!"

"Why?"

"May *I* answer that question?" interrupted a new, dry, rather quizzical voice.

Dan had taken a step toward her, intensely conscious of her attractiveness. He stopped, burned with embarrassment, as one of the five doors opened.

Mr. Edmund Ireton, shortish and thin and dandified in his middle fifties, emerged with his usual briskness. There was not much gray in his polished black hair. His face was a benevolent satyr's.

"Forgive me," he said.

Behind him towered Toby Curtis, heavy and handsome and fair-haired, in a bulky tweed jacket. Toby began to speak, but Mr. Ireton's gesture silenced him before he could utter a sound.

"Forgive me," he repeated. "But what Joyce says is quite true. Every word can be overheard here, even with the rain pouring down. If you go on shouting and Dr. Fell hears it, you will land that girl in serious danger."

"Danger?" demanded Toby Curtis. He had to clear his throat. "What danger could *Dan* get her into?"

Mr. Ireton, immaculate in flannels and shirt and thin pullover, stalked to the mantelpiece. He stared up hard at *The Lovers* before turning round.

"The Psalmist tells us," he said dryly, "that all is vanity. Has none of you ever noticed—God forgive me for saying so—that Brenda's most outstanding trait was her vanity?"

His glance flashed toward Joyce, who abruptly turned away and pressed her hands over her face.

"Appalling vanity. Scratch that vanity deeply enough and our dearest Brenda would have committed murder."

"Aren't you getting this backwards?" asked Dan. "Brenda didn't commit any murder. It was Brenda—"

"Ah!" Mr. Ireton pounced. "And there might be a lesson in that, don't you think?"

"Look here, you're not saying she strangled herself with her own scarf?"

"No—but hear what I do say. Our Brenda, no doubt, had many passions and many fancies. But there was only one man she loved or ever wanted to marry. It was not Mr. Dan Fraser."

"Then who was it?" asked Toby.

"You."

Toby's amazement was too genuine to be assumed. The color drained out of his face. Once more he had to clear his throat.

"So help me," he said, "I never knew it! I never imagined—"

"No, of course you didn't," Mr. Ireton said even more dryly. A goatish amusement flashed across his face and was gone. "Brenda, as a rule, could get any man she chose. So she turned Mr. Fraser's head and became engaged to him. It was to sting you, Mr. Curtis, to make you jealous. And you never noticed. While all the time Joyce Ray and Dan Fraser were eating their hearts out for each other; and *he* never noticed either."

Edmund Ireton wheeled round.

"You may lament my bluntness, Mr. Fraser. You may want to wring my neck, as I see you do. But can you deny one word I say?"

"No." In honesty Dan could not deny it.

"Well! Then be very careful when you face the police, both of you, or they will see it too. Joyce already has a strong motive. She is Brenda's only relative, and inherits Brenda's money. If they learn she wanted Brenda's fiancé, they will have her in the dock for murder."

"That's enough!" blurted Dan, who dared not look at Joyce. "You've made it clear. All right, stop there!"

"Oh, I had intended to stop. If you are such fools that you won't help yourselves, I must help you. That's all."

It was Toby Curtis who strode forward.

"Dan, don't let him bluff you!" Toby said. "In the first place, they can't arrest anybody for this. You weren't here. I know—"

"I've heard about it, Toby."

"Look," insisted Toby. "When the police finished measuring and photographing and taking casts of Brenda's footprints, I did some measuring myself."

Edmund Ireton smiled. "Are *you* attempting to solve this mystery, Mr. Curtis?"

"I didn't say that." Toby spoke coolly. "But I might have a question or two for you. Why have you had your knife into me all day?"

"Frankly, Mr. Curtis, because I envy you."

"You—*what?*"

"So far as women are concerned, young man, I have not your advantages. *I* had no romantic boyhood on a veldt-farm in South Africa. *I* never learned to drive a span of oxen and flick a fly off the leader's ear with my whip. *I* was never taught to be a spectacular horseman and rifle shot."

"Oh, turn it up!"

" 'Turn it up?' Ah, I see. And was that the sinister question you had for me?"

"No. Not yet. You're too tricky."

"My profoundest thanks."

"Look, Dan," Toby insisted. "You've seen that rock formation they call King Arthur's Chair?"

"Toby, I've seen it fifty times," Dan said. "But I still don't understand—"

"And I don't understand," suddenly interrupted Joyce, without turning round, "why they made me sit there where Brenda had been sitting. It was horrible."

"Oh, they were only reconstructing the crime." Toby spoke rather grandly. "But the question, Dan, is how anybody came near that chair without leaving a footprint?"

"Quite."

"Nobody could have," Toby said just as grandly. "The murderer, for instance, couldn't have come from the direction of the sea. Why? Because the highest point at high tide, where the water might have blotted out footprints, is more than twenty feet in front of the chair. More than twenty feet!"

"Er—one moment," said Mr. Ireton, twitching up a finger. "Surely Inspector Tregellis said the murderer must have crept up and caught her from the back? Before she knew it?"

"That won't do either. From the flagstones of the terrace to the back of the chair is at least twenty feet, too. Well, Dan? Do you see any way out of that one?"

Dan, not normally slow-witted, was so concentrating on Joyce that he could think of little else. She was cut off from him, drifting away from him, forever out of reach just when he had found her. But he tried to think.

"Well . . . could somebody have jumped there?"

"Ho!" scoffed Toby, who was himself a broad jumper and knew better. "That was the first thing they thought of."

"And that's out, too?"

"Definitely. An Olympic champion in good form might have done it, if he'd had any place for a running start and any place to land. But he hadn't. There was *no* mark in the sand. He couldn't have landed on the chair, strangled Brenda at his leisure, and then hopped back like a jumping bean. Now could he?"

"But somebody did it, Toby! It happened!"

"How?"

"I don't know."

"You seem rather proud of this, Mr. Curtis," Edmund Ireton said smoothly.

"Proud?" exclaimed Toby, losing color again.

"These romantic boyhoods—"

Toby did not lose his temper. But he had declared war.

"All right, gaffer. I've been very grateful for your hospitality, at that bungalow of yours, when we've come down here for weekends. All the same, you've been going on for hours about who I am and what I am. Who are *you?*"

"I beg your pardon?"

"For two or three years," Toby said, "you've been hanging about with us. Especially with Brenda and Joyce. Who are you? What are you?"

"I am an observer of life," Mr. Ireton answered tranquilly. "A student of human nature. And—shall I say?—a courtesy uncle to both young ladies."

"Is that all you were? To either of them?"

"Toby!" exclaimed Joyce, shocked out of her fear.

She whirled round, her gaze going instinctively to Dan, then back to Toby.

"Don't worry, old girl," said Toby, waving his hand at her. "This is no reflection on you." He kept looking steadily at Mr. Ireton.

"Continue," Mr. Ireton said politely.

"You claim Joyce is in danger. She isn't in any danger at all," said Toby, "as long as the police don't know how Brenda was strangled."

"They will discover it, Mr. Curtis. Be sure they will discover it!"

"You're trying to protect Joyce?"

"Naturally."

"And that's why you warned Dan not to say he was in love with her?"

"Of course. What else?"

Toby straightened up, his hand inside the bulky tweed jacket.

"Then why didn't you take him outside, rain or no, and tell him on the quiet? Why did *you* shout out that Dan was in love with Joyce, and she was in love with him, and give 'em a motive for the whole house to hear?"

Edmund Ireton opened his mouth, and shut it again.

It was a blow under the guard, all the more unexpected because it came from Toby Curtis.

Mr. Ireton stood motionless under the painting of *The Lovers*. The expression of the pictured Brenda, elusive and mocking, no longer matched his own. Whereupon, while nerves were strained and still nobody spoke, Dan Fraser realized that there was a dead silence because the rain had stopped.

Small night-noises, the creak of woodwork or a drip of water from the eaves, intensified the stillness. Then they heard footsteps, as heavy as those of an elephant, slowly approaching behind another of the doors. The footfalls, heavy and slow and creaking, brought a note of doom.

Into the room, wheezing and leaning on a stick, lumbered a man so enormous that he had to maneuver himself sideways through the door.

His big mop of gray-streaked hair had tumbled over one ear. His eyeglasses, with a broad black ribbon, were stuck askew on his nose. His big face would ordinarily have been red and beaming, with chuckles animating several chins. Now it was only absent-minded, his bandit's moustache outthrust.

"Aha!" he said in a rumbling voice. He blinked at Dan with an air of refreshed interest. "I think you must be Mr. Fraser, the last of this rather curious weekend party? H'm. Yes. Your obedient servant, sir. I am Gideon Fell."

Dr. Fell wore a black cloak as big as a tent and carried a shovel-hat in his other hand. He tried to bow and make a flourish with his stick, endangering all the furniture near him.

The others stood very still. Fear was as palpable as the scent after rain.

"Yes, I've heard of you," said Dan. His voice rose in spite of himself. "But you're rather far from home, aren't you? I suppose you had some—er—antiquarian interest in King Arthur's Chair?"

Still Dr. Fell blinked at him. For a second it seemed that chuckles would jiggle his chins and waistcoat, but he only shook his head.

"Antiquarian interest? My dear sir!" Dr. Fell wheezed gently. "If there were any association with a semi-legendary King Arthur, it would be at Tintagel much farther south. No, I was here on holiday. This morning Inspector Tregellis fascinated me with the story of a fantastic murder. I returned tonight for my own reasons."

Mr. Ireton, at ease again, matched the other's courtesy. "May I ask what these reasons were?"

"First, I wished to question the two maids. They have a room at the back, as Miss Ray has; and this afternoon, you may remember, they were still rather hysterical."

"And that is all?"

"H'mf. Well, no." Dr. Fell scowled. "Second, I wanted to detain all of you here for an hour or two. Third, I must make sure of the motive for this crime. And I am happy to say that I have made very sure."

Joyce could not control herself. "Then you did overhear everything!"

"Eh?"

"Every word that man said!"

Despite Dan's signals, Joyce nodded toward Mr. Ireton and poured out the words. "But I swear I hadn't anything to do with Brenda's death. What I told you today was perfectly true: I don't want her money and I won't touch it. As for my—my private affairs," and Joyce's face flamed, "everybody seems to know all about them except Dan and me. Please, please pay no attention to what that man has been saying."

Dr. Fell blinked at her in an astonishment which changed to vast distress.

"But, my dear young lady!" he rumbled. "We never for a moment believed you did. No, no! Archons of Athens, no!" exclaimed Dr. Fell, as though at incredible absurdity. "As for what your friend Mr. Ireton may have been saying, I did not hear it. I suspect it was only what he told me today, and it did supply the motive. But it was not your motive."

"Please, is this true? You're not trying to trap me?"

"Do I really strike you," Dr. Fell asked gently, "as being that sort of person? Nothing was more unlikely than that you killed your cousin, especially in the way she was killed."

"Do you know how she was killed?"

"Oh, *that,*" grunted Dr. Fell, waving the point away too. "That was the simplest part of the whole business."

He lumbered over, reflected in the mirrors, and put down stick and shovel-hat on a table. Afterward he faced them with a mixture of distress and apology.

"It may surprise you," he said, "that an old scatterbrain like myself can observe anything at all. But I have an unfair advantage over the police. I began life as a schoolmaster: I have had more experience with habitual liars. Hang it all, think!"

"Of what?"

"The facts!" said Dr. Fell, making a hideous face. "According to the maids, Sonia and Dolly, Miss Brenda Lestrange went down to swim at ten minutes to seven this morning. Both Dolly and Sonia were awake, but did not get up. Some eight or ten minutes later, Mr. Toby Curtis began practising with a target rifle some distance away behind the bungalow."

"Don't look at me!" exclaimed Toby. "That rifle has nothing to do with it. Brenda wasn't shot."

"Sir," said Dr. Fell with much patience, "I am aware of that."

"Then what are you hinting at?"

"Sir," said Dr. Fell, "you will oblige me if you too don't regard every question as a trap. I have a trap for the murderer, and the murderer alone. You fired a number of shots—the maids heard you and saw you." He turned to Joyce. "I believe you heard too?"

"I heard one shot," answered the bewildered Joyce, "as I told Dan. About seven o'clock, when I got up and dressed."

"Did you look out of the windows?"

"No."

"What happened to that rifle afterwards? Is it here now?"

"No," Toby almost yelled. "I took it back to Ireton's after we found Brenda. But if the rifle had nothing to do with it, and I had nothing to do with it, then what the hell's the point?"

Dr. Fell did not reply for a moment. Then he made another hideous face. "We know," he rumbled, "that Brenda Lestrange wore a beach robe, a bathing suit, and a heavy silk scarf knotted round her neck. Miss Ray?"

"Y-yes?"

"I am not precisely an authority on women's clothes," said Dr. Fell. "As a rule I should notice nothing odd unless I passed Madge Wildfire or Lady Godiva. I have seen men wear a scarf with a beach robe, but is it customary for women to wear a scarf as well?"

There was a pause.

"No, of course it isn't," said Joyce. "I can't speak for everybody, but I never do. It was just one of Brenda's fancies. She always did."

"Aha!" said Dr. Fell. "The murderer was counting on that."

"On what?"

"On her known conduct. Let me show you rather a grisly picture of a murder."

Dr. Fell's eyes were squeezed shut. From inside his cloak and pocket he fished out an immense meerschaum pipe. Firmly under the impression that he had filled and lighted the pipe, he put the stem in his mouth and drew at it.

"Miss Lestrange," he said, "goes down to the beach. She takes off her robe. Remember that, it's very important. She spreads out the robe in King Arthur's Chair and sits down. She is still wearing the scarf, knotted tightly in a broad band round her neck. She is about the same height as you, Miss Ray. She is held there, at the height of her shoulders, by a curving rock formation deeply bedded in sand."

Dr. Fell paused and opened his eyes.

"The murderer, we believe, catches her from the back. She sees and hears nothing until she is seized. Intense pressure on the carotid arteries, here at either side of the neck under the chin, will strike her unconscious within seconds and dead within minutes. When her body is released, it should fall straight forward. Instead, what happens?"

To Dan, full of relief ever since danger had seemed to leave Joyce, it was as if a shutter had flown open in his brain.

"She was lying on her back," Dan said. "Joyce told me so. Brenda was lying flat on her back with her head towards the sea. And that means—"

"Yes?"

"It means she was twisted or spun round in some way when she fell. It has something to do with that infernal scarf—I've thought so from the first. Dr. Fell! Was Brenda killed with the scarf?"

"In one sense, yes. In another sense, no."

"You can't have it both ways! Either she was killed with the scarf, or she wasn't."

"Not necessarily," said Dr. Fell.

"Then let's all retire to a loony bin," Dan suggested, "because nothing makes any sense at all. The murderer still couldn't have walked out there without leaving tracks. Finally, I agree with Toby: what's the point of the rifle? How does a .22 rifle figure in all this?"

"Because of its sound."

Dr. Fell took the pipe out of his mouth. Dan wondered why he had ever thought the learned doctor's eyes were vague. Magnified behind the glasses on the broad black ribbon, they were not vague at all.

"A .22 rifle," he went on in his big voice, "has a distinctive noise. Fired in the open air or anywhere else, it sounds exactly like the noise made by the real instrument used in this crime."

"Real instrument? What noise?"

"The crack of a blacksnake whip," replied Dr. Fell.

Edmund Ireton, looking very tired and ten years older, went over and sat down in an easy chair. Toby Curtis took one step backward, then another.

"In South Africa," said Dr. Fell, "I have never seen the very long whip which drivers of long ox spans use. But in America I have seen the blacksnake whip, and it can be twenty-four feet long. You yourselves must have watched it used in a variety turn on the stage."

Dr. Fell pointed his pipe at them.

"Remember?" he asked. "The user of the whip stands some distance away facing his girl-assistant. There is a vicious crack. The end of the whip coils two or three times round the girl's neck. She is not hurt. But she would be in difficulties if he pulled the whip towards him. She would be in grave danger if she were held back and could not move.

"Somebody planned a murder with a whip like that. He came here early in the morning. The whip, coiled round his waist, was hidden by a loose and bulky tweed jacket. Please observe the jacket Toby Curtis is wearing now."

Toby's voice went high when he screeched out one word. It may have been protest, defiance, a jeer, or all three.

"Stop this!" cried Joyce, who had again turned away.

"Continue, I beg," Mr. Ireton said.

"In the dead hush of morning," said Dr. Fell, "he could not hide the loud crack of the whip. But what could he do?"

"He could mask it," said Edmund Ireton.

"Just that! He was always practising with a .22 rifle. So he fired several shots, behind the bungalow, to establish his presence. Afterwards nobody would notice when the crack of the whip—that single, isolated 'shot' heard by Miss Ray—only seemed to come from behind the house."

"Then, actually, he was—?"

"On the terrace, twenty feet behind a victim held immovable in the curve of a stone chair. The end of the whip coiled round the scarf. Miss Lestrange's breath was cut off instantly. Under the pull of a powerful arm she died in seconds.

"On the stage, you recall, a lift and twist dislodges the whip from the girl-assistant's neck. Toby Curtis had a harder task; the scarf was so embedded in her neck that she seemed to have been strangled with it. He *could* dislodge it. But only with a powerful whirl and lift of the arm which spun her up and round, to fall face upwards. The whip snaked back to him with no trace in the sand. Afterwards he had only to take the whip back to Mr. Ireton's house, under pretext of returning the rifle. He had committed a murder which, in his vanity, he thought undetectable. That's all."

"But it can't be all!" said Dan. "Why should Toby have killed her? His motive—"

"His motive was offended vanity. Mr. Edmund Ireton as good as told you so, I fancy. He had certainly hinted as much to me."

Edmund Ireton rose shakily from the chair.

"I am no judge or executioner," he said. "I—I am detached from life. I only observe. If I guessed why this was done—"

"You could never speak straight out?" Dr. Fell asked sardonically.

"No!"

"And yet that was the tragic irony of the whole affair. Miss Lestrange wanted Toby Curtis, as he wanted her. But, being a woman, her pretense of indifference and contempt was too good. He believed it. Scratch her vanity deeply enough and she would have committed murder. Scratch *his* vanity deeply enough—"

"Lies!" said Toby.

"Look at him, all of you!" said Dr. Fell. "Even when he's accused of murder, he can't take his eyes off a mirror."

*"Lies!"*

"She laughed at him," the big voice went on, "and so she had to die. Brutally and senselessly he killed a girl who would have been his for the asking. That is what I meant by tragic irony."

Toby had retreated across the room until his back bumped against a wall. Startled, he looked behind him; he had banged against another mirror.

"Lies!" he kept repeating. "You can talk and talk and talk. But there's not a single damned thing you can prove!"

"Sir," inquired Dr. Fell, "are you sure?"

"Yes!"

"I warned you," said Dr. Fell, "that I returned tonight partly to detain all of you for an hour or so. It gave Inspector Tregellis time to search Mr. Ireton's house, and the Inspector has since returned. I further warned you that I questioned the maids, Sonia and Dolly, who today were only incoherent. My dear sir, you underestimate your personal attractions."

Now it was Joyce who seemed to understand. But she did not speak.

"Sonia, it seems," and Dr. Fell looked hard at Toby, "has quite a fondness for you. When she heard that last isolated 'shot' this morning, she looked out of the window again. You weren't there. This was so strange that she ran out to the front terrace to discover where you were. She saw you."

The door by which Dr. Fell had entered was still open. His voice lifted and echoed through the hall.

"Come in, Sonia!" he called. "After all, you are a witness to the murder. You, Inspector, had better come in too."

Toby Curtis blundered back, but there was no way out. There was only a brief glimpse of Sonia's swollen, tear-stained face. Past her marched a massive figure in uniform, carrying what he had found hidden in the other house.

Inspector Tregellis was reflected everywhere in the mirrors, with the long coils of the whip over his arm. And he seemed to be carrying not a whip but a coil of rope—gallows rope.

# HISTORICAL MYSTERY AND ROMANCE

# The Dim Queen

"The Dim Queen" is one of John Dickson Carr's earliest stories. He was only nineteen years old when it was published in his college literary magazine, *The Haverfordian,* May 1926; this is its first book publication. As a young man, Carr was almost equally drawn between writing historical romance and detective stories. At Haverford, he wrote at least six tales with period settings, and in Paris from 1927 to 1928 he wrote and then destroyed a historical novel filled with what he described as "gadzookses and horseplay." "The Dim Queen" is a youthful work, especially in its viewpoint of women (which could have been written only by an inexperienced man) and in its heaping helpings of atmospheric writing, but it is a gripping story.

# The Dim Queen

## I

He lost a fortune at the gaming-table and won the cross of honor at Austerlitz. The banners of France went flaring on, but he was left in the wake of the army where the men with the bandaged heads lie and do not move. Often they would see him, with his gait that stumbled from the musket-balls, go limping around to the stricken, and he would smile dimly like the somnambulist of a mighty dream and say, "La patrie." That is all.

The tramp of the army passed. There was no martial music for the women with the wild wet eyes. Napoleon had gone to Elba; a Bourbon ruled in France. And while Europe was furrowed with the track of cannon that had marked the conqueror's way, Retif of Picardy mounted his horse. When they saw him ride to the south they knew that he would return, and his black figure up against the sky was a symbol. It was in Spain that for the first time he laughed—Spain which is gray and old as the beards of kings, but splendid as the sunset is splendid. The armadas have gone into the twilight, and faint comes the ghostly drum of Moorish hoofs. But somewhere the dim queen is waiting, with the roses in her hair . . .

Into Seville rode Retif, for Seville is the Paris of Andalusia. And atop the Giralda the bronze figure of Faith swings in every wind, and Don Juan whispers at the lattice, and the stars are the eyes of sultanas from Granada. There are men who smoke idle cigarettes, with their brown faces dreamy as the smoke. At the windows sing the nightingales to a sky that is bluer than the Mediterranean; at the windows hover the dusky ladies whose combs glitter above their heads. For all Seville is a nightingale in a cage, singing the joy and dance of life. Retif of Picardy heard it as he rode into the streets that day.

"What, señor!" cried a rollicking blade, swinging his hat at Retif's horse, "what, señor, you are sad? Then you shall come with me for wine, and I will play you the song I have made for the fairest in Spain."

High on his horse like a character of old romance sat Retif, sombre and broken with battle. But at the words the warm melody went into him.

"I give you thanks," he said, and laughed as he dismounted; "your hand, my good friend. You give me the glow of life. I was thinking of wars and bloodshed—"

"Oh, then you were foolish! War is a child's game, and we are grown men. We shall have wine. I have no money; nor have you, I perceive by your ragged costume. Good, I will sell my sash."

"More fool I!" Retif exclaimed. "Yes, I am a ragged picture, I do not doubt. But I have money, much money, for in my country they call me seigneur. See!" he added, and flung a piece of gold to a beggar; "you behold it. I will buy the wine."

"Señor, beware! I am a swordsman; do not insult my hospitality. Why," said the Spaniard, whipping off his sash, "here is a merchant, sunning himself in his own door. How much for this?"

"Ten pistoles," replied the man, who wore a yellow robe and puffed out clouds of smoke like a catfish with a cigarette, leering at them. The owner of the sash tossed it to him. Then, tall and lazy-eyed and scarlet of mouth, he stood disdainfully while the money was counted out. Juggling the coins, he laughed and put an arm about Retif's shoulders. They sauntered down the street with the horse trailing behind—an ill-assorted pair out of a fantastic painting, the laughing cavalier and the foolish dreamer, such as one meets only in old Seville.

Music lighted the air now like bright lamps, whirling in a dance of crowds and color. Still the swashbuckling men, some wearing rapiers. The two roysterers turned in beneath a lattice. Beyond it was a patio with tables, and sweeping below the blue of the Guadalquivir, flaunting clouds that winged the sky like the sails of Philip's galleons when the armada was young. At one of the tables, across which lay a mandolin, sat Retif and his companion. A dark daring girl brought them wine. And through the white tracery of arches that framed river and clouds they watched the fleets of shadow come up out of the sunset until the arches swam in dimness. Retif sat entranced. And the white patio was a pool of dusk filled with trembling lights, and the great hush of starlight hung upon it, and faint forms began to move about it in the laughter that is the voice of Spain.

"Señor," murmured the young man, who was visible only by the flourishing red tip of his cigarette, "I have as much reason to be sad as yourself. But I am not sad, because no man who is in love is ever sad. Listen, adventurer of France, and you shall hear my story."

Retif was silent.

"Tonight you must meet her. Tonight when the ghosts are back in Seville. No one can be romantic by day . . .

"In Seville there is a woman. She is old, old as the Alhambra, old as the art of poison. But there is in her the fiery, swirling beauty of Castille, the passion of the Moor, the cruelty of the Inquisition. She is a swordswoman. Yes, and she is the matador—conceive it, señor!—she is the matador whom all Spain cheers at the Corrida de Torros. At times she is languishing, under the moon, all softness and pretty words. But I, who have seen her in the arena, and seen her poised for the thrust of the blade that blocks the great bulls and crushes them to their knees in blood—I know! Ah, she is magnificent! . . ."

"Your pardon?" said Retif, startled, but the other did not notice. He went on:

"Once in Seville there were two men who loved her. They never saw each other, because one had gone out into the world before the other came to woo her. Rodrigo de Vega remained, and was laughed at; for though she loved him, she mocked him. The other man, Don Garcia Esteban, became a wanderer. He became a citizen of all lands. Because he had tattooed upon the back of his right hand the figure of a dove, they called him La Paloma; but ah, amigo!" cried the Spaniard, "his is the cunningest sword-arm in Europe. He has conquered Dansart, Gallivan, D'Elville, every living master of fence. In Spain all would recognize the dove upon his hand. But he never knew of this woman's love for him . . ."

The flick of fire was motionless. Then the young man said:

"You know me, señor?"

Retif laughed.

"I saw this Don Garcia Esteban once. He was tall, and wore a beard. You have no beard now, but—Señor Esteban, your hand!"

"Diable!" exclaimed his companion, "diable, but you flatter me! . . . I am Rodrigo de Vega."

And he rose with a flourish and bowed as a thrum of hidden guitars smote the patio like a shock of steel. Along the balconies a shadow moved about with a glowing wick, lighting the candles until a world of tiny flames was flung in chains round them. A troop of students came clattering in, knocking over tables and taking possession of others. They laughed under their wide hats; they strummed guitars, and their cigarette smoke drifted like incense across the candlelight. A cigarette girl whisked among them, too, smiling and shaking her head so violently that her earrings flashed. Across the stones in the middle of the tables the shadow of a beam lay black like a crucifix . . .

"See," Don Rodrigo remarked, laughing into his wine; "tonight you will find them all; the fauns and the satyrs, the grotesquerie that dances the night before el toro is slain. We are a strange people. We love our devils."

The sensuous song whirled and burst like a leap of the heart. Wine-glasses gleamed aloft as a dancer in scarlet shawl whipped to the center of the tables, and the castanets clicked time to the spin of her feet along the black shadow that was the shadow of a cross. Against the background of white costumes she made a great play of flashing heels and back-thrown head, whose hair was somehow warm and brown over a tea-rose face . . .

"Amigo," Don Rodrigo said suddenly, "she is here. She is the only woman in Spain who would dare come, but there she sits. Up by the rail of the gallery, where the candles shine on her hair; you see her?"

Retif looked. The candles lit the white unmoving face as before the Shrine of a Madonna; there was a faint blur of smoke before it, and the lifted cigarette was just beneath the dim deep eyes.

"We will go to her," decided Retif's companion. They rose, moving through the crowded aisles until they reached a stair. At the top step they could see a table through shifting shadows, where sat the woman. There was power about her, and dominance, and cruelty. The pale face was cameo under an arch of tight black hair. She did not smile . . .

"Carito mio, I have brought you a friend," Don Rodrigo said. "Give him welcome. He is a soldier of France, but a gentleman."

"Soldier of France!" she repeated, and her voice gave it a heroic ring. They sat down. At the end of the long gallery, beyond the woman, there was a stairway blue with starlight . . .

"You said, did you not, that you were called Retif?" de Vega asked. "I have been speaking of you to him, Dolores."

Retif bent to kiss the hand that brushed his lips.

"Your Bonaparte was cruel to us, M. Retif," she said, and the words came out distinctly as the music below swept to a low thrumming.

. . . At the end of the gallery there was a stair blue with starlight, and a man lounged on it with wan face upturned as he sang with a mandolin to a window above. Below, on the lowest step where the candles found it, was a shrunken bundle of a man, and a red stain crawled slowly around the knife-blade in his side.

## II

It was very late. In their sockets the candles had sunk to wide sheets of flame; the dangerous hours of night were upon the patio. It was the time when kisses are long over balconies. At the tables in the court the crowd had reached its maddest, cheeks flushed, voices clashing. There had been a brilliant flicker of swordplay . . .

Retif of Picardy and the woman Dolores sat in the gallery alone, for Rodrigo de Vega had gone to join the throng below. Cigarette stubs floated sodden in their wine-glasses. His hat and gloves lay before them.

"You love this Don Garcia Esteban?" Retif questioned. He sat there thin and worn, and his eyes were sad as a dim strain of music.

"In Spain we have a proverb, 'Death, not inconstancy'," she returned, "yet I am very lonely. Were you ever lonely?"

"Señorita Dolores," he answered, "the loneliest man in Europe is my emperor. Am I better than he?"

"Why do you follow him?"

"In France, señorita, in France I had a friend; his name was Du Verde. He loved wine, and life, and laughter. He died at Friedlands."

Retif paused. When he spoke again it was in the same monotone.

"And I had another very dear friend, who hated war, who trembled when he heard the cannon. He was killed at Leipzig, and when the horses trampled him down he was still in front with his drum, beating a charge until he died . . ." Suddenly his voice took fire. "Then I realized, señorita, why Du Verde, who had so much of to live for, went down in the charge; and why Malvorin, who hated death, went on beating his drum into eternity . . . That is why I follow my emperor. If I were not so determined, my new friend, then I would say, 'I love you' . . ."

The long hush was shattered by the sickening noise that stuns like heartbreak. It was laughter. Señorita Dolores had burst into a laugh which rang and echoed in the gallery. She rose; statue-quiet no longer, but vibrant and flame-lipped, a thing that mocked and dazzled in its splendid life. She was unapproachable; ice and fire and a song from thundering hordes.

"M. Retif," she cried, "diable! but you are the most sentimental fool I have ever met . . . Caballeros!" she twirled to the railing and threw up an arm; he saw that she was small, of a pallor that her black shawl accentuated. "Caballeros, come and drink me a toast to the height of French gallantry! To the man who says, 'I live only to die for my emperor; I yearn to die, I long passionately to die, but if I were not determined to die, I should lay my heart at your feet!' Oh, this is magnificent!"

There was an answering shout from the patio, the sound of overturning tables and wild acclaim. Men came tumbling up the stairs, filling the gallery with a nightmare of faces. And in the midst of it Retif sat looking stupidly at his glass . . .

A tall, jet-haired Spaniard lurched to the front, holding up a light that dappled Dolores' face and made blue vistas of her eyes.

"You see him?" she demanded. "Here is one of Bonaparte's sweet-voiced murderers, come to steal Spanish virtue as well as Spanish gold!"

The tall Spaniard was quite drunk. As Retif rose he thrust the light into his face.

"Eh, a Frenchman! Now, by the mercy of God, señor, you tempt much to come here! And so you insult our lady Dolores—"

"But wait!" the woman cried, and made a pretty, mocking gesture. "I am going to test this soldier's bravery. You accustom yourselves to making war on women; well, then, will you do it now? How would Don Garcia Esteban treat this person, do you think, if he were here?"

There was a laugh, in which she joined. You saw a sort of pride to her in the thought that she could do as she wished with these men. She clapped her hands.

"Come, then—swords! I will give this gallant a chance to defend himself as all gallants should!"

"Señorita—" said Retif queerly.

"Why," she interrupted, "Don Garcia will not be here for many months. This is a splendid joke; to let his lady defend herself. What, señor? Have we anything more precious than our virtue?"

"Some persons," Retif replied in his monotone, "believe that they possess a thing more precious."

"But I am not one of them!" she said proudly.

"No," said Retif. "No, you are not one of them . . ."

She stood regarding him, and from her the anger curled like a whiplash. She caught up his gloves from the table, and then suddenly she stung them into his face. Then she went to a door opening on the gallery.

"Bring swords, if you please . . ."

The shout of laughter was broken when the tall Spaniard bowed elaborately to Retif. He said: "May I offer the señor my services? I have a stout blade, and should be able to defeat our lady, if the quarrel be transferred."

"Señorita Dolores is mad!" Retif cried, and there was panic to him. "I cannot fight her . . . for the the love of God! I beg of you . . ." He was struggling as they caught him up and bore him to the door. Beyond it, in a long, white-walled room under the light of many lamps, stood the woman. She had thrown off her shawl, so that her bare shoulders gleamed, and her head was tossed back. A supple figure, like one awaiting an embrace to which the white arms would respond and the blue eyes close, she provoked a burst of admiration.

They flung Retif against one wall, and thrust a sword into his hand.

"Dolores," he kept repeating, "I tell you I cannot! . . . I know not swordplay . . ."

"The light hurts my eyes," she said fretfully. "Take away all the lamps but one. Now—shut the door against the keeper of the hotel. Monsieur le français, you are ready, then? Oh, this is fine French gallantry!"

It was Don Rodrigo de Vega who made a mild protest.

"Come," he said, "this grows fantastic . . . Well, well, M. Retif, if it must be, you at least know how to hold a blade. Up—so."

"I will not . . ." Retif began, and paused. His white face swept the circle about him; he made a tiny vague gesture. "Señorita," he went on, and quite suddenly they stopped laughing at him, "I am ready."

There was an odd hush, until someone else giggled in a rather silly way, like a school-girl. One of the mandolins began strumming a love song . . .

Only a faint gasping lamp lit the big bodies in the room, and the yellow oblong of matting, and the white walls with the shadows of the duellists, but it made glittering fierce streaks of the blades. Retif was a shapeless thing, holding his sword awkwardly, amateur-like with full body exposed to his opponent, arm loose, palm upwards. And in an instant it was over, sickening as surgeon's work.

Abnormally long, the steel seemed, the Spanish rapier that is thin and double-edged. A tingle and shudder of it before the woman's blade came flashing round. It was no stroke of fencing, that slash which seared her antagonist's face just across the eyes . . .

Retif gave a kind of shaking gasp that clogged his throat and set him shuddering. There were tiny drops upon the yellow matting. But Retif stood very straight, without moving.

"Señorita," he said, "you have touched me. *I cannot see you any longer, señorita . . .*"

The woman was the only one there who laughed.

"Your gloves," she said, and threw them at his feet; "pick them up, if you can. I suppose I should keep them as a token. Eh, well, you may return them when you have proved yourself a swordsman; say, when you have met Don Garcia Esteban!" She put on her shawl. "Oh, it is abominably dark in here! Bring lamps; or let us go downstairs. Where is the music?"

The door was knocked open; over the lamplight and the sudden clash of voices a mandolin wove a wandering air, a sweet Spanish song of maidens who wept for the warriors who had laughed and died among the swords . . .

"A doctor—" Rodrigo de Vega murmured vaguely, but he forgot it when he caught Señorita Dolores to his lips. And the men were kissing Dolores' hands, whereat she trembled deliciously, and smiled.

"Por dios, but you are cold! And it is vilely dark in there! . . ."

They closed the door. Still Retif stood quite straight. Then he began to grope about the room, slowly, just a tiny bit unsteadily. When Conchita, the little dancer from downstairs, crept in with wide stricken eyes, she saw him lying there by a chair, and he did not notice that the lamp had gone out.

### III

In all the strange bright years kings had grown accustomed to treat Messire Death as a necessary man, for he was a court fool to cut capers, and amuse them when they could not get what they wanted. But the fool was always the wisest man at court. So when he set the bugles blowing again the kings clapped their hands for a dance very merrily, but the soldiers' wives did not smile. In the March of 1815, when the snow gnaws at France, a small grim person returned. The hosts of the gay cockade

marched him to Paris, singing songs of glory and crying, "Vive l'Empér-
eur!"

Then it was the cry of the bugles that swept the world. Men and guns,
men and guns, rolling of cannon on the roads like the sound of a colossal
game of ninepins for a man who bowled with God! Beneath the shine of
bayonets marched the red-coats in a storm of flags, and the terrible fair
Uhlans under Blücher whose name is a roar of guns came pounding out
of Prussia, and the swords of Austria rang in their scabbards, and the
lean plumed fighting-men from Italy grinned to meet the Gaul once
more, and the earth was mad. Drum-beat and heart-beat, fleeting kiss of
sweetheart, swing of marching column past the old, old men who stand
with proud smiling lips and brimming eyes! Foaming songs and foaming
tankards, all drunk with wine or death when the trains of artillery smash
past windows like the black beasts that bay on the last trail! Poured in
one terrific plunging mass, spurted and raked with shot, over the crumpled cannon in the leap of horses—on to Waterloo! . . . And, hidden,
the thresholds over which small feet pass gaily, and move on in echoes
that forever remain . . .

It had been many days since the messenger had ridden into Seville with
the news that Napoleon had returned. In a room of the hotel far above
the street Conchita the dancer had hidden away a man whose eyes were
bandaged, and who was very ill. Conchita did not tell him that the great
emperor was back, for Retif of Picardy was blind. In Seville they thought
that he had gone, and they made merry over the soldier who was beaten
by a woman. Retif lay in the big black bedstead among the shadows. He
dreamed, and wove mighty cities in whose applause rode a grim little
man on a white horse; Conchita dreamed, too, when she brushed his
hand . . .

That afternoon Conchita had put up the shutters fast against all the
windows. There were noises in the street; fresh news had come down
from France in a blast that hushed the merriment of Seville. And the high
room had been darkened except for a lamp. Conchita sat near it, a wisp
of girl that sometimes one sees in Spain like a leaf blown there—warm
and brown-haired, with eyes that see much of the world, but only its
great aching beauty. She was reading to Retif, who sat in his big chair
with eyes from which he still refused to remove the bandage. Finally she
put down the book.

"It is a silly story, Retif," she said . . . and then, quite suddenly, she
heard stirrings in the street. There were mad fellows who boasted of
braving the journey to join Blücher, mustering in squadrons of gold lace
to a beat of drums.

"Another festival?" asked Retif petulantly; "they are singing—"

"It is nothing, my friend! I tell you it is nothing." Alarm was in her eyes. She hurried to the table and took up a mandolin. "Listen, and I will sing to you, as you like."

She began to strum the mandolin so that the noise rang loudly in the room. Slim as a dryad she stood by the window, and her voice was like a bell of silver that pealed for vanished kings, and rose in the wind . . .

"Please . . ." said Retif; "more softly, if you will . . ."

But she answered eagerly: "No, my Retif; not a love-song. I will sing to you of your emperor, and it shall drown out any reality. But it shall be of romance; are you not pleased to call her your dim queen? Yes, as romance always drowns reality!" And the strains soared aloft with a power that was the great groping of the troubadour for stars. The voice throbbed with a note which suddenly made Retif unquiet; it thrilled and shook him, for there was that in it which he had never heard in her songs before.

"Conchita," he exclaimed, "down there in the street—a festival? . . . I have heard that sound—somewhere before—why is it so faint?"

"It is nothing! Listen . . ."

"Conchita, you have put up the shutters!"

He rose unsteadily, seizing the arms of his chair. He heard the mandolin jangle into silence on the floor. And he heard, as she had, the footfalls outside the door; the thump at its panels and rattle at its knob. It was the proprietor's voice . . .

Click of key, then a louder burst from the fat proprietor. But most distinctly came the voice of Don Rodrigo de Vega:

"Dios, señorita! Must we seek you out even here to dance for the soldiers of Spain?"

The room went silent. Don Rodrigo, lazy in uniform, was staring at the thin white man who stood by the chair, right hand uplifted.

"Conchita," cried Retif, and his sightless eyes were not for the figures in the doorway, "you are crying!"

Rodrigo de Vega came forward. He looked huge and awkward, a bright-clad figure in a halo of yellow light; his hands trembled. And his eyes had not left off staring at Retif.

"I think," said Rodrigo, "I think I ought to kneel; yes, assuredly I ought to kneel . . . *You see it, Conchita? On the back of monsieur's hand —the figure of a dove!"*

IV

The heat of afternoon, which makes Spain hard and brittle and somehow tawdry, had not softened when Rodrigo de Vega strode into the patio of the house where Dolores lived. She was sitting among the palms where a fountain brushed its spray. She was an irritable figure now; there was too much of the painted doll about her, and the set mocking smile had grown just a bit wearisome. There could be no alluring gestures under the beat of the sun. But Dolores made a mistake, a rather hollow grotesque mistake in attempting one.

"You have come to say good-bye?" she asked softly.

"Oh, for the love of God," said de Vega. He laughed as she sat there wistful. Then he lighted a cigarette.

"But you march tonight?" She was plaintive, and he laughed again.

"Are you prepared, Dolores, for an emotional scene? This should be emotional, and I am prepared to see you draw a dagger to flourish at me. Then you will threaten me with the sword of Garcia Esteban . . .

"Listen to me," he added, abruptly harsh. "You are a liar, señorita. A bluffer; not that I object to bluffers, when they mean no harm. But you never knew Don Garcia Esteban."

She was on her feet, horribly and rather absurdly fierce.

". . . You never knew him. You never saw him. But, eh, did it not make you much sought-after by the lovers when they thought that the greatest swordsman in Europe was madly—oh, so madly! you said—enamored of you? It is what certain people would call good business."

"He will kill you for this!"

"He will never fight another duel," the Spaniard responded, snapping the words at her. "You put out his eyes. Be quiet, now, and hear me! You knew him as Retif; so did I, because he always wore gloves except that night. That night, when he, being a gallant fool, would not give you away before the crowd. That night, when he dared not meet you with the blades because he would have had to expose the back of his hand! Did you not notice, how he fenced? He did not anticipate, I dare say, that you would blind him with the foulest stroke known to fencers . . . Did you never think, Dolores, *why* he came into Spain after the wars? Why does a soldier of France venture into a hostile country, except that it was once his own country before he began to follow a mad ideal?"

She was quite ghastly now, for the whole weight of it had fallen.

"You are tricking me! . . ."

"Well, I am not concerned. It does not matter if you wish to doubt me, Dolores; not one cigarette does it matter. Oh, but I am speaking the truth. Now, does it not occur to you after these weeks that you loved him?"

Dolores was shaken, but she steadied herself for a yearning smile.

"You, too, will doubt me . . . but yes, I think I have loved him . . ."

"Unfortunate!" cried Don Rodrigo, laughing; "he has already set out for France, señorita, with the dancer who loves him . . . Yes, he is a soldier of Napoleon," added the Spaniard, and suddenly his voice grew soft, "but all Seville would have given him God-speed when he left. Is not that a great triumph?"

The fountain sang . . .

"Pathetic, the man was," said de Vega oddly, after a while, "when he left, striving to reach his emperor. Well, well, the whole world is directed for a shambles, with the Englishman Wellington black as thunder . . ."

"You do not think," she asked hopefully, "that if I went to the inn—"

Don Rodrigo flipped away his cigarette.

"I have no more time to waste here," he observed, and drew something from his pocket. "Señorita, his gloves!" They fell at her feet.

"Well," continued the Spaniard after another silence, "Why the devil don't you cry?"

. . . It was not until darkness had blurred the patio that he held her in his arms fervently, and whispered that the world did not matter, and damned himself for doubting a love that cannot fly into the window at midday.

# The Other Hangman

John Dickson Carr wrote "The Other Hangman" for *A Century of Detective Stories,* published in 1935 with the G. K. Chesterton introduction which is quoted earlier in this book. The first American printing of the story was in *The Department of Queer Complaints* (1940) by "Carter Dickson." Set in nineteenth-century Pennsylvania, "The Other Hangman" is based on various cronies of his father, a lawyer and politician, in his hometown of Uniontown, Pennsylvania. Carr said that the short story has "one of my best plots, which I should have been sensible enough to reserve for a novel."

# The Other Hangman

"Why do they electrocute 'em instead of hanging 'em in Pennsylvania? What" (said my old friend, Judge Murchison, dexterously hooking the spittoon closer with his foot) "do they teach you youngsters in these new-fangled law schools, anyway? That, son, *was* a murder case. It turned the Supreme Court's whiskers grey to find a final ruling, and for thirty years it's been argued about by lawyers in the back room of every saloon from here to the Pacific coast. It happened right here in this county—when they hanged Fred Joliffe for the murder of Randall Fraser.

"It was in '92 or '93; anyway, it was the year they put the first telephone in the court-house, and you could talk as far as Pittsburgh except when the wires blew down. Considering it was the county seat, we were mighty proud of our town (population 3,500). The hustlers were always bragging about how thriving and growing our town was, and we had just got to the point of enthusiasm where every ten years we were certain the census-taker must have forgotten half our population. Old Mark Sturgis, who owned the *Bugle Gazette* then, carried on something awful in an editorial when they printed in the almanac that we had a population of only 3,265. We were all pretty riled about it, naturally.

"We were proud of plenty of other things, too. We had good reason to brag about the McClellan House, which was the finest hotel in the county; and I mind when you could get room and board, with apple pie for breakfast every morning, for two dollars a week. We were proud of our old county families, that came over the mountains when Braddock's army was scalped by the Indians in seventeen fifty-five, and settled down in log huts to dry their wounds. But most of all we were proud of our legal batteries.

"Son, it was a grand assembly! Mind, I won't say that all of 'em were long on knowledge of the Statute Books; but they knew their *Blackstone* and their *Greenleaf on Evidence,* and they were powerful speakers. *And* there were some—the top-notchers—full of graces and book-knowledge and dignity, who were hell on the exact letter of the law. Scotch-Irish Presbyterians, all of us, who loved a good debate and a bottle o' whisky. There was Charley Connell, a Harvard graduate and the district attorney, who had fine white hands, and wore a fine high collar, and made such pathetic addresses to the jury that people flocked for miles around to hear him; though he generally lost his cases. There was Judge Hunt, who prided himself on his resemblance to Abe Lincoln, and in consequence always wore a frock coat and an elegant plug hat. Why, there was your own grandfather, who had over two hundred books in his library, and people used to go up nights to borrow volumes of the encyclopaedia.

"You know the big stone court-house at the top of the street, with the flowers round it, and the jail adjoining? People went there as they'd go to a picture-show nowadays; it was a lot better, too. Well, from there it was only two minutes' walk across the meadow to Jim Riley's saloon. All the cronies gathered there—in the back room, of course, where Jim had an elegant brass spittoon and a picture of George Washington on the wall to make it dignified. You could see the footpath worn across the grass until they built over that meadow. Besides the usual crowd, there was Bob Moran, the sheriff, a fine, strapping big fellow, but very nervous about doing his duty strictly. And there was poor old Nabors, a big, quiet, reddish-eyed fellow, who'd been a doctor before he took to drink. He was always broke, and he had two daughters—one of 'em consumptive—and Jim Riley pitied him so much that he gave him all he wanted to drink for nothing. Those were fine, happy days, with a power of eloquence and theorizing and solving the problems of the nation in that back room, until our wives came to fetch us home.

"Then Randall Fraser was murdered, and there was hell to pay.

"Now if it had been anybody else but Fred Joliffe who killed him, naturally we wouldn't have convicted. You can't do it, son, not in a little community. It's all very well to talk about the power and grandeur of justice, and sounds fine in a speech. But here's somebody you've seen walking the streets about his business every day for years; and you know when his kids were born, and saw him crying when one of 'em died; and you remember how he loaned you ten dollars when you needed it. . . . Well, you can't take that person out in the cold light of day and string him up by the neck until he's dead. You'd always be seeing the look on his face afterwards. And you'd find excuses for him no matter what he did.

"But with Fred Joliffe it was different. Fred Joliffe was the worst and nastiest customer we ever had, with the possible exception of Randall Fraser himself. Ever seen a copperhead curled up on a flat stone? And a copperhead's worse than a rattlesnake—that won't strike unless you step on it, and gives warning before it does. Fred Joliffe had the same brownish color and sliding movements. You always remembered his pale little eye and his nasty grin. When he drove his cart through town—he had some sort of rag-and-bone business, you understand—you'd see him sitting up there, a skinny little man in a brown coat, peeping round the side of his nose to find something for gossip. And grinning.

"It wasn't merely the things he said about people behind their backs. Or to their faces, for that matter, because he relied on the fact that he was too small to be thrashed. He was a slick customer. It was believed that he wrote those anonymous letters that caused . . . but never mind that. Anyhow, I can tell you his little smirk *did* drive Will Farmer crazy one time, and Will *did* beat him within an inch of his life. Will's livery stable was burnt down one night about a month later, with eleven horses inside, but nothing could ever be proved. He was too smart for us.

"That brings me to Fred Joliffe's only companion—I don't mean friend. Randall Fraser had a harness-and-saddle store in Market Street, a dusty place with a big dummy horse in the window. I reckon the only thing in the world Randall liked was that dummy horse, which was a dappled mare with vicious-looking glass eyes. He used to keep its mane combed. Randall was a big man with a fine mustache, a horseshoe pin in his tie, and sporty checked clothes. He was buttery polite, and mean as sin. He thought a dirty trick or a swindle was the funniest joke he ever heard. But the women liked him—a lot of them, it's no denying, sneaked in at the back door of that harness store. Randall itched to tell it at the barber shop, to show what fools they were and how virile he was; but he had to be careful. He and Fred Joliffe did a lot of drinking together.

"Then the news came. It was in October, I think, and I heard it in the morning, when I was putting on my hat to go down to the office. Old Withers was the town constable then. He got up early in the morning, although there was no need for it; and, when he was going down Market Street in the mist about five o'clock, he saw the gas still burning in the back room of Randall's store. The front door was wide open. Withers went in and found Randall lying on a pile of harness in his shirt-sleeves, and his forehead and face bashed in with a wedging-mallet. There wasn't much left of the face, but you could recognize him by his mustache and his horseshoe pin.

"I was in my office when somebody yelled up from the street that they had found Fred Joliffe drunk and asleep in the flour-mill, with blood on his hands and an empty bottle of Randall Fraser's whisky in his pocket. He was still in bad shape, and couldn't walk or understand what was going on, when the sheriff—that was Bob Moran I told you about—came to take him to the lock-up. Bob had to drive him in his own rag-and-bone cart. I saw them drive up Market Street in the rain, Fred lying in the back of the cart all white with flour, and rolling and cursing. People were very quiet. They were pleased, but they couldn't show it.

"That is, all except Will Farmer, who had owned the livery stable that was burnt down.

" 'Now they'll hang him,' says Will. 'Now, by God they'll hang him.'

"It's a funny thing, son: I didn't realize the force of that until I heard Judge Hunt pronounce sentence after the trial. They appointed me to defend him, because I was a young man without any particular practice, and somebody had to do it. The evidence was all over town before I got a chance to speak with Fred. You could see he was done for. A scissors-grinder who lived across the street (I forget his name now) had seen Fred go into Randall's place about eleven o'clock. An old couple who lived up over the store had heard 'em drinking and yelling downstairs; at near on midnight they'd heard a noise like a fight and a fall; but they knew better than to interfere. Finally, a couple of farmers driving home from town at midnight had seen Fred stumble out of the front door, slapping his clothes and wiping his hands on his coat like a man with delirium tremens.

"I went to see Fred at the jail. He was sober, although he jerked a good deal. Those pale watery eyes of his were as poisonous as ever. I can still see him sitting on the bunk in his cell, sucking a brown-paper cigarette, wriggling his neck, and jeering at me. He wouldn't tell me anything, because he said I would go and tell the judge if he did.

" 'Hang *me?*' he says, and wrinkled his nose and jeered again. 'Hang *me?* Don't you worry about that, mister. Them so-and-so's will never hang me. They're too much afraid of me, them so-and-so's are. Eh, mister?'

"And the fool couldn't get it through his head right up until the sentence. He strutted away in court; making smart remarks, and threatening to tell what he knew about people, and calling the judge by his first name. He wore a new dickey shirt-front he bought to look spruce in.

"I was surprised how quietly everybody took it. The people who came to the trial didn't whisper or shove; they just sat still as death, and looked at him. All you could hear was a kind of breathing. It's funny about a court-room, son: it has its own particular smell, which won't bother you unless you get to thinking about what it means, but you notice worn places and cracks in the walls more than you would anywhere else. You would hear Charley Connell's voice for the prosecution, a little thin sound in a big room, and Charley's footsteps creaking. You would hear a cough in the audience, or a woman's dress rustle, or the gas-jets whistling. It was dark in the rainy season, so they lit the gas-jets by two o'clock in the afternoon.

"The only defence I could make was that Fred had been too drunk to be responsible, and remembered nothing of that night (which he admitted was true). But, in addition to being no defence in law, it was a terrible frost besides. My own voice sounded wrong. I remember that six of the jury had whiskers, and six hadn't; and Judge Hunt, up on the bench with the flag draped on the wall behind his head, looked more like Abe Lincoln than ever. Even Fred Joliffe began to notice. He kept twitching round to look at people, a little uneasy-like. Once he stuck out his neck at the jury and screeched: '*Say* something, can'tcha? Do something, can'tcha?'

"They did.

"When the foreman of the jury said: 'Guilty of murder in the first degree,' there was just a little noise from those people. Not a cheer, or anything like that. It hissed out all together, only once, like breath released, but it was terrible to hear. It didn't hit Fred until Judge Hunt was half-way through pronouncing sentence. Fred stood looking round with a wild, half-witted expression until he heard Judge Hunt say: *'And may God have mercy on your soul.'* Then he burst out, kind of pleading and kidding as though this was carrying the joke too far. He said: 'Listen, now, you don't *mean* that, do you? You can't fool me. You're only Jerry Hunt; I know who you are. You can't do that to me.' All of a sudden he began pounding the table and screaming: 'You ain't really agoing to hang me, are you?'

"But we were.

"The date of execution was fixed for the twelfth of November. The order was all signed. '. . . within the precincts of the said county jail, between the hours of eight and nine A.M., the said Frederick Joliffe shall be hanged by the neck until he is dead; an executioner to be commissioned by the sheriff for this purpose, and the sentence to be carried out in the presence of a qualified medical practitioner; the body to be interred . . .' And the rest of it. Everybody was nervous. There hadn't been a hanging since any of that crowd had been in office, and nobody knew how to go about it exactly. Old Doc Macdonald, the coroner, was to be there; and of course they got hold of Reverend Phelps the preacher; and Bob Moran's wife was going to cook pancakes and sausage for the last breakfast. Maybe you think that's fool talk. But think for a minute of taking somebody you've known all your life, and binding his arms one cold morning, and walking him out in your own backyard to crack his neck on a rope—all religious and legal, with not a soul to interfere. Then you begin to get scared of the powers of life and death, and the thin partition between.

"Bob Moran was scared white for fear things wouldn't go off properly. He had appointed big, slow-moving, tipsy Ed Nabors as hangman. This was partly because Ed Nabors needed the fifty dollars that was the fee, and partly because Bob had a vague idea that an ex-medical man would be better able to manage an execution. Ed had sworn to keep sober; Bob Moran said he wouldn't get a dime unless he *was* sober; but you couldn't always tell.

"Nabors seemed in earnest. He had studied up the matter of scientific hanging in an old book he borrowed from your grandfather, and he and the carpenter had knocked together a big, shaky-looking contraption in the jail yard. It worked all right in practice, with sacks of meal; the trap went down with a boom that brought your heart up in your throat. But once they allowed for too much spring in the rope, and it tore a sack apart. Then old Doc Macdonald chipped in about that fellow John Lee, in England—and it nearly finished Bob Moran.

"That was late on the night before the execution. We were sitting round the lamp in Bob's office, trying to play stud poker. There were tops and skipping-ropes, all kinds of toys, all over that office. Bob let his kids play in there—which he shouldn't have done, because the door out of it led to a corridor of cells with Fred Joliffe in the last one. Of course the few other prisoners, disorderlies and chicken-thieves and the like, had been moved upstairs. Somebody had told Bob that the scent of an execution affects 'em like a cage of wild animals. Whoever it was, he was right. We could hear 'em shifting and stamping over our heads, and one old black man singing hymns all night long.

"Well, it was raining hard on the tin roof; maybe that was what put Doc Macdonald in mind of it. Doc was a cynical old devil. When he saw that Bob couldn't sit still, and would throw in his hand without even looking at the buried card, Doc says:

" 'Yes, I hope it'll go off all right. But you want to be careful about that rain. Did you read about that fellow they tried to hang in England?—and the rain had swelled the boards so's the trap wouldn't fall? They stuck him on it three times, but still it wouldn't work . . .'

"Ed Nabors slammed his hand down on the table. I reckon he felt bad enough as it was, because one of his daughters had run away and left him, and the other was dying of consumption. But he was twitchy and reddish about the eyes, he hadn't had a drink for two days, although there was a bottle on the table. He says:

" 'You shut up or I'll kill you. Damn you, Macdonald,' he says, and grabs the edge of the table. 'I tell you nothing *can* go wrong. I'll go out and test the thing again, if you'll let me put the rope round your neck.'

"And Bob Moran says: 'What do you want to talk like that for, anyway, Doc? Ain't it bad enough as it is?' he says. 'Now you've got me worrying about something else,' he says. 'I went down there a while ago to look at him, and he said the funniest thing I ever heard Fred Joliffe say. He's crazy. He giggled and said God wouldn't let them so-and-so's hang him. It was terrible, hearing Fred Joliffe talk like that. What time is it, somebody?'

"I was cold that night. I dozed off in a chair, hearing the rain, and that animal-cage snuffling upstairs. The black man was singing that part of the hymn about while the nearer waters roll, while the tempest still is high.

"They woke me about half-past eight to say that Judge Hunt and all the witnesses were out in the jail yard, and they were ready to start the march. Then I realized that they were really going to hang him after all. I had to join behind the procession as I was sworn, but I didn't see Fred Joliffe's face and I didn't want to see it. They had given him a good wash, and a clean flannel shirt that they tucked under at the neck. He stumbled coming out of the cell, and started to go in the wrong direction; but Bob Moran and the constable each had him by one arm. It was a cold, dark, windy morning. His hands were tied behind.

"The preacher was saying something I couldn't catch; everything went off smoothly enough until they got half-way across the jail yard. It's a pretty big yard. I didn't look at the contraption in the middle, but at the witnesses standing over against the wall with their hats off; and I smelled the clean air after the rain, and looked up at the mountains where the sky was getting pink. But Fred Joliffe did look at it, and went down flat on his knees. They hauled him up again. I heard them keep on walking, and go up the steps, which were creaky.

"I didn't look at the contraption until I heard a thumping sound, and we all knew something was wrong.

"Fred Joliffe was not standing on the trap, nor was the bag pulled over his head, although his legs were strapped. He stood with his eyes closed and his face towards the pink sky. Ed Nabors was clinging with both hands to the rope, twirling round a little and stamping on the trap. It didn't budge. Just as I heard Ed crying something about the rain having swelled the boards, Judge Hunt ran past me to the foot of the contraption.

"Bob Moran started cursing pretty obscenely. 'Put him on and try it, anyway,' he says, and grabs Fred's arm. 'Stick that bag over his head and give the thing a chance.'

" 'In His name,' says the preacher pretty steadily, 'you'll not do it if I can help it.'

"Bob ran over like a crazy man and jumped on the trap with both feet. It was stuck fast. Then Bob turned round and pulled an Ivor-Johnson .45 out of his hip-pocket. Judge Hunt got in front of Fred, whose lips were moving a little.

" 'He'll have the law, and nothing but the law,' says Judge Hunt. 'Put that gun away, you lunatic, and take him back to the cell until you can make the thing work. Easy with him, now.'

"To this day I don't think Fred Joliffe had realized what happened. I believe he only had his belief confirmed that they never meant to hang him after all. When he found himself going down the steps again, he opened his eyes. His face looked shrunken and dazed-like, but all of a sudden it came to him in a blaze.

" 'I knew them so-and-so's would never hang me,' says he. His throat was so dry he couldn't spit at Judge Hunt, as he tried to do; but he marched straight and giggling across the yard. 'I knew them so-and-so's would never hang me,' he says.

"We all had to sit down a minute, and we had to give Ed Nabors a drink. Bob made him hurry up, although we didn't say much, and he was leaving to fix the trap again when the court-house janitor came bustling into Bob's office.

" 'Call,' says he, 'on the new machine over there. Telephone.'

" 'Lemme out of here!' yells Bob. 'I can't listen to no telephone calls now. Come out and give us a hand.'

" 'But it's from Harrisburg,' says the janitor. 'It's from the Governor's office. You got to go.'

" 'Stay here, Bob,' says Judge Hunt. He beckons to me. 'Stay here, and I'll answer it,' he says. We looked at each other in a queer way when we went across the Bridge of Sighs. The court-house clock was striking nine, and I could look down into the yard and see people hammering at the trap. After Judge Hunt had listened to that telephone call he had a hard time putting the receiver back on the hook.

" 'I always believed in Providence, in a way,' says he, 'but I never thought it was so personal-like. Fred Joliffe is innocent. We're to call off this business,' says he, 'and wait for a messenger from the Governor. He's got the evidence of a woman. . . . Anyway, we'll hear it later.'

"Now, I'm not much of a hand at describing mental states, so I can't tell you exactly what we felt then. Most of all was a fever and horror for fear they had already whisked Fred out and strung him up. But when we looked down into the yard from the Bridge of Sighs we saw Ed Nabors and the carpenter arguing over a cross-cut saw on the trap itself; and the blessed morning light coming up in a glory to show us we could knock the ugly contraption to pieces and burn it.

"The corridor downstairs was deserted. Judge Hunt had got his wind back, and, being one of those stern elocutionists who like to make complimentary remarks about God, he was going on something powerful. He sobered up when he saw that the door to Fred Joliffe's cell was open.

" 'Even Joliffe,' says the judge, 'deserves to get this news first.'

"But Fred never did get that news, unless his ghost was listening. I told you he was very small and light. His heels were a good eighteen inches off the floor as he hung by the neck from an iron peg in the wall of the cell. He was hanging from a noose made in a child's skipping-rope; black-faced, dead already, with the whites of his eyes showing in slits, and his heels swinging over a kicked-away stool.

"No, son, we didn't think it was suicide for long. For a little while we were stunned, half crazy, naturally. It was like thinking about your troubles at three o'clock in the morning.

"But, you see, Fred's hands were still tied behind him. There was a bump on the back of his head, from a hammer that lay beside the stool. Somebody had walked in there with the hammer concealed behind his back, had stunned Fred when he wasn't looking, had run a slip-knot in that skipping-rope, and jerked him up a-flapping to strangle there. It was the creepiest part of the business, when we'd got that through our heads, and we began loudly to tell each other where we'd been during the confusion. Nobody had noticed much. I was scared green.

"When we gathered round the table in Bob's office, Judge Hunt took hold of his nerve with both hands. He looked at Bob Moran, at Ed Nabors, at Doc Macdonald, and at me. One of us was the other hangman.

" 'This is a bad business, gentlemen,' says he, clearing his throat a couple of times like a nervous orator before he starts. 'What I want to know is, who under sanity would strangle a man when he thought we intended to do it, anyway, on a gallows?'

"Then Doc Macdonald turned nasty. 'Well,' says he, 'if it comes to that, you might inquire where that skipping-rope came from, to begin with.'

" 'I don't get you,' says Bob Moran, bewildered-like.

" 'Oh, don't you?' says Doc, and sticks out his whiskers. 'Well, then, who was so dead set on this execution going through as scheduled that he wanted to use a gun when the trap wouldn't drop?'

"Bob made a noise as though he'd been hit in the stomach. He stood looking at Doc for a minute, with his hands hanging down—and then he went for him. He had Doc back across the table, banging his head on the edge, when people began to crowd into the room at the yells. Funny, too; the first one in was the jail carpenter, who was pretty sore at not being told that the hanging had been called off.

" 'What do you want to start fighting for?' he says, fretful-like. He was bigger than Bob, and had him off Doc with a couple of heaves. 'Why didn't you tell me what was going on? They say there ain't going to be any hanging. Is that right?'

"Judge Hunt nodded, and the carpenter—Barney Hicks, that's who it was; I remember now—Barney Hicks looked pretty peevish, and says:

" 'All right, all right, but you hadn't ought to fight all over the joint like that.' Then he looks at Ed Nabors. 'What I want is my hammer. Where's my hammer, Ed? I been looking all over the place for it. What did you do with it?'

"Ed Nabors sits up, pours himself four fingers of rye, and swallows it.

" 'Beg pardon, Barney,' says he in the coolest voice I ever heard. 'I must have left it in the cell,' he says, 'when I killed Fred Joliffe.'

"Talk about silences! It was like one of those silences when the magician at the Opera House fires a gun and six doves fly out of an empty box. I couldn't believe it. But I remember Ed Nabors sitting big in the corner by the barred window, in his shiny black coat and string tie. His hands were on his knees, and he was looking from one to the other of us, smiling a little. He looked as old as the prophets then; and he'd got enough liquor to keep the nerve from twitching beside his eye. So he just sat there, very quietly, shifting the plug of tobacco around in his cheek, and smiling.

" 'Judge,' he says in a reflective way, 'you got a call from the Governor at Harrisburg, didn't you? Uh-huh. I knew what it would be. A woman had come forward, hadn't she, to confess Fred Joliffe was innocent and she had killed Randall Fraser? Uh-huh. The woman was my daughter. Jessie couldn't face telling it here, you see. That was why she ran away from me and went to the Governor. She'd have kept quiet if you hadn't convicted Fred.'

" 'But why . . .' shouts the judge. *'Why . . .'*

" 'It was like this,' Ed goes on in that slow way of his. 'She'd been on pretty intimate terms with Randall Fraser, Jessie had. And both Randall and Fred were having a whooping lot of fun threatening to tell the whole town about it. She was pretty near crazy, I think. And, you see, on the night of the murder Fred Joliffe was too drunk to remember anything that happened. He thought he *had* killed Randall, I suppose, when he woke up and found Randall dead and blood on his hands.

" 'It's all got to come out now, I suppose,' says he, nodding. 'What did happen was that the three of 'em were in that back room, which Fred didn't remember. He and Randall had a fight while they were baiting Jessie; Fred whacked him hard enough with that mallet to lay him out, but all the blood he got was from a big splash over Randall's eye. Jessie . . . Well, Jessie finished the job when Fred ran away, that's all.'

" ' 'But, you damned fool,' cried Bob Moran, and begins to pound the table, 'why did you have to go and kill Fred when Jessie had confessed?'

" 'You fellows wouldn't have convicted Jessie, would you?' says Ed, blinking round at us. 'No. But, if Fred had lived after her confession, you'd have *had* to, boys. That was how I figured it out. Once Fred learned what did happen, that he wasn't guilty and she was, he'd never have let up until he'd carried that case to the Superior Court out of your hands. He'd have screamed all over the State until they either had to hang her or send her up for life. I couldn't stand that. As I say, that was how I figured it out, although my brain's not so clear these days. So,' says he, nodding and leaning over to take aim at the cuspidor, 'when I heard about that telephone call, I went into Fred's cell and finished *my* job.'

" 'But don't you understand,' says Judge Hunt, in the way you'd reason with a lunatic, 'that Bob Moran will have to arrest you for murder, and—'

"It was the peacefulness of Ed's expression that scared us then. He got up from his chair, and dusted his shiny black coat, and smiled at us.

" 'Oh, no,' says he very clearly. 'That's what you don't understand. You can't do a single damned thing to me. You can't even arrest me.'

" 'He's bughouse,' says Bob Moran.

" 'Am I?' says Ed affably. 'Listen to me. I've committed what you might call a perfect murder, because I've done it legally . . . Judge, what time did you talk to the Governor's office, and get the order for the execution to be called off? Be careful now.'

"And I said, with the whole idea of the business suddenly hitting me:

" 'It was maybe five minutes past nine, wasn't it, Judge? I remember the court-house clock striking when we were going over the Bridge of Sighs.'

" 'I remember it too,' says Ed Nabors. 'And Doc Macdonald will tell you that Fred Joliffe was dead before ever that clock struck nine. I have in my pocket,' says he, unbuttoning his coat, 'a court order which authorizes me to kill Fred Joliffe, by means of hanging by the neck—which I did—between the hours of eight and nine in the morning—which I also did. And I did it in full legal style before the order was countermanded. Well?'

"Judge Hunt took off his stovepipe hat and wiped his face with a bandana. We all looked at him.

" 'You can't get away with this,' says the judge, and grabs the sheriff's orders off the table. 'You can't trifle with the law in that way. And you can't execute sentence alone. Look here! "In the presence of a qualified medical practitioner." What do you say to that?'

" 'Well, I can produce my medical diploma,' says Ed, nodding again. 'I may be a booze-hister, and mighty unreliable, but they haven't struck me off the register yet. . . . You lawyers are hell on the wording of the law,' says he admiringly, 'and it's the wording that's done for you this time. Until you get the law altered with some fancy words, there's nothing in that document to say that the doctor and the hangman can't be the same person.'

"After a while Bob Moran turned round to the judge with a funny expression on his face. It might have been a grin.

" 'This ain't according to morals,' says he. 'A fine citizen like Fred shouldn't get murdered like that. It's awful. Something's got to be done about it. As you said yourself this morning, Judge, he ought to have the law and nothing but the law. Is Ed right, Judge?'

" 'Frankly, I don't know,' says Judge Hunt, wiping his face again. 'But, so far as I know, he is. What are you doing, Robert?'

" 'I'm writing him out a cheque for fifty dollars,' says Bob Moran, surprised-like. 'We got to have it all nice and legal, haven't we?' "

## *Persons or Things Unknown*

"Persons or Things Unknown" was published in the Christmas 1938 issue of the British magazine *The Sketch*. The first U.S. printing was in *The Department of Queer Complaints* (1940). The glossy British weeklies at this time usually included a Christmas ghost story at the end of the year, and Carr wrote at least three such tales. Being John Dickson Carr, however, he felt it necessary to include at least the possibility of a rational solution. The ghost-story form allowed Carr to begin in the present but quickly go back in time to events taking place in the England of the Merry Monarch, Charles II.

# Persons or Things Unknown

"After all," said our host, "it's Christmas. Why not let the skeleton out of the bag?"

"Or the cat out of the closet," said the historian, who likes to be precise even about clichés. "Are you serious?"

"Yes," said our host. "I want to know whether it's safe for anyone to sleep in that little room at the head of the stairs."

He had just bought the place. This party was in the nature of a house-warming; and I had already decided privately that the place needed one. It was a long, damp, high-windowed house, hidden behind a hill in Sussex. The drawing-room, where a group of us had gathered round the fire after dinner, was much too long and much too draughty. It had fine panelling—a rich brown where the firelight was always finding new gleams—and a hundred little reflections trembled down its length, as in so many small gloomy mirrors. But it remained draughty.

Of course, we all liked the house. It had the most modern of lighting and heating arrangements, though the plumbing sent ghostly noises and clanks far down into its interior whenever you turned on a tap. But the smell of the past was in it; and you could not get over the idea that somebody was following you about. Now, at the host's flat mention of a certain possibility, we all looked at our wives.

"But you never told us," said the historian's wife, rather shocked, "you never told us you had a ghost here!"

"I don't know that I have," replied our host quite seriously. "All I have is a bundle of evidence about something queer that once happened. It's all right; I haven't put anyone in that little room at the head of the stairs. So we can drop the discussion, if you'd rather."

"You know we can't," said the inspector: who, as a matter of strict fact, is an Assistant Commissioner of the Metropolitan Police. He smoked a large cigar, and contemplated ghosts with satisfaction. "This is exactly the time and place to hear about it. What is it?"

"It's rather in your line," our host told him slowly. Then he looked at the historian. "And in your line, too. It's a historical story. I suppose you'd call it a historical romance."

"I probably should. What is the date?"

"The date is the year sixteen hundred and sixty."

"That's Charles the Second, isn't it, Will?" demanded the historian's wife; she annoys him sometimes by asking these questions. "I'm terribly fond of them. I hope it has lots of big names in it. You know: Charles the Second and Buckingham and the rest of them. I remember, when I was a little girl, going to see"—she mentioned a great actor—"play David Garrick. I was looking forward to it. I expected to see the programme and the cast of characters positively bristling with people like Dr. Johnson and Goldsmith, and Burke and Gibbon and Reynolds, going in and out every minute. There wasn't a single one of them in it, and I felt swindled before the play had begun."

The trouble was that she spoke without conviction. The historian looked sceptically over his pince-nez.

"I warn you," he said, "if this is something you claim to have found in a drawer, in a crabbed old handwriting and all the rest of it, I'm going to be all over you professionally. Let me hear one anachronism—"

But he spoke without conviction, too. Our host was so serious that there was a slight, uneasy silence, in the group.

"No. I didn't find it in a drawer; the parson gave it to me. And the handwriting isn't particularly crabbed. I can't show it to you, because it's being typed, but it's a diary: a great, hefty mass of stuff. Most of it is rather dull, though I'm steeped in the seventeenth century, and I confess I enjoy it. The diary was begun in the summer of '60—just after the Restoration—and goes on to the end of '64. It was kept by Mr. Everard Poynter, who owned Manfred Manor (that's six or seven miles from here) when it was a farm.

"I know that fellow," he added, looking thoughtfully at the fire. "I know about him and his sciatica and his views on mutton and politics. I know why he went up to London to dance on Oliver Cromwell's grave, and I can guess who stole the two sacks of malt out of his brew-house while he was away. I see him as half a Hat; the old boy had a beaver hat he wore on his wedding day, and I'll bet he wore it to his death. It's out of all this that I got the details about people. The actual facts I got from the report of the coroner's inquest, which the parson lent me."

"Hold on!" said the Inspector, sitting up straight. "Did this fellow Poynter see the ghost and die?"

"No, no. Nothing like that. But he was one of the witnesses. He saw a man hacked to death, with thirteen stab-wounds in his body, from a hand that wasn't there and a weapon that didn't exist."

There was a silence.

"A murder?" asked the Inspector.

"A murder."

"Where?"

"In that little room at the head of the stairs. It used to be called the Ladies' Withdrawing Room."

Now, it is all very well to sit in your well-lighted flat in town and say we were hypnotized by an atmosphere. You can hear motor-cars crashing their gears, or curse somebody's wireless. You did not sit in that house, with a great wind rushing up off the downs, and a wall of darkness built up for three miles around you: knowing that at a certain hour you would have to retire to your room and put out the light, completing the wall.

"I regret to say," went on our host, "that there are no great names. These people were no more concerned with the Court of Charles the Second—with one exception—than we are concerned with the Court of George the Sixth. They lived in a little, busy, possibly ignorant world. They were fierce, fire-eating Royalists, most of them, who cut the Stuart arms over their chimney-pieces again and only made a gala trip to town to see the regicides executed in October of '60. Poynter's diary is crowded with them. Among others there is Squire Radlow, who owned this house then and was a great friend of Poynter. There was Squire Radlow's wife, Martha, and his daughter Mary.

"Mistress Mary Radlow was seventeen years old. She was not one of your fainting girls. Poynter—used to giving details—records that she was five feet tall, and thirty-two inches round the bust. 'Pretty and delicate,' Poynter says, with hazel eyes and a small mouth. But she could spin flax against any woman in the county; she once drained a pint of wine at a draught, for a wager; and she took eager pleasure in any good spectacle, like a bear-baiting or a hanging. I don't say that flippantly, but as a plain matter of fact. She was also fond of fine clothes, and danced well.

"In the summer of '60 Mistress Mary was engaged to be married to Richard Oakley, of Rawndene. Nobody seems to have known much about Oakley. There are any number of references to him in the diary, but Poynter gives up trying to make him out. Oakley was older than the girl; of genial disposition, though he wore his hair like a Puritan; and a great reader of books. He had a good estate at Rawndene, which he managed well, but his candle burned late over his books; and he wandered abroad in all weathers, summer or frost, in as black a study as the Black Man.

"You might have thought that Mistress Mary would have preferred somebody livelier. But Oakley was good enough company, by all accounts, and he suited her exactly—they tell me that wives understand this.

"And here is where the trouble enters. At the Restoration, Oakley was looking a little white. Not that his loyalty was exactly suspect; but he had bought his estate under the Commonwealth. If sales made under the Commonwealth were now declared null and void by the new Government, it meant ruin for Oakley; and also, under the business-like standards of the time, it meant the end of his prospective marriage to Mistress Mary.

"Then Gerald Vanning appeared.

"Hoy, what a blaze he must have made! He was fresh and oiled from Versailles, from Cologne, from Bruges, from Brussels, from Breda, from everywhere he had gone in the train of the formerly exiled king. Vanning was one of those 'confident young men' about whom we hear so much complaint from old-style Cavaliers in the early years of the Restoration. His family had been very powerful in Kent before the Civil Wars. Everybody knew he would be well rewarded, as he was.

"If this were a romance, I could now tell you how Mistress Mary fell in love with the handsome young Cavalier, and forgot about Oakley. But the truth seems to be that she never liked Vanning. Vanning disgusted Poynter by a habit of bowing and curvetting, with a superior smile, every time he made a remark. It is probable that Mistress Mary understood him no better than Poynter did.

"There is a description in the diary of a dinner Squire Radlow gave to welcome him here at this house. Vanning came over in a coach, despite the appalling state of the roads, with a dozen lackeys in attendance. This helped to impress the Squire, though nothing had as yet been settled on him by the new regime. Vanning already wore his hair long, whereas the others were just growing theirs. They must have looked odd and patchy, like men beginning to grow beards, and rustic enough to amuse him.

"But Mistress Mary was there. Vanning took one look at her, clapped his hand on the back of a chair, bowed, rolled up his eyes, and began to lay siege to her in the full-dress style of the French king taking a town. He slid *bons mots* on his tongue like sweetmeats; he hiccoughed; he strutted; he directed killing ogles. Squire Radlow and his wife were enraptured. They liked Oakley of Rawndene—but it was possible that Oakley might be penniless in a month. Whereas Vanning was to be heaped with preferments, a matter of which he made no secret. Throughout this dinner Richard Oakley looked unhappy, and 'shifted his eyes.'

"When the men got drunk after dinner, Vanning spoke frankly to Squire Radlow. Oakley staggered out to get some air under the apple-trees; what between liquor and crowding misfortunes, he did not feel well. Together among the fumes, Vanning and Squire Radlow shouted friendship at each other, and wept. Vanning swore he would never wed anybody but Mistress Mary, not if his soul rotted deep in hell as Oliver's. The Squire was stern, but not too stern. 'Sir,' said the Squire, 'you abuse my hospitality; my daughter is pledged to the gentleman who has just left us; but it may be that we must speak of this presently.' Poynter, though he saw the justice of the argument, went home disturbed.

"Now, Gerald Vanning was not a fool. I have seen his portrait, painted a few years later when periwigs came into fashion. It is a shiny, shrewd, razorish kind of face. He had some genuine classical learning, and a smattering of scientific monkey-tricks, the new toy of the time. But, above all, he had foresight. In the first place, he was genuinely smitten with hazel eyes and other charms. In the second place, Mistress Mary Radlow was a catch. When awarding bounty to the faithful, doubtless the

King and Sir Edward Hyde would not forget Vanning of Mallingford; on the other hand, it was just possible they might.

"During the next three weeks it was almost taken for granted that Vanning should eventually become the Squire's son-in-law. Nothing was said or done, of course. But Vanning dined a dozen times here, drank with the Squire, and gave to the Squire's wife a brooch once owned by Charles the First. Mistress Mary spoke of it furiously to Poynter.

"Then the unexpected news came.

"Oakley was safe in his house and lands. An Act had been passed to confirm all sales and leases of property since the Civil Wars. It meant that Oakley was once more the well-to-do son-in-law; and the Squire could no longer object to his bargain.

"I have here an account of how this news was received at the manor. I did not get it from Poynter's diary. I got it from the records of the coroner's inquest. What astonishes us when we read these chronicles is the blunt directness, the violence, like a wind, or a pistol clapped to the head, with which people set about getting what they wanted. For, just two months afterwards, there was murder done."

Our host paused. The room was full of the reflections of firelight. He glanced at the ceiling; what we heard up there was merely the sound of a servant walking overhead.

"Vanning," he went on, "seems to have taken the fact quietly enough. He was here at the manor when Oakley arrived with the news. It was five or six o'clock in the afternoon. Mistress Mary, the Squire, the Squire's wife, and Vanning were sitting in the Ladies' Withdrawing Room. This was (and is) the room at the head of the stairs—a little square place, with two 'panel' windows that would not open. It was furnished with chairs of oak and brocade; a needlework-frame; and a sideboard chastely bearing a plate of oranges, a glass jug of water, and some glasses.

"There was only one candle burning, at some distance from Vanning, so that nobody had a good view of his face. He sat in his riding-coat, with his sword across his lap. When Oakley came in with the news, he was observed to put his hand on his sword; but afterwards he 'made a leg' and left without more words.

"The wedding had originally been set for the end of November; both Oakley and Mistress Mary still claimed this date. It was accepted with all the more cheerfulness by the Squire, since, in the intervening months, Vanning had not yet received any dazzling benefits. True, he had been awarded £500 a year by the Healing and Blessed Parliament. But he was little better off than Oakley; a bargain was a bargain, said the Squire, and Oakley was his own dear son. Nobody seems to know what Vanning did in the interim, except that he settled down quietly at Mallingford.

"But from this time curious rumours began to go about the country-side. They all centred round Richard Oakley. Poynter records some of them, at first evidently not even realizing their direction. They were as light as dandelion-clocks blown off, but they floated and settled.

"Who was Oakley? What did anybody know about him, except that he had come here and bought land under Oliver? He had vast learning, and above a hundred books in his house; what need did he have of that? What had he been? A parson? A doctor of letters of physic? Or letters of a more unnatural kind? Why did he go for long walks in the wood, particularly after dusk?

"Oakley, if questioned, said that this was his nature. But an honest man, meaning an ordinary man, could understand no such nature. A wood was thick; you could not tell what might be in it after nightfall; an honest man preferred the tavern. Such whispers were all the more rapid-moving because of the troubled times. The broken bones of a Revolution are not easily healed. Then there was the unnatural state of the weather. In winter there was no cold at all: the roads dusty; a swarm of flies; and the rose-bushes full of leaves into the following January.

"Oakley heard none of the rumours, or pretended to hear none. It was Jamy Achen, a lad of weak mind and therefore afraid of nothing, who saw something following Richard Oakley through Gallows Copse. The boy said he had not got a good look at it, since the time was after dusk. But he heard it rustle behind the trees, peering out at intervals after Mr. Oakley. He said that it seemed human, but that he was not sure it was alive.

"On the night of Friday, the 26th November, Gerald Vanning rode over to this house alone. It was seven o'clock, a late hour for the country. He was admitted to the lower hall by Kitts, the Squire's steward, and he asked for Mr. Oakley. Kitts told him that Mr. Oakley was above-stairs with Mistress Mary, and that the Squire was asleep over supper with Mr. Poynter.

"It is certain that Vanning was wearing no sword. Kitts held the candle high and looked at him narrowly, for he seemed on a wire of apprehension and kept glancing over his shoulder as he pulled off his gloves. He wore jack-boots, a riding-coat half-buttoned, a lace band at the neck, and a flat-crowned beaver hat with a gold band. Under his sharp nose there was a little edge of moustache, and he was sweating.

" 'Mr. Oakley has brought a friend with him, I think,' says Vanning.

" 'No, sir,' says Kitts, 'he is alone.'

" 'But I am sure his friend has followed him,' says Vanning, again twitching his head round and looking over his shoulder. He also jumped as though something had touched him, and kept turning round and round and looking sharply into corners as though he were playing hide-and-seek.

" 'Well!' says Mr. Vanning, with a whistle of breath through his nose. 'Take me to Mistress Mary. Stop! First fetch two or three brisk lads from the kitchen, and you shall go with me.'

"The steward was alarmed, and asked what was the matter. Vanning would not tell him, but instructed him to see that the servants carried cudgels and lights. Four of them went above-stairs. Vanning knocked at the door of the Withdrawing Room, and was bidden to enter. The servants remained outside, and both the lights and the cudgels trembled in their hands: later they did not know why.

"As the door opened and closed, Kitts caught a glimpse of Mistress Mary sitting by the table in the rose-brocade dress she reserved usually for Sundays, and Oakley sitting on the edge of the table beside her. Both looked round as though surprised.

"Presently Kitts heard voices talking, but so low he could not make out what was said. The voices spoke more rapidly; then there was a sound of moving about. The next thing to which Kitts could testify was a noise as though a candlestick had been knocked over. There was a thud; a high-pitched kind of noise; muffled breathing sounds and a sort of thrashing on the floor; and Mistress Mary suddenly beginning to scream over it.

"Kitts and his three followers laid hold of the door, but someone had bolted it. They attacked the door in a way that roused the Squire in the dining-room below, but it held. Inside, after a silence, someone was heard to stumble and grope towards the door. Squire Radlow and Mr. Poynter came running up the stairs just as the door was unbolted from inside.

"Mistress Mary was standing there, panting, with her eyes wide and staring. She was holding up one edge of her full skirt, where it was stained with blood as though someone had scoured and polished a weapon there. She cried to them to bring lights; and one of the servants held up a lantern in the doorway.

"Vanning was half-lying, half-crouching over against the far wall, with a face like oiled paper as he lifted round his head to look at them. But they were looking at Oakley, or what was left of Oakley. He had fallen near the table, with the candle smashed beside him. They could not tell how many wounds there were in Oakley's neck and body; above a dozen, Poynter thought, and he was right. Vanning stumbled over and tried to lift him up, but of course, it was too late. Now listen to Poynter's own words:

" 'Mr. Radlow ran to Mr. Vanning and laid hold of him, crying: "You are a murderer! You have murdered him!" Mr. Vanning cried to him: "By

God and His mercy, I have not touched him! I have no sword or dagger by me!" And indeed, this was true. For he was flung down on the floor by this bloody work, and ordered to be searched, but not so much as a pin was there in his clothes.

" 'I had observed by the nature of the wide, gaping wounds that some such blade as a broad knife had inflicted them, or the like. But what had done this was a puzzle, for every inch of the room did we search, high, low and turnover; and still not so much as a pin in crack or crevice.

" 'Mr. Vanning deposed that as he was speaking with Mr. Oakley, something struck out the light, and over-threw Mr. Oakley, and knelt on his chest. But who or what this was, or where it had gone when the light was brought, he could not say.' "

Bending close to the firelight, our host finished reading the notes from the sheet of paper in his hands. He folded up the paper, put it back in his pocket, and looked at us.

The historian's wife, who had drawn closer to her husband, shifted uneasily. "I wish you wouldn't tell us these things," she complained. "But tell us, anyway. I still don't understand. What was the man killed with, then?"

"That," said our host, lighting his pipe, "is the question. If you accept natural laws as governing this world, there wasn't anything that could have killed him. Look here a moment!"

(For we were all looking at the ceiling.)

"The Squire begged Mistress Mary to tell him what had happened. First she began to whimper a little, and for the first time in her life she fainted. The Squire wanted to throw some water over her, but Vanning carried her downstairs and they forced brandy between her teeth. When she recovered she was a trifle wandering, with no story at all.

"Something had put out the light. There had been a sound like a fall and a scuffling. Then the noise of moving about, and the smell of blood in a close, confined room. Something seemed to be plucking or pulling at her skirts. She does not appear to have remembered anything more.

"Of course, Vanning was put under restraint, and a magistrate sent for. They gathered in this room, which was a good deal bleaker and barer than it is to-day; but they pinned Vanning in the chimney-corner of that fireplace. The Squire drew his sword and attempted to run Vanning through: while both of them wept, as the fashion was. But Poynter ordered two of the lads to hold the Squire back, quoting himself later as saying: 'This must be done in good order.'

"Now, what I want to impress on you is that these people were not fools. They had possibly a cruder turn of thought and speech; but they were used to dealing with realities like wood and beef and leather. Here was a reality. Oakley's wounds were six inches deep and an inch wide, from a thick, flat blade that in places had scraped the bone. But there wasn't any such blade, and they knew it.

"Four men stood in the door and held lights while they searched for that knife (if there was such a thing): and they didn't find it. They pulled the room to pieces; and they didn't find it. Nobody could have whisked it out, past the men in the door. The windows didn't open, being set into the wall like panels, so nobody could have got rid of the knife there. There was only one door, outside which the servants had been standing. Something had cut a man to pieces; yet it simply wasn't there.

"Vanning, pale but calmer, repeated his account. Questioned as to why he had come to the house that night, he answered that there had been a matter to settle with Oakley. Asked what it was, he said he had not liked the conditions in his own home for the past month: he would beg Mr. Oakley to mend them. He had done Mr. Oakley no harm, beyond trying to take a bride from him, and therefore he would ask Mr. Oakley to call off his dogs. What dogs? Vanning explained that he did not precisely mean dogs. He meant something that had got into his bedroom cupboard, but was only there at night; and he had reasons for thinking Mr. Oakley had whistled it there. It had been there only since he had been paying attentions to Mistress Mary.

"These men were only human. Poynter ordered the steward to go up and search the little room again—and the steward wouldn't go.

"That little seed of terror had begun to grow like a mango-tree under a cloth, and push up the cloth and stir out tentacles. It was easy to forget the broad, smiling face of Richard Oakley, and to remember the curious 'shifting' of his eyes. When you recalled that, after all, Oakley was twice Mistress Mary's age, you might begin to wonder just whom you had been entertaining at bread and meat.

"Even Squire Radlow did not care to go upstairs again in his own house. Vanning, sweating and squirming in the chimney corner, plucked up courage as a confident young man and volunteered to go. They let him. But no sooner had he got into the little room than the door clapped again, and he came out running. It was touch-and-go whether they would desert the house in a body."

Again our host paused. In the silence it was the Inspector who spoke, examining his cigar and speaking with some scepticism. He had a common-sense voice, which restored reasonable values.

"Look here," he said, "are you telling us local bogy-tales, or are you seriously putting this forward as evidence?"

"As evidence given at a coroner's inquest."

"Reliable evidence?"

"I believe so."

"I don't," returned the Inspector, drawing the air through a hollow tooth. "After all, I suppose we've got to admit that a man was murdered, since there was an inquest. But if he died of being hacked or slashed with thirteen wounds, some instrument made those wounds. What happened to that weapon? You say it wasn't in the room; but how do we know that? How do we know it wasn't hidden away somewhere, and they simply couldn't find it?"

"I think I can give you my word," said our host slowly, "that no weapon was hidden there."

"Then what the devil happened to it? A knife at least six inches in the blade, and an inch broad—"

"Yes. But the fact is, nobody could see it."

"It wasn't hidden anywhere, and yet nobody could see it?"

"That's right."

"An invisible weapon?"

"Yes," answered our host, with a curious shining in his eyes. "A quite literally invisible weapon."

"How do you know?" demanded his wife abruptly.

"Hitherto she had taken no part in the conversation. But she had been studying him in an odd way, sitting on a hassock; and, as he hesitated, she rose at him in a glory of accusation.

"You villain!" she cried. "Ooh, you unutterable villain! You've been making it all up! Just to make everybody afraid to go to bed, and because *I* didn't know anything about the place, you've been telling us a pack of lies—"

But he stopped her.

"No. If I had been making it up, I should have told you it was a story." Again he hesitated, almost biting his nails. "I'll admit that I may have been trying to mystify you a bit. That's reasonable, because I honestly don't know the truth myself. I can make a guess at it, that's all. I can make a guess at how those wounds came there. But that isn't the real problem. That isn't what bothers me, don't you see?"

Here the historian intervened. "A wide acquaintance with sensational fiction," he said, "gives me the line on which you're working. I submit that the victim was stabbed with an icicle, as in several tales I could mention. Afterwards the ice melted—and was, in consequence, an invisible weapon."

"No," said our host.

"I mean," he went on, "that it's not feasible. You would hardly find an icicle in such unnaturally warm weather as they were having. And icicles are brittle: you wouldn't get a flat, broad icicle of such steel-strength and sharpness that thirteen stabs could be made and the bone scraped in some of them. And an icicle isn't invisible. Under the circumstances, this knife was invisible—despite its size."

"Bosh!" said the historian's wife. "There isn't any such thing."

"There is if you come to think about it. Of course, it's only an idea of mine, and it may be all wrong. Also, as I say, it's not the real problem, though it's so closely associated with the real problem that—

"But you haven't heard the rest of the story. Shall I conclude it?"

"By all means."

"I am afraid there are no great alarms or sensations," our host went on, "though the very name of Richard Oakley became a nightmare to keep people indoors at night. 'Oakley's friend' became a local synonym for anything that might get you if you didn't look sharp. One or two people saw him walking in the woods afterwards, his head was on one side and the stab-wounds were still there.

"A grand jury of Sussex gentlemen, headed by Sir Benedict Skene, completely exonerated Gerald Vanning. The coroner's jury had already said 'persons or things unknown,' and added words of sympathy with Mistress Mary to the effect that she was luckily quit of a dangerous bargain. It may not surprise you to hear that eighteen months after Oakley's death she married Vanning.

"She was completely docile, though her old vivacity had gone. In those days young ladies did not remain spinsters through choice. She smiled, nodded, and made the proper responses, though it seems probable that she never got over what had happened.

"Matters became settled, even humdrum. Vanning waxed prosperous and respectable. His subsequent career I have had to look up in other sources, since Poynter's diary breaks off at the end of '64. But a grateful Government made him Sir Gerald Vanning, Bart. He became a leading member of the Royal Society, tinkering with the toys of science. His cheeks filled out, the slyness left his eyes, a periwig adorned his head, and four Flanders mares drew his coach to Gresham House. At home he often chose this house to live in when Squire Radlow died; he moved between here and Mallingford with the soberest grace. The little room, once such a cause of terror, he seldom visited; but its door was not locked.

"His wife saw to it that these flagstones were kept scrubbed, and every stick of wood shining. She was a good wife. He for his part was a good husband: he treated her well and drank only for his thirst, though she often pressed him to drink more than he did. It is at this pitch of domesticity that we get the record of another coroner's inquest.

"Vanning's throat was cut on the night of the 5th October, '67.

"On an evening of high winds, he and his wife came here from Mallingford. He was in unusually good spirits, having just done a profitable piece of business. They had supper together, and Vanning drank a great deal. His wife kept him company at it. (Didn't I tell you she once drank off a pint of wine at a draught, for a wager?) She said it would make him sleep soundly; for it seems to be true that he sometimes talked in his sleep. At eight o'clock, she tells us, she went up to bed, leaving him still at the table. At what time he went upstairs we do not know, and neither do the servants. Kitts, the steward, thought he heard him stumbling up that staircase out there at a very late hour. Kitts also thought he heard someone crying out, but a high October gale was blowing and he could not be sure.

"On the morning of the 6th October, a cowherd named Coates was coming round the side of this house in a sodden daybreak from which the storm had just cleared. He was on his way to the west meadow, and stopped to drink at a rain-water barrel under the eaves just below the little room at the head of the stairs. As he was about to drink, he noticed a curious colour in the water. Looking up to find out how it had come there, he saw Sir Gerald Vanning's face looking down at him under the shadow of the yellow trees. Sir Gerald's head was sticking out of the window, and did not move; neither did the eyes. Some of the glass in the window was still intact, though his head had been run through it, and—"

It was at this point that the Inspector uttered an exclamation.

It was an exclamation of enlightenment. Our host looked at him with a certain grimness, and nodded.

"Yes," he said. "You know the truth now, don't you?"

"The truth?" repeated the historian's wife, almost screaming with perplexity. "The truth about what?"

"About the murder of Oakley," said our host. "About the trick Vanning used to murder Oakley seven years before.

"I'm fairly sure he did it," our host went on, nodding reflectively. "Nothing delighted the people of that time so much as tricks and gadgets of that very sort. A clock that ran by rolling bullets down an inclined plane; a diving-bell; a burglar-alarm; the Royal Society played with all of them. And Vanning (study his portrait one day) profited by the monkey-tricks he learned in exile. He invented an invisible knife."

"But see here—!" protested the historian.

"Of course he planned the whole thing against Oakley. Oakley was no more a necromancer or a consorter with devils than I am. All those rumours about him were started with a definite purpose by Vanning himself. A crop of whispers, a weak-minded lad to be bribed, the whole power of suggestion set going; and Vanning was ready for business.

"On the given night he rode over to this house, alone, with a certain kind of knife in his pocket. He made a great show of pretending he was chased by imaginary monsters, and he alarmed the steward. With the servants for witnesses, he went upstairs to see Oakley and Mistress Mary. He bolted the door. He spoke pleasantly to them. When he had managed to distract the girl's attention, he knocked out the light, tripped up Oakley, and set upon him with that certain kind of knife. There had to be many wounds and much blood, so he could later account for blood on himself. The girl was too terrified in the dark to move. He had only to clean his knife on a soft but stiff-brocaded gown, and then put down the knife in full view. Nobody noticed it."

The historian blinked. "Admirable!" he said. "Nobody noticed it, eh? Can you tell me the sort of blade that can be placed in full view without anybody noticing it?"

"Yes," said our host. "A blade made of ordinary plain glass, placed in the large glass jug full of water standing on a sideboard table."

There was a silence.

"I told you about that glass water-jug. It was a familiar fixture. Nobody examines a transparent jug of water. Vanning could have made a glass knife with the crudest of cutting tools; and glass is murderous stuff —strong, flat, sharp-edged, and as sharp-pointed as you want to make it. There was only candle-light, remember. Any minute traces of blood that might be left on the glass knife would sink as sediment in the water, while everybody looked straight at the weapon in the water and never noticed it. But Vanning (you also remember?) prevented Squire Radlow from throwing water on the girl when she fainted. Instead he carried her downstairs. Afterwards he told an admirable series of horror-tales; he found an excuse to go back to the room again alone, slip the knife into his sleeve, and get rid of it in the confusion."

The Inspector frowned thoughtfully. "But the real problem—" he said.

"Yes. If that was the way it was done, did the wife know? Vanning talked in his sleep, remember."

We looked at each other. The historian's wife, after a glance round, asked the question that was in our minds.

"And what was the verdict of *that* inquest?"

"Oh, that was simple," said our host. "Death by misadventure, from falling through a window while drunk and cutting his throat on the glass. Somebody observed that there were marks of heels on the board floor as though he might have been dragged there, but this wasn't insisted on. Mistress Mary lived on in complete happiness, and died at the ripe age of eighty-six, full of benevolence and sleep. These are natural explanations. Everything is natural. There's nothing wrong with that little room at the head of the stairs. It's been turned into a bedroom now; I assure you it's comfortable; and anyone who cares to sleep there is free to do so. But at the same time—"

"Quite," we said.

# The Gentleman From Paris

"The Gentleman from Paris," set in New York City in 1849, is often considered John Dickson Carr's best short story. It received first prize in the annual contest run by *Ellery Queen's Mystery Magazine,* and it was published in the April 1950 issue. The first British printing seems to have been in *Majority, 1931–1952,* an anthology honoring his British publisher's twenty-first anniversary. The story became the basis for *The Man with a Cloak,* an MGM movie released in 1951, starring Joseph Cotten, Leslie Caron, Jim Backus, and Barbara Stanwyck.

# The Gentleman from Paris

Carlton House Hotel
Broadway, New York
14 April 1849

My dear brother:

Were my hand more steady, Maurice, or my soul less agitated, I should have written to you before this. *All is safe:* so much I tell you at once. For the rest, I seek sleep in vain; and this is not merely because I find myself a stranger and a foreigner in New York. Listen and judge.

We discussed, I think, the humiliation that a Frenchman must go to England ere he could take passage in a reliable ship for America. The *Britannia* steam-packet departed from Liverpool on the second of the month, and arrived here on the seventeenth. Do not smile, I implore you, when I tell you that my first visit on American soil was to Platt's Saloon, under Wallack's Theater.

Great God, that voyage!

On my stomach I could hold not even champagne. For one of my height and breadth I was as weak as a child.

"Be good enough," I said to a fur-capped coachman, when I had struggled through the horde of Irish immigrants, "to drive me to some fashionable place of refreshment."

The coachman had no difficulty in understanding my English, which pleased me. And how extraordinary are these "saloons"!

The saloon of M. Platt was loud with the thump of hammers cracking ice, which is delivered in large blocks. Though the hand-colored gas globes, and the rose paintings on the front of the bar-counter, were as fine as we could see at the Three Provincial Brothers in Paris, yet I confess that the place did not smell so agreeably. A number of gentlemen, wearing hats perhaps a trifle taller than is fashionable at home, lounged at the bar-counter and shouted. I attracted no attention until I called for a sherry cobbler.

One of the "bartenders," as they are called in New York, gave me a sharp glance as he prepared the glass.

"Just arrived from the Old Country, I bet?" he said in no unfriendly tone.

Though it seemed strange to hear France mentioned in this way, I smiled and bowed assent.

"Italian, maybe?" said he.

This bartender, of course, could not know how deadly was the insult.

"Sir," I replied, "I am a Frenchman."

And now in truth he was pleased! His fat face opened and smiled like a distorted, gold-toothed flower.

"Is that so, now!" he exclaimed. "And what might your name be?

Unless"—and here his face darkened with that sudden defensiveness and suspicion which, for no reason I can discern, will often strike into American hearts—"unless," said he, "you don't want to give it?"

"Not at all," I assured him earnestly. "I am Armand de Lafayette, at your service."

My dear brother, what an extraordinary effect!

It was silence. All sounds, even the faint whistling of the gas jets, seemed to die away in that stone-flagged room. Every man along the line of the bar was looking at me. I was conscious only of faces, mostly with whiskers under the chin instead of down the cheekbones, turned on me in basilisk stare.

"Well, well, well!" almost sneered the bartender. "You wouldn't be no relation of the *Marquis* de Lafayette, would you?"

It was my turn to be astonished. Though our father has always forbidden us to mention the name of our late uncle, due to his republican sympathies, yet I knew he occupied small place in the history of France and it puzzled me to comprehend how these people had heard of him.

"The late Marquis de Lafayette," I was obliged to admit, "was my uncle."

"You better be careful, young feller," suddenly yelled a grimy little man with a pistol buckled under his long coat. "We don't like being diddled, we don't."

"Sir," I replied, taking my bundle of papers from my pocket and whacking them down on the bar-counter, "have the goodness to examine my credentials. Should you still doubt my identity, we can then debate the matter in any way which pleases you."

"This is furrin writing," shouted the bartender. *"I* can't read it!"

And then—how sweet was the musical sound on my ear!—I heard a voice addressing me in my own language.

"Perhaps, sir," said the voice, in excellent French and with great stateliness, "I may be able to render you some small service."

The newcomer, a slight man of dark complexion, drawn up under an old shabby cloak of military cut, stood a little way behind me. If I had met him on the boulevards, I might not have found him very prepossessing. He had a wild and wandering eye, with an even wilder shimmer of brandy. He was not very steady on his feet. And yet, Maurice, his manner! It was such that I instinctively raised my hat, and the stranger very gravely did the same.

"And to whom," said I, "have I the honor . . . ?"

"I am Thaddeus Perley, sir, at your service."

"Another furriner!" said the grimy little man, in disgust.

"I am indeed a foreigner," said M. Perley in English, with an accent like a knife. "A foreigner to this dram shop. A foreigner to this neighborhood. A foreigner to—" Here he paused, and his eyes acquired an almost frightening blaze of loathing. "Yet I never heard that the reading of French was so very singular an accomplishment."

Imperiously—and yet, it seemed to me, with a certain shrinking nervousness—M. Perley came closer and lifted the bundle of papers.

"Doubtless," he said loftily, "I should not be credited were I to translate these. But here," and he scanned several of the papers, "is a letter of introduction in English. It is addressed to President Zachary Taylor from the American minister at Paris."

Again, my brother, what an enormous silence! It was interrupted by a cry from the bartender, who had snatched the documents from M. Perley.

"Boys, this is no diddle," said he. "This gent is the real thing!"

"He ain't!" thundered the little grimy man, with incredulity.

"He is!" said the bartender. "I'll be a son of a roe *(i.e., biche)* if he ain't!"

Well, Maurice, you and I have seen how Paris mobs can change. Americans are even more emotional. In the wink of an eye hostility became frantic affection. My back was slapped, my hand wrung, my person jammed against the bar by a crowd fighting to order me more refreshment.

The name of Lafayette, again and again, rose like a holy diapason. In vain I asked why this should be so. They appeared to think I was joking, and roared with laughter. I thought of M. Thaddeus Perley, as one who could supply an explanation.

But in the first rush toward me M. Perley had been flung backward. He fell sprawling in some wet stains of tobacco juice on the floor, and now I could not see him at all. For myself, I was weak from lack of food. A full beaker of whisky, which I was obliged to drink because all eyes were on me, made my head reel. Yet I felt compelled to raise my voice above the clamor.

"Gentlemen," I implored them, "will you hear me?"

"Silence for Lafayette!" said a big but very old man, with faded red whiskers. He had tears in his eyes, and he had been humming a catch called "Yankee Doodle." "Silence for Lafayette!"

"Believe me," said I, "I am full of gratitude for your hospitality. But I have business in New York, business of immediate and desperate urgency. If you will allow me to pay my reckoning . . ."

"Your money's no good here, monseer," said the bartender. "You're going to get liquored-up good and proper."

"But I have no wish, believe me, to become liquored up! It might well endanger my mission! In effect, I wish to go!"

"Wait a minute," said the little grimy man, with a cunning look. "What *is* this here business?"

You, Maurice, have called me quixotic. I deny this. You have also called me imprudent. Perhaps you are right; but what choice was left to me?

"Has any gentleman here," I asked, "heard of Mme Thevenet? Mme Thevenet, who lives at Number 23 Thomas Street, near Hudson Street?"

I had not, of course, expected an affirmative reply. Yet, in addition to one or two sniggers at mention of the street, several nodded their heads.

"Old miser woman?" asked a sportif character, who wore checkered trousers.

"I regret, sir, that you correctly describe her. Mme Thevenet is very rich. And I have come here," cried I, "to put right a damnable injustice!"

Struggle as I might, I could not free myself.

"How's that?" asked half a dozen.

"Mme Thevenet's daughter, Mlle Claudine, lives in the worst of poverty at Paris. Madame herself has been brought here, under some spell, by a devil of a woman calling herself . . . Gentlemen, I implore you!"

"And I bet you," cried the little grimy man with the pistol, "you're sweet on this daughter what's-her-name?" He seemed delighted. "Ain't you, now?"

How, I ask of all Providence, could these people have surprised my secret? Yet I felt obliged to tell the truth.

"I will not conceal from you," I said, "that I have in truth a high regard for Mlle Claudine. But this lady, believe me, is engaged to a friend of mine, an officer of artillery."

"Then what do you get out of it? Eh?" asked the grimy little man, with another cunning look.

The question puzzled me. I could not reply. But the bartender with the gold teeth leaned over.

"If you want to see the old Frenchie alive, monseer," said he, "you'd better git." *(Sic,* Maurice.) "I hearn tell she had a stroke this morning."

But a dozen voices clamored to keep me there, though this last intelligence sent me into despair. Then up rose the big and very old man with the faded whiskers: indeed, I had never realized how old, because he seemed so hale.

"Which of you was with Washington?" said he, suddenly taking hold of the fierce little man's neckcloth, and speaking with contempt. "Make way for the nephew of Lafayette!"

They cheered me then, Maurice. They hurried me to the door, they begged me to return, they promised they would await me. One glance I sought—nor can I say why—for M. Thaddeus Perley. He was sitting at a table by a pillar, under an open gas jet; his face whiter than ever, still wiping stains of tobacco juice from his cloak.

Never have I seen a more mournful prospect than Thomas Street, when my cab set me down there. Perhaps it was my state of mind; for if Mme Thevenet had died without a sou left to her daughter: you conceive it?

The houses of Thomas Street were faced with dingy yellow brick, and a muddy sky hung over the chimney pots. It had been warm all day, yet I found my spirit intolerably oppressed. Though heaven knows our Parisian streets are dirty enough, we do not allow pigs in them. Except for these, nothing moved in the forsaken street save a blind street musician, with his dog and an instrument called a banjo; but even he was silent too.

For some minutes, it seemed to me, I plied the knocker at Number 23, with hideous noise. Nothing stirred. Finally, one part of the door swung open a little, as for an eye. Whereupon I heard the shifting of a floor bolt, and both doors were swung open.

Need I say that facing me stood the woman whom we have agreed to call Mlle Jezebel?

She said to me: "And then, M. Armand?"

"Mme Thevenet!" cried I. "She is still alive?"

"She is alive," replied my companion, looking up at me from under the lids of her greenish eyes. "But she is completely paralyzed."

I have never denied, Maurice, that Mlle Jezebel has a certain attractiveness. She is not old or even middle aged. Were it not that her complexion is as muddy as was the sky above us then, she would have been pretty.

"And as for Claudine," I said to her, "the daughter of madame—"

"You have come too late, M. Armand."

And well I remember that at this moment there rose up, in the mournful street outside, the tinkle of the banjo played by the street musician. It moved closer, playing a popular catch whose words run something thus:

> Oh, I come from Alabama
>   With my banjo on my knee;
> I depart for Louisiana
>   My Susannah for to see.

Across the lips of mademoiselle flashed a smile of peculiar quality, like a razor cut before the blood comes.

"Gold," she whispered. "Ninety thousand persons, one hears, have gone to seek it. Go to California, M. Armand. It is the only place you will find gold."

This tune, they say, is a merry tune. It did not seem so, as the dreary twanging faded away. Mlle Jezebel, with her muddy blonde hair parted in the middle and drawn over her ears after the best fashion, faced me implacably. Her greenish eyes were wide open. Her old brown taffeta dress, full at the bust, narrow at the waist, rustled its wide skirts as she glided a step forward.

"Have the kindness," I said, "to stand aside. I wish to enter."

Hitherto in my life I had seen her docile and meek.

"You are no relative," she said. "I will not allow you to enter."

"In that case, I regret, I must."

"If you had ever spoken one kind word to *me,*" whispered mademoiselle, looking up from under her eyelids, and with her breast heaving, "one gesture of love—that is to say, of affection—you might have shared five million francs."

"Stand aside, I say!"

"As it is, you prefer a doll-faced consumptive at Paris. So be it!"

I was raging, Maurice; I confess it; yet I drew myself up with coldness.

"You refer, perhaps, to Claudine Thevenet?"

"And to whom else?"

"I might remind you, mademoiselle, that the lady is pledged to my good friend Lieutenant Delage. I have forgotten her."

"Have you?" asked our Jezebel, with her eyes on my face and a strange hungry look in them. Mlle Jezebel added, with more pleasure: "Well, she will die. Unless you can solve a mystery."

"A mystery?"

"I should not have said mystery, M. Armand. Because it is impossible of all solution. It is an Act of God!"

Up to this time the glass-fronted doors of the vestibule had stood open behind her, against a darkness of closed shutters in the house. There breathed out of it an odor of unswept carpets, a sourness of stale living. Someone was approaching, carrying a lighted candle.

"Who speaks?" called a man's voice; shaky, but as French as Mlle Jezebel's. "Who speaks concerning an Act of God?"

I stepped across the threshold. Mademoiselle, who never left my side, immediately closed and locked the front doors. As the candle glimmer moved still closer in gloom, I could have shouted for joy to see the man whom (as I correctly guessed) I had come to meet.

"You are M. Duroc, the lawyer!" I said. "You are my brother's friend!"

M. Duroc held the candle higher, to inspect me.

He was a big, heavy man who seemed to sag in all his flesh. In compensation for his bald head, the grayish-brown mustache flowed down and parted into two hairy fans of beard on either side of his chin. He looked at me through oval gold-rimmed spectacles; in a friendly way, but yet frightened. His voice was deep and gruff, clipping the syllables, despite his fright.

"And you"—*clip-clip;* the candle holder trembled—"you are Armand de Lafayette. I had expected you by the steam packet today. Well! You are here. On a fool's errand, I regret."

"But why?" (And I shouted at him, Maurice.)

I looked at mademoiselle, who was faintly smiling.

"M. Duroc!" I protested. "You wrote to my brother. You said you had persuaded madame to repent of her harshness toward her daughter!"

"Was that your duty?" asked the Jezebel, looking full at M. Duroc with her greenish eyes. "Was that your right?"

"I am a man of law," said M. Duroc. The deep monosyllables rapped, in ghostly bursts, through his parted beard. He was perspiring. "I am correct. Very correct! And yet—"

"Who nursed her?" asked the Jezebel. "Who soothed her, fed her, wore her filthy clothes, calmed her tempers and endured her interminable abuse? *I* did!"

And yet, all the time she was speaking, this woman kept sidling and sidling against me, brushing my side, as though she would make sure of my presence there.

"Well!" said the lawyer. "It matters little now! This mystery . . ."

You may well believe that all these cryptic remarks, as well as reference to a mystery or an Act of God, had driven me almost frantic. I demanded to know what he meant.

"Last night," said M. Duroc, "a certain article disappeared."

"Well, well?"

"It disappeared," said M. Duroc, drawn up like a grenadier. "But it could not conceivably have disappeared. I myself swear this! Our only suggestions as to how it might have disappeared are a toy rabbit and a barometer."

"Sir," I said, "I do not wish to be discourteous. But—"

"Am I mad, you ask?"

I bowed. If any man can manage at once to look sagging and uncertain, yet stately and dignified, M. Duroc managed it then. And dignity won, I think.

"Sir," he replied, gesturing the candle toward the rear of the house, "Mme Thevenet lies there in her bed. She is paralyzed. She can move only her eyes or partially the lips, without speech. Do you wish to see her?"

"If I am permitted."

"Yes. That would be correct. Accompany me."

And I saw the poor old woman, Maurice. Call her harridan if you like. It was a square room of good size, whose shutters had remained closed and locked for years. Can one smell rust? In that room, with faded green wallpaper, I felt I could.

One solitary candle did little more than dispel shadow. It burned atop the mantelpiece well opposite the foot of the bed; and a shaggy man, whom I afterward learned to be a police officer, sat in a green-upholstered armchair by an unlighted coal fire in the fireplace grate, picking his teeth with a knife.

"If you please, Dr. Harding!" M. Duroc called softly in English.

The long and lean American doctor, who had been bending over the bed so as to conceal from our sight the head and shoulders of Madame Thevenet, turned round. But this cadaverous body—in such fashion were madame's head and shoulders propped up against pillows—his cadaverous body, I say, still concealed her face.

"Has there been any change?" persisted M. Duroc in English.

"There has been no change," replied the dark-complexioned Dr. Harding, "except for the worse."

"Do you want her to be moved?"

"There has never been any necessity," said the physician, picking up his beaver hat from the bed. He spoke dryly. "However, if you want to learn anything more about the toy rabbit or the barometer, I should hurry. The lady will die in a matter of hours, probably less."

And he stood to one side.

It was a heavy bed with four posts and a canopy. The bed curtains, of some dullish-green material, were closely drawn on every side except the long side by which we saw Madame Thevenet in profile. Lean as a post, rigid, the strings of her cotton nightcap tightly tied under her chin, Madame Thevenet lay propped up there. But one eye rolled towards us, and it rolled horribly.

Up to this time the woman we call the Jezebel had said little. She chose this moment again to come brushing against my side. Her greenish eyes, lids half-closed, shone in the light of M. Duroc's candle. What she whispered was: "You don't really hate me, do you?"

Maurice, I make a pause here.

Since I wrote the sentence, I put down my pen, and pressed my hands over my eyes, and once more I thought. But let me try again.

I spent just two hours in the bedroom of Madame Thevenet. At the end of the time—oh, you shall hear why!—I rushed out of that bedroom, and out of Number 23 Thomas Street, like the maniac I was.

The streets were full of people, of carriages, of omnibuses, at early evening. Knowing no place of refuge save the saloon from which I had come, I gave its address to a cabdriver. Since still I had swallowed no food, I may have been lightheaded. Yet I wished to pour out my heart to the friends who had bidden me return there. And where were they now?

A new group, all new, lounged against the bar-counter under brighter gaslight and brighter paint. Of all those who smote me on the back and cheered, none remained save the ancient giant who had implied friendship with General Washington. *He,* alas, lay helplessly drunk with his head near a sawdust spitting box. Nevertheless I was so moved that I took the liberty of thrusting a handful of bank notes into his pocket. He alone remained.

Wait, there was another!

I do not believe he had remained there because of me. Yet M. Thaddeus Perley, still sitting alone at the little table by the pillar, with the open gas jet above, stared vacantly at the empty glass in his hand.

He had named himself a foreigner; he was probably French. That was as well. For, as I lurched against the table, I was befuddled and all English had fled my wits.

"Sir," said I, "will you permit a madman to share your table?"

M. Perley gave a great start, as though roused out of thought. He was now sober: this I saw. Indeed, his shiver and haggard face were due to lack of stimulant rather than too much of it.

"Sir," he stammered, getting to his feet, "I shall be—I shall be honored by your company." Automatically he opened his mouth to call for a waiter; his hand went to his pocket; he stopped.

"No, no, no!" said I. "If you insist, M. Perley, you may pay for the second bottle. The first is mine. I am sick at heart, and I would speak with a gentleman."

At these last words M. Perley's whole expression changed. He sat down, and gave me a grave courtly nod. His eyes, which were his most expressive feature, studied my face and my disarray.

"You are ill, M. de Lafayette," he said. "Have you so soon come to grief in this—this *civilized* country?"

"I have come to grief, yes. But not through civilization or the lack of it." And I banged my fist on the table. "I have come to grief, M. Perley, through miracles or magic. I have come to grief with a problem which no man's ingenuity can solve!"

M. Perley looked at me in a strange way. But someone had brought a bottle of brandy, with its accessories. M. Perley's trembling hand slopped a generous allowance into my glass, and an even more generous one into his own.

"That is very curious," he remarked, eying the glass. "A murder, was it?"

"No. But a valuable document has disappeared. The most thorough search by the police cannot find it."

Touch him anywhere, and he flinched. M. Perley, for some extraordinary reason, appeared to think I was mocking him.

"A document, you say?" His laugh was a trifle unearthly. "Come, now. Was it by any chance—a letter?"

"No, no! It was a will. Three large sheets of parchment, of the size you call foolscap. Listen!"

And as M. Perley added water to his brandy and gulped down about a third of it, I leaned across the table.

"Mme Thevenet, of whom you may have heard me speak in this café, was an invalid. But (until the early hours of this morning) she was not bedridden. She could move, and walk about her room, and so on. She had been lured away from Paris and her family by a green-eyed woman named the Jezebel.

"But a kindly lawyer of this city, M. Duroc, believed that madame suffered and had a bad conscience about her own daughter. Last night, despite the Jezebel, he persuaded madame at last to sign a will leaving all her money to this daughter.

"And the daughter, Claudine, is in mortal need of it! From my brother and myself, who have more than enough, she will not accept a sou. Her affianced, Lieutenant Delage, is as poor as she. But, unless she leaves France for Switzerland, she will die. I will not conceal from you that Claudine suffers from that dread disease we politely call consumption."

M. Perley stopped with his glass again halfway to his mouth.

He believed me now; I sensed it. Yet under the dark hair, tumbled on his forehead, his face had gone as white as his neat, mended shirt frill.

"So very little a thing is money!" he whispered. "So very little a thing!"

And he lifted the glass and drained it.

"You do not think I am mocking you, sir?"

"No, no!" says M. Perley, shading his eyes with one hand. "I knew myself of one such case. She is dead. Pray continue."

"Last night, I repeat, Mme Thevenet changed her mind. When M. Duroc paid his weekly evening visit with the news that I should arrive today, madame fairly chattered with eagerness and a kind of terror. Death was approaching, she said; she had a presentiment."

As I spoke, Maurice, there returned to me the image of that shadowy, arsenic-green bedroom in the shuttered house; and what M. Duroc had told me.

"Madame," I continued, "cried out to M. Duroc that he must bolt the bedroom door. She feared the Jezebel, who lurked but said nothing. M. Duroc drew up to her bedside a portable writing desk, with two good candles. For a long time madame spoke, pouring out contrition, self-abasement, the story of an unhappy marriage, all of which M. Duroc (sweating with embarrassment) was obliged to write down until it covered three large parchment sheets.

"But it was done, Mr. Perley!

"The will, in effect, left everything to her daughter, Claudine. It revoked a previous will by which all had been left (and this can be done in French law, as we both know) to Jezebel of the muddy complexion and the muddy yellow hair.

"Well, then! . . ."

"M. Duroc sallies out into the street, where he finds two sober fellows who come in. Madame signs the will, M. Duroc sands it, and the two men from the street affix their signatures as witnesses. Then *they* are gone. M. Duroc folds the will lengthways, and prepares to put it into his carpetbag. Now, M. Perley, mark what follows!

" 'No, no, no!' cries madame, with the shadow of her peaked nightcap wagging on the locked shutters beyond. 'I wish to keep it—for this one night!'

" 'For this one might, madame?' asks M. Duroc.

" 'I wish to press it against my heart,' says Mme Thevenet. 'I wish to read it once, twice, a thousand times! M. Duroc, what time is it?'

"Whereupon he takes out his gold repeater, and opens it. To his astonishment it is one o'clock in the morning. Yet he touches the spring of the repeater, and its pulse beat rings one.

" 'M. Duroc,' pleads Mme Thevenet, 'remain here with me for the rest of the night!'

" 'Madame!' cried M. Duroc, shocked to the very fans of his beard. 'That would not be correct.'

" 'Yes, you are right,' says madame. And never, swears the lawyer, has he seen her less bleary of eye, more alive with wit and cunning, more the great lady of ruin, than there in that green and shadowy and foul-smelling room.

"Yet this very fact puts her in more and more terror of the Jezebel, who is never seen. She points to M. Duroc's carpetbag.

" 'I think you have much work to do, dear sir?'

"M. Duroc groaned. 'The Good Lord knows that I have!'

" 'Outside the only door of this room,' says madame, 'there is a small dressing room. Set up your writing desk beside the door there, so that no one may enter without your knowledge. Do your work there; you shall have a lamp or many candles. Do it,' shrieks madame, 'for the sake of Claudine and for the sake of an old friendship!'

"Very naturally, M. Duroc hesitated.

" '*She* will be hovering,' pleads Mme Thevenet, pressing the will against her breast. '*This* I shall read and read and read, and sanctify with my tears. If I find I am falling asleep,' and here the old lady looked cunning, 'I shall hide it. But no matter! Even *she* cannot penetrate through locked shutters and a guarded door.'

"Well, in fine, the lawyer at length yielded.

"He set up his writing desk against the very doorpost outside that door. When he last saw madame, before closing the door, he saw her in profile with the green bed curtains drawn except on that side, propped up with a tall candle burning on a table at her right hand.

"Ah, that night! I think I see M. Duroc at his writing desk, as he has told me, in an airless dressing room where no clock ticked. I see him, at times, removing his oval spectacles to press his smarting eyes. I see him returning to his legal papers, while his pen scratched through the wicked hours of the night.

"He heard nothing, or virtually nothing, until five o'clock in the morning. Then, which turned him cold and flabby, he heard a cry which he describes as being like that of a deaf-mute.

"The communicating door had not been bolted on Mme Thevenet's side, in case she needed help. M. Duroc rushed into the other room.

"On the table, at madame's right hand, the tall candle had burned down to a flattish mass of wax over which still hovered a faint bluish flame. Madame herself lay rigid in her peaked nightcap. That revival of spirit last night, or remorse in her bitter heart, had brought on the last paralysis. Though M. Duroc tried to question her, she could move only her eyes.

"Then M. Duroc noticed that the will, which she had clutched as a doomed religious might clutch a crucifix, was not in her hand or on the bed.

" 'Where is the will?' he shouted at her, as though she were deaf too. 'Where is the will?'

"Mme Thevenet's eyes fixed on him. Then they moved down, and looked steadily at a trumpery toy—a rabbit, perhaps four inches high, made of pink velours or the like—which lay on the bed. Again she looked at M. Duroc, as though to emphasize this. Then her eyes rolled, this time with dreadful effort, toward a large barometer, shaped like a warming pan, which hung on the wall beside the door. Three times she did this before the bluish candle flame flickered and went out."

And I, Armand de Lafayette, paused here in my recital to M. Perley.

Again I became aware that I was seated in a garish saloon, swilling brandy, amid loud talk that beat the air. There was a thumping noise from the theater above our heads, and faint strains of music.

"The will," I said, "was not stolen. Not even the Jezebel could have melted through locked shutters or a guarded door. The will was not hidden, because no inch of the room remains unsearched. *Yet the will is gone!*"

I threw a glance across the table at M. Perley.

To me, I am sure, the brandy had given strength and steadied my nerves. With M. Perley I was not so sure. He was a little flushed. That slightly wild look, which I had observed before, had crept up especially into one eye, giving his whole face a somewhat lopsided appearance. Yet all his self-confidence had returned. He gave me a little crooked smile.

I struck the table.

"Do you honor me with your attention, M. Perley?"

"What song the Syrens sang," he said to me, "or what name Achilles assumed when he hid himself among women, although puzzling questions, are not beyond *all* conjecture."

"They are beyond *my* conjecture!" I cried. "And so is this!"

M. Perley extended his hand, spread the fingers, and examined them as one who owns the universe.

"It is some little time," he remarked, "since I have concerned myself with these trifles." His eyes retreated into a dream. "Yet I have given some trifling aid, in the past, to the Prefect of the Parisian police."

"You are a Frenchman! I knew it! And the police!" Seeing his lofty look, I added: "As an amateur, understood?"

"Understood!" Then his delicate hand—it would be unjust to call it clawlike—shot across the table and fastened on my arm. The strange eyes burned toward my face. "A little more detail!" he pleaded humbly. "A little more, I beg of you! This woman, for instance, you call the Jezebel?"

"It was she who met me at the house."

"And then?"

I described for him my meeting with the Jezebel, with M. Duroc, and our entrance to the sickroom, where the shaggy police officer sat in the armchair and the saturnine doctor faced us from beside the bed.

"This woman," I exclaimed, with the room vividly before my eyes as I described it, "seems to have conceived for me (forgive me) a kind of passion. No doubt it was due to some idle compliments I once paid her at Paris.

"As I have explained, the Jezebel is *not* unattractive, even if she would only (again forgive me) wash her hair. Nevertheless, when once more she brushed my side and whispered, 'You don't really hate me, do you?' I felt little less than horror. It seemed to me that in some fashion I was responsible for the whole tragedy.

"While we stood beside the bed, M. Duroc the lawyer poured out the story I have recounted. There lay the poor paralytic, and confirmed it with her eyes. The toy rabbit, a detestable pink color, lay in its same position on the bed. Behind me, hung against the wall by the door, was the large barometer.

"Apparently for my benefit, Mme Thevenet again went through her

dumb show with imploring eyes. She would look at the rabbit; next (as
M. Duroc had not mentioned), she would roll her eyes all round her, for
some desperate yet impenetrable reason, before fixing her gaze on the
barometer.

"It meant . . . what?

"The lawyer spoke then. 'More light!' gulped out M. Duroc. 'If you
must have closed shutters and windows, then let us at least have more
light!'

"The Jezebel glided out to fetch candles. During M. Duroc's explanation he had several times mentioned my name. At first mention of it the
shaggy police officer jumped and put away his clasp knife. He beckoned
to the physician, Dr. Harding, who went over for a whispered conference.

"Whereupon the police officer sprang up.

" 'Mr. Lafayette!' And he swung my hand pompously. 'If I'd known it
was you, Mr. Lafayette, I wouldn't 'a' sat there like a bump on a log.'

" 'You are an officer of police, sir,' said I. 'Can *you* think of no explanation?'

"He shook his head.

" 'These people are Frenchies, Mr. Lafayette, and you're an American,' he said, with somewhat conspicuous lack of logic. '*If* they're telling
the truth—'

" 'Let us assume that!'

" 'I can't tell you where the old lady's will is,' he stated positively. 'But
I can tell you where it ain't. It ain't hidden in this room!'

" 'But surely . . . !' I began in despair.

"At this moment the Jezebel, her brown taffeta dress rustling, glided
back into the room with a handful of candles and a tin box of the new-
style lucifer matches. She lighted several candles, sticking them on any
surface in their own grease.

"There were one or two fine pieces of furniture; but the mottled-marble
tops were chipped and stained, the gilt sides cracked. There were a few
mirrors, creating mimic spectral life. I saw a little more clearly the faded
green paper of the walls, and what I perceived to be the partly open door
of a cupboard. The floor was of bare boards.

"All this while I was conscious of two pairs of eyes: the imploring gaze
of Mme Thevenet, and the amorous gaze of the Jezebel. One or the other
I could have endured, but both together seemed to suffocate me.

" 'Mr. Duroc here,' said the shaggy police officer, clapping the distressed advocate on the shoulder, 'sent a messenger in a cab at half-past
five this morning. And what time did we get here? I ask you and I tell
you! Six o'clock!'

"Then he shook his finger at me, in a kind of pride and fury of efficiency.

" 'Why, Mr. Lafayette, there's been fourteen men at this room from six this morning until just before you got here!'

" 'To search for Mme Thevenet's will, you mean?'

"The shaggy man nodded portentously, and folded his arms.

" 'Floor's solid.' He stamped on the bare boards. 'Walls and ceiling? Nary a inch missed. We reckon we're remarkable smart; and we are.'

" 'But Mme Thevenet,' I persisted, 'was not a complete invalid until this morning. She could move about. If she became afraid of—the name of the Jezebel choked me—'if she became afraid, and *did* hide the will . . .'

" 'Where'd she hide it? Tell me!'

" 'In the furniture, then?'

" 'Cabinetmakers in, Mr. Lafayette. No secret compartments.'

" 'In one of the mirrors?'

" 'Took the backs of 'em off. No will hid there.'

" 'Up the chimney!' I cried.

" 'Sent a chimney-sweep up there,' replied my companion in a ruminating way. Each time I guessed, he would leer at me in friendly and complacent challenge. 'Ye-es, I reckon we're pretty smart. But we didn't find no will.'

"The pink rabbit also seemed to leer from the bed. I saw madame's eyes. Once again, as a desperate mind will fasten on trifles, I observed the strings of the nightcap beneath her scrawny chin. But I looked again at the toy rabbit.

" 'Has it occurred to you,' I said triumphantly, 'to examine the bed and bedstead of Mme Thevenet herself?'

"My shaggy friend went to her bedside.

" 'Poor old woman,' he said. He spoke as though she were already a corpse. Then he turned round. 'We lifted her out, just as gentle as a newborn babe (didn't we, ma'am?). No hollow bedposts! Nothing in the canopy! Nothing in the frame or the feather beds or the curtains or the bedclothes!'

"Suddenly the shaggy police officer became angry, as though he wished to be rid of the whole matter.

" 'And it ain't in the toy rabbit,' he said, 'because you can see we slit it up, if you look close. And it ain't in that barometer there. It just—ain't here.'

"There was a silence as heavy as the dusty, hot air of this room.

" 'It is here,' murmured M. Duroc in his gruff voice. 'It must be here!'

"The Jezebel stood there meekly, with downcast eyes.

"And I, in my turn, confess that *I* lost my head. I stalked over to the barometer, and tapped it. Its needle, which already indicated, 'Rain; cold,' moved still further toward that point.

"I was not insane enough to hit it with my fist. But I crawled on the floor, in search of a secret hiding place. I felt along the wall. The police officer—who kept repeating that nobody must touch anything and he would take no responsibility until he went off duty at something o'clock —the police officer I ignored.

"What at length gave me pause was the cupboard, already thoroughly searched. In the cupboard hung a few withered dresses and gowns, as though they had shriveled with Mme Thevenet's body. But on the shelf of the cupboard . . .

"On the shelf stood a great number of perfume bottles: even today, I fear, many of our countrymen think perfume a substitute for water and soap; and the state of madame's hands would have confirmed this. *But,* on the shelf, were a few dusty novels. There was a crumpled and be-grimed copy of yesterday's New York *Sun.* This newspaper did not contain a will; but it did contain a black beetle, which ran out across my hand.

"In a disgust past describing, I flung down the beetle and stamped on it. I closed the cupboard door, acknowledging defeat. Mme Thevenet's will was gone. And at the same second, in that dim green room—still badly lighted, with only a few more candles—two voices cried out.

"One was my own voice:

" *'In God's name, where is it?'*

"The other was the deep voice of M. Duroc:

" *'Look at that woman! She knows!'*

"And he meant the Jezebel.

"M. Duroc, with his beard fans atremble, was pointing to a mirror; a little blurred, as these mirrors were. Our Jezebel had been looking into the mirror, her back turned to us. Now she dodged, as at a stone thrown.

"With good poise our Jezebel writhed this movement into a curtsy, turning to face us. But not before I also had seen that smile—like a razor cut before the blood comes—as well as full knowledge, mocking knowledge, shining out of wide-open eyes in the mirror.

" 'You spoke to me, M. Duroc?' She murmured the reply, also in French.

" 'Listen to me!' the lawyer said formally. 'This will is *not* missing. It is in this room. You were not here last night. Something has made you guess. You know where it is.'

" 'Are you unable to find it?' asked the Jezebel in surprise.

" 'Stand back, young man!' M. Duroc said to me. 'I ask you something, mademoiselle, in the name of justice.'

" 'Ask!' said the Jezebel.

" 'If Claudine Thevenet inherits the money to which she is entitled, you will be well paid; yes, overpaid! You know Claudine. You know that!'

" 'I know it.'

" 'But if the new will be *not* found,' said M. Duroc, again waving me back, 'then you inherit everything. And Claudine will die. For it will be assumed—'

" 'Yes!' said the Jezebel, with one hand pressed against her breast. 'You yourself, M. Duroc, testify that all night a candle was burning at madame's bedside. Well! The poor woman, whom *I* loved and cherished, repented of her ingratitude toward me. She burned this new will at the candle flame; she crushed its ashes to powder and blew them away!'

" 'Is that true?" cried M. Duroc.

" 'They will assume it,' smiled the Jezebel, 'as you say.' She looked at me. 'And for you, M. Armand!'

"She glided closer. I can only say that I saw her eyes uncovered; or, if you wish to put it so, her soul and flesh together.

" 'I would give you everything on earth,' she said. 'I will not give you the doll face in Paris.'

" 'Listen to me!' I said to her, so agitated that I seized her shoulders. 'You are out of your senses! You cannot give Claudine to me! She will marry another man!'

" 'And do you think that matters to me,' asked the Jezebel, with her green eyes full on mine, 'as long as you still love her?'

"There was a small crash as someone dropped a knife on the floor.

"We three, I think, had completely forgotten that we were not alone. There were two spectators, although they did not comprehend our speech.

"The saturnine Dr. Harding now occupied the green armchair. His long thin legs, in tight black trousers with strap under the boot instep, were crossed and looked spidery; his high beaver hat glimmered on his head. The police officer, who was picking his teeth with a knife when I first saw him, had now dropped the knife when he tried to trim his nails.

"But both men sensed the atmosphere. Both were alert, feeling out with the tentacles of their nerves. The police officer shouted at me.

" 'What's this gabble?' he said. 'What's a-gitting into your head?'

"Grotesquely, it was that word 'head' which gave me my inspiration.

" 'The nightcap!' I exclaimed in English.

" 'What nightcap?'

"For the nightcap of Mme Thevenet had a peak; it was large; it was tightly tied under the chin; it might well conceal a flat-pressed document which—but you understand. The police officer, dull-witted as he appeared, grasped the meaning in a flash. And how I wished I had never spoken! For the fellow meant well, but he was not gentle.

"As I raced round the curtained sides of the bed, the police officer was holding a candle in one hand and tearing off madame's nightcap with the other. He found no will there, no document at all; only straggly wisps of hair on a skull grown old before its time.

"Mme Thevenet had been a great lady, once. It must have been the last humiliation. Two tears overflowed her eyes and ran down her cheeks. She lay propped up there in a nearly sitting position; but something seemed to wrench inside her.

"And she closed her eyes forever. And the Jezebel laughed.

"That is the end of my story. That is why I rushed out of the house like a madman. The will has vanished as though by magic; or is it still there by magic? In any case, you find me at this table: grubby and disheveled and much ashamed."

For a little time after I had finished my narrative to M. Perley in the saloon it seemed to me that the bar-counter was a trifle quieter. But a faint stamping continued from the theater above our heads. Then all was hushed, until a chorus rose to a tinkle of many banjos.

> Oh, I come from Alabama
>   With my banjo on my knee;
> I depart for Louisiana . . .

Enough! The song soon died away, and M. Thaddeus Perley did not even hear it.

M. Perley sat looking downward into an empty glass, so that I could not see his face.

"Sir," he remarked almost bitterly, "you are a man of good heart. I am glad to be of service in a problem so trifling as this."

*"Trifling!"*

His voice was a little husky, but not slurred. His hand slowly turned the glass round and round.

"Will you permit two questions?" asked M. Perley.

"Two questions? Ten thousand!"

"More than two will be unnecessary." Still M. Perley did not look up. "This toy rabbit, of which so much was made: I would know its exact position on the bed?"

"It was almost at the foot of the bed, and about the middle in a crossways direction."

"Ah, so I had imagined. Were the three sheets of parchment, forming the will, written upon two sides or upon only one?"

"I had not told you, M. Perley. But M. Duroc said: upon one side only."

M. Perley raised his head.

His face was now flushed and distorted with drink, his eye grown wild. In his cups he was as proud as Satan, and as disdainful of others' intelligence; yet he spoke with dignity, and with careful clearness.

"It is ironic, M. de Lafayette, that I should tell you how to lay your hand on the missing will and the elusive money; since, upon my word, I have never been able to perform a like service for myself." And he smiled, as at some secret joke. "Perhaps," he added, "it is the very simplicity of the thing which puts you at fault."

I could only look at him in bewilderment.

"Perhaps the mystery is a little *too* plain! A little *too* self-evident!"

"You mock me, sir! I will not . . ."

"Take me as I am," said M. Perley, whacking the foot of the glass on the table, "or leave me. Besides," here his wandering eye encountered a list of steam sailings pasted against the wall, "I—I leave tomorrow by the *Parnassus* for England, and then for France."

"I meant no offence, M. Perley! If you have knowledge, speak!"

"Mme Thevenet," he said, carefully pouring himself some more brandy, "hid the will in the middle of the night. Does it puzzle you that she took such precautions to hide the will? But the element of the outré must always betray itself. The Jezebel *must not* find that will! Yet Mme Thevenet trusted nobody—not even the worthy physician who attended her. If madame were to die of a stroke, the police would be there and must soon, she was sure, discover her simple device. Even if she were paralyzed, it would ensure the presence of other persons in the room to act as unwitting guards.

"Your cardinal error," M. Perley continued dispassionately, "was one of ratiocination. You tell me that Mme Thevenet, to give you a hint, looked fixedly at some point near the foot of the bed. Why do you assume that she was looking at the toy rabbit?"

"Because," I replied hotly, "the toy rabbit was the only object she could have looked at!"

"Pardon me; but it was *not*. You several times informed me that the bed curtains were closely drawn together on three sides. They were drawn on all but the 'long' side toward the door. Therefore the ideal reasoner, without having seen the room, may safely say that the curtains were drawn together at the foot of the bed?"

"Yes, true!"

"After looking fixedly at this point represented by the toy, Mme Thevenet then 'rolls her eyes all round her'—in your phrase. May we assume that she wishes the curtains to be drawn back, so that she may see something *beyond* the bed?"

"It is—possible, yes!"

"It is more than possible, as I shall demonstrate. Let us direct our attention, briefly, to the incongruous phenomenon of the barometer on another wall. The barometer indicates, 'Rain; cold.' "

Here M. Perley's thin shoulders drew together under the old military cloak.

"Well," he said, "the cold is on its way. Yet this day, for April, has been warm outside and indoors, oppressively hot?"

"Yes! Of course!"

"You yourself," continued M. Perley, inspecting his fingernails, "told me what was directly opposite the foot of the bed. Let us suppose that the bed curtains are drawn open. Mme Thevenet, in her nearly seated position, is looking *downward*. What would she have seen?"

"The fireplace!" I cried. "The grate of the fireplace!"

"Already we have a link with the weather. And what, as you have specifically informed me, was in the grate of the fireplace?"

"An unlighted coal fire!"

"Exactly. And what is essential for the composition of such a fire? We need coal; we need wood; but primarily and above all, we need . . ."

*"Paper!"* I cried.

"In the cupboard of that room," said M. Perley, with his disdainful little smile, "was a very crumpled and begrimed (mark that; not dusty) copy of *yesterday's* New York Sun. To light fires is the most common, and indeed the best, use for our daily press. That copy had been used to build yesterday's fire. But something else, during the night, was substituted for it. You yourself remarked the extraordinarily dirty state of Mme Thevenet's hands."

M. Perley swallowed the brandy, and his flush deepened.

"Sir," he said loudly, "you will find the will crumpled up, with ends most obviously protruding, under the coal and wood in the fireplace grate. Even had anyone taken the fire to pieces, he would have found only what appeared to be dirty blank paper, written side undermost, which could never be a valuable will. It was too self-evident to be seen.— Now go!"

"Go?" I echoed stupidly.

M. Perley rose from his chair.

"Go, I say!" he shouted, with an even wilder eye. "The Jezebel could not light that fire. It was too warm, for one thing; and all day there were police officers with instructions that an outsider must touch nothing. But now? *Mme Thevenet kept warning you that the fire must not be lighted, or the will would be destroyed!"*

"Will you await me here?" I called over my shoulder.

"Yes, yes! And perhaps there will be peace for the wretched girl with—with the lung trouble."

Even as I ran out of the door I saw him, grotesque and pitiful, slump across the table. Hope, rising and surging, seemed to sweep me along like the crack of the cabman's whip. But when I reached my destination, hope receded.

The shaggy police officer was just descending the front steps.

"None of us coming back here, Mr. Lafayette!" he called cheerily. "Old Mrs. What's-her-name went and burned that will at a candle last night.—Here, what's o'clock?"

The front door was unlocked. I raced through that dark house, and burst into the rear bedroom.

The corpse still lay in the big, gloomy bed. Every candle had flickered almost down to its socket. The police officer's clasp knife, forgotten since he had dropped it, still lay on bare boards. But the Jezebel was there.

She knelt on the hearth, with the tin box of lucifer matches she had brought there earlier. The match spurted, a bluish fire; I saw her eagerness; she held the match to the grate.

"A lucifer," I said, "in the hand of a Jezebel!"

And I struck her away from the grate, so that she reeled against a chair and fell. Large coals, small coals rattled down in puffs of dust as I plunged my hands into the unlighted fire. Little sticks, sawed sticks; and I found it there: crumpled parchment sheets, but incontestably madame's will.

"M. Duroc!" I called. "M. Duroc!"

You and I, my brother Maurice, have fought the Citizen-King with bayonets as we now fight the upstart Bonapartist; we need not be ashamed of tears. I confess, then, that the tears overran my eyes and blinded me. I scarcely saw M. Duroc as he hurried into the room.

Certainly I did not see the Jezebel stealthily pick up the police officer's knife. I noticed nothing at all until she flew at me, and stabbed me in the back.

Peace, my brother: I have assured you all is well. At that time, faith, I was not much conscious of any hurt. I bade M. Duroc, who was trembling, to wrench out the knife; I borrowed his roomy greatcoat to hide the blood; I must hurry, hurry, hurry back to that little table under the gas jet.

I planned it all on my way back. M. Perley, apparently a stranger in this country, disliked it and was evidently very poor even in France. But *we* are not precisely paupers. Even with his intense pride, he could not refuse (for such a service) a sum which would comfort him for the rest of his life.

Back I plunged into the saloon, and hurried down it. Then I stopped. The little round table by the pillar, under the flaring gas jet, was empty.

How long I stood there I cannot tell. The back of my shirt, which at first had seemed full of blood, now stuck to the borrowed greatcoat. All of a sudden I caught sight of the fat-faced bartender with the gold teeth, who had been on service that afternoon and had returned now. As a mark of respect, he came out from behind the bar-counter to greet me.

"Where is the gentleman who was sitting at that table?"

I pointed to it. My voice, in truth, must have sounded so hoarse and strange that he mistook it for anger.

"Don't you worry about that, monseer!" said he reassuringly. *"That's* been tended to! We threw the drunken tramp out of here!"

"You threw . . ."

"Right bang in the gutter. Had to crawl along in it before he could stand up." My bartender's face was pleased and vicious. "Ordered a bottle of best brandy, and couldn't pay for it." The face changed again. "Goddelmighty, monseer, what's wrong?"

*"I* ordered that brandy."

*"He* didn't say so, when the waiter brought me over. Just looked me up and down, crazy-like, and said a gentleman would give his I.O.U. Gentleman!"

"M. Perley," I said, restraining an impulse to kill that bartender, "is a friend of mine. He departs for France early tomorrow morning. Where is his hotel? Where can I find him?"

"Perley!" sneered my companion. "That ain't even his real name, I hearn tell. Gits high-and-mighty ideas from upper Broadway. But his real name's on the I.O.U."

A surge of hope, once more, almost blinded me. "Did you keep that I.O.U. ?"

"Yes, I kepp it," growled the bartender, fishing in his pocket. "God knows why, but I kepp it."

And at last, Maurice, I triumphed!

True, I collapsed from my wound; and the fever would not let me remember that I must be at the dock when the *Parnassus* steam packet departed from New York next morning. I must remain here, shut up in a hotel room and unable to sleep at night, until I can take ship for home. But where I failed, you can succeed. He was to leave on the morrow by the *Parnassus* for England, and then for France—so he told me. You can find him—in six months at the most. In six months, I give you my word, he will be out of misery for ever!

*"I.O.U.,"* reads the little slip, *"for one bottle of your best brandy, forty-five cents. Signed: Edgar A. Poe."*

I remain, Maurice,
Your affectionate brother,
Armand

# *The Black Cabinet*

"The Black Cabinet," which takes place in the Paris of the Emperor Napoleon III, was first published in the 1951 Mystery Writers of America anthology, *Twenty Great Tales of Murder.* The first British printing was in *MacKill's Mystery Magazine,* November 1952. It is a story of intrigue and suspense; that it concerns a mystery is revealed only in the tale's final line, though Carr, faithful to the fair-play tradition, provides clues to the ending.

# The Black Cabinet

As the Emperor's closed carriage swung toward the private entrance at the Opera, with the gentlemen's carriages ahead and the white horses of the Imperial Guard clattering behind, three bombs were thrown from the direction of the Opera steps.

And, only a minute before, a small nine-year-old girl in the crowd had been almost mutinous.

She was too grownup, Nina thought, to be lifted up in *maman's* arms as though she were four years old or even six. True, the fusty-smelling coats and tall hats of the men, even the bonnets and crinolines of the women, made so high a black hedge that Nina could see little except the gas jets illuminating the façade of the Opera and the bright lamps of the Parisian street. But it was warm down here: warm, at least, for a night in mid-January of 1858.

Then up Nina went, on the arm of *maman.* Already they could hear in the distance the measured applause—the slow, steady clap-clap of hands, as at a play—and a ragged cheer as the procession approached.

But Nina did not even know what it was, or why they were here.

"Mother, I . . ." she began in French.

*Maman's* bonnet, lined with ruffles, was so long-sided that Nina could not see her mother's face until it was turned around. Then *maman's* dark Italian eyes, always so kindly, took on a glassy bulging glare of hatred and triumph as she pressed her lips against Nina's long curls; bright brown curls, like the hair of Nina's American father.

"Look well!" whispered the handsome Signora Maddalena Bennett, in the Italian language. "At last you will see the death of the devil."

And Nina understood. She too hated, as she had been taught to hate, without knowing why. She had been schooled not to sob or tremble. Yet tears welled up in her eyes, because Nina was sick with fear. In one of those carriages must be Napoleon the Third, Emperor of the French.

*Clop-clop, clop-clop* moved the horses; slowly, but ever nearer the carpet of white sand spread in front and at the side of the Opera. Then, suddenly, Signora Bennett's whole expression changed. She had never dreamed that the murderers—Orsini and his conspirators—would hold their hands so long, or might throw bombs from the very side or steps of the Opera itself.

"No!" she shrieked aloud.

Holding the child closely, Signora Bennett flung the side of her fur pelisse over Nina's head and dropped down into the half-frozen mud among the spectators. Just as she fell, a black object flew over the heads of the crowd, high-sailing against gas lamps.

Through a crack between the fur pelisse and *maman's* fashionable deep-bosomed gown with the steel buttons, Nina saw the edge of a white flash. Though they were protected, the first explosion seemed to crush rather than crash, driving steel needles through her eardrums. There were two more explosions, at seconds' intervals. But the street went dark at the first crash, blinding the gas lamps, setting the air a-sing with flying glass from lamps or windows. Nina's scream was lost amid other screams.

Afterward the small girl felt little or nothing.

A curtain of nightmare, now called shock, wrapped soothingly round Nina's mind and nerves. She looked without surprise, or with very little surprise, at anything she saw. Though her mother, also unhurt, still crouched and breathed heavily, Nina stood up on shaky legs.

Most of the black hedge of tall shiny hats had fallen away. It lay motionless, or tried to crawl across bloodied white sand. And, as Nina turned sideways, she saw the Emperor's state coach near the foot of the steps.

"Sire! Sire!" she heard military voices shouting, amid other shouts. And, above it, the bellow of a military policeman: "Sire!"

The great closed carriage was at a standstill. Stabbed with blast and steel splinters and needles of glass, it had toppled partly toward Nina but remained intact except for its windows. Also, by some miracle, one great gold-bound carriage lantern was still burning on this side.

Before the officers of the Emperor's bodyguard could reach the handle of the coach door, the door opened. There emerged a stately-looking man, plump rather than stout, who jumped to the coach step and thence to the ground.

The carriage lamp gleamed on gold epaulets against a blue coat, and white trousers. His (apparently) steady hand was just putting back on his head the overdecorated cocked hat he wore fore-and-aft. Nina knew, if only from pictures, that he was the Emperor. Though he might be sallow-faced and growing puffy under the eyes, yet between his heavy black moustaches and fox-brush of imperial beard there appeared the edge of a cool smile.

"He is not hurt, the Emperor! Louis Napoleon is unhurt!"

"Long live the Emperor!"

Gravely the sallow-faced man handed down from the carriage a pretty, bad-tempered lady, her countenance as white as her long pearl earrings; she must be the Empress Eugénie. Officers, their uniform coats torn and their faces slashed, whipped out sabers in salute.

"Long live the Empress!"

"And the Emperor! And the Emperor!"

A thick, low rattle of drums ran urgently along the line. Foot-soldiers, dark silhouettes, flowed across and stood up at present-arms, so that the Emperor might not see fallen men with half faces or women carrying bomb splinters where they might have carried children. Around that wrecked carriage, with its two dead horses, lay one hundred and fifty persons, dead or wounded.

The Emperor smiled broadly, concealing agitation.

For the first time genuine hatred, a hatred of what she saw for herself, entered into Nina Bennett and never left her. It made her small body squirm, choking back her voice. It may have been due partly to the teaching of her mother's friends of Young Italy, of the *Carbonari,* who derisively called Napoleon the Third "the sick parrot" when they did not call him devil. But now it was Nina's own hatred.

She could not have explained what had happened, even now. Though she had heard something of bombs, she did not even think of bombs—or of the men who had thrown them. Nina felt only that a white lightning bolt had struck down beside her, hurting, *hurting* these people and perhaps even making them die as her own father had died a year ago in Naples.

Yet the yellow-faced Emperor, with his black moustaches and imperial, had taken no scathe. He stood there and (to Nina) smiled hatefully. He had caused this. It was his fault. His!

Instinctively, amid the reek and the drum-beating, Nina cried out in English, the language her father had taught her, and which she spoke far better than French or even Italian.

"Sick parrot!" the small lungs screeched, the words lost. "Devil! Usurper!"

And then her mother enfolded her, feeling over her for wounds and whispering furiously.

"Be silent, my child! Not another word, I tell thee!"

Gathering up Nina under her fur pelisse, and adding indignity to hysteria, *maman* fought and butted her way out of the crowd with such fury that suspicious eyes turned. Up in front of them loomed a military policeman, his immense cocked hat worn sideways.

"The child!" cried Signora Bennett, clutching Nina with true stage effect, and tragically raised dark eyes to a dark muffled sky. "The child," she lied, "is injured!"

"Pass, madame," gruffly. "Regret."

Though the distance was not great, it took them almost an hour in the crowds to reach their fine furnished lodgings in the rue de Rivoli. There waited Aunt Maria, also Italian and *maman's* maid-companion, fiercely twisting the point of a knife into a rosewood table as she awaited news. Afterward Nina could remember little except a bumping of portmanteaux and a horrible seasickness.

For Signora Bennett, Nina, and Aunt Maria left Paris next day. They had long been safe in England when two of the bomb-assassins—Orsini and Pieri—dropped on the plank and looked out through the everlasting window of the guillotine.

And that had been just over ten years ago.

So reflected Miss Nina Bennett, at the very mature age of nineteen, on the warm evening early in July which was the third evening after her return to Paris. Nobody could have denied that she was beautiful. But all those years in England had made her even more reserved than the English, with a horror of elaborate gestures like those of her late mother.

Though the sky was still bright over the Place de la Concorde, Nina Bennett had told Aunt Maria to close the heavy striped curtains on the windows. Aunt Maria was very fat now. She had a faint moustache of vertical hairs, like a tiny portcullis between nose and mouth. As she waddled over to scrape shut the curtains and waddled back to her chair, wrath exuded from her like a bad perfume.

Nina sat at the dressing-table before a mirror edged in gold leaf. Two gas jets, one in the wall on either side of the mirror, set up yellow flames in flattish glass dishes. They shone on Nina's pink-and-white complexion, her dark blue eyes, her bright brown hair parted in the middle and drawn across the ears to a soft, heavy pad along the nape of the neck. The evening gown of that year was cut just an inch and a half below each shoulder, curving down in lace across the breast; and Nina's gown was so dark a red that it seemed black except when the gaslight rippled or flashed.

Yet her intense composure gave Nina's beauty a chilly quality like marble. She sat motionless, unsmiling, her arms stretched out and hands lightly crossed on the dressing-table.

"No," she thought, "I am not unattractive." The thought, or so she imagined, gave her neither pleasure nor displeasure.

At her left on the dressing-table stood a great bouquet of yellow roses in a glass vase of water. Nina Bennett had bought them herself, as a part of her plan of death. In the dressing-table drawer lay the weapon of death.

"I have no heroics," she thought, looking at the reflection of her blue eyes. "I do not think of myself as Joan of Arc or Charlotte Corday. Though I may be insane, I do not believe so. But I will kill this puff-ball Emperor, who still mysteriously reigns over the French. I will kill him. I will kill him. I will kill him."

Her intensity was so great that she breathed faster, and faint color tinged her pink-and-white face. Suddenly, out of the darkling background in the mirror, she saw fat Aunt Maria, with gray-streaked hair and fishbone moustache, writhing and flapping with anger.

Aunt Maria's hoarse, harsh voice spoke in Italian.

"Now I wonder," sneered Aunt Maria, "why you must close the curtains, and dare not look on the beauty of Paris."

Nina hesitated before she replied, moistening her lips. Despite her flawless English speech and her tolerable French, she had half-forgotten her mother's Italian and must grope for it.

"You are at liberty," she said, "to wonder what you like."

Again Aunt Maria slapped the chair-arms and writhed, almost in tears. Never in her life could Nina believe that these gesticulations were real, as they were, and not mere theatricalism. Intensely she disliked them.

"Out there," panted Aunt Maria, "is the city of light, the city of pleasure. And who made it so? It was your loathed Louis Napoleon and Baron Haussmann, planning their wide boulevards and their lamps and greenery. If we now have the Wood of Boulogne, it is because Louis Napoleon loves trees."

Nina raised her brown eyebrows so slightly that they hardly seemed to move.

"Do you tell *me*," she asked, "the history of the sick parrot?"

The gas jets whistled thinly, in a shadowy room with black satin wall panels figured in gold. Gracefully, with a studied grace, Nina Bennett rose from the dressing-table, and turned around. The monstrous crinolines of the past decade had dwindled into smaller, more manageable hoopskirts which rustled with petticoats at each step. Glints of crimson darted along Nina's dark, close-fitting gown.

"Have you forgotten, Maria?" she asked, in a passionately repressed voice. "In these rooms, these very rooms, where we lived ten years ago? How you took a great knife, and stabbed a dozen times into the top of a rosewood table, when you heard Orsini had failed? Can you deny it?"

"Ah, blood of the Madonna!"

"Can you deny it?"

"I was younger; I was foolish!" The harsh voice rose in pleading. "See, now! This Emperor, in his youth, worshipped the memory of his uncle, the war-lord, the first Napoleon. The first Napoleon they exiled . . ."

"Yes," agreed Nina, "and kings crept out again to feel the sun."

Aunt Maria was galvanized. "That is a noble line; that is a heart-shaking line!"

"It is the late Mrs. Browning's. A trifle. No matter."

"Well! This young man—yes, yes, it is the way of all young men!—was also a republican; a lover of liberty; a member of the *Carbonari* itself. Once he promised us a united Italy. But he wavered, and more than a few of us tried to kill him. He wavers always; I say it! But has he not done much in these past few years to redeem his promise? Body of Bacchus! Has he not?"

Though Nina was not tall, she stood high above Maria in the chair and looked down at her indifferently. Nina's white shoulders rose very slightly in the dark red gown.

"Ah, God, your mother has taught you well!" cried Aunt Maria. "Too well!" She hesitated. "And yet, when she died six months ago, it did not seem to me that you were much affected."

"I did not weep or tear my hair, if that is what you mean."

"Unnatural! Pah, I spit! What do you care for Italy?"

"A little, perhaps. But I am an American, as was my father before me."

"So I have heard you say."

"And so I mean!" Nina drew a deep breath; the gown seemed to be constricting her heart as well as her flesh. "My father was of what they call New England, in the state of Massachusetts. His money, though my mother sneered, has kept us above poverty all these years." Her tone changed. "Poor Maria; do the closed curtains stifle you?"

Whereupon Nina, with the same grace in managing her hoopskirt, went to the left-hand window and threw back the curtains. The fustiness of the room, the fustiness of the curtains, for some reason reminded her of men's greatcoats; Nina shivered without knowing why. Then she opened the curtains of the other window.

Outside, to the little wrought-iron balcony above the rue de Rivoli, was fastened a flagstaff at an oblique angle. From it floated the beloved flag, the flag of the Union, the stars and stripes little more than three years triumphant in bitter war.

"Now what patriotism," jeered Aunt Maria, "for a country you have never seen!"

"It is more than that," said Nina, wanting to laugh. "In a sense it protects us. Have you not heard . . . ?"

"Speak!"

"This is our Day of Independence, the Fourth of July."

"Mad! Mad! Mad!"

"I think not. His Majesty Napoleon the Third made a futile stupid attempt to establish an empire in Mexico. That did not please the States of America." Nina lifted her exquisite hands and dropped them. "But the traditional friendship of France and America has been renewed. This evening, less than an hour from now, your hypocritical Emperor drives in state to the Opera, for a French-American ball, with ceremonies. As his carriage crosses the Place de la Concorde into the rue Royale . . ."

Aunt Maria heaved her laundry-bag shape up out of the chair.

"Blood of the Madonna!" she screamed. "You do not mean this mad-woman's gamble for tonight?"

"Oh, but I do." And for the first time Nina Bennett smiled.

There was a silence, while Nina stood with her back to the window, with the soft and magical sky glow competing with these harsh-singing gaslights. And Nina was uneasy.

She had expected Aunt Maria to stamp, to howl, even possibly to shout from the window for help. But the aging woman only fell back into the chair, not speaking. Tears flowed out of her eyes, tears running down grotesquely past her nose and the hair-spikes of her moustache. Nina Bennett spoke sharply.

"Come, Aunt Maria. This is ridiculous! Why should you weep?"

"Because you are beautiful," Aunt Maria said simply.

There was a silence.

"Well! I—I thank you, Maria. Still . . . !"

"Oh, your plan is good." Aunt Maria turned her streaming eyes toward the great bouquet of yellow roses on the dressing-table, and the drawer which held the weapon. "No doubt you will kill him, my dear. Then you will go to the guillotine, in bare feet and with a black veil over your head, because to kill the Emperor is an act of parricide. You will have had no life, none! No laughter. No affection. No love of men."

Nina's face had gone white. For some reason she retorted cruelly.

"And your own vast experience of love, dear Maria . . . ?"

"That too is ridiculous, eh? Oho, that is comic; yes? This to you!" Aunt Maria made the gesture. "For I have known love more than you think! And the good strong passion, and the heartache too. But *you* will not know it. You are poisoned; your veins are poisoned. If an honest lover bit your arm until the blood flowed, he would die. Ah, behold! You shrink in disgust like a cold Englishwoman!"

"No, good Maria. And Englishwomen are not cold, save perhaps in public. It is as stupid a legend as the legend that they are all fair-haired."

"Listen!" blurted Maria, dabbing at her eyes. "Do you know who poisoned you?"

"If you please, Maria . . . !"

"It was your own mother. Yes! Do you think she knew no man except your father? Body of Venus, she had enough lovers to fill a prison! I startled you? But, because she must dedicate you to her 'cause' of murder, she would turn you against men. How long she spoke to you, when you were thirteen or fourteen, in the accursed great cold house in London! Have I not seen you rush out of the drawing-room, crimson-faced, and your sainted mother laughing secretly?"

"I—I have thought of love," she said calmly. "I would love well, perhaps, if I did not hate. And now, Maria, it is time to fetch my jewel box; and set out my hat and cloak."

Aunt Maria paid no attention.

There was a wild shining of inspiration in her eyes, as though at last she had seen some way to turn this inflexible girl from a mad course. But the time was going, the time was going!

"Come, a test!" panted Aunt Maria. "Are you in truth as poisoned as I said?"

"Did you hear my command, Maria?"

"No! Listen! You remember three nights ago, the evening of the first day we came to Paris? How we returned from our walk, and the young man you met in the courtyard? Well, I saw your eyes kindle!" Aunt Maria cackled with mirth. "You an American? You are a Latin of the Latins! And this young man: was he French—or Italian?"

Nina Bennett grew rigid.

"You have strange fancies," she said. "I cannot remember this at all."

But she did remember it. As Nina turned around briefly to look out of the long window, where a faint breeze rippled the vivid colors of the stars and stripes, that whole brief scene was re-created in every detail.

As the courtesy-aunt said, it had been at about this time on the evening of July second. Aunt Maria had marched beside Nina as they returned from their walk. Even in this modern age, the most emancipated American or English girl would not have gone through such tree-bewitched streets, full of summer's breath and mirrors a-wink in cafés, without a formidable chaperone.

The house in which they had taken furnished lodgings was unlike most of those in the same street. It was of an older day, patterned after a nobleman's *hôtel*. Through a smaller door in high-arched wooden doors you passed through a cool tunnel smelling of old stone, with the *concierge's* lodge on the right. Then you emerged into a green courtyard; it had galleries built around on three sides, and stone balustrades carved with faces. An outside staircase led up to each gallery. In the middle of the green, scented turf was a dead fountain.

As Aunt Maria creaked up the staircase, Nina followed her. Vaguely Nina had noticed a young man standing a little distance away, smoking a cigar and leaning on a gold-headed stick. But she paid little attention. In both hands, if only for practice's sake, she carried a large bouquet of red roses in which was hidden a small but heavy object, and two fingers of her right hand held the chains of her reticule. Though strung-up and alert, Nina was very tired.

Perhaps that was why the accident happened. When she had gone six steps up behind Aunt Maria, Nina's reticule—a heavy, flower-painted handbag—slipped through her fingers, bounced down the steps, and landed on the lowermost one.

"Ah, so-and-so!" exclaimed Aunt Maria, and wheeled around her moustache.

There was a flick in the air as the dark-complexioned young man flung away his cigar. He had suffered some injury to his left leg. But, so deft was his use of the stick, that he scarcely seemed to limp when he made haste. In an instant he was at the foot of the staircase.

The cane was laid down. With his left hand he swept off his high, glossy hat, and his right hand scooped up the reticule. His eyes strayed to Nina's ringless left hand.

"If you will permit me, mademoiselle . . . ?" he said.

The man, whether French or Italian, had a fine resonant voice, fashioning each French syllable clearly. His dark hair, parted on one side, was so thick that it rose up on the other side of the parting. A heavy moustache followed the line of his delicate upper lip. His somber dark clothes, though carelessly worn, were of fine quality.

Nina Bennett, who had turned around, looked down the stairs straight into his eyes. Nina, in a dress of dark purple taffeta and a boat-shaped hat with a flat plume, would have denied coldly that she was a romantic.

"But he is undeniably handsome," she was thinking, "and without oiliness or exaggeration. He has endured great suffering, by the whiteness of his face and the little gray in his hair. And yet his mockery of eye, as though he knew too much of women . . . !"

Abruptly Nina straightened up.

"I thank . . ." she began coldly; and then the worst happened.

Nina, still holding the bouquet of red roses, either by accident or nervousness, jerked her left wrist against the stair-balustrade. The roses seemed to spill apart. Out of their stems leaped a derringer, short of barrel but large of bore. It banged on the step, and clattered down to the lowermost one. Though it was loaded with wad, powder, and heavy ball, it did not explode; there was no percussion-cap on the firing-nipple.

Nina stood rigid with horror, like Aunt Maria. For a moment, in that shadowy green courtyard under the light of a pink sunset, it was as silent as though they stood in the Forest of Marly.

The young man looked strangely at the pistol, and suddenly jumped back as though he feared it might still go off. Then he smiled. After a swift glance at the lodge of the *concierge,* he dropped the reticule on top of the derringer, concealing it. He picked up both, advanced up the stairs, and gravely handed the fallen objects to Nina.

"Permit me, mademoiselle, to return your reticule and your—your protection against footpads. If I might suggest . . ."

"I thank you, monsieur. But it is not necessary to suggest."

"Alas, I have already done so," he said, and again looked her in the eyes. His French voice both pointed the double meaning, yet smilingly robbed the words of offense. Pressing the brim of his hat against the black broadcloth over his heart, he bowed slightly. "Until a re-meeting, made-moiselle!"

"Until a re- . . ." said Nina, and stopped. She had not meant to speak at all.

Whirling around her skirts, the roses and pistol and reticule like a mortifying weight in her arms, Nina marched up the stairs after Aunt Maria.

And this was the brief scene which returned in every detail to Nina Bennett, in the dark old room with the gas jets, during the moment when she looked out of the long window over the rue de Rivoli. She had only to concentrate, and it was gone forever. But she felt the pressure of Aunt Maria's eyes, wet and crafty, boring into her back; and anger rose again.

Turning around, Nina took four steps and stood over Aunt Maria in the chair.

"Why do you remind me of this?" Nina asked.

"Oh, then we *were* smitten!"

"Hardly." The voice was dry. But when Nina opened her blue eyes wide, Maria shrank back because they were maniacal and terrifying. "Do you imagine that some sordid affair of love would keep me back from the only cause I have for living?"

"This 'cause'!" sneered Aunt Maria. "I tell you, it is a cold warming-pan for a long night, instead of a husband. Away with it! With your looks and your money: body of Bacchus, you might wed any man you chose." Abruptly, amid her tears, the fat woman began to cackle again with laughter. "But not the young Italian of the courtyard, poor Nina! No, no! Not that one!"

"And why not?" demanded Nina.

"Listen, my child. Pay heed to an old conspirator like me! For I have seen them all. I know the ingratiating air, the cringing approach, the mark of the almost-gentleman . . ."

"How dare you!" Nina amazed herself by crying out. Then she controlled her voice. "You will allow me, please, to pass my own judgment on a gentleman."

"Oh, then we were not smitten! Oh, no!" cackled Aunt Maria. Then her laughter died. "Shall I tell you what this young man really is?"

"Well?"

"He is what the French call a *mouchard*. A police spy."

"You lie!" A pause. "In any event," Nina added casually, "it is of no importance. Since you disobey my order to fetch my hat and cloak and jewel box . . ."

"No, no, I will find them!" said Aunt Maria, and surged up out of the chair.

On creaking slippers she wheezed across to an immense dark wardrobe beside the door and opposite the windows. Opening one door of the wardrobe, she plucked out a waist-length cape of rich material in stripes of silver and wine-red.

"Well!" snorted Aunt Maria, examining the cape and giving no sign of furious thought. "You will go to kill the Emperor. I have promised not to interfere; good, I keep my promise! But it will be sad for you, hot-blood, when they arrest you—as they will, mark it!—before you have fired the shot."

Nina's gaze had gone to the grandfather clock, near the alcove which housed the big curtained bed. The time—the time was running out. True, she still had many minutes. But there would be a crowd. She must be in place, the exact spot she had chosen, long before the Imperial procession went past.

Now the meaning of Maria's words stabbed into her brain for the first time.

"What did you say, fuss-budget?"

"Enough," muttered the fat woman darkly. "I said enough!"

"Come, good Maria. Is this another of your childish tricks to divert me?"

"Childish!" cried Aunt Maria, now in a real temper. "Was I your mother's companion for twenty years, or was I not? Do I know every dog's-tail of plotting, or do I not?"

"Of old and clumsy plotting, yes. But my device . . ."

"Faugh!" snorted Aunt Maria, past patience. "How do you think Louis Napoleon keeps so quiet his bright city, his toy? Ask the Prefect of Police, M. Pietri—yes, I said Pietri, not Pieri—but above all ask M. Lagrange, the chief of the political police! They buy more spies than the sand-grains at Dieppe! By my immortal soul, Lagrange will stir up a riot for the very joy of showing how quickly he can suppress it!"

Aunt Maria shook the cape. With her own version of a haughty shrug, she reached again into the wardrobe and drew out a very wide-brimmed velvet hat of the same dark red as Nina's gown.

"You don't believe an old woman, eh?" she taunted. "Good! For I have finished with you. But this I swear on the Cross: you have been betrayed."

"Lies and lies and lies! Betrayed by whom?"

"Why, by your young man down in the courtyard."

She was going dangerously far, to judge by Nina's eyes and breathing.

"Little stupid!" she continued to taunt. "Did you not observe how he started and jumped, when the pistol fell at his feet? He thought there might be a bullet for *him.* Did you not see how he looked with quickness towards the lodge of the *concierge,* who was watching? The *concierge,* who feeds the police with a spoon! You a plotter, when you gave your true name of Bennett? Pah! The name of your mother is a very passport to the Prefecture!"

Now Aunt Maria did not actually believe one word of what she had said about the young man. In fact, three nights ago she had scarcely noticed him except as a possible moustache-twisting sinner of the boulevards. But these ideas foamed into her brain; she could not stop; she must speak faster and faster.

For it seemed to her that there was a hesitation in Nina's eyes . . .

Nina moved slowly to the side of the dressing-table, still looking steadily at the other woman. Gaslight burnished the wings of Nina's soft brown hair. With her left hand she pulled open the drawer of the dressing-table, in which the derringer pistol lay fully loaded, and with a percussion-cap resting under the light pressure of its hammer.

"What do you do?" Aunt Maria screamed out. Then, abruptly glancing at the door and holding up cape and hat as though to call for silence, she added: "Listen!"

Outside the door, the only door in the room, was a drawing room with a polished hardwood floor unmuffled by any carpet. There was a sound. Both women heard the soft thump of the cane as the visitor slid forward a lame leg; then silence; then again the bump of the cane. Someone was slowly but steadily approaching the bedroom door. Both women knew who it was.

"My God!" thought the staggered Aunt Maria. "He really *is* a *mouchard* after all!"

A fist, not loudly, but firmly and with authority, knocked at the bedroom door.

Aunt Maria, terrified, backed away towards the bed alcove and held up cape and hat as though they might shield her.

If there had ever been any uncertainty in Nina's face, it was gone now. Her cold movements were swift but unhurried. From the vase she whipped the bouquet of yellow roses, squeezing the water from the stems and wrapping them in heavy tissue paper from the drawer. Gripping the stems in her left hand, she plucked out the pistol. There was a soft click as she drew back the hammer. She made an opening in the roses, hiding the derringer so that nothing should catch in the hammer when she snatched it out.

There would still be time to reload if she must dispose of an intruder first.

"Enter!" Nina calmly called in French. It was the language they spoke afterwards.

Their visitor, the man of the courtyard, came in and closed the door behind him. He was in full evening dress, partly covered by his ankle-length black cloak, which yet showed his white frilled shirtfront and a carelessly tied stock. In one white-gloved hand he held his hat, in the other his gold-headed stick.

Again Nina noted the delicacy of his white, handsome face, in contrast to the heavy dark hair and moustache. Even his figure was somewhat slight, though well-made.

"For this intrusion," he said in his fine voice, "I deeply apologize to mademoiselle; and, understood," bowing towards Aunt Maria, "to madame."

Nina's pink lips went back over fine teeth.

"Your best apology lies behind you." She nodded towards the door.

"Unfortunately, no." The stranger, at leisure, put down his hat and stick on a table at the left of the door. His dark eyes, with that odd life-in-death quality, grew strong with a fierce sincerity; and so did his voice. "For I presume to have an interest in you, mademoiselle."

"Who are you? What do you want?"

The stranger leaned his back against the door, seeming to lounge rather than lean, in a devil-may-care swagger which to Nina seemed vaguely familiar.

"Let us say that I am the detective Lecoq, in the admirable police-romances of M. Gaboriau. Lecoq is a real person, remember, as was the character D'Artagnan. Well! I am Lecoq."

Nina breathed a little faster. Her finger tightened round the trigger of the pistol.

"How did you enter by a locked front door?"

"Believe me, I have passed through more difficult doors than that. Stop!" His white-gloved hand went up to forestall her, and he smiled. "Let us suppose (I say merely let us suppose!) that Mademoiselle Nina Bennett had intent to kill the Emperor of the French. I who speak to you, I also live in this house. I can put questions to a *concierge.*"

"Did I not tell you?" screamed Aunt Maria, hiding her face behind cape and hat.

Neither of them looked at her.

"To any reader of the French journals, the name of your mother is well known. The nationality of your father," and he nodded toward the flag outside the window, his nostrils thin and bitter, "you too obviously display. However! If it be your intent to kill the Emperor, where would you go? Assuredly not far from here, or you would have been gone now."

("If you must kill this sly one here," Aunt Maria thought wildly, "kill him now! Shoot!")

"I think," continued the stranger, "you have chosen the corner of the rue Royale and the rue de Rivoli. Every journal in Paris will have told you, with exactness, the route and time of the procession. It is summer; there will be an open carriage, low-built. The Emperor, a fact well known, sits always on the right-hand side facing forward, the Empress on the left.

"How lovely . . ." His strong voice shook; he checked himself. "How innocent you will look, in your finery and jewels, chattering English and deliberately bad French, on the curbstone! The military, even the military police, will only smile when you walk out slowly toward the slow-moving carriage, and speak English as you offer—is it not so?—the bouquet of roses to the Empress Eugénie of Montijo."

("I was mad, I was mad!" mentally moaned Aunt Maria. "Let him take the damned pistol from her now!")

"Holding the bouquet in your left hand," he went on quietly, "you must lean partly across His Majesty. With your right hand you will take out an old-style single-shot pistol, and fire it at the Emperor's head so closely that you cannot miss. Have I, M. Lecoq, correctly deduced your plan?"

Nina Bennett cast a swift glance at the clock.

Time, time, time! A while ago, when she had looked out of the window, far up to the right there had been a red sky over Neuilly beyond the top of the Champs-Elysées. Now the whole sky was tinged with pink amid white and pale blue. It brightened the gaslights in that black-silk-paneled room, which might have been a symbol of espionage since the days of Savary and Napoleon the First.

"Are you the only one," Nina asked levelly, "who knows of this—this plan?"

"The only one, mademoiselle."

With a steady hand Nina took the derringer from among the roses, moving aside the yellow bouquet. It is a sober fact that the young man did not even notice it.

"And now," he said in that hypnotic voice, "I must tell you of my interest in you. It is very easy." He straightened up, his face whiter, and clenched his gloved fists. "You are Venus in the body of Diana; you are Galatea not yet kissed to true life. You are—I will not say the most beautiful woman I have ever met—but the most maddening and stimulating." Cynicism showed in his eyes. "And I have known so many women."

"How modest you are!" Nina cried furiously.

"I state a fact. But I tell you one of the reasons, my love, why I will not permit you to go from this room for at least half an hour."

Again Nina started, almost dropping the pistol.

From the street below, and from the open spaces beyond, there were cries and shouts. She heard the confused running of feet, seeming to come from every direction at once, which can conjure up a Paris crowd in one finger-snap. Very faintly, in the distance, she also heard the slow clop-clop of many horses in procession.

According to every newspaper, the procession to the Opera would be headed by the Imperial Band. The instruments of the band were clear rather than brassy; already they had begun with the swinging tune, *"Partant pour la Syrie,"* which was the official song of Napoleon the Third.

> Setting out for Syria
> Young and brave Dunois . . .

There was still time. Nina Bennett's hand was as steady as a statue's.

"You call yourself a detective, M. Lecoq. But you are only a police spy. Now stand away from that door!"

"No, my dear," smiled the other, and folded his arms lazily.

"I will count to three . . ."

"Count to five thousand; I would hear your voice. What matter if you kill me? Most people," and his dark eyes seemed to wander out to the boulevards, "think me already dead. Put your hand in mine; let fools flourish pistols or knives."

"One!" said Nina, and thought she meant it.

The clop-clop of the procession, though still not loud, was drawing nearer. What sent a shiver through Nina's body was the tune into which the band changed, in honor of the French-American ball at the Opera. There were no words. There were only dreams and memories. Slow, somber, the great battle-hymn rolled out.

> Mine eyes have seen the glory of the coming of the Lord,
> He is trampling out the vintage where the grapes of wrath
> are stored . . .

"In a moment," continued the visitor, unhearing, "I will come and take that pistol from you. It does not become you. But first hear what I have to say." His tone changed, fiercely. "This political assassination is more than wrong. It changes nothing. It is the act of an idiot. If I could make you understand . . ."

Abruptly he paused.

He, too, had heard the music, clear in the hush of evening. His face darkened. Had Aunt Maria been watching, she would have seen in his eyes the same maniacal glitter as in those of Nina Bennett. And he spoke the only words which could have ended his life.

"By God!" he snarled. "You might have been a human being, without your mother and your damned Yankee father!"

Nina pulled the trigger, firing straight for his heart at less than ten feet's distance. The percussion-cap flared into the bang of the explosion, amid heavy smoke. The stranger, flung back against the door, still stood upright and emerged through smoke.

She had missed the heart. But the pistol-ball, smashing ribs on the right of his chest, had torn open his right lung. And Nina knew that never, never in her life, could she have fired at the Emperor unless he had first uttered some maddening insult.

"I thank you, my dear," gravely said the stranger, pressing his reddening fingers to his chest, and white-faced at his own choked breathing. "Now be quick! Put that derringer into my hand; and I shall have time to say I did it myself."

Then another realization struck Nina.

"You've been speaking in English!" she cried in that language. "Ever since you said 'damned Yankee.' Are you English?"

"I am an American, my dear," he answered, drawing himself up and swallowing blood. "And at least no one can call me a police spy. My name," he added casually, "is John Wilkes Booth."

# A LOCKED-ROOM NOVELLA

# The Third Bullet

The novella that follows first appeared in 1937 as a separately published paperback under the "Carter Dickson" pseudonym. The British publishers, Hodder & Stoughton, issued twelve volumes of original stories, advertised as "the new at ninepence illustrated thrillers." Margery Allingham and such then well-known writers as Francis Beeding, George Goodchild and G. D. H. and M. Cole also wrote novellas for the series, but it was unsuccessful and the first edition of *The Third Bullet* is probably Carr's rarest book. The story has never been republished in its entirety—until *Fell and Foul Play,* that is. When Frederic Dannay printed it in the January 1948 issue of *Ellery Queen's Mystery Magazine,* he omitted large chunks of the story, including in several instances entire pages. Character descriptions, details of the murder site, red herrings, and even some clues to the solution—all disappeared. Since Carr himself no longer had a copy of the full "The Third Bullet," it was Dannay's abridgment that was used for all subsequent magazine and book reprints. We are very pleased that, for the first time since 1937, Carr's original text is presented to the reader on the following pages.

"I remember 'The Third Bullet,' Carr wrote some nine years after its first publication, "as being not a bad story at all." That is, of course, an understatement. The case of the murder in the pavilion near Hampstead Heath is among Carr's most ingenious.

# The Third Bullet

## Chapter 1

On the edge of the Assistant Commissioner's desk, a folded newspaper lay so as to expose a part of a headline: *Mr. Justice Mortlake Murdered.* . . . On top of it was an official report sheet covered with Inspector Page's trim handwriting. And on top of the report sheet, trigger guard to trigger guard, lay two pistols. One was an Ivor-Johnson .38 revolver. The other was a Browning .32 automatic of Belgian manufacture.

Though it was not yet eleven in the morning, a raw and rainy day looked in at the windows over the Embankment, and the green-shaded lamp was burning above the desk. Colonel Marquis, the Assistant Commissioner of Metropolitan Police, leaned back at ease and smoked a cigarette with an air of doing so cynically. Colonel Marquis was a long, stringy man whose thick and wrinkled eyelids gave him a sardonic look not altogether deserved. Though he was not bald, his white hair had begun to recede from the skull, as though in sympathy with the close cropping of the gray mustache. His bony face was as unmistakably of the Army as it was now unmistakably out of it; and the reason became plain whenever he got up—he limped. But he had a bright little eye, which was amused.

"Yes?" he said.

Inspector Page, though young and not particularly ambitious, was as gloomy as the day outside.

"The Superintendent said he'd warn you, sir," John Page answered. "I'm here with two purposes. First, to offer you my resignation—"

Colonel Marquis snorted.

"—and second," said Page, looking at him, "to ask for it back again."

"Ah, that's better," said the Assistant Commissioner, opening his eyes with an air of refreshed interest. "But why the double offer?"

"Because of this Mortlake case, sir. It doesn't make sense. As you can see by my report . . ."

"I have not read your report," said the Assistant Commissioner. "God willing, I do not intend to read your report. Inspector Page, I am bored; bloody bored; bored stiff and green. And this Mortlake case does not appear to offer anything very startling. It's unfortunate, of course," he added rather hurriedly. "Yes, yes. But correct me if I am wrong. Mr. Justice Mortlake, recently retired, was a judge of the King's Bench Division, officiating at the Central Criminal Court. He was what they call the 'red judge,' and sat in Courtroom Number One on serious offenses like murder or manslaughter. Some time ago he sentenced a man called White to fifteen strokes of the cat and eighteen months' hard labor for robbery with violence. White made threats against the judge. Which is nothing new; all the old lags do it. The only difference here is that, when

White got out of jail, he really did keep his threat. He came back and killed the judge." Colonel Marquis scowled. "Well? Any doubt about that?"

Page shook his head.

"No, sir, apparently not," he admitted. "*I* can testify to that. Mortlake was shot through the chest yesterday afternoon at half-past five. Sergeant Borden and I practically saw the thing done. Mortlake was alone—with White—in a sort of pavilion on the grounds of his house. It is absolutely impossible for anyone else to have reached him, let alone shot him. So, if White didn't kill him, the case is a monstrosity. But that's just the trouble. For if White did kill him—well, it's still a monstrosity."

Colonel Marquis's rather speckled face was alight with new pleasure. He pushed across a cigarette box to the other. "Go on," he said.

"First of all, to give you the background," said Page. He now uncovered the newspaper, on the front page of which was a large photograph of the dead judge in his robes. It showed a little man dwarfed by a great flowing wig. Out of the wig peered a face with a parrot-like curiosity in it, but with a mildness approaching meekness. "I don't know whether you knew him?"

"No. I've heard he was active in the Bar Mess."

"He retired at seventy-two, which is early for a judge. Apparently he was as sharp-witted as ever. But the most important point about him was his leniency on the bench—his extreme leniency. It's been said that he never put the case for the prosecution to the jury, and the old lags used to dance a hornpipe when they heard they were to be tried by him. It is known, from a speech I looked up, that he disapproved of using the cat-o'-nine-tails even in extreme cases."

"Yet he sentenced this fellow White to fifteen of the best?"

"Yes, sir. That's the other side of the picture, the side nobody can understand." Page hesitated. "Now, take this fellow Gabriel White. He's not an old lag; it was his first offense, mind you. He's young, and handsome as a film actor, and a cursed sight too artistic to suit me. Also, he's well educated and it seems certain that 'Gabriel White' isn't his real name—though we didn't bother with that beyond making sure he wasn't in the files.

"The robbery-with-violence charge was a pretty ugly business, *if* White was guilty. It was done on an old woman who kept a tobacconist's shop in Poplar, and was reputed to be a very wealthy miser: the old stuff. Well, someone came into her shop on a foggy evening, under pretense of buying cigarettes—bashed up her face pretty badly even after she was unconscious—and got away with only two pound-notes and some loose silver out of the till. Gabriel White was caught running away from the place. In his pocket was found one of the stolen notes, identified by the number;

and an unopened packet of cigarettes, although it was shown he did not smoke."

For some reason Colonel Marquis frowned. His bright little eye was fixed on the inspector.

"And did he admit the robbery?"

"No. His story was that, as he was walking along, somebody cannoned into him in the fog, stuck a hand into his pocket, and ran. He thought he was the victim of a running pickpocket. He automatically started to run after the man, until he felt in his pocket and found something had been put there. This was just before a constable stopped him."

Again Page hesitated.

"You see, sir, there were several weak points in the prosecution. For one thing, the old woman couldn't identify him beyond doubt as the right man. If he'd had competent counsel, and if it hadn't been for the judge, I don't think there's much doubt that he'd have been acquitted. But, instead of taking any one of the good men the court was willing to appoint to defend him, the fool insisted on defending himself. Also, his manner in court wasn't liked. And the judge turned dead against him. Old Mortlake made out a devilish case against him in his charge to the jury, and practically directed them to find him guilty. When he was asked whether he had anything to say why sentence should not be passed against him, he said just this: *'You are a fool, and I will see you presently.'* I suppose that could be taken as a threat. All the same, he nearly fainted—and so did several others—when Mortlake calmly gave him fifteen strokes of the cat."

The Assistant Commissioner said: "Look here, Page, I don't like this. Weren't there grounds for an appeal?"

"White didn't appeal. He said nothing more, though they tell me he didn't stand the flogging at all well. But the damned trouble is, sir, that all opinions about White are conflicting. People are either dead in his favor, or dead against him. They think he's a thoroughly wronged man, or else a thorough wrong 'un. He served his time at Wormwood Scrubs. Now, the governor of the prison and the prison doctor both think he's a fine type, and would back him anywhere. But the chaplain of the prison, and Sergeant Borden (the officer who arrested him) both think he's a complete rotter. Anyway, he was a model prisoner. He got the customary one-sixth of his sentence remitted for good behavior, and he was released six weeks ago—on September twenty-fourth."

"Still threatening?"

Page was positive of this. "No, sir. Of course, he was on ticket of leave and we kept an eye on him. But everything seemed to be going well until yesterday afternoon. At just four o'clock we got a phone message from a pawnbroker we know only too well (you see?) that Gabriel White had just bought a gun in his place. This gun."

Across the table Page pushed the Ivor-Johnson .38 revolver. With a glance of curiosity at the little automatic beside it, Colonel Marquis picked up the revolver. One shot had been fired from an otherwise fully loaded magazine. Colonel Marquis took the brass cartridge-case from the drum, turned it over in his palm, and replaced it.

"So," Page went on, "we sent out orders to pick him up—just in case. But that was no sooner done than we got another message by phone. It was from a woman, and it was pretty hysterical. It said that Gabriel White was going to kill old Mortlake, and couldn't we do anything about it?"

"Woman? What woman?"

Page spoke carefully. He said. "It was from Miss Ida Mortlake, the judge's daughter."

"H'm. I do not wish," observed the other, with a sour and sardonic inflection, "to jump to conclusions. But are you going to tell me that Miss Ida Mortlake is young and charming; that our Adonis with the painful name, Gabriel White, is well acquainted with her; and that the judge knew it when he issued that whacking sentence?"

"Yes, sir. But I'll come to that in a moment. As soon as that message came in, the Superintendent thought I had better get out to Hampstead at once—that's where the Mortlakes live. I took along Sergeant Borden because he had handled White before. We hopped into a police car and got out there in double time.

"Now, the lay of the land is important. The house has fairly extensive grounds around it. But the suburbs round Hampstead Heath have grown in such a way that houses and villas crowd right up against the grounds; and there's a stone wall, all of fifteen feet high, round the judge's property.

"And there are only two entrances: a main carriage drive, and a tradesman's entrance. The first is presided over by an old retainer, named Robinson, who lives at a lodge just inside. He opened the gates for us. It was nearly half-past five when we got there, and almost dark. Also, it was raining and blowing in full November style.

"Robinson, the caretaker, told us where the judge was. He was in a pavilion, a kind of glorified outbuilding, in a clump of trees about two hundred yards from the house. It's a small place: there are only two rooms, with a hallway dividing them. The judge used one of the rooms as a study. Robinson was sure he was there. It seems that the judge was expecting an old crony of his to tea; and so, about half-past three, he had phoned Robinson at the lodge gates. He said that he was going from the house across to the pavilion; and when the crony showed up, Robinson was to direct the visitor straight across to the pavilion.

"Borden and I went up a path to the left. We could see the pavilion straight ahead. Though there were trees round it, none of the trees came within a dozen feet of the pavilion, and we had a good view of the place. There was a door in the middle, with a fanlight up over it; and on each side of the door there were two windows. The two windows to the right of the door were dark. The two windows of the room to the left, though they had heavy curtains drawn over them, showed chinks of light. Also, there was a light in the hall; you could see it in that glass pane up over the top of the door. And that was how we saw a tall man duck out of the belt of trees toward the right, and run straight for the front door.

"But it wasn't all. The rain was blowing straight down the back of our necks, and there was a good deal of thunder. The lightning came just before that man got his hand on the front door. It was a real blaze, too. For a couple of seconds the whole place was as dead-bright as a photographer's studio. As soon as we had seen the man duck out from the trees, Borden let out a bellow. The man heard us, and he turned round.

"It was Gabriel White, right enough; the lightning made no doubt of that. He'd got on a long coat, but he had no hat. He wears his hair rather long, and the rain plastered it down. And when he saw us, he took that revolver out of his pocket. But he didn't go for us. He opened the door of the pavilion, and now we could see him fully. From where we were standing (or running, now) we could see straight down the little hall inside; he was making for the door to the judge's study on the left.

"Well, sir, it's easy to get a wrong conception of distances when you quote them in feet or yards. So I'll try to give a distance that's easier to fix in the mind. When we first saw White, we were about as far away from the front door of the pavilion as from one end of a tennis-court to the other. We started running—Borden was well ahead of me—and Borden let out another bellow as loud as doomsday.

"That was what brought the judge to the window. In the room on the left-hand side Mr. Justice Mortlake drew back the curtains of the window nearest the front door and looked out. I want to emphasize this to show there had been no funny business or hocus-pocus. It was old Mortlake: I've seen him too many times in court, and at this time he was alive and well. He pushed up the window a little way and looked out; I saw his bald head shine. He called out, 'Who's there?' Then something else took his attention away from the window. He turned back into the room.

"What took his attention was the fact that Gabriel White had opened the hall door to his study, had run into the study, and had turned the key in the lock as he went through. Sergeant Borden was on White's tail, but a few seconds too late to get him before he locked the door. I saw that *my* quickest way into the study, if I wanted to head off anything, would be through that window—now partly open. Then I heard the first shot.

"Yes, sir: I said the *first* shot. I heard it when I was about twenty running paces away from the window. Then, when I was ten paces from the window, I heard the second shot. The black curtains were only partly drawn and I couldn't see inside until I had drawn level with the window.

"Inside, a little way out and to my left, old Mortlake was lying forward on his face across a flat-topped desk. In the middle of the room Gabriel White stood holding the Ivor-Johnson revolver out stiffly in front of him, and looking stupid."

Page stopped, a little uncomfortable at the vigor he was putting into his narrative. But he could see it too vividly: the muddy stuccoed house under the lightning, and the tall rain-sodden figure of White, with his draggled fair hair, staring and dripping over the pistol in the judge's study. But at this point the Assistant Commissioner looked at him sharply.

"That's a curious choice of words," said Colonel Marquis. "Why do you say he looked stupid?"

"It's the only word that describes him," replied Page, hesitating. "He wasn't savage, or defiant, or even weepy; he'd only got a silly sort of look on his face. Well, sir, the only thing for me to do was to climb through the window. There wasn't much danger in it. White paid no attention to me, and I doubt if he even saw me. The first thing I did was to go over and take the gun out of White's hand. He didn't resist. The next thing I did was to unlock the door leading into the hallway—Borden was still hammering at it outside—so that Borden could get in.

"Then I went to the body of Mr. Justice Mortlake.

"He was lying on his face across a big writing table. From the ceiling over the desk hung a big brass lamp shaped like a Chinese dragon, with a powerful electric bulb inside. It poured down a flood of light on the writing desk, and it was the only light in the room. At the judge's left hand was a standing dictaphone, with its rubber cover off. And the judge was dead, right enough. He had been shot through the heart at fairly close range, and death had been almost instantaneous. There had been two shots. One of the bullets had killed him. The other bullet had smashed the glass mouth of the speaking tube hung on the dictaphone, and was embedded in the wall behind him. I dug it out later.

"If you look at the plan I've drawn, you will get a good general idea of the room. It was a large, square room, furnished chiefly with bookcases and leather chairs. There was no fireplace, but in the north wall a two-bar electric fire (turned on) had been let into the wall. In the west wall there were two windows. (But both of these windows were locked on the inside; and in addition, their heavy wooden shutters were also locked on

## PLAN OF STUDY IN PAVILION

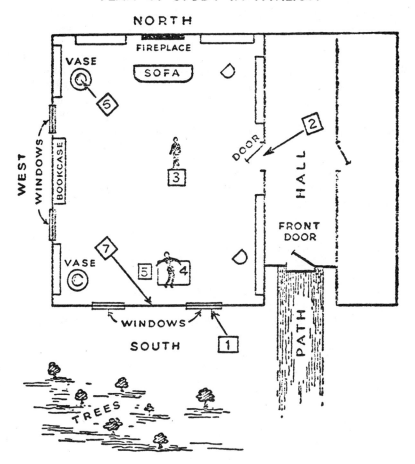

1. Window by which Inspector Page entered.
2. Door outside which Sergeant Borden stood.
3. Where White was standing when police entered.
4. Position of body across writing-table.
5. Dictaphone.
6. Vase in which Browning .32 automatic was found.
7. Arrow shows position in wall where bullet from Ivor-Johnson .38 revolver lodged.

the inside.) In the south wall there were two windows. (But this was the side by which I had entered myself. One of these windows was locked and shuttered; the other, through which I climbed, I had kept under observation the whole time.) There was only one other exit from the room—the door to the hall. (But this door had been under the observation of Sergeant Borden from the moment White ran inside and locked it.)

"Of course, sir, all this was routine. We knew the answer. We had White in a closed circle with his victim. Nobody else could have escaped from that room. Nobody was hiding there when we entered; as a matter of routine, we searched that room thoroughly. Gabriel White had fired two bullets, one of which had killed the old man, and the other had missed him and stuck in the wall. It was all smooth, easy sailing—until it occurred to me, purely as routine, to break open the Ivor-Johnson revolver and look at the cylinder."

"Well?" inquired Colonel Marquis.

"Well," Inspector Page said grimly, "only one bullet had been fired from White's gun."

## Chapter 2

That his chief was enjoying this Page had no doubt. Colonel Marquis had sat up straighter; and his speckled shiny face, showing a high framework of bones, had grown less sardonic.

"Admirable," he said, lighting another cigarette. "What I like, Inspector, is your informal style of making a report. I recall a young subaltern of the Guards—Cranley, I think his name was—who was taking great pride in marching his company from one barracks to another. Unfortunately, at a critical moment he could not think of the proper order to give. While he racked his brains fiendishly to think of the precise wording of that order, the company was marching steadily into a blank wall; and Cranley cut the knot by shouting, 'Oh, hell, turn to the right and go up Birdcage Walk.' The advantage of this was that everybody knew precisely what he meant. Continue in the same vein. I like it."

Page was never certain how to take the man, but he went at it with a grin.

"Frankly, sir, we couldn't believe our eyes. The gun was just as you see it now: fully loaded except for one exploded cartridge case. Theoretically, of course, he *might* have walked into that room and fired one bullet; then he might have carefully opened the cylinder, extracted the spent cartridge case, put another bullet in its place, and fired that—leaving the cylinder as we found it."

"Rubbish," said Colonel Marquis.

"Yes, sir. Why should anybody have done such a crazy trick as that, when the cylinder was full to begin with? Besides, he couldn't have done it. In that case, there'd have been an extra shell to account for—the cartridge case of the first bullet—and it wasn't anywhere in the room or on his person. We made sure of that."

"What did the accused say to all this?"

Page took a notebook out of his pocket and got the right place.

"I'll read you his testimony verbatim," Page said, "although he was in pretty bad shape and what he said wasn't any more coherent than the rest of this business. First, I warned him that anything he said would be taken down and might be used in evidence. And here it is:

Q. So you shot him after all?
A. I don't know.
Q. What do you mean, you don't know? You don't deny you shot him?
A. I shot *at* him. Then things all went queer. I don't know.
Q. And you shot at him twice?
A. No, I didn't. So help me God, I didn't. I only shot at him once. I don't know whether I hit him; but he didn't fall or anything.
Q. Are you trying to tell me there was only one shot?
A. No, no, there were two shots right enough. I heard them.
Q. Which one of them did you fire?
A. The first one. I shot at the old swine as soon as I got in here. He was just turning round from that window and he put out his hands toward me and I shot at him.
Q. Do you mean that there was somebody in here who fired a second shot?
A. I don't know.
Q. Well, did you see anybody else in here?
A. No. There isn't any light except that one directly over the desk, and I couldn't see.
Q. Do you mean to say that if somebody let off a gun in this room right under your nose, you wouldn't see the man or the gun or anything else?
A. I don't know. I'm just telling you. I shot at the old swine and he didn't fall. He started to run over to the other window to get away from me, and shouted at me. Then I heard another shot. He stopped, and put his hands up to his chest, and took a couple of steps forward again, and fell over, on his face across that table.
Q. What direction did this shot come from?
A. I don't know.

"I had just asked him this question—he was pulling at his wet hair as though he were massaging it, and looking like Beau Brummell after a bad night—when Sergeant Borden made a discovery. Borden had been prowling over along the west wall, near those two enormous yellow porcelain vases. They were standing in the two corners of the room along that wall *(see the plan)*. Borden bent over beside one of them, in the northwest angle of the wall. And he picked up a spent cartridge case.

"At first, of course, Borden thought it was the shell we were looking for out of the Ivor-Johnson revolver. But as soon as I glanced at it I saw it wasn't. It was a shell ejected from a .32 automatic. And then we looked inside that vase and we found this."

Again grinning wryly, Page pushed across the table the Browning .32 automatic.

"This pistol was lying at the bottom of the vase, where somebody had dropped it. The vase was too high to reach down inside with an arm. But the judge had brought an umbrella to the pavilion; we found it leaning up against the wall in the hall, so we reached down and fished out the gun with the crook of the umbrella.

"By the smell of the barrel I could tell that the Browning .32 had been fired within the last few minutes. One bullet was missing from the clip. The cartridge case from that bullet (our firearms expert swears to this) was the one we found lying beside the vase. The cartridge case, when I touched it, was still very faintly warm: in other words, sir, it had been fired within the last few seconds."

Page tapped one finger on the edge of the desk.

"Consequently, sir," he said, "there is absolutely no doubt that a second shot was fired from that Browning automatic; that it was fired by somebody *inside the room;* and that afterwards somebody dropped the gun into that vase."

There was a silence. Colonel Marquis got up from his desk, unsteady on his lame leg until he propped himself up with his cane. He limped across the room, a thin and stoop-shouldered figure in pepper-and-salt clothes. His eyes were half-shut, but he seemed pleased. For a moment he remained staring out of the window at the drizzle on the Embankment.

He asked, without turning from the window: "Which bullet killed him?"

"That's the point, sir; we don't know."

"You don't know?" repeated the other sharply. He turned round. "I should think it would be fairly easy. There were two bullets, a .38 revolver and a .32 automatic. One of them was, to put it in an undignified way, in the judge; the other was embedded in the wall. You tell me you dug out the one in the wall. Which was it?"

From his pocket Page took a labeled envelope and shook out of it a lead pellet which had been flattened and partly chipped.

"This was in the wall," he said. "It's a brick wall, and the bullet's been splintered a little. So we can't go entirely by weight—that is, not beyond any doubt. I'm almost certain this is the .38 bullet from White's revolver. But it can't be put into record until I get the post-mortem report from

Dr. Blaine and get my claws on the one in the judge's body. Dr. Blaine is doing the post-mortem this morning."

Colonel Marquis's expression became a broad grin, changing to extreme gravity.

"You are thorough, Inspector," he said. "All the same, where do you think we stand? If that bullet turns out to be the .38 revolver, then Gabriel White fired and missed. So far, so good. But what happened afterwards? Not more than a few seconds afterwards, according to your story, someone blazed away with the Browning automatic and killed Mr. Justice Mortlake. By the way, were there fingerprints on that Browning?"

"No, sir. But then White was wearing gloves."

Colonel Marquis whistled a bar or two, and raised his eyebrows. "I see. You think White may have fired both shots after all?"

"I think it's a possibility. He may have come to the pavilion equipped with two guns and done all that funny business as a deliberate blind, to make us think that the second shot which really killed the judge was fired by somebody else. And yet—"

"It's a very large 'and yet,' " grunted the other. "I agree. If he had indulged in any such elaborate hocus-pocus as that, he would have taken good care to see that the room wasn't sealed up like a box; he wouldn't have taken such precautions to prove that nobody else *could* have fired the shot. His actions, in blazing away directly under the noses of the police, sound more like a deliberate bid for martyrdom. That's reasonable enough; there are plenty of cranks. But the use of two pistols, under such circumstances, would be rank insanity. Whether Gabriel White is a crank or whether he isn't, I presume you don't think he is three times madder than a March hare."

Page was disturbed. "I know, sir. Also, they talk about 'acting,' but I would be willing to swear that the expression on White's face—when I looked through that window—was absolutely genuine. There isn't an actor alive who could have managed it. The man was staggered with surprise—half out of his wits at what he saw. But there it is! What else can we believe? The room was, as you say, sealed up like a box. So White must have fired both shots because nobody else could have done it."

"You don't see any alternative?"

A curious tone in Colonel Marquis's voice made his subordinate chuckle to himself. A noted taker of thieves was the Assistant Commissioner, and some were disposed to call him Old Man River for reasons which will be found in the words of the song.

"Yes, sir," said Page. "I do."

"Ah, I hoped you would," said Colonel Marquis in an equable tone. "Well?"

"There's the possibility that White might be shielding somebody. For instance, suppose somebody else had been in that room, armed with the Browning. White fires, and misses. X, the unknown, fires and rings the bell. Whereupon—the police being at the door—X hops out one of the windows in the west wall, and White locks the windows and the shutters after X has gone."

He raised his eyes and the other nodded.

"Yes. Let's suppose, just for the sake of argument," said Colonel Marquis, "that White didn't kill the judge after all. Let's have a little personal information. Was anyone else interested in killing him? What about his household, or his personal friends?"

"His household is small. He's a widower; he married rather late in life, and his wife died about five years ago. He leaves two daughters—Carolyn, the elder (twenty-eight), and Ida, the younger (twenty-five). Aside from servants, the only other member of the household is an old man by the name of Penney: he's been the judge's legal clerk for years, and was taken into the house after the judge's retirement to help Mortlake on his book about *Fifty Years at Bench and Bar,* or some such thing—"

"Inevitable, of course," said the colonel. "What about friends?"

"He's got only one close friend. You remember my telling you, sir, that a crony of the judge was expected to come to tea yesterday afternoon and the judge sent word that he should come over to the pavilion as soon as he arrived? That's the man. He's a good deal younger than Mortlake. You may be interested to know that he's Sir Andrew Travers—the greatest criminal lawyer of 'em all. He's upset more than one of our best-prepared cases."

The Assistant Commissioner limped back to his chair, sat down, and stared.

"I *am* interested," he said. "Travers. Yes. I don't know him personally, but I know a good deal about him. Spectacular stuff of the Marshall Hall variety, isn't it?—Yes. So Travers was invited to tea yesterday. Did he get there?"

"No. He was delayed; he phoned afterwards, I understand."

Colonel Marquis reflected. "What about this household? I don't suppose you've had a chance to interview all of them; but one lead stands and shines. You say that the younger daughter, Ida, got in touch with you and told you Gabriel White was going to kill her father; you also think she knew White personally?"

"Yes, sir. I've seen Miss Ida Mortlake. She's the only one of the household I have seen, because both Miss Carolyn Mortlake and Penney, the clerk, were out yesterday afternoon. You want my honest opinion of her? Well, she's grand," said Page, dropping into humanity with such violence that the Assistant Commissioner blinked at him.

"Do you mean," asked the other, "that she has the grand manner, or merely what I think you mean?"

"Grand manner? Far from it. I mean I'd back her against any field," replied Page. He could admit how much he had been impressed. He remembered the big house in the park, a sort of larger and more ornate version of the pavilion itself; and Ida Mortlake, white-faced, coming down the stairs to meet him. "Whatever happened at the pavilion," he went on, "it's certain she had nothing to do with it. There's nothing hard-boiled or modern about her. She's fine. She's more in the Victorian style, except that she didn't—you know—faint or carry on or anything like that. She—"

"One moment," interrupted Colonel Marquis, with some asperity. "The young lady is good-looking, I suppose?"

"I don't know," said Page, honestly doubtful. "I didn't notice. She's certainly attractive."

"Blonde or brunette?"

"Blonde."

"I see. Anyhow, I take it you questioned her? You asked her about her association with White, if there was any association?"

"The fact is, sir, I didn't question her too closely. She was rather upset, as you can imagine, and she promised to tell me the whole story today. She admitted that she knew White, but she knows him only slightly and acknowledges that she doesn't particularly like him. I gather that he's been attentive. She met him at a studio party in Chelsea. Studio parties seem to be a craze of the elder daughter, who appears to be along the hard-boiled line. On this occasion Ida Mortlake went along and met—"

Whenever there appeared on Colonel Marquis's face a wolfish grin, as happened now, it seemed to crackle the face like the skin of a roast pig. He remained sitting bolt upright, studying Page with a bleak eye.

"Inspector," he said, "your record has been good and I will refrain from comment. I say nothing against the young lady. All I should like to know is, why are you so certain she couldn't have had anything to do with this? You yourself admitted the possibility that White might be shielding somebody. You yourself admitted that there might have been somebody else in the room who got out of a window after the shot was fired, and that White might have locked the window afterwards."

"Did I?" said Page, glad to hit back at the old so-and-so. "I don't think I said that, Colonel. I considered it. I also found, later, that it wouldn't work and that it's the rankest impossibility of all."

"Why?"

"Before and after the shots, I had the two south windows under my eye. Nobody came out of either window at any time. Borden was watching the door. The only remaining way out would be one of the west windows. But we learned from Robinson, the gatekeeper, that neither of the west windows had been touched for over a year. It seems that those two windows were loose in the frame and let in bad drafts. The judge used that pavilion, as a rule, only in the evening; and he was afraid of drafts. So the windows were always locked and the shutters always bolted into place outside them. You see, when Borden and I came to examine them, the locks were so rusted that it took our combined strength to budge them. The shutters outside the windows had their bolts so rusted from exposure that we couldn't move them at all. So that's definitely o-u-t. Whatever light and ventilation the room got, it got from the south windows. As for the other two, you might as well have tried to open a part of the wall."

Colonel Marquis used an unofficial word. "So we come directly round in a circle again?"

"I'm afraid so, sir. It really does seal the room up. Out of four sides of a square, one was a blank wall, one was impregnable with rusted bolts, and the other two were watched. We have got to believe Gabriel White fired both those shots—or go crazy."

The telephone on the Assistant Commissioner's desk rang sharply. Colonel Marquis, evidently about to hold forth on his refusal to go crazy, answered it with some annoyance; but his expression changed. He put a hand over the mouthpiece of the phone.

"Where is White now? You're holding him, naturally?"

"Naturally, sir. He's downstairs now. I thought you might like to have a talk with him."

"Send them both in," Marquis said to the telephone, and hung up in some satisfaction. "I think," he went on to Page, "it will be a good idea, presently, to confront everybody with everybody else. And I am very curious to form my own opinion of this saint-martyr, or rotter-murderer, Mr. Gabriel White. But at the moment we have visitors. No, don't get up. Miss Ida Mortlake and Sir Andrew Travers are on their way in."

## Chapter 3

Though Page was afraid he might have pitched it too strongly in his description of Ida Mortlake, her appearance reassured him. She had been wrong, he thought, to use that word "Victorian," yet it was something she conveyed rather than what she was. Seen now for the second time, she was a slender girl with a coolness and delicacy like Dresden china. Though she was rather tall, she did not seem tall. Her skin was very fair, her hair clear yellow under a black close-fitting hat with a short veil, her eyes blue; and she had a smile capable of loosening Page's judgment. Though her manner was anxious and somewhat deprecating, mixed with a good deal of shyness, it was that of complete honesty. She wore a mink coat which Page—who had been out after fur thieves in the West India Dock Road the week before—valued at fifteen hundred guineas.

This depressed him. For the first time it occurred to him that, with the old judge out of the way, Ida Mortlake would be a very rich woman.

"Colonel Marquis?" she said, her color rising. "I thought—"

A clearing of the throat behind her interrupted the speech, for someone towered there. Page had never seen Sir Andrew Travers without his barrister's wig and gown; yet he had the same mannerisms in private life as in court. They had become, evidently, a part of him. Sir Andrew Travers had a massive head, a massive chest, a blue jowl, and an inscrutable eye. His wiry black hair was so thick that you expected it to be long, but it was cropped off just above the ears. He was formidable, but he was also affable. He had a trick of lifting up his chin, hooking his thumbs in his lapels as though he were hitching up a gown, and studying you. His movements were slow, like those of a battleship which is so heavy that it goes ahead and rams something before anybody can get the engines reversed. He wore a dark overcoat, through which showed a gray cravat; and he formally carried top hat and gloves. His full, rich voice compassed the room.

"In such a shocking affair, Colonel Marquis," he said, "you will readily understand Miss Mortlake's feelings. As a personal friend of poor Mortlake's, I asked the liberty of accompanying her here—"

Page had got up hastily to stand at attention against the wall, while Marquis indicated chairs. Ida recognized him and gave him a smile. As Sir Andrew Travers lowered himself into a chair, Page seemed to see a manservant at work brushing him to give him that gloss. Sir Andrew assumed his most winning air.

"Frankly, Colonel Marquis, we are here to ask for information—"

"Oh, no," said Ida. She flushed again, and her eyes were bright. "It isn't that. But I do want to tell you that I can't believe Gabriel White killed father."

Travers looked slightly annoyed and Colonel Marquis was very bland. He addressed himself to Travers. There was an air of intense formality about the whole proceeding which reminded Page of a courtroom and made him uncomfortable.

"You are familiar with the details?" the Assistant Commissioner asked.

"Only, I regret to say, what I have read here," said Travers. He reached out and touched the newspaper. Page thought that his inscrutable eye rested for more than a glance at the Browning automatic. But at this moment Ida Mortlake caught sight of the two guns, and such obvious distress came into her face that Colonel Marquis shut them into a drawer. "You can understand," Travers went on, "that I am in a position of some delicacy. I am a barrister, not a solicitor. I may not appear in this officially without instructions from a solicitor—unless, of course, we care to make it a 'legal aid' case. But at the moment I am here only as a friend of Miss Mortlake. Frankly, is there some doubt of this unfortunate young man's guilt?"

The Assistant Commissioner considered. "There is," he said, "what I can only call—an unreasonable doubt. Do you follow me?"

"Ah," said Sir Andrew Travers.

"And therefore," Colonel Marquis went on, "would Miss Mortlake mind answering a few questions?"

"Of course not," the girl replied promptly. "That's why I'm here; that's why I wanted to come, although Andrew advised me not to. I tell you, I *know* Gabriel White couldn't have done it."

"Why are you so certain of that, Miss Mortlake?"

"I know him, you see."

"Forgive the question, but are you interested in him?"

Her face became still more pink and she spoke with eagerness. "No! No, honestly I'm not: not in the way you mean, that is. In the way you mean, I think I rather dislike him, though he's been very nice to me. I shouldn't say it, but it's the truth, and it's all the more reason why I know he couldn't have done it."

"Yet you knew that he was sentenced to flogging and imprisonment for a particularly brutal case of robbery with violence."

"Yes, I knew it," she said calmly. "I know all about that. He told me. He was innocent, of course. You see, it's not in Gabriel's nature; he's too much of an idealist; a thing like that is directly opposed to all he believes in most strongly. He hates war and he hates violence of all kinds. He's a member of all kinds of societies opposed to war and violence and capital punishment. There's one political society, called the Utopians—he says it's the political science of the future—and he's the leading member of that. You remember when he was tried, the prosecution asked what a respectable citizen was *doing* in a slum district like Poplar on the night that poor old woman was robbed? And he refused to answer. And they made quite a lot of that." She was speaking in a somewhat breathless rush. "Actually, he was going to a meeting of the Utopians. But most of their members are very poor, and a lot of them are foreigners. Gabriel said that, if he had answered, the jury would merely have thought they were a lot of anarchists. He says English juries think all foreigners are anarchists and terribly wicked. And it would only have prejudiced the case still more against him."

"H'm," said Colonel Marquis, after a pause. "How long have you known him, Miss Mortlake?"

"Oh, nearly three years, I should think. I mean, I knew him about a year before he—before they put him in prison."

"What do you know about him?"

"He's an artist."

"One more point, doubtless, for the jury," interposed Travers dryly. Page had the feeling that Travers was watching with tense alertness, waiting to intervene.

"There is just one thing," pursued Colonel Marquis, examining his hands, "which does not seem to square with this. You are willing to swear, Miss Mortlake, that White could not have killed your father. And yet, if I understand correctly, you were the one who rang up here yesterday afternoon at four-thirty o'clock and begged for men to protect your father because White had threatened to kill him. Is that true?"

"I know I said so," answered the girl, with a sort of astounding simplicity which never turned a hair; "but, of course, I never thought he would really."

She spoke as though this were the most natural thing in the world. There was a silence, during which the Assistant Commissioner regarded her with a satirical indulgence, and Page was frankly amazed. Both these glances seemed to awake in her a certain impatience; almost a pettishness which, even so, was not unbecoming.

"Oh, don't you understand? I was panicky, horribly panicky. The more I thought of it, the worse it seemed—you see, I met Gabriel yesterday afternoon between three-thirty and four o'clock, I think it was. If you remember, it started to rain about four or a little past. Up to that time, the weather had been decent and there was even a little sun. We had been having so much rain that I thought I should get out the car and get a little air. So I went out for a drive, but I wasn't very far down North End Road when I saw Gabriel. He was walking along with his head down, looking like thunder. I stopped the car. At first he didn't want to speak to me. But the car was right outside a Lyons', and he said in that curt way of his, 'Oh, come in and have some tea.' We did. There weren't many people there at that hour. At first he wouldn't talk much, but at last he broke out raving against my father. He said he was going to kill him—"

"And you weren't impressed?"

"Gabriel always talks like that," she answered. She made a slight, sharp gesture of her gloved hand. "But I didn't want a row in a public place like that. At last I said, 'Well, if you can't behave any better than this, perhaps I'd better go.' I left him sitting there with his elbows stuck out on the table. By that time it had begun to rain and lightning, and I'm frightened of storms. So I drove straight back home as soon as I'd got a book from the lending library."

"Yes?" he prompted, as she hesitated.

"Well, I warned Robinson—the gatekeeper—not to let anybody in, anybody at all, even by the tradesman's entrance. There's a big wall all around, with glass on the top. As a matter of fact, I still don't see how Gabriel got in. I went up to the house. There was nobody there except the servants; Carolyn and old Mr. Penney, the clerk, were both out; and father was at the pavilion. I suppose it was the fact that there was nobody in the house, and there was a storm outside that made me get panicky and still more panicky. At last I simply grabbed the phone, and—" She sat back, breathing hard. "I lost my silly head, that was all."

Colonel Marquis frowned. "But didn't you go to the pavilion and warn your father, Miss Mortlake?"

"No."

"Even though you believed his life was in danger?"

"No." She was almost on the edge of tears. If she had not kept herself so well in hand, Page felt she would have made a sort of fighting gesture. "In the first place I was afraid of the storm—out there. In the second place I didn't want my father to know I had talked to Gabriel. I was afraid to. But I thought that, if Scotland Yard knew, he couldn't be in any danger."

"Ah," said Marquis, taking in a rich inhalation of smoke. "Now we come to it. You know, of course, that your father sat in judgment on White in the robbery case. H'm, yes. At this time I suppose your father was acquainted with White, or knew that White knew you?"

Sir Andrew Travers sat up straight and bristling.

"That, sir," he interposed, with great suavity nevertheless, "is an insult to the judicial system. Of course Charles Mortlake knew nothing of the sort. He had no knowledge of, or acquaintance with, White. If he had, do you think he would have sat on the bench in that robbery case? It is not only an insult to the judicial system; it is an insult to poor Mortlake himself."

Colonel Marquis looked at him mildly. "If it comes to that," he said, "his murder was an insult to him. I take it, Sir Andrew, you are willing to be briefed for the defense?"

"I shall do whatever Miss Mortlake wishes."

"Then you shouldn't object to the idea that Mortlake might have known White and given him that heavy sentence with deliberate intent—should you? It's one for the defense. It shows extreme provocation."

Page had a feeling that swords were being crossed: that Marquis was enjoying it, and Travers was not. Yet he also felt that the barrister was stiffening himself for battle, after first underestimating his adversary. Travers's blue-jowled face grew very bland.

"Did your father know White, Miss Mortlake?" asked Marquis. "It won't take long to deny it, you know."

She was troubled. "Yes, I'm pretty sure he did. At least, he knew I had been—seeing Gabriel."

"And he didn't approve?"

"No; I'm sure I don't know why. He certainly never saw Gabriel in my presence."

"So you think there might have been a personal reason why he ordered a flogging? I am aware," Marquis snapped quickly, as Travers opened his mouth, "that you don't have to answer that, Miss Mortlake. Sir Andrew was going to advise you not to answer. But it strikes me the defense will need all the help it can get. In spite of your gallant words in White's favor, he admits firing one of the shots. You knew that?"

The girl's blue eyes widened and the color went out of her face, leaving it soft-looking and (for a second) curiously ineffectual. She glanced at Page. "No, I didn't," she said. "But this is horrible! If he really admits doing it after all—"

"No, he doesn't admit firing the shot that actually killed your father. That's the trouble." Colonel Marquis took the two pistols out of the desk drawer, and he very rapidly gave a summary of the case. "So, you see, it seems we shall have to prosecute White or, as the Inspector says, go crazy. Do you know of anyone else who might have wished to kill your father?"

"Nobody in the world," she admitted. "Quite to the contrary, everybody in public life loved him. You've heard how lenient he was. He never had any animosity from any of the people he sentenced. He was always helping people too; giving them money, and things like that."

"And in private life?"

This evidently surprised her. "Private life? What on earth? Certainly not! Of course," she hesitated, "sometimes—there's no harm in my saying it, is there?—sometimes he was difficult. I mean, he had splendid humanitarian principles and he was always trying to make the world better; but I did wish sometimes he would be less gentle in court and at banquets and a little more humanitarian at home. Please don't misunderstand me! He was a wonderful man and I don't think he ever spoke an unkind word to us in his life. But he loved to lecture: on and on in that smooth, easy voice of his. I—I suppose it was for our own good, though."

For the first time, and with a sort of shock, it occurred to Page that the liberal and lenient Mr. Justice Charles Mortlake might have been a holy terror to live with. Colonel Marquis looked at Travers.

"You agree with that, Sir Andrew?"

Travers clearly had to draw back his attention from other matters. He had picked up the little Browning automatic from the desk and was turning it over in his fingers. His big face was indecipherable, but it looked blacker. He cleared his throat.

"Agree? About Mortlake having any enemies? Oh, emphatically."

"You have nothing to add to that?"

"I have a great deal to add to it," said Travers with sharpness. He seemed to have developed a number of little wheezes in his throat. "So the second shot was fired from this? Well, it alters matters. I don't know whether or not White is guilty. But I know that now I can't undertake his defense . . . my friend, this Browning automatic belongs to me."

## Chapter 4

Ida Mortlake let out an exclamation. With great urbanity Travers reached into his breast pocket, drew out a wallet, and showed the card of a firearms license. There was a curious smile on his face.

"If you will compare the serial numbers," he said, "you will see that they agree. I don't know what to say about this, except that it's damned awkward."

"H'm," said Marquis, and grunted. "Are you going to confess to the murder, then?"

Travers's smile grew broader and more human. "God love us, *I* didn't kill him, if that's what you think. I liked him too well. But this is an unusual position for me, and I can't say it's a pleasant one. I thought I recognized this little weapon as soon as I came in here, although I thought it couldn't possibly be the same one. The last time I saw it, it was in my chambers at the Inner Temple. To be exact, it was in the lowest left-hand drawer of the desk in my study."

"Could White have stolen it from there?"

Travers shook his head. He seemed completely frank.

"I don't think so. I should regard it as extremely unlikely. I don't know White; to my knowledge, I've never even seen him. And he's never been in my chambers, unless it was burglary. My study is an inner room; the clerk would never have let him in. I can't say it's impossible for him to have taken it, but my opinion is that he didn't."

"When did you last see the gun?"

"I'm afraid I can't answer that," said Travers. He was now at his ease, studying the matter as though in luxurious debate. But Page thought he was watchful. "The pistol was too much part of—the domestic furniture, so to speak. I think I can say I haven't taken it out of the drawer for over a year; I had no use for it. If I ever opened the drawer, as I probably did any number of times, I can't even tell you whether I noticed the pistol there. It may have been gone for a year. It may have been gone for no longer than a few days."

"Who could have stolen it?"

There was a heavy cloud on Travers's face. He looked up and down, but the movement of his foot on the carpet was the only sign of uneasiness.

"I can hardly answer that, can I? Anyone with free access to my rooms might have done it."

"A member of Mr. Justice Mortlake's household, for instance?"

"Come!" protested the other, unrolling the full richness of his voice. He smiled, but Colonel Marquis was not impressed.

"Come on yourself," said Marquis. "You can't be very surprised at that. It's the first question you yourself would have asked anybody in the witness-box. A member of the judge's household?"

"Oh, yes, it's possible," replied Travers. He turned to Ida with amused irony. "Take care, my girl. They will be suspecting you next."

"But that's absurd!" cried the girl, who had evidently never considered this before. "You—you don't, do you? That is . . ."

Page had a distinct feeling that his chief, usually restrained, was about to explode in a rich panorama of profanity. Colonel Marquis's years in the army had brought his vocabulary to a pitch of excellence. But he only remained looking at them, his wrinkled eyelids moving a little.

"Sorry," said Sir Andrew Travers grimly. "I don't want you to accuse me, of all people, of evading your questions. As a possibility, yes: any of them might have taken it. Ida might have. Carolyn might have—though Carolyn doesn't particularly like me and seldom comes there. Even old Penney, Mortlake's clerk, might have; he sometimes came with a new half chapter of manuscript for me to read. Mortlake was writing his reminiscences. And—" He leaned forward, his mirth broadening. "And Mortlake himself might have taken it. Has that occurred to you? The obvious thing, isn't it? If he thought he was in danger of attack, he may very well have taken my pistol and said nothing about it because he did not wish to alarm anyone."

"When did you think of that?" asked Colonel Marquis.

"I beg your pardon?"

"I asked when that explanation occurred to *you*. To me it sounds a little like an afterthought," observed the other, with that disconcerting habit he had of seeming to read people's thoughts. "It wasn't the obvious suggestion, or you'd have made it as soon as you heard the gun had disappeared. Other possibilities occurred to you before that did. So you didn't think it was likely Mortlake himself had taken the gun?"

Travers looked at him.

"Man," he said, "I'm afraid we can't make any progress if you care to argue about the precise second a thought entered my head." Again his tone was one of gentle irony. "Certainly I think it likely. Can you advance a better explanation?"

"Oh, it merely occurred to me. Very well," said the Assistant Commissioner dully. "Would you mind, Sir Andrew, giving an account of your movements yesterday afternoon?"

The barrister reflected. "I was in court until about half-past three in the afternoon. Michaelmas Term began a week ago, and I've been rather busy. Afterwards I walked across the street—I was at the Law Courts over the way, not the Central Criminal Court—to the Temple. It was not raining then. Let me see. When I passed through Fountain Court, I remember noticing by the sundial on the wall that it was twenty minutes to four. I had promised to be at Hampstead, for tea with Mortlake, by four-thirty at the latest."

Sir Andrew Travers paused, a gleam of interest in his stolid face. It seemed to kindle the big body and animate him.

"By Jove, Colonel, there's an idea! The sundial: I hadn't thought of it before. In stories we've heard a lot about alibis being manufactured by some ingenious trick of altering clocks; but has anybody ever manufactured an alibi by tampering with a sun-dial?—No, I am not trying to throw you off. At twenty minutes to four I went to my chambers, intending to go from there to Hampstead. Unfortunately, my clerk told me that Gordon Bates had gone on the sick list and had insisted on turning the brief in the Lake case over to me. The Lake case comes up for trial today, and it's rather a complicated business. I knew that I should have to swot up on it all yesterday afternoon and probably all night, to be in shape to argue it today. Which killed any possibility of my going to Hampstead for tea. So I stayed in my chambers with the brief—"

"Just a moment. Did you phone Hampstead to tell the judge you weren't coming?"

Travers frowned. "Not at the moment, I regret to say. I wondered how much of the brief I might be able to master. So I put it off. It was twenty minutes to six when I suddenly realized I hadn't made any excuses over the phone. But by that time—well, poor Mortlake was dead. I understand he was shot about half-past five."

"And all this time you were in your chambers? Have you any confirmation of this?"

"I believe I have," the other affirmed with grave attention. "My clerk should confirm it. He was in the outer room until nearly six o'clock. I was in the inner part of the chambers: my living quarters. There is only one way out of the chambers; and to leave them, I should have had to pass through the room where my clerk was. I believe he will give me an alibi." Travers spread out his hands, and regarded the Assistant Commissioner with a sort of whimsical keenness. "Does that set your mind at rest?"

Supporting himself on his cane, Colonel Marquis got up with great formality and nodded.

"Right," he said. "I have just one request. I wonder whether I can trespass on your time by asking you to wait in another room for about ten minutes? There is something I must do, and then I should like to speak with both of you again."

He pressed a buzzer on his desk. He swept them out of the room with such effortless smoothness that even Travers had scarcely time to protest. Page remembered Ida Mortlake, puzzled and lovely, also making protests; but she did not forget to give Page a smile which made the inspector's scalp tingle. In short, here was a respectable police-officer very badly smitten with a Burne-Jones girl who wore fifteen-hundred-guinea mink coats. But he had not even time to reflect gloomily on this.

"Remarkable! Excellent!" said Colonel Marquis, who was rubbing his hands with fiendish glee. Page felt that if his chief had not been lame, he would have danced. Marquis pointed a long forefinger at his subordinate. "You are shocked," he went on. "In the depths of your soul you are shocked at my lack of dignity. Wait until you are my age. Then you will realize that the greatest joy of passing sixty is being able to act as you jolly well please. Inspector, this case is a sizzler; it has leads; it has possibilities; and doubtless you see them?"

"I'm not shocked," said Page, annoyed. He considered. "As for the possibilities, sir, there seems to be something very fishy about that theft of Sir Andrew Travers's gun. If White couldn't have done it—"

"Ah, White. Yes. That's why I wanted our friends out of the room; I should like to have a little talk with White, alone."

He got on the telephone again and gave orders for White to be brought up.

There was little change in the young man's appearance since last night, Page noticed, except that he was now dry and brushed. Two constables brought him in: a tall, rather lanky figure still wearing his shabby topcoat. His darkish fair hair was worn rather long, brushed back from the forehead, and he smoothed at it nervously. His face was strong, with a delicate nose but a strong jaw; and he had good gray eyes under pinched brows. The face was slightly hollow, his movements jerky. At the moment he seemed half belligerent, half despairing; he did not seem to know how to take Colonel Marquis's affability; he seemed dejected, he seemed defiant, in a whole succession of attitudes; and at length he merely sat down and looked at the Assistant Commissioner.

"That's better," said the latter. "You know, young fellow, you're in a bit of a tight spot."

He spoke with such geniality that it seemed to tickle some nerve of humor in White. A faint smile dawned on White's face. For the first time

White seemed suddenly at ease, and it made a transformation in his pale earnestness. There was an honest charm about him.

"I know it," said White.

"Why don't you tell us what really happened at that pavilion?"

"I wish you'd tell *me,*" the other said simply. "Do you think I've been pounding my head about anything else since they nabbed me? Whatever happens, I'm due for a long stretch at the Moor, because I really did take a crack at the old swine. But, believe it or not, *I—did—not—kill—him.*"

"Well, that's what we're here to discover," Marquis said comfortably, and pushed across the cigarette-box. "Smoke?"

"Thanks."

"Light? There you are. By the way, I thought it was shown at your last trial that you didn't smoke?"

"A lot of things were shown at that trial," said White, and hesitated abruptly. He did not seem to care to discuss that. For the first time, strangely, there had come into his manner a curious touch of that stiffness which is associated in humor with the old-school-tie. Page wondered at it. "I didn't smoke because I couldn't afford to," White added shortly. "Not that it matters."

"You are an artist, I've heard?"

"I am a painter," said White, still shortly. "Whether or not I am an artist remains to be seen." The light of the fanatic came into his eyes. "By heaven, I wish Philistines would not persist in misusing terms they do not understand! I wish—"

"We are coming to that. I understand you've got some strong political views. What do you believe in?"

White regarded him. "Something tells me you're not altogether the Colonel Blimp you want to appear. As to what I believe in," he said politely, "I should require a month to complete your conversion. And by that time I shall probably be sentenced to be hanged by the neck until I am dead. So there is no need to discuss what I believe in." He broke off. "You want to know what I believe in?" he demanded. "I believe in a new world, an enlightened world, a world free from the muddle we have made of this. I want a world of light and progress, that a man can breathe decently in; a world without violence or war; a world, in that fine phrase of Wells's, 'waste, austere and wonderful.' That's all I want, and it's little enough."

"And how would you bring this about?"

"First," said White, "all capitalists would be taken out and hanged. Those who opposed us, of course, would merely be shot. But capitalists would be hanged, because they have brought about this muddle and made us their tools. I say it again: we are tools, tools, tools, TOOLS."

Page thought: The fellow's off his onion. But there was about Gabriel

White such a complete and flaming earnestness that it carried conviction. White stopped, breathing so hard that it choked him.

"And you think Mr. Justice Mortlake deserved death?"

"He was a swine," answered White calmly. "You don't need political science to tell you that."

"Did you know him personally?"

"No," said White, after a hesitation.

"Be careful! Look here, young fellow: try to do yourself some good and help your case. It would help you if you could show he knew you when you were tried for robbery: it would show he had bias."

"I'm sorry," said White. That weird stiffness of the old-school-tie had shut him up again, and made his answers short. "I've already told you I didn't know him."

"But you know Miss Mortlake?"

"Which Miss Mortlake?"

"Ida."

"I know her slightly." He was still inscrutable. "Not that it matters. There is no need to drag her into this; she knows nothing of it."

"Naturally not. Well, suppose you tell us exactly what happened yesterday afternoon. To begin with, how did you get inside the grounds?"

White looked dogged. "I'd better tell you about that, yes, because it's the one thing I'm ashamed of. You see, I met Ida yesterday afternoon. We were at a Lyons' in Hampstead. Naturally I didn't want to meet her just then; but I felt bound to warn her I was going to kill the old man if I could." There was a dull flush under his cheekbones. His fine, rather large-knuckled hands were fidgeting on his knees. "The fact is, I hid in the back of her car. She didn't know it. After she'd left the teashop, she was going to a lending library just down the road. I knew that. So I followed. While she was in the library, I nipped into the back of the car and got down under a rug. It was a very dark day and raining hard, so I knew she wouldn't notice me. Otherwise I couldn't have got inside the grounds at all. The gatekeeper keeps a sharp lookout."

"Go on."

"She drove through the gates and up to the house. When she put the car in the garage, I sneaked out. The trouble was I didn't know *where* the old swine was. How was I to know he was at the pavilion? I thought I should find him in the house.

"I wasted nearly an hour trying to get into that house. There seemed to be servants all over the place. Finally I did get in—through a side window. And I nearly walked into the butler. He was just going into a front room, drawing room or the like, where Ida Mortlake was sitting. He said it was getting very late, and asked whether she wanted tea served? She said yes; she said to go ahead and serve it, because her father was at the pavilion and probably wouldn't be up for tea. That was how I knew, you see. So I hopped out the side window again."

"What time was this?"

"God knows; I wasn't paying any attention to that. Stop a bit, though." White reflected. "You can easily enough find out. I ran straight down to the pavilion, as hard as I could pelt. There I ran into your police officers—I supposed they were police officers—and by that time I was determined to kill the old devil if it was the last thing I ever did."

The breath whistled out of his nostrils. Colonel Marquis asked:

"We can put it, then, at half-past five? Good. Go on. Everything!"

"I've gone over it a hundred times since then," said White. He shut his eyes, and spoke slowly. "I ran back to the door of the study. I ran inside and locked the door. Mortlake had been standing at the window, shouting something to the police officer outside. When he heard me come in, he turned round from the window. . . ."

"Did he say anything?"

"Yes. He said, 'What is the meaning of this?' or 'What do you want here?' or something of that sort. I can't remember the exact words. Then he put his hand up in front of him, as though I were going to hit him, when he saw the gun in my hand. Then I fired. With that pistol," said White, touching the Ivor-Johnson .38 on the table.

"H'm, yes. D'you hit him?"

"Sir, I'm practically certain I didn't," declared the other, bringing down his fist on the edge of the desk. "Look here: there was a very bright light up over the desk. It was in a brass holder of some kind, and it left most of the room pretty dark because it was concentrated. But it lit up the desk and the space between the windows. The paper on the walls is a light yellowish-brown. I've thought and thought about it. Just as I pulled the trigger, I saw the bullet hole jump up black in the wall behind him. It was like a painting. And he was still moving and running. Besides . . ."

"Well?"

"It isn't as easy," said White, suddenly looking like an old man, "to kill a man as you might think. It's all right until your hand is actually on the trigger. Then something seems to wash all out of you. It seems as though you can't, physically can't, do it. It's like hitting a man when he's down. And it's a queer thing—just at that second, I almost pitied the old beggar. He looked so *scared,* flapping away from my gun like a bat trying to get out."

"Just a moment," interposed Marquis, studying the other with a hard, dead stare. "Are you accustomed to use firearms?"

White was puzzled. "No. I don't suppose I've ever handled anything more deadly than an air rifle when I was a boy. But I thought, shut up in a room, I couldn't very well miss. Then—I did miss. Do you want me to go on? Right. He started to run away from me, along the back wall. He was alive then, all right. I want you to understand that the whole thing was such a brief matter of seconds, all compressed, that it's a bit confused. At this time he was facing, slightly sideways, the wall behind me on my right . . ."

"Facing, then, the corner where the yellow vase stood? The vase where the automatic was later found?"

"Yes. It seemed as though he'd turned round to swing out into the room. Then I heard another shot. Actually, I thought I had fired it myself. Then I realized that I couldn't be as crazy as that, because the gun was hanging down in my hand. Also, it seemed to come from behind me and to my right. I felt—a kind of wind, if you know what I mean.

"After this—it seemed rather *longer* after this than you might have expected, if you could split seconds—he put his hands up to his chest. He turned round and took a few steps back the way he'd come, and swung a little back again, and then fell headfirst across the desk. Just as he fell, your police officer"—White nodded toward Page—"came in through the window. And that's the best I can do."

"Did you see anybody else in the room, either before or after this shot?"

"No."

"Did you see the flash of it?"

"No. It was behind me. I felt the vibration, if you can call it that."

The Assistant Commissioner's somber eyes wandered over to Page. "A question for you, Inspector. Would it be possible for there to have been any mechanical device in that room, hidden somewhere, which could have fired a shot and concealed the pistol without anyone else being there?"

Page was prompt. He and Borden had searched that room too well.

"It's absolutely impossible, sir," he answered. "We nearly took that pavilion to pieces. Also," he smiled a little, "you can rule out any idea of a secret passage or a trap door. There wasn't so much as a mousehole. . . . Besides, there's the gun in the yellow vase, which really was fired inside that room."

Colonel Marquis put his hands up to his temples and ruffled the sparse white hair that grew far back on his skull. He nodded dully. He said:

"Yes, I think we have got to acknowledge that the second shot was fired by somebody inside the room. Look here, White: how far were you away from the judge when you shot at him?"

"About fifteen feet, I should think."

"And how far was it, in a diagonal line, from where the judge was lying to the yellow vase where the second shot came from?"

"It must have been close on twenty-five feet. That's a big room. About that—?" said White, looking at Page for confirmation. The inspector nodded.

"H'm, yes. Very well. We assume somebody dropped that pistol into the vase. You say the vase was much too high for anybody's arm to reach down inside and deposit the gun there. So it must have made some noise when it fell." He looked at White. "Did you hear any noise?"

White was troubled. "I don't know. I honestly don't know. If I keep thinking about this I may convince myself of something or other, and put something in my head that isn't true. I can't remember—"

"You realize," said Marquis, with sudden harshness, "that you are telling us an absolutely impossible thing? You are saying that somebody must have escaped from a room which was locked and guarded on all sides? *How?* . . . Yes, yes, what is it?"

He broke off as his secretary came into the room and spoke in a low tone. Colonel Marquis nodded, becoming affable again.

"It's the police surgeon," he said to Page. "He's performed the post-mortem. And the results seem to be so interesting that he wants to see me directly. Most unusual. Send him in."

There was a silence. White sat quietly in his chair; but he had braced his elbows against the back of the chair and his heavy handsome face had a blankness of waiting. Page knew what goblins had come into the room to surround the prisoner. If the bullet in the judge's body turned out to be a .38 after all, it meant the end of him. Dr. Gallatin, the police surgeon, a worried bustling man, came into the room with a briefcase in his hand.

"Good morning, Doctor," said Colonel Marquis. "We were waiting for you. We can't go any further until we know. What's the verdict?"

"That's up to you, sir," Dr. Gallatin told him. He took out of his brief-case a written report and a small cardboard box. "But I don't think you're going to like it."

White made a sound which seemed to proceed out of a dry and furred mouth. Colonel Marquis pushed the two pistols across the desk.

"Public opinion is divided. One branch thinks Mr. Justice Mortlake was killed by a bullet from an Ivor-Johnson .38 revolver, fired from a distance of about fifteen feet. The other branch denies this and says he was killed by a bullet from a Browning .32 automatic, fired from a distance of about twenty-five feet. Which side is right?"

"Neither," said the doctor.

Colonel Marquis sat up very slowly. "What the devil do you mean, neither? Kindly endeavor to cultivate—"

"I said neither," replied the doctor, "because both sides are wrong, sir. As a matter of fact, he was killed by a bullet from an Erckmann air pistol, roughly corresponding to a .22 caliber fired from a distance of about ten feet."

## Chapter 5

Although Marquis did not bat an eyelid, Page felt that the old so-and-so had seldom in his life received so unexpected an announcement. He remained sitting bolt upright, looking coldly at the doctor.

"I trust, Dr. Gallatin," he said, "that you are sober?"

"Quite sober, worse luck," agreed the doctor.

"And you are seriously trying to tell me that there was still a *third* shot fired in that room?"

"I don't know anything about the case, sir. All I know is that he was plugged at fairly short range"—Gallatin opened the little cardboard box and took out a flattish lump of lead—"by this bullet from an Erckmann air pistol. The Erckmann people—it's a German firm, of course—used to turn out a lot of them during the war. There are some still knocking about in this country. As a rule you see the Erckmann army pistol, which is a lot heavier than this. But this one is a dangerous job, because it's got much more power than an ordinary firearm, and it's almost noiseless."

Colonel Marquis turned to White. "What have you got to say to this?"

White was evidently so strung up that he had forgotten his role as light bringer and social reformer; he spoke like a schoolboy, with sullen petulance. "Here, I say! Fair play! I don't know any more about it than you do. If—"

"Did you hear or see another shot fired in that room?"

"No, I did not."

"Inspector Page: you searched the room immediately after you went in. Did you find any air pistol, or any such gun?"

"No, sir," said Page firmly. "If there had been any, I'm pretty certain we should have found it."

"And you also searched the prisoner. Did he have any such pistol on him, or could he have disposed of it in any way?"

"He did not and he could not," replied Page. "Besides, three pistols carried by one man would be coming it a little too strong. In a case like that, I should think it would have been simpler to have used a machine gun." He saw the Colonel's eye grow dangerous, and added: "May I ask a question? Doctor, would it have been possible for that air-pistol bullet to have been fired either from a Browning .32 or an Ivor-Johnson .38? A sort of fraud to make us think a third gun had been used?"

Dr. Gallatin grinned. "You don't know much about ballistics, do you?" he asked. "It's not only impossible, it's mad. Ask your firearms man. This little pellet had to be fired, and was fired, from an Erckmann air pistol."

Now that the reaction had set in, White was deadly pale. He looked from one to the other of them.

"Excuse me," he said, with the first trace of humility he had shown, "but does this mean I'm cleared of the actual—murder?"

"Yes," said Colonel Marquis. "Brace up, man! Here, pull yourself together. I'm sending you downstairs for a while. This alters matters considerably."

He pressed the buzzer on his desk. White was escorted out, talking volubly but incomprehensibly about nothing at all. The Assistant Commissioner remained staring after him with somber concentration, and knocking his knuckles against his desk. Page and the doctor watched him.

"This is insanity," he went on. "Let us see where we stand:

"There is now no doubt that three shots were fired: from the Ivor-Johnson, *and* the Browning, *and* the missing Erckmann. The trouble is that we lack a bullet, for only two of the three bullets have been found. By the way, Inspector, pass me over that pellet you found stuck in the wall." Page gave it to him and Colonel Marquis weighed it in his hand. "You say this is from the Ivor-Johnson .38. I agree, decidedly. We'll get a third opinion; what's your guess, Doctor?"

Gallatin took the bullet and studied it.

"It's a .38, all right," he agreed. "No doubt of it. I've handled too many of them. This has been chipped a bit, that's all."

"Right, then. This is the one White admits having fired at the judge, as soon as he walked into the judge's study. So far, so good. But what about afterward? What sort of witchcraft or hocus-pocus happened in the next two or three seconds?—By the way, Doctor, you said an Erckmann air pistol is almost noiseless. *How* noiseless?"

Gallatin was cautious. "That's out of my department, you know. But I think I can give you an idea. It isn't a great deal louder than the noise you make when you press the catch of an electric-light switch."

"Not nearly loud enough, then, to be mistaken for an ordinary pistol shot?"

"Good God, no!"

"Then, sir," interposed Page slowly, "you mean the Erckmann might have been fired in that room almost under White's nose, and (especially with a storm going on outside) he mightn't have heard it at all?"

Marquis nodded. "But take it in order," he said. "After White fires his revolver, the judge starts to run away. Then someone else—standing behind and to the right of White, over in the corner by the yellow vase—fires a shot with the Browning automatic. This shot is heard by Inspector Page, who is within ten steps of the window. But the *bullet* from the Browning disappears. If it didn't kill the judge, where did it go? Where did it lodge? Where is it now?

"Finally, someone cuts loose with an Erckmann air pistol and fires the shot which really does kill Mortlake. But this time the *gun* disappears. Whoosh!" said Colonel Marquis, with an imaginative flourish. "Just as Mortlake falls forward dead across the writing table, Inspector Page arrives at the window, in time to find the room sealed up impregnably from every side—the only point being that the *murderer* has disappeared."

He paused, letting them picture the scene for themselves. Page saw it only too vividly.

"Gentlemen, I don't believe it. I cannot believe that djinns and afreets were fooling about in a bewitched house. But there it is. Have you any suggestions?"

"Only questions," Page said gloomily. "I take it we agree, sir, that White can't be the murderer?"

"Yes, I think we can safely say that."

Page took out his notebook and wrote: "Three questions seem to be indicated, all tied up with each other. (1) Did the same person who fired the Browning automatic also fire the Erckmann air pistol? And, if not, were there two people in the room besides White? (2) Was the fatal shot fired immediately before, or immediately after, the shot from the Browning? (3) In either case, where was the actual murderer standing?"

He looked up from his notebook, and Marquis nodded.

"Yes, I see the point. Number three is the hardest question of the lot," the Assistant Commissioner said. "According to the doctor here, Mortlake was shot through the heart at a distance of about ten feet. (Right? Good.) White, by his own confession, was standing fifteen feet away from Mortlake. How the devil does it happen, then, that White didn't see the murderer? Gentlemen, there is something so infernally fishy about this case that it is beginning to scent the whole of Scotland Yard."

"You mean," Page volunteered, "you mean the old idea that White might be shielding somebody?"

"But that's the trouble. Even if White is shielding anybody, how did anybody get out of the room? There was certainly one other person in there, and possibly two. Suppose one, or two, or six people took a shot at the judge: where did the whole procession vanish to—in the course of about eight or ten seconds?" He shook his head. "I say, Doctor, is there anything in the medical evidence that would help us?"

"Not about the vanishing, certainly," said Gallatin. "And not much about anything. Death was almost instantaneous. He might have taken a step or two afterward, or made a movement; but not much more."

Page made an aimless design in the margin of his notebook. He was trying to sketch out a plan of crossing bullets by which sense could be made of the position. He said:

"According to that, Doctor, the shot that killed him probably came immediately after the shot from the Browning—the last of the three?"

"Probably. But I can't tell."

"In that case," said the colonel, "*I* am going to find out. Let's have a car round here, Page, and run out to Hampstead. This interests me."

He limped across after his hat and coat. In his dark blue overcoat and soft gray hat, Colonel Marquis presented a figure of great sartorial elegance, except for the fact that he jammed on the hat so malevolently as to give it a high crown like Guy Fawkes's. First, Page had to issue instructions: a man must be sent to verify Travers's alibi, and the files of the firearms department ransacked to find any record of who might own an Erckmann air pistol. Then Colonel Marquis went limping out, towering over nearly everyone in the office. When Page protested that Ida Mortlake and Sir Andrew Travers were still waiting, he grunted.

"Let 'em wait," he said impolitely. "The case has taken such a turn that they will only confuse matters. Between ourselves, Inspector, I don't care to have Travers about when I examine the scene. Travers is a trifle too shrewd." He said little more while the police car moved through wet and gusty streets toward Hampstead. Page prompted him.

"It seems," the Inspector said, "that we've now got a very restricted circle."

"Restricted circle?"

"Like this, sir. There seems no reason why Travers should have killed the judge; and, on top of it, he's got a sound alibi. I'm assuming the alibi is straight, because it's so easily checked and Travers (who's no fool) would be a first-class fathead to lie about a point so easily established. Next, Ida Mortlake has an alibi—an unintentional alibi—"

"Ah; you noticed that," observed Colonel Marquis, looking at him.

"Provided, unintentionally, by White himself. You remember what White said. He got through a window into the judge's house, not knowing the judge was at the pavilion. And he didn't learn the truth until he heard the butler asking Ida whether tea should be served. As soon as he heard this, he nipped out of the window and ran straight to the pavilion. This was at five-thirty, for he met Borden and myself on the way. Consequently, Ida must still have been at the house; and we can probably get the butler's corroboration. That's a sound alibi."

"Quite. Anything else?"

"If," answered Page thoughtfully, "if, as seems likely, no outsider could have got into the grounds—well, it looks as though he must have been killed either by one of the servants or by Miss Carolyn Mortlake or by old Penney, the clerk."

Colonel Marquis grunted out something which might have been assent or disagreement and pointed out that they would soon know. The car had swung into the broad suburban thoroughfare along one side of which ran the high wall of the judge's house. It was a busy street, where a tram line and a bus route crossed. Along one side were several shops, contrasting with the lonely stone wall across the street, beyond which elms showed tattered against a drizzling sky. They stopped before iron-grilled gates; and old Robinson, recognizing the police car, hastened to open.

"Anything new?" Page asked.

Robinson, the gatekeeper, a little man with a veined forehead and a dogged eye, thrust his head into the back of the car. He remained doubled in and half out, his corduroy backside splashed with rain.

"Nossir," he said. "Except your sergeant is still dead set trying to find out whether anybody could have sneaked in here yesterday afternoon without my knowing—"

"And could anybody have done that?" asked Colonel Marquis.

Robinson studied him, wondering. "Well, sir, they told me to keep people out—or Miss Ida did, yesterday—and I *did* keep people out. That's my job. You just take a look at them walls. Anybody'd need a ladder to get over 'em, and there's no side of the walls where you could prop up a ladder without being seen by half the people in Hampstead. There's a main road in front and there's people's back gardens coming up against the walls on every other side." He cleared his throat, like a man about to spit, and grew more dogged. "There's only two gates, as you can see for yourself, and I was sitting right by one of them."

"What about the other gate—the tradesmen's entrance?"

"Locked," said Robinson promptly. "When Miss Ida come back from her drive yesterday, about four-twenty, no more, she told me to lock it and I did. There's only one other key besides mine, and Miss Ida's got that. I do my job."

Page took out his notebook. The rain continued to splash, and Robinson's hinder quarters shifted uncomfortably outside the car, but he continued to lean through and stare at them.

"You said that both Miss Carolyn Mortlake and Mr. Penney weren't here yesterday afternoon?"

"I don't remember whether I said so to you. But it's true."

"What time did they go?"

"Miss Carolyn—'bout quarter to four. Yes. Becos she'd wanted the car. And Miss Ida had already taken the car and gone out a quarter of an hour before that. Miss Carolyn, she was pretty mad; she was going to a cocktail party (people name o' Fischer at Golder's Green); and she wanted that car." Some faint amusement seemed to stir the swollen veins in his forehead; but it died away, and was replaced by dislike, when his thoughts moved on to the clerk. "As for Alfred Eric Penney, don't ask me when *he* went out. About ten minutes past four, I think. But I don't know where he went; he didn't tell me, and I'm not the one to ask."

Colonel Marquis was bland. "For the sake of clearness, we had better make this a timetable. The judge went from his house across to the pavilion—when?"

"Half-past three," answered Robinson firmly. "That's certain."

"Good. Ida Mortlake leaves here in the car about the same time. Correct? Good. Carolyn Mortlake leaves for a cocktail party at fifteen minutes to four. At ten minutes past four, Penney also leaves. At twenty minutes past four, the rain having then begun, Ida Mortlake returns in the car. They all seem to have missed each other most conveniently; but that, I take it, is the timetable of events?"

"I suppose it is; yes, sir," Robinson admitted.

"Drive on," said Colonel Marquis.

The car sped up a gravel drive between doleful elms. Page indicated where a branch of this path turned towards the pavilion, but the pavilion was some distance away, hidden in an ornamental clump of trees, and Marquis could not see it. The house itself would not have pleased an architect. It was of three stories, stuccoed, and built in that bastard style of Gothic architecture first seen at Strawberry Hill, but revived with gusto by designers during the middle of the nineteenth century. Its discolored pinnacles huddled together under the rain. Most of the long windows were shuttered, but smoke drooped down from all the chimneys. Though it was a landmark of solid Victorian respectability and prosperity, Page did not like it. There was about it no sense of death or regret. Despite the respectability of its starched curtains, there was about it something close-lipped and definitely evil.

Page saw his companion look at it curiously, but Marquis did not comment. The height of respectability also was the grizzled, heavy-headed manservant who admitted them. He fitted; you would have expected him. Page had seen him yesterday, although he had taken no statement. They now learned his name, which was Davies; and something of his nervousness as well.

"If you don't mind, sir," he said, "I'll call Miss Carolyn. As a matter of fact, Miss Carolyn was just about to set out to see you or someone at Scotland Yard. She—"

"And if *you* don't mind," said a new voice, "I should prefer to handle this myself, please."

The hall was heavy and shadowed by a window of red glass at the back. A woman came out between the bead curtains (which still exist) of an archway to the right. Carolyn Mortlake was one of those startling family contrasts (which, also, still exist). Where Ida was rather tall and soft, Carolyn was short, stocky, and hard. Where Ida was fair, Carolyn was dark. She had a square, very good-looking but very hard face; with black eyes of a snapping luminousness and a mouth painted dark red. They could see her jaw muscles. She came forward at a free stride, wearing a tilted hat and a plain dark coat with a fur collar. But Page noticed, curiously enough, that her eyelids were puffy and reddish. She appraised them coolly, a heavy handbag under her arm.

"You are—?" she said.

Colonel Marquis made the introductions, and in his politeness the girl seemed to find something suspicious.

"We are honored," she told him, "to have the Assistant Commissioner visit us in person. Perhaps, then, I had better give you this."

With a decisive snap she opened the catch of her handbag, and took out a nickeled pistol with a rather long and top-heavy barrel.

"It is an Erckmann air pistol," she said.

"So it is, Miss Mortlake. Where did you get it?"

"From the bottom drawer of the bureau in my bedroom," replied Carolyn Mortlake, and lifted her head to stare at him defiantly.

## Chapter 6

"Perhaps," she said after a pause, "you had better come this way." In spite of her defiance, it was clear that she was shaking with some strong inner strain. But she was as cool as ever when she led them through the bead curtains into a thick-cluttered drawing room. However, there were easy chairs, and a bright fire burned. Carolyn Mortlake sat down, crossing her legs and (as though in defiance) exposing more flesh than was necessary. She continued to look at them steadily. Her eyes, which had long lashes, were her best feature; but they were glazed over with a calm sneer.

"I don't know quite what the game is," she went on. "I can't see why anybody should want to do it, because obviously my father wasn't killed with that gun. . . . No, I didn't put the gun there. It wasn't there last night. But I think I know what I was intended to do when I found it. I was supposed to become panicky, and hide the gun away again in case I should be suspected of something, and generally behave like a silly ass. Well, you jolly well won't find me doing things like that; I'm not such a fool." She smiled, without humor, and reached for a cigarette box. "There's the gun and you may take it or leave it. But why? That's what I should like to know. No, I don't think you'll find any fingerprints on it. I looked."

Colonel Marquis turned the pistol over in his fingers. "You think, then," he said, "that somebody deliberately hid this in your room?"

She opened her mouth to speak; then she hesitated and shrugged her shoulders.

"You want me to commit myself," she said, with a faint jeer; "and I have no intention of doing anything of the kind. No; considering our household, I shouldn't consider that very likely—should you? Besides, suspicion of what? Where's the point?"

"If you have observed that there are no fingerprints on it, Miss Mortlake, you have probably observed that one bullet has been fired from it."

She had taken a cigarette from the box; and she broke the cigarette in two. Still she did not take her eyes from his face. "I am not going to pretend to misunderstand when I understand perfectly well what you mean. Or what I think you mean. Yes. I thought of that too. But it's absolutely impossible. There were only two guns, a .32 and a .38; and this isn't either."

"Well . . . waiving that for a moment: you don't happen to know who owns this gun? You've never seen it before?"

"Of course I've seen it before—dozens of times. It belonged to father."

Page stared at this extraordinary witness who seemed to speak with such a contempt that she could hardly pack it into words. But the Assistant Commissioner only nodded, with an appreciative smile.

"Ah, yes. Where did your father keep it?"

"In the drawer of his writing table at the pavilion."

"And when did you see it last, if you can remember?"

"I saw it yesterday afternoon, in the writing-table drawer as usual."

"You will perceive, by the haste with which Inspector Page goes after his notebook," Marquis told her suavely, "that these discoveries are coming fast. Suppose, Miss Mortlake, we keep from going too fast, and get these things in order? First of all, naturally, I should like to convey my sympathies in the death of your father . . ."

Whether or not this was bait, she did not rise to it; she remained unblinking and acknowledged it only with a slight twist of the lip. What possessed her was curiosity. It was clear to Page that she did not believe Marquis's suggestion that Mr. Justice Mortlake might have been killed by an Erckmann bullet: she thought he was bluffing, as she believed that the whole world bluffed. But no trace of curiosity appeared on her sallow, cynical face.

"Thank you," she said.

"Were you fond of him?"

"Yes and no."

Marquis frowned. By this time their eyes were used to the firelight in the room, and Marquis glanced at a large painting on one wall. It was a full length, seated, portrait of the judge in his robes. The mild face, turned slightly sideways, seemed to peer with attention out of the wig, as though it was listening; firelight made rich color of the robes.

"Can you give any reason, Miss Mortlake, why your father seems to have been disliked in his own house? Neither you nor your sister seems to show any great grief at his death."

"Whether I felt any grief or whether I didn't," said Carolyn dispassionately, "I should not be inclined to discuss it with someone I had just met. But didn't you know? He is not our father, really. We were very young when he married our mother; but our real father is dead. I do not see that it matters, but you had better have the facts straight."

This was news both to Page and Marquis, who looked at each other. The Assistant Commissioner ignored the justifiable thrust in reply to his question.

"I have no intention, Miss Mortlake, of trying to trap you or hide things from you. Your father—we'll call him that—really was shot with the air pistol." He gave a very terse but very clever account of the affair, up to the point they had reached. "That," he added, "is why I need your help."

She had been staring at him, her face dark and rather terrible. But she spoke calmly enough. "So someone really was trying to throw suspicion on me?"

"It would seem so. Again, while it's *possible* that an outsider could have committed the crime, still you'll agree with me that it's very improbable. It would appear to be somebody in this house. Is there anybody here who has a grudge against you?"

"No, certainly not!"

"Tell me frankly, then: how did you get on with your father?"

"As well as people do in most families, I dare say." For the first time she looked troubled and rather hunted. "Do you understand?"

"There was no outright quarrel?"

"No, never. That I'll swear to."

"You and your sister, I take it, are your father's heirs?"

She tried to force a hard smile. "The old problem of the will, eh?" she inquired, with a mocking ghastliness of waggery. "Yes, so far as I know we were. He made no secret of that. There are small legacies for the servants and a substantial one for Penney, but Ida and I inherit jointly. That's how it used to be, anyhow. He made a will when my mother died. Of course, he may have changed it since, but I don't think so."

Colonel Marquis nodded, and held up the air pistol. "This pistol, Miss Mortlake . . . you say your father kept it constantly by him?"

"Good Lord, no! I didn't say that." She roused herself out of some private fog and perplexity, focusing her mind with difficulty on the question. "No; or he wouldn't have kept it at the pavilion. He kept it as a kind of curio. You see, a friend of his was in the Secret Service during the war, and made him a present of it; I believe those air guns are a rarity. The— the judge," she looked at the past, and made an odd grimace, "for all his dryness, had rather a romantic mind. He was always reading murder mysteries, and he was proud of that pistol. He used to show it to his friends sometimes."

"Yes. What I meant was, he didn't keep the gun by him because he feared an attack?"

"No, I'm positive he didn't."

"What about the threats made by Gabriel White?"

"Oh, Gabriel!—" she said. Her gestures seemed to sum up a great deal; then she considered. "Besides, until I saw Ida last night and read the newspapers this morning, I didn't know Gabriel *had* made any threats. Not that he would not have had reason to. There will be an interesting and beautiful mess, my dear Colonel, when the truth about that comes out. I'll anticipate your question: my father knew Gabriel—or, at least he knew of him. I don't know how. He never spoke much about it. But he never troubled to conceal his belief that Gabriel was a swine."

"What was your own belief, Miss Mortlake? What did you think when you heard White was supposed to have killed your father?"

Her eyes narrowed. "Frankly, I didn't see how even Gabriel could have been such a fool. But there it was—or seemed to be."

"You liked White?"

"Yes. No. I don't know." She paused, and her square handsome face had an expression of cynicism so deep that it seemed to have been put there with a stamp. "My opinion! You flatter me, Colonel. I have been asked my opinion more times in the last ten minutes than I have been asked for it in the last ten months. I rather like Gabriel, to tell you the truth; and I think he's quite straight. But, my God, I hate lame ducks!"

"You mean failures?"

"If you prefer the term."

Colonel Marquis was sitting bolt upright, his gloved hands folded over his cane. His expression was indecipherable. He said:

"One last question, Miss Mortlake, before we come to the account of your movements yesterday afternoon. I have told you that the .32 Browning automatic, the one found in the yellow vase, belongs to Sir Andrew Travers. Apparently someone stole it out of Sir Andrew's chambers in the Temple. It has been suggested that your father himself might have stolen the pistol, and kept the theft a secret so as not to alarm anyone. What do you think of it?"

"I think it's rubbish," she answered promptly. "If you had known him, you'd have agreed with me. The idea of him *stealing* a pistol—no: decidedly not. Do not think, please, that I mean he could not be dishonest. But he wouldn't have been guilty of that particular kind of dishonesty. It would have been a breach of good manners." Her voice had almost reached a mimicking note, but she checked herself. "He would no more have stolen a gun out of Andrew's desk than he would have stolen a book off his shelves. Besides, if he had been alarmed, he certainly wouldn't have concealed it. He wasn't like that. If he ever had so much as a touch of stomach-ache, he howled the house down—in a refined way, of course."

"I see. Now, for the benefit of Inspector Page's notebook, how did you spend yesterday afternoon?"

"Ah, the alibi," murmured Carolyn, slightly showing her teeth. "Well, let's see. The earlier part of the afternoon I spent interviewing a horde of prospective servants. Our maid—we boast only one—is leaving us next month to get married. Ah, romance! So we've got to replace her; the judge insisted on the absolute smooth-running of the house in the old style. The agency couldn't supply us with exactly what we wanted, so we've been forced to advertise as well. Yesterday I had my brains buffeted by a succession of females of all sizes. Actually, the managing of the house is Ida's job—I hate housework and management, and I don't trouble to conceal it—but Ida said I was such a wonderful judge of character that I was flattered into doing the dirty work."

Inspector Page interposed.

"There seem to be a lot of things we haven't heard of, Miss Mortlake," he said. "You mean there were a number of outsiders here in the grounds yesterday afternoon?"

She studied him and at length decided to be civil. "You may set your mind and notebook at rest, Inspector," she informed him. "All of the lot were out of the house and out of the grounds at least two hours before my father was shot. Robinson at the gate can tell you that, if he overcomes his usual closed-mouth tactics. He let 'em in, and counted 'em, and let 'em out." Her face lighted up with impish amusement. "Besides, even the most modern housemaid could hardly hope to get a situation by first murdering her prospective employer. But, if you're suspicious, I have a list of names and addresses. Shall I go on? Thank you.

"The last of them left between half-past three and a quarter to four. I know that, because I was anxious to get out of the house myself. Then I discovered that Ida had gone out and taken the car. That was a bloody bore"—the snapping luminousness had come back into her dark eyes—"because I had been rather under the impression it was promised to me. But there it was. I could get a taxi, anyhow. First, however, I went down to the pavilion. . . ."

"Why did you go to the pavilion, Miss Mortlake?"

She flushed a little. "I wanted some money. Respectable young ladies need pocket money, and I am not particularly expensive. Besides, I wanted to tell him, in a dutiful way, that I had engaged a new maid."

"Go on, please."

"He had only been at the pavilion five minutes or so when I got there;

he went down about half-past three. You may be interested to know that I got the money. That, incidentally, is how I happen to know the air pistol was in the drawer of his writing table at that time. He opened the drawer to get his check-book. It was too late for the bank, but I knew where I could get the check cashed. When he opened the drawer I saw the gun."

"Was the drawer locked or unlocked?"

She reflected, her hand shading her eyes. "It was locked. I remember: he got a bunch of keys out of his pocket and opened it."

"Did he lock it afterwards?"

"I'm not sure. I didn't notice—after I'd got the check. But I rather think he did; yes, I'm inclined to think he did. His precious manuscript was there."

"I see. Did he do or say anything notable that you remember?"

"Notable is good. No, not that I remember. He was a little short, because he doesn't like being interrupted when he's down there reciting chapters of his book to that dictaphone. He wrote down the name of the maid I was going to engage: he wanted to check her credentials before she came here next month. . . . Oh, yes; and he mentioned that Sir Andrew Travers was coming there to tea. They were going to have tea at the pavilion. In the other room at the pavilion—the one across the hall from the study—he has an electric kettle and all the doings. I suggested that he'd better switch on the electric fire in the room across the hall or it would be freezing cold when Andrew got there."

"And did he switch it on?"

She was puzzled. "Yes. Or, rather, I did it for him."

"How was your father dressed at this time, Miss Mortlake?"

Page could not understand the drift of his superior officer's questions, and, it was plain, neither did Carolyn Mortlake. They both stared at him; but Colonel Marquis's face was rapt with a sudden idea which pleased him.

"Dressed?" the girl repeated, after a pause. "Well, he'd got on the usual smoking-jacket he wears when he's down there; dark heavy thing; old-fashioned. A wing collar. A black bow tie. Striped trousers, I think, but I'm not certain."

Colonel Marquis turned to Page. "That was the costume he was wearing when you found him?"

"Yes, sir."

"Also, Inspector, when you and Sergeant Borden searched the pavilion, I suppose you looked into this other room across the hall? Was the electric fire burning in that room as well as the one in the study?"

Page saw an angry flush come into Carolyn Mortlake's face, but he checked her outburst. He could remember very well how he and Borden had plunged into every corner; of how he had opened the door across the hall and seen the orange-red square of a fire glowing in the darkness. It was, as they discovered when they turned up the lights, a sort of sitting room.

"Yes, sir, the fire was on."

"Thank you," snapped Carolyn Mortlake.

"I don't think you quite understand the meaning of the last question," the Colonel told her calmly. "One more question, Inspector. When you discovered the body, was the smoking jacket buttoned?"

"Yes, sir."

"Good. Now," said the other, turning back to Carolyn, "will you go on with your story, please?"

"I left the pavilion, and I left the grounds; that was about a quarter to four."

"Yes; and afterwards?"

She folded her hands in her lap with great nicety. Taking a deep breath, she lifted her head and looked him in the eye. Something had blazed and hardened, like the effect of a fire.

"I'm sorry," she said; "but that's where the story stops. That's all I have to say."

### Chapter 7

"I don't understand this," said Colonel Marquis sharply. "You mean you won't tell us what you did after you left the house?"

"Yes."

"But that's absurd. Don't be a young fool! Your gatekeeper himself told us you were going to a cocktail party at Golder's Green."

"He had no right to tell you any such thing," she flared, and hesitated. "You'll only waste your time inquiring after me at the Fischers'. I didn't go. I intended to go, but an hour or so before I left the house I got a telephone message which made me change my mind. That's all I can tell you."

"But why shouldn't you tell us?"

"In the first place, because you wouldn't believe me. In the second place, because I can't prove where I was during the afternoon, so it's no good as an alibi. In the third place—well, that's what I prefer to keep to myself. It's no good coming the high official over me. I've said I won't tell you, and I mean it."

"You realize, Miss Mortlake, that this puts you under suspicion for murder?"

"Yes."

Page felt that she was about to add something else; but at that moment all emotion, protest, or explanation was washed out of her. She became again a person of shuttered defiance. For someone had come into the room—they heard hesitant footsteps, and the faint clicking of the bead curtains at the door.

The newcomer was a little, deprecating man with a stoop and a nervously complaisant manner. They felt that it must be Alfred Penney, the clerk. It has been said that long association with a particular person will give a secretary, an employee, a companion, most of the mannerisms and even some of the looks of the master. When the firelight rose on the walls, there was undeniably a resemblance in Penney to the picture of the judge: giving a somewhat ghostly effect to his entrance through the bead curtains. But it was a weak and ill-brushed copy. Where Mr. Justice Mortlake had been almost delicate of feature, Penney's feet were enormous and his hands seemed all knuckles. The judge had been bald; Penney had a few strands of iron-gray hair brushed across his skull like the skeleton of a fish, and something suspiciously like side whiskers. But he had a faithful eye, blinking at them while he dabbed his hand at it.

"I beg your pardon," he said, wheeling round quickly.

Carolyn Mortlake rose. "Alfred, this is Colonel Marquis, the Assistant Commissioner of Police, and Inspector Page. Tell them what you can. For the moment, I think they will excuse *me.*"

While Penney blinked at them, his mouth a little open, she strode past out of the room. Then his face assumed his legal manner.

"I really beg your pardon," he repeated. "I should not have intruded, but I saw Davies, the butler, in the hall intently listening to what was going on in here, and—no matter. You are the police? Yes; of course."

"Sit down, Mr. Penney," said Colonel Marquis.

"This is a terrible thing, gentlemen. Terrible," said Penney, balancing himself gingerly on the edge of a chair. "You cannot realize what a shock it has been to me. I have been associated with him for thirty years. Twenty-nine and a half, to be exact." His voice grew even more mild. "I trust you will not think me vindictive, gentlemen, if I ask you whether you have taken any steps with regard to this young—young hound who killed him?"

"Gabriel White?"

"If you prefer to call him that."

"So?" prompted Marquis, with a gleam of interest. He lifted his eyebrows. "It has been suggested, Mr. Penney, that 'Gabriel White' is not the man's real name. The judge knew him?"

The little man nodded. "I am not ashamed to tell you," he replied, tilting up his chin, "that he did. If he condemned him, he dealt out moral justice; and moral justice was always Charles Mortlake's aim. Charles Mortlake knew the young man's father very well and has been acquainted with the young man since he was a boy. 'Gabriel White' is really Lord Edward Whiteford, a son of the Earl of Cray."

There was a pause, while Penney stared sideways at the fire. "Fortunately," he went on, knitting the baggy skin of his forehead, "the Earl of Cray does not know where his son is, or how he has sunk; and Charles Mortlake was not so inhumane as to enlighten him. . . . Gabriel White, since he prefers to call himself that, started in the world with every advantage. At Oxford he had a distinguished career. He was a leading member of the Union and great things were predicted for him. Also, he was a popular athlete. I believe he holds the university record for the broad jump; and he was also an expert swordsman and pistol shot. But, like so many who start with advantages—"

"Hold on," interrupted Marquis in a voice so sharp and official that Penney jumped a little. "I want to get this straight. You say he was an expert pistol shot? In my office this morning he told us that he had never handled a gun in his life."

"I am afraid he lied, then," Penney said without rancor. "Lying is a habit of his." Then Penney smiled. "Pray forgive me, gentlemen. I am a lawyer, and I am aware that you will require proof beyond my bare word. Excuse me just a moment."

For a moment after he had gone out of the room, neither Page nor Marquis spoke. The colonel was whistling softly between his teeth, his forehead puzzled. Page had a feeling of the whole riddle descending on them again like a vacuum. Then Marquis looked at his subordinate. At the entrance of Penney he had thrust the air-pistol behind him in the chair, but now he took it out again.

"This is growing much worse," he observed. "Look here, Inspector: you say you searched that study when you found the judge shot. Did you look in the drawer of the writing-table, or was it locked?"

"Yes, I looked in the drawer. I tell you, sir, we looked everywhere. The drawer wasn't locked. And the pistol certainly wasn't in it. There was nothing in the drawer but some sheets of manuscript; and, I think, a memorandum-pad and a check-book."

The other reflected. "Which confirms a part of Carolyn Mortlake's story, anyhow. I'm inclined to accept that story, Inspector—in spite of some asinine idea she seems to have got into her head about refusing to talk. Well . . . she saw the air pistol in that drawer about a quarter to four. At half-past five it was used to shoot the judge. But where the devil did it evaporate to afterwards, along with the murderer?"

He paused again as Penney returned, holding out an old photograph. Against the background of a park stood two men, an old man with a moustache and a younger one who was obviously Gabriel White. Each had a pistol in his hand; and each was holding up—self-consciously—a cardboard practice-target. The old man's target was speckled with some-what erratic shooting, but the young man's target had its bull's-eye so drilled out that Page could see daylight through it.

"I noticed this in Charles Mortlake's scrap-book some weeks ago," Penney explained. "It is some years old, of course. It was taken at Whiteford Park, the Earl of Cray's seat. That is his Lordship on the left. . . . As for 'Gabriel White's' prowess with firearms, I am afraid you have only my humble word beside this photograph, but at Whiteford Park, in the cellar where there is—or used to be—a pistol-range, I have seen him pin an ace of diamonds to the wall and shoot the center out of it from thirty feet away. He used what is called—I believe—an army pistol. I have—ah—no knowledge of firearms myself."

As though feeling that he had said too much, Penney folded his arms and eyed Marquis with a respectful doggedness.

"I see. Then can you explain how he missed a human body at half the distance?"

"Missed? Oh, ah, I presume you refer to the fact that—" Here Penney checked himself, and a slight change went over his dusty face. "I should be inclined to call it another trick, sir. His tricks are notorious."

Marquis took the air pistol from the chair and held it up.

"Ever see this before?"

"Yes, sir. Often," said Penney, taken aback. "It belonged to Charles Mortlake. May I ask why—?"

"When did you last see it?"

"A few days ago, I think; but I am afraid I cannot swear to the exact time. He kept it in the drawer of his writing table at the pavilion. May I ask why—?"

"Were you at the pavilion yesterday afternoon? Sit down, man, and don't look so alarmed!"

"I should like to point out that I am not in the least alarmed," Penney corrected him with dignity. "Yes, I was at the pavilion yesterday after-noon—for a very brief time. Five minutes, perhaps. This was shortly before I left the house. And I have something to tell you, which I venture to think is important."

He arranged his thoughts, as though he were arranging papers.

"Yesterday afternoon I was going to the Guildhall Library to verify a series of references for the book he was writing: and which, I fear, will now remain unfinished. But I was obliged to write some letters first. It was four o'clock when I found myself free to go. That was late, of course, but I knew it would not require a great time to verify the references once I had reached the library. I left the house at shortly after four o'clock—it had begun to rain, I may remark—and on my way down to the gate it occurred to me that I had better go to the pavilion and inquire whether there were any additional material he wished me to consult.

"I found him alone at the pavilion, speaking to the dictaphone." The clerk paused and something like the edge of a tear appeared in the corner of each eye. "He said there was nothing further he wished me to do at the library. So I left the grounds, about ten minutes past four. It was the last time I ever saw him alive. But . . ."

"But?"

"I should have been warned," said Penney, fixing his questioner with grave attention. "There was somebody prowling round the pavilion even then."

It was a commonplace enough statement, it was a commonplace enough pavilion where the judge sat under his dragon-lamp, but something in the words made Page shiver. Penney regarded them with quavering earnestness.

"I am aware, gentlemen, that my statement may sound fanciful and even—ah—sensational. I cannot help it. It is true. While we were speaking together, I distinctly heard footsteps approaching the windows."

"Which windows?"

"The west windows, sir. The windows whose locks and shutters are so rusted it is impossible to open them."

"Go on."

"Immediately after that, I was under the impression that I heard a sound of someone softly pulling or rattling at one of the west windows, as though trying to open it. But the rain was making some noise then, and I am not certain of this."

"The judge heard it as well?"

"Yes. I am afraid he regarded it as imagination. But only a few seconds afterward something struck the outer shutter of one of the *other* windows. I am under the impression that it was a pebble, or light stone of some kind, which had been thrown. This window was one of those in the south wall. . . . Judging from accounts I have heard," he turned mildly to Page, "it was the window through which you, Inspector, were obliged to climb nearly an hour and a half afterwards. When Charles Mortlake heard this noise, he pushed back the curtains, pushed up the window, unlocked the shutters, and looked out. There was nothing to be seen."

"What did he do then?"

"He closed and relocked the window, although he did not relock the shutters. He left them open against the wall. He was . . . I fear he was somewhat annoyed. He accused me of entertaining fancies. There is a tree some dozen or so feet away from the window; and he declared that a twig or the like had probably come loose in the storm, and had blown against the shutter. It is true that there was a strong wind, but I could not credit this explanation."

"You feared an attack?"

Penney spread out his knuckly hands, and looked muddled. "Sir, I do not know what I feared. I can only say that I was uneasy. Nor, I confess, did I think of Gabriel White then; I fear I had completely forgotten him."

"Do you know whether this air pistol was then in the table drawer?"

"I don't know; I should suppose so. He had no occasion to open the drawer. But my thoughts did not go—well, quite to the edge of violence in that line." His eyes did not fall before Marquis's steady stare; and presently he went on: "You will wish to know what I did afterward. I went from here, by Underground, to Mansion House station, and thence to the Guildhall Library on foot. I arrived there at four-thirty-five, since I happened to notice the clock. I left the library at just five o'clock. In coming home I experienced some delay and did not arrive here until five-forty, when I heard Charles Mortlake was dead. It was a terrible shock to me; so much so that, though I knew there was an inspector of police in the house, I locked myself up in my room and could not face him. I am afraid that is all I have to say. . . . And now may I ask a question? Why are you concerned with that air pistol?"

Again Colonel Marquis told the familiar story. As he did so, Penney did not look startled; he only looked witless. He remained sitting by the fire, a gnome with veined hands, and he hardly seemed to breathe. Marquis concluded:

"You see, we are compelled to accept White's innocence. Even if you argue that the air pistol was in the table drawer and White might have used it himself, still he would not have had the time to fire *three* shots. Next, though he was seized by police officers instantly, the air pistol had completely vanished; and he could not have concealed it. Finally, he was at once taken to the police station; so that he could not have conveyed the air pistol to this house. But it was actually found here this morning."

Penney said, "Good heaven!—" and somehow the expletive seemed as weak and ineffectual as himself. "But this is surely the most preposterous thing I have heard of," he stammered. "I cannot imagine you are serious. You are? You are? But there is no reason in it! Life works by reason and system. You cannot believe that there were three prospective murderers shut up in that room?"

At this point Page had the impression that Marquis was playing with his witness; that he was juggling facts for his own amusement, or to show his skill; and that the colonel had an excellent idea of what really happened in the locked room. Marquis remained urbane.

"Will you argue theories, Mr. Penney? Not necessarily *three,* but certainly two. Has it occurred to you, for example, that the same person who fired the Browning may also have fired the Erckmann air pistol?"

"I do not know what has occurred to me," Penney retorted simply. He lifted up his arms and dropped them with an oddly flapping gesture. "I only know that, however my poor friend was killed, Lord Edward Whiteford—or Gabriel White, if you prefer—killed him. Sir, you do not know that young man. I do. It sounds exactly like him. He would, and he could, deceive the devil himself! I cannot tell you how strongly I feel about this, or how clever that young hound is. With him it is always the twisted way, the ingenious way. If poor Mortlake had not laid him by the heels, he would have got off scot free from beating an old woman's face to a pulp in that tobacconist's shop: not, mind you, because he needed to do so in order to steal a few poor shillings out of her till, but because he took pleasure in doing it."

"Still, you don't maintain he can perform miracles?"

"Apparent miracles, yes," Penney replied quite seriously. "You don't know his cleverness, I repeat; and you won't know it until he somehow hoodwinks and humiliates you as well. For instance, how did he get into the grounds at all? I have heard from Robinson that they were locked up as tight as a prison, and that nobody could have got over the wall. There is a problem for you. How did he get in?"

"He has already answered that himself. While Miss Ida Mortlake was getting a book at a lending library, he got into her car and crouched down under a rug in the tonneau. When she drove up to the garage, he waited until she had gone and then got out. The day was too dark for her to notice him."

At the doorway someone coughed. It was hardly a cough at all, so modest and self-effacing was the sound. They looked up to see the grizzled and heavy-faced Davies, the butler.

"May I say a word, sir?" he inquired.

"Eh?" said Colonel Marquis irritably. "All right: yes; what is it?"

"Well, sir, under the circumstances I'll make no bones about saying I overheard what was being said. I mean about the man White, sir, and how he got in by hiding under the rug in Miss Ida's car. However he got into the grounds, it certainly wasn't that way. He wasn't hiding in the back of the car—and I can prove it."

## Chapter 8

As Davies came into the room, his hands folded in front of him, Penney gave a mutter of petulant protest which changed to interest as soon as he appeared to understand what Davies was talking about. Beyond any doubt Davies looked competent; he was bulbous-nosed and bulbous-eyed, but he had a strong jaw. For the moment, he had dropped the well-brushed airs of his calling. Though he remained quite respectful he shook his head with such a look of scepticism that it was almost like amusement.

"Yes, sir, I admit I listened," he said. "But I look at it like this. We're all shut up in here. Like a ship, as it were. It's to our advantage, servants most of all, to show we didn't have anything to do with killing the poor judge. If you see what I mean, sir. We've got to do it. Besides, it isn't as though I was a proper *butler*. I'm not even allowed to engage a maid, as a proper butler would. Fact is, sir, I was a court crier down on my luck (the drink did it, in Leeds) when the judge picked me up and gave me this job to make good. And I think I did make good, though all I ever knew about being a butler I got from the judge and out of a book. Now that he's dead, my lady friend and I are going to marry and settle down. But, just because he is dead, it doesn't mean we don't care who killed him and that we don't appreciate what he's done for us. So—I listened."

Penney almost sputtered. He acted as though a picture on the wall had suddenly made a face at him.

"You never acted like this before. You never talked like this before—"

"No, sir," said Davies. "But I never had occasion to talk like this before. The judge would've sacked me." He looked at Marquis steadily. "But I think I can do a bit of good."

Colonel Marquis was interested. "A court crier turned butler, eh?" he said, turning the idea over in his mind. "Look here, I should like to hear your autobiography one day. Been with the judge long?"

"Eleven years, sir."

"Benefit under the judge's will?"

"Yes, sir: five hundred pounds. He showed me the will. And I've got a bit saved as well."

This time it was Marquis's turn to blink. "H'm. I suppose *you* didn't kill him, did you?"

"No, sir," replied Davies with complete seriousness. "I've seen five men sentenced to death in court. And that cured me of any desire to kill anybody. If I ever had a desire to kill anybody, that is."

"All right. Let's hear about this business of White, or Lord Edward Whiteford; and how he didn't get in here by hiding in Miss Mortlake's car, and how you knew about it."

Davies nodded, not relaxing his butleresque stance. "The thing is, sir, she went out in the car yesterday afternoon. It started to rain, and I knew she hadn't an umbrella with her. Now, the garage is twenty yards or so from the house. At near on half-past four—maybe twenty or twenty-five minutes past—I saw her drive back. I was in the kitchen, looking out of the window, when I saw the car swing round the drive. So I got an umbrella and went out to the garage and held it over her coming back to the house so she shouldn't get wet."

"Yes; go on."

"Now, I was out to the garage before she'd even got out of the car. The car is a big Vauxhall saloon—the judge used to use it for going to the courts, before he retired and let his chauffeur go—and I admit somebody *could* hide in the back as easy as easy. But nobody did. I did what you naturally do; as soon as Miss Ida got out, I opened the door of the back and looked to see whether she'd brought any parcels. There was nobody in the back of that car. And nobody could have nipped out before I looked in, because there was nowhere to go."

"Since Davies insists on speaking," Penney interposed coolly, "at least you can see for yourselves, gentlemen, just how reliable 'Gabriel White' is. He has told you at least two lies. Probably a hundred more, but at least two. First he said he had never handled a pistol. Then he said he came to the grounds hidden in that car."

Page was doubtful. White, beyond question, had lied; but they were not the sort of lies which seemed likely to do him any good. They did not seem the sort of lies a man would tell to save his own skin.

"Would it have been possible," Page asked, "for him to have slipped out of the car as it came through the gates, or somewhere on the drive before Miss Mortlake reached the garage?"

"I can't tell you that, sir. You'd better ask Robinson or Miss Ida. But if he *said* he didn't slip out until the car came to the garage—?"

Colonel Marquis did not comment. For a brief time he stared across the room. "Anything else?" he prompted.

"Yes, sir. A bit of exoneration," replied Davies promptly. "Even though I'm not a proper butler, still I feel responsible for the other servants. If you see what I mean. Now, sir, there's only three of us, excluding Robinson, of course, but then he rarely comes to the house. There used to be four, when the judge kept a chauffeur; but he let the chauffeur go and pensioned him handsome. At present, then, there's the cook, the maid, and me. Can I take it for granted that the judge was killed between, say, twenty minutes past five and twenty minutes to six?"

"You can," Colonel Marquis agreed, and glanced at Page. "Did you note, Inspector, the exact time to the minute or second when all the shots were being fired?"

Page nodded. "I looked at my watch as soon as I got into the pavilion and took the gun out of White's hand. It was half-past five, almost to the second."

"Thank you, sir," said Davies, with heartiness and almost with a smile. "Because all three of us, cook, maid and me, happened to be in the kitchen at that time. We were together until a quarter to six, as a matter of fact. I know that, because it's the time the evening post arrives, and I went to the door to see whether there were any letters. So we can produce a corporate alibi, if you see what I mean."

Marquis spoke musingly, his fingertips together and his cane propped against his leg. "By the way, we might check up on another part of White's story and see whether it tallies. He admits that he came here in order to kill the judge—"

"Ah," said Penney softly.

"—and thinking the judge was here in the house, he prowled round until he got through a side window. He says that at close to half-past five he was here in hiding, and heard you ask Miss Ida Mortlake whether tea should be served at last. Is that true?"

"So that's why the window was unfastened," muttered Davies, and pulled himself up. "Yes, sir: quite true. It was at twenty minutes past five. Just after I asked her that, I went out to the kitchen; that's how I know all the servants were together. She also told me she had telephoned the police about this man White—or whoever he is—and the cook was in a considerable flutter."

"There's something on your mind," Marquis said quietly. "Better speak up. What is it?"

For the first time Davies was showing signs of discomfort. He started to glance over his shoulder; but, evidently thinking that would be unbecoming, he assumed a stolid expression.

"Yes, sir, I know I've got to speak up. I don't like it a little bit, and I won't say I've got any particular affection for the person named; but I did like the judge, and I want to see fair. It's about Miss Carolyn. I think I can tell you where she went yesterday.

"You'll say that everybody in this house is listening to everybody's business. Maybe in a way it's true; but in this case I think it's understandable. As you heard, sir, the maid is leaving next month to get married. Yesterday Miss Carolyn was interviewing a lot of applicants. Now, it happens that the maid's got a cousin—a nice girl—and she was anxious for her cousin to get the place. But Miss Carolyn said sentiment has no business in a thing like that. Well, Millie Reilly (that's the maid) wasn't afraid of her cousin being beat out of it by casual applicants who might come here, but she *was* afraid the Agency might dig up somebody with references a yard long. And the Agency has been phoning here several times. So the long and short of it is," Davies squirmed a little but spoke in his best court voice, "that Millie's got into the habit of listening in to all the phone conversations, in case it should be the Agency. There's a phone extension upstairs."

Colonel Marquis leaned forward.

"Good," he said. "I was hoping we should come across something like that. Don't apologize for the delinquencies. Miss Mortlake told us that she intended to go to a cocktail party, but that she received a phone message which caused her to change her mind. Did Millie hear that message?"

"Yes, sir." Davies's discomfort had grown acute, and he fiddled with his cuffs; he spoke almost violently: "And not only about the murder, but the judge would turn in his grave if he knew some of the things the rest of us know. . . . She listened. I'll fetch the girl in here so that she can tell it to you herself, but I can give you the gist of what she heard. A man's voice spoke. Millie didn't recognize the voice. It said, 'If you want to know something that vitally concerns you and Ralph Stratfield, go to the stationer's shop at 66 Hastings Street, W.C.1, and ask for a letter written to you under the name of Carolyn Baer. Don't fail, or it may be the worse for you.' "

Colonel Marquis sat up and Page almost whistled. Unless there was a coincidence of names, here was again a crossing of the ways with the C.I.D. The Ralph Stratfield he knew was well known to Scotland Yard, although they had never been able to obtain a conviction and Stratfield swanked it in the West End with his thumb to his nose. Ralph Stratfield was a supergigolo who lived off women. Several times he had skirted the line of blackmail and once he had been brought to court for it. But he had been ably defended—by Sir Andrew Travers, Page now remembered —and had come off scot-free. Page remembered having seen Stratfield once, and thought him rather a repulsive type, but women seemed to agree that he was a great lover. Also, Page realized why Carolyn Mortlake might have been so determined to keep her mouth shut, even under bad risks. Page looked at Davies, and was about to ask a question, but the butler anticipated him.

"Yes, sir, it's the same man," Davies said grimly.

Colonel Marquis scowled. "I like it as little as you do," he acknowledged. "But what did Esmond say? 'I can't but accept the world as I find it, including a rope's end, as long as it is the fashion.' Damnation. By the way, you're sure of that, Davies? And also the address?"

"Yes, sir, Millie remembered it. You can see why. If there'd been a '10' tacked on to it it would have been 'Hastings, 1066'; and that's pretty easy to remember. If you want to know where she went, that's probably the place."

Subconsciously Page had been expecting an outburst from another direction, but he was not too pleased when it occurred. The bead curtains were swept aside. Carolyn Mortlake came into the room with short, quick steps. Her face was sallow with rage and the eyes so dead that they looked like currants in dough. With difficulty she mastered her breathing, for they heard it. She stood trying to control her voice, but behind this shaking there was an inner emotion; and that inner emotion was shame.

"You may go, Davies," she said, calmly enough. "I will speak to you later. But I should advise you to begin packing at once. You will have to accept a month's wages in place of notice."

"Stay here, Davies," said Colonel Marquis.

He hoisted himself to his feet, supporting himself on his cane. He towered over her in the firelight.

"I'm afraid the police have first claim, Miss Mortlake," he went on, after an explosive pause. "You can't order the witnesses about like that, you know, when they have something to tell us. You are at liberty to discharge him, naturally; but I should be sorry to see you do it. He was only trying to protect you."

"You ———," said the girl. It was an ugly word, and it had even more startling a quality in this sheltered Victorian room.

"Ralph Stratfield is poor company, Miss Mortlake."

"I think," she said with sudden politeness, "it is none of your damned business with whom I choose to go, or whom I see. Or is it?"

"Under the circumstances, yes. Look here, you know how you're feeling as well as I do. Now that it's said and done, there's no reason why it should come out. All we care about is where you happened to be yesterday afternoon. Will it do any great harm to tell us whether you really went there?"

She had herself well in hand now. "I'm sure I don't know. I'm sure it won't do any particular good. You needn't preach about Ralph Stratfield: Ralph had nothing to do with that message. It was a fake. In other words, Mr. Clever, I was got out of the way by one of the oldest, most bewhiskered tricks ever used in shilling shockers. There is no such address as 66 Hastings Street. There is only one stationer's in the street and that wasn't the place. It took me quite a time to tumble to it, unfortunately, and it succeeded. For, you see, I can't prove where I was yesterday and I'm in exactly the same situation I was before. Why anyone should—"

She stopped, and for a moment Page had an uncomfortable feeling that this hardheaded, savage young lady was going to collapse in tears. Only her inexpressible rage seemed to save her; that, or a certain bewilderment. But she did not wait to see. She almost ran out of the room. Penney, muttering inarticulately, followed her. When they had gone the force of her emotion surcharged the room still. Davies made a feint of mopping his forehead.

"It's a good thing I've got a bit of money saved," he said.

"It would appear," mused Colonel Marquis, "that neither of Mr. Justice Mortlake's daughters selected the company he would have chosen for them. By the way, did you ever see Gabriel White?"

"Oh, I suppose it's only natural, sir," Davies observed philosophically, "like clergymen's sons. Playing the giddy goat, I mean. Or at least they always do in the books, though I can't say *I* ever knew a clergyman's son who was a rip-roarer. Mostly they seem a pretty quiet lot. Gabriel White? No, sir. He never came here. The only time I ever saw him was yesterday afternoon, between two police officers. Mr. Penney says he's a lord?"

Marquis smiled with tight-lipped amusement. "No, my lad. No: you're not supposed to question me. I'm supposed to question you. And I dare say you've kept your ears and eyes open. Who do you think killed the judge?"

Davies looked somewhat apprehensive.

"Here, I say, sir, you're not suspecting me, are you? I tell you, I've got a perfect alibi. I ask that because—well, because in the butler-business you've got to read notes in people's voices, like notes in music. If you see an expression on a face that seems to say, 'I want a match,' you've got to get out that match and have it in front of the person's cigar before he knows he wants a match himself. If you see what I mean. That's why I asked."

"I'm sorry to hear my face is such an open book," said Colonel Marquis as though saluting an antagonist with a sword. "But I didn't say I suspected you. I want you to read the notes you've seen hereabouts. Who do you think killed the judge?

"Just between ourselves, sir?"

"Naturally."

"The only thing I've got, I admit, is a germ of an idea, and it may not be worth much. But if I were you, sir, I should keep a sharp eye out for Sir Andrew Travers."

"So? You think he's the murderer?"

"N-no, no, I don't mean that, exactly." Davies seemed a trifle hurried, and he was certainly not anxious to commit himself. "I only said, keep a sharp eye out. Because why? I'll tell you. From what I heard while I—while I—"

"Lurked."

"Yes, sir: lurked. From what I heard while I lurked, it struck me that there's one thing that doesn't seem to fit anywhere. It's this: it's one of them shots, *and* Sir Andrew's gun. That's what's throwing you all skew-wiff. It's that one shot, from the Browning automatic, which won't fit in anywhere no matter how you explain the case. It's a kind of excrescence, if I've got the right word. Don't ask me to explain how the murderer got out of the locked room. I don't know. But why on earth was the Browning, Sir Andrew's gun, fired at all? This Gabriel White fires with the .38.

The murderer fires with that funny-looking gun you've got in your hand. But where does the Browning come into it? . . . Incidentally, sir, everybody seems all hot and bothered about one thing which seems fairly simple to me."

"I'm glad to hear it. What is that?"

"Well, you're wondering what happened to the bullet out of the Browning. Everything seems to have vanished, and that bullet vanished with it. But common sense must tell you where it went."

"Yes?"

"It went out the window," returned Davies promptly. "You didn't find it in the room and it can't have melted or anything. But—if you'll excuse my saying so—there was one slightly open space where a bullet could have flown. After the judge had opened the window, he turned back to see White, and White shot at him, and then everybody started firing all over the room. But the window was up a little way—with the Inspector here running towards it. So, when somebody took a shot with the Browning, the bullet missed the judge and went out the window."

Colonel Marquis seemed genuinely delighted. He rubbed his hands, he jabbed the ferrule of his cane against the floor; and at length he consulted Page.

"What do you think of that suggestion, Inspector? Is it possible?"

Page felt a retrospective shiver. "*If* it happened," he said, "all I've got to say is, it's a wonder I'm not a dead man now. I don't see how it could have missed me. I was running in a dead-straight line for that window. And as I told you, when I heard that shot I wasn't ten steps away from the window. Of course, it may have gone in a diagonal line. It probably did, being fired from the corner where the vase stands. But it's odd that I didn't hear it, or any sound to indicate it, if it came so close to me as that. I didn't notice anything."

"You say it's impossible?"

"I don't say that, considering that somehow the murderer vanished out of the room with less noise or trace. But I should be inclined to call it the next thing to impossible, because—"

Somewhere in the depths of the house a doorbell began to ring. It was a discreet, muffled doorbell, like the house and like the judge. When he heard it, Davies's big body stiffened back into its official posture, as though by an effect of magic or plaster of paris. Though he had been about to speak, he went gravely to answer the bell. And then Sergeant Borden burst into the room.

It is not quite accurate to say he burst into the room, for Borden was a heavy man with a bowler hat which seemed permanently stuck to his head. Besides, the presence of the Assistant Commissioner made him walk lightly and as though with corns. But he was excited. Though he addressed himself to Page, his talk was for the Assistant Commissioner.

"Robinson told me you were here, sir," he said. "I wish you would come down to the pavilion. I've found something that changes the whole case."

"Well?"

"First, there's some footprints. Pretty good footprints. But that's not the main thing. The judge can't have been killed by the bullet from the .32 automatic after all. I don't understand how it happened, unless somebody else was doing the shooting, but if you'll come down with me you'll see. All I can say is I've found a bullet fired from a .32 automatic, and probably the Browning."

"Where did you find it, sergeant?" asked Colonel Marquis.

"Stuck in a tree some distance away from the window where you"—he nodded toward Page—"climbed through, sir." After a pause (while Davies, in the background, grinned broadly) Borden continued: "But some of the footprints don't make sense either, sir. It looks as though the murderer must have got in and out through one of the west windows— the ones that are so locked and rusted that you can't open them even now."

Chapter 9

They walked down to the pavilion, taking a branch of the gravel path which led them to the back of it. Though the rain had cleared, the sky was still gray and heavy-looking, and what wet foliage still remained clinging to the trees hung down dispirited. A faint drip of water whispered all around them when they stopped at the back of the pavilion. Colonel Marquis studied it for a moment.

"We'll take the footprints by the west windows first," he announced. "To the right here? I thought so. What have you done about the prints, sergeant?"

Borden was dubious. "Sent for plaster of paris, sir, to take a cast. Robinson is standing by them now, on guard. But I doubt if we'll get anything like an impression at all. It's been raining most of the time since yesterday afternoon, and they're pretty well blurred out."

Rounding the side of the pavilion, they came on Robinson, in a cap and a big sou'wester, morosely regarding the ground. Under the west window nearest the northern end—just inside was the vase in which the Browning had been found—a few wooden boxes had been upended in a line to protect the exhibits from rain. Borden lifted the boxes almost reverently. Along the side of the wall ran what in summer must have been a flower bed, terminating in a brick border below the window. The flower bed was a big one, running out ten feet from the window. Five footprints were visible in the uneven soil, though they were so churned and blurred by the rain that they could be distinguished as little more than outlines of feet. But the toes were all pointing away from the pavilion, and all were made by the same pair of shoes.

Borden snapped on a flashlight, following the ragged line across the ten-foot expanse of flower bed, and Colonel Marquis studied it.

"Were those tracks here yesterday afternoon, sergeant?"

The sergeant hesitated and looked at Page, who undertook the responsibility. "I don't know, sir," Page answered. "I imagine they must have been, but we didn't go outside the pavilion once we found it was locked up from the inside. It's another oversight, but there it is. Anyhow, it seems to corroborate one thing Penney said, if you remember. He said that when he was talking to the judge yesterday a few minutes past four, he heard somebody prowling round the house; also, that he thought he heard the prowler testing the shutters on one of the west windows." Then Page stopped and looked at the tracks. "Hold on, though! That won't do. Because—"

"Exactly," said Marquis, with dry politeness. "Every one of these tracks comes away from the window, as though somebody got out the window and slogged back. Well, how did the prowler get *to* the window? He didn't fly across that immense space. Ergo, he must have come out of the window and run away." He turned round almost savagely. "Let's understand things. Inspector, are you certain beyond any doubt that those windows haven't been tampered with?"

"Beyond any doubt," said Page, and Borden agreed with him. "They were locked and shuttered on the inside when we arrived, and all you've got to do is test the shutters. You'll see for yourself."

"Robinson!"

The gatekeeper made an inquiring sound like "Yow?" and thrust out his neck.

"Robinson, do you agree with that?"

"I do," said the man. "I'm gardener and general handyman here, and I do any repairs that has to be done." He pondered. "Here! Point o' fact, there was trouble about those same windows only a few days ago. Miss Ida, she wanted the judge to get new frames put in 'em, because the old ones are bad and that's why the shutters have to be kept up. She said it was sense, because then the judge could have light instead of being half-dark all the time. I was going to do it, but the judge wouldn't hear of it. He said he'd be driven out of his workroom for two or three days just when he was at the most important part of his book; and he wouldn't hear of it."

In the gloom Page could see that a slight transformation had gone over the Assistant Commissioner's face: an expression as though he were blinking, or making a face—or seeing light. He turned away, poking at the ground with his cane. When he turned back again, he was calm and almost brisk.

"Put your light on those tracks again," he ordered. "What do you make of them, Inspector?"

"It's a big shoe," said Page. "A number ten at the smallest. The trouble is that you can't make any clear estimate about the weight of the man who wore it, because the tracks are flooded and there's no indication of what their depth was."

"Does anyone we know wear a number ten?"

"White doesn't: I can tell you that. He's tall, but he doesn't wear more than a number seven or eight."

"Very well. For the moment . . . what other exhibits have you to show us, sergeant?"

"Round to the front, now, sir," said Borden. "There's that bullet in the tree; and to round it off, there's more footprints."

"More footprints?"

"Yes, sir. And a woman's this time."

Colonel Marquis did not seem so surprised as Page would have expected. "Ah, I rather thought we should come to that," he remarked, with almost a comfortable air. "We were too long without 'em. They were certain to turn up. Lead the way."

The front of the pavilion was unchanged, except that now the shutters on both windows of the study were folded back against the wall. Page tried to visualize the scene as it had been yesterday. But he was astonished at the tree to which Borden led them. This was a thick-waisted elm some fifteen feet away from the window in a direct line. Page remembered the tree well enough. When he had been running for the window, he had passed that tree so closely as to brush it; and retracing every step in his mind, he realized that he had been passing the tree at just about the time the second shot had been fired. He was sure of this, because its distance would make about ten running steps from the window.

Sergeant Borden pointed with a pardonable air of triumph and directed the beam of his flashlight at the bole of the tree.

"Now look sharp, sir—some little distance up. If you reach up you can touch it. That makes about the height if it came out through the window. That's a bullet hole, and it's pretty sure to be a .32 Browning bullet embedded in there. I didn't dig it out, though; I thought you'd better see it first."

Colonel Marquis studied the crumbled and sodden little hole, and then looked back towards the window.

"Dig it out now," he said.

When Borden's penknife had produced another lead pellet, not quite so flattened by the soft wood in which it had been buried, it was passed from hand to hand and weighed. Page now had no doubt. "Subject to examination," he said cautiously, "I'd say that's certainly the .32 Browning bullet. But," he added with some explosiveness, "how in the name of God—?"

"You have doubts? H'm, yes," grinned the Colonel. "But wait until we have finished. Borden, as soon as you've shown us the footprints, get on the phone to the Yard and have the photographer out here. I want photographs and measurements of that bullet hole. You see the queer thing about it? The bullet went in an almost direct line."

"Photographer's coming, sir," Borden told him. "And here's the other footprints."

Moving his companions back a little, Borden threw his light to indicate a spot some distance behind and to the right of the tree as you faced the pavilion. The grass under the tree was soft and sparse, well protected by the branches above. Impressed in the soil was the clear print of a woman's shoe, narrow, pointed, and high-heeled. It was the right shoe, a smudged toe print of the left one being about six inches away from it. It looked as though someone had been hiding behind the tree and peering round it. But—the moment Page saw that print—his skepticism increased to complete unbelief.

"We'd better go easy, sir," he said calmly. "This thing's fake."

Sergeant Borden made a protesting noise, but Marquis regarded him with bright and steady eyes of interest.

"Exactly what do you mean by that, Inspector?"

"I mean that somebody's been manufacturing evidence since yesterday afternoon. I'll take my oath there was nobody standing behind that tree. I know, because I passed within a couple of inches of it, and I should have seen anybody in that whole vicinity." He knelt beside the two prints and studied them. "Besides, take a look at the marks. (Got a tape measure, Borden?) They're much too deep. If a woman made that right-hand one, the woman must have been an Amazon or a fat lady out of a circus; whoever made those prints weighed twelve or thirteen stone. Or else—"

Marquis, who had been beating his hands together softly and peering round him, nodded. "Yes; I don't think there's much doubt of that. The person who made the marks was either a man, or else a woman who stamped violently on the ground with the right foot in order to leave a sharp, unmistakable impression. . . . It's manufactured evidence, right enough. So, I am inclined to think, are those other number-ten footprints on the far side of the pavilion. We were intended to find both sets of prints. But there's one thing which doesn't seem to fit in. What about the .32 bullet in the tree? Is that manufactured evidence too?—and if so, why?"

Page contemplated Old Man River, wondering whether this was a catechism or whether Old Man River really did not know the answer.

"I'll admit, sir," he said, "that Davies's deductions seem to have been right. He said we'd find a bullet outside somewhere and here it is. But it's very fishy all the same. I was passing that tree when the shot was fired. How is it I didn't hear anything: the vibration of it or the sound of the bullet hitting the tree? It *might* have been done without my knowing it. It's possible. But there's one thing that's not possible at all. . . ."

"The line of the bullet?"

"The line of the bullet. As you say, it's gone into the tree on a dead straight line from that window. Well, the Browning was fired from the far corner of the room. As we stand here facing the pavilion, that corner is on our left. In order to get into the tree in this position, that bullet must have curved in the air like a boomerang—a kind of parabola, or whatever they call it. Which is nonsense."

During this debate Sergeant Borden had been looking from one to the other of them, plainly taken back by the casualness with which his proud evidence had been treated. He settled his bowler hat more firmly on his head, scowled, and addressed Page.

"But here *is* the stuff," he insisted. "Here and here and here. It's real. You can see it. What I meantersay; if there's funny business, why should anyone be up to funny business?"

"To get somebody hanged," said Colonel Marquis. "Into the pavilion, now."

They tramped in during a gloomy silence. Page switched up the lights in the little central hall, and opened the door of the study on the left. Nothing had been altered. The big room smelt close and stuffy. When Page touched another switch, a flood of light poured down from the dragon-lamp hanging above the judge's writing table. It was true that little could be seen beyond the immediate neighborhood of the table; the opaque sides of the lamp gave it the effect of a spotlight, and the room became a masked shadow of bookshelves from which the big yellow vases gleamed faintly. A rich Kurdistan carpet added a touch of the barbaric to the study. In the hard brightness round the desk, they could see the hole in the yellow paper where the .38 bullet had gone, a little way beyond the dictaphone.

First Colonel Marquis went across to the west windows, and satisfied himself that these were impregnable.

"Yes," he growled. "Unless the murderer made himself as thin as a picture postcard, he didn't go out there. Also, this room is genuinely dark. We'll try a little experiment. I was careful to bring this along." With sour suavity he produced Sir Andrew Travers's Browning from his coat pocket. "With all the guns we're finding, I've become a walking arsenal. But our friend Davies is right: this pistol is the excrescence; this pistol is causing all the trouble. So we'll try a shot on our own. But before we do . . ."

He juggled the pistol in one hand, his eye measuring distances. He then walked slowly round the room, examining each window. At the writing table he paused, and the other two followed him there. A chalk outline had been drawn across desk and blotter to show how Mr. Justice Mortlake's body had lain. After examining that, Colonel Marquis laid his hand on the dictaphone.

"I haven't the least idea," he said, "that there will be anything here, but, just to test it—"

He picked up the flexible tube at the end of which the glass mouthpiece had been chipped by the bullet. Adjusting the pointer on the wax cylinder of the record, he started the cylinder whirling, and pressed a button on the speaking tube. After a hoarse pause and a click, a thin voice came up in measured squeakings.

*"The Act of 1834, section 3, provides for a new district to be considered as one county for the purpose of venue,"* said the voice, *"which is to be laid as the Central Criminal Court. This district comprises by section 2 and the Local Government Act, 1888, section 89—ahem."*

"Bah," said Colonel Marquis, slamming the tube back on its hook. "Where are all the sinister secrets that might have been breathed out of that? I consider that we've been badly treated. Perhaps this will be better."

The drawer of the writing table was unlocked. He pulled it out, exposing neat sheets of typewritten manuscript. On top of them lay a memorandum-pad and a check-book on the Whitehall Bank. On the memorandum-pad were a few lines of small, precise handwriting:

> Sara Samuels,
>     36d, Hare Road, Putney.

> Refs.: Lady Emma Markleton, "Flowerdene," 18 Sheffield Terrace, Kensington, W. 8. (Have Penney write.)

"The new maid and her references," said Colonel Marquis. "Not much there. Nor in the check-book, I'm afraid. The last counterfoil is a check for £10 to Carolyn Mortlake, and dated yesterday. She's not paying blackmail to Ralph Stratfield, or *that* wouldn't pay it." He put the objects back and shut up the drawer with a snap. "As a last hope let's try our reconstruction."

"Reconstruction?"

The other limped across the room to the corner by the yellow vase in the far corner, and again he juggled Sir Andrew Travers's Browning.

"I am going to stand here and fire a shot in the general direction of where the judge was standing. Afterwards I will drop the pistol into the vase. Inspector, you will represent White. Stand where White was standing, about the middle of the room, with your back towards me and your face towards the phantom judge. When you hear the shot, whirl around —and tell me whether you can see me. Stop a bit! First put up the window about as high as it was when you climbed through."

After putting the window some half way up, Page returned to the middle of the room and took up his position. He had expected the shot immediately, but no shot came. Colonel Marquis was playing for time so as to take him off guard; so much he realized while he waited. It was very quiet in the room. He could hear his own watch. Even Sergeant Borden was out of his line of view. Uneasy qualms began to stir through him as his imagination set to work; and he was suddenly conscious of a hope that the Assistant Commissioner would not shoot him through the back of the head. Since Colonel Marquis was behind him in just about the position of a tennis player in a doubles match beginning to serve behind his companion at the net—no farther away—it was not impossible. He fixed his attention on the illuminated table. No one spoke. A wind, smelling of sodden leaves, stirred the curtains at the window.

The shot was so loud that it seemed to make the room shake like a cabin at sea. Also, it seemed to close behind his ear; he could have sworn the powder grains stung him. Startled in spite of himself, he swung round against the vibrations. He had been looking at the brilliant beam of light from the dragon-lamp, and he was a quarter blind when he stared into the corner. He could see absolutely nothing, for the darkness appeared to have speckles in it; but he heard a faint noise as of someone putting an umbrella into a porcelain umbrella stand.

"Nerves are curious things," rumbled a drawling voice out of the darkness. "I gave you two minutes, and it must have seemed like ten. If you had flinched or moved a step to the right, you might have got it through the head. I will not say any more, in case you should feel inclined, justifiably, to hit me over the head with a chair.—Well, can you see me?"

Page's eyes were growing accustomed to the dark. "No, sir," he answered. "By this time I can see a kind of shadow along the vase. I think I can make out an outline; but that's because I know you're there."

"Did you hear the gun drop into the vase?"

"Yes, faintly. If I hadn't been expecting it, though, I don't know what I'd have thought it was. Remember, it was storming when the shot was fired yesterday."

Colonel Marquis limped forward, twirling the pistol with his finger through the trigger guard. He put out a long arm and pointed. "You observe, Inspector, that the bullet did not go out of the window. It's unfortunate that we have to bang up walls like this, but . . . there you are."

A much-annoyed Sergeant Borden was already examining the fresh scar. In the yellow-papered wall between the south windows there were now two bullet holes. The bullet fired by Colonel Marquis was close to the left-hand window, it is true; but it had not come within a foot of going out the open space.

"Yes, but if it didn't go there," insisted Borden doggedly, "now, I ask you, sir, where did the other one go? I'm fair sick of bullets. It's raining bullets. And there's no sense in any of 'em."

## Chapter 10

At half-past five that afternoon Inspector Page emerged from the Underground at Westminster Station and tramped wearily up the Embankment to New Scotland Yard. He had made undeniable progress; his notebook contained evidence of both acquittal and accusation. But he had got no lunch and no beer. After the "reconstruction" of the shots at about one o'clock, the old so-and-so had gone off amiably to a good lunch, and Page had remained to do the routine work.

The note of the half hour, clashing and vibrating from the great clock over his head, gave him an idea. Not more than a popgun's shot away from Scotland Yard there is a public house, tucked away in such fashion that it is not generally noticed; and, in fact, there is a pretense that it does not exist at all. But it is much patronized by members of the Force. Pushing up through the chilly dampness which was bringing fog off the river, Page found that the pub had just opened its doors. He did not go into the public bar. He was a sociable soul, but he wanted to pore over his notes. Moving on to a private room, where a bright fire burned, he was surprised to find it occupied. A figure sat with its long legs stretched out to the fire, showing a head with sparse white hair over the back of the chair, a pint tankard in a speckled hand, and a cloud of cigarette smoke over all. Then the figure craned round, revealing the grinning face of Colonel Marquis.

Now this was unheard of. If Assistant Commissioners go into pubs, they do not go into pubs patronized by their subordinates; and it would cause surprise to see them drinking with anybody less than a chief inspector. But Colonel Marquis enjoyed above all things to break rules.

"Ah, Inspector," he said. "Come in. Yes, it is the old man in the flesh; don't stare. I had been rather expecting you." You recall the old chestnut about the idiot boy who surprised everybody by finding the lost horse. 'Well, I thought of where I'd go if I were a horse; and I went there; and he had.' That's police work in a nutshell; I do not draw the analogy further. What'll you have?"

He took charge of matters. "Beer," he went on. "And take a long pull before you start to talk." When the beer was brought, he smoked thoughtfully while Page attacked it. "Now then. What luck? This case has been bothering me like a fly. I can't forget it. That's why I'm here."

"Aaah," said Page, relaxing. "I don't know about luck, but there have certainly been plenty of developments. The case has gone pfft."

"What the devil do you mean, 'pfft'?" inquired Marquis with austerity. "Kindly stop making strange noises and answer my question. It is a regrettable thing if an inspector of Metropolitan Police—"

"Sorry, sir. I mean that two of our calculations have been upset. Two of the things we regarded as certain are turned the wrong way round. The person who looked most suspicious, and didn't have an alibi, is pretty well exonerated entirely. The person we regarded as being more or less above suspicion is—well, not above suspicion now."

Marquis opened his eyes. "H'm. I'm not surprised. Who is exonerated?"

"Carolyn Mortlake," Page answered wearily. "I wish she hadn't given us all that trouble. Maybe she doesn't know it herself, but she's got a cast-iron alibi. . . . You remember Davies's story about what the maid heard over the phone? Carolyn was supposed to go to number 66, Hastings Street, a stationer's shop, and ask for a letter in the name of Carolyn Baer. According to her own story, she went there but there wasn't any such place as number 66. She swore she was hoaxed—and she was. She really did go to Hastings Street. I went there myself this afternoon to see whether I could pick up any trace of her. I was equipped with a photograph; I snaffled it out of an album at the house, to be frank. There's no stationer's at number 66, but there is a newsagent's at number 32: which is the closest anybody could find to it. And she tried that as a last resort. The woman who keeps the shop had noticed a woman prowling up and down the street, looking at numbers and acting queerly. Finally this stranger made a dash, came into the newsagent's, and asked for a letter in the name of Carolyn Baer. I got out my photograph. There's no doubt of it; the proprietress of the shop identifies her as Carolyn Mortlake. . . . There was no letter, of course. The thing was a trumped-up job. But she was in that shop at twenty minutes past five yesterday, a shop in Bloomsbury. Not even if she had flown or used seven-leagued boots could she have got to Hampstead by five-thirty. And she's out of it."

Colonel Marquis drew a deep breath. For a brief time he remained staring at the fire, and then he nodded. "It clears the air, anyhow," he said. "What's next? If one person is exonerated, who's the one to go back under suspicion?"

"Sir Andrew Travers."

"Good God!" said Marquis.

He had clearly not expected this. He got up out of his chair and limped up and down the room with angry bumps of his cane. Stopping by the table, he took a deep draught out of his tankard; hesitated, drank again, and set down the tankard with a thump.

"I see, sir," remarked Page, with a broad smile. "I'll lay you a small bet. I'll bet you thought I was going to say Miss Ida Mortlake."

"Shrewd lad," said Marquis, looking at him. "You're not a fool, then?"

"Not altogether," said Page, considering this. "I know you've been thinking that I've rather too pointedly overlooked her, and never given her a moment's consideration, even though she was slap-bang in the middle of the whole mess. You'll adduce evidence—of contradictory times. White says she was in the house, talking to the butler, at close on five-thirty; just before White himself rushed down to the pavilion. Result: alibi. Davies says she was talking to him at twenty minutes past five, and after that Davies left her. Result: no alibi."

"Yes, I'd thought of it," agreed the other shortly. "Waiter! More beer!"

"You could even say that there seems to be a woman's touch about this crime. It's there; you can feel it, in addition to the fake evidence of the shoes. (I'll come to the shoes in just a moment, sir.) And it's certain there was a strong effort to throw suspicion on Carolyn Mortlake. But my early opinion of Ida holds. And I'll tell you something more," continued Page with fierce earnestness, and tapped the table. "The brain behind this business is a man's."

"I agree," said Colonel Marquis explosively.

Page was a trifle surprised. It was the first time Old Man River had been betrayed from his rolling course, to show where his thoughts really went. Marquis was scowling, still on his feet and restless.

"I agree, yes. But go on about Travers. Why is he back under suspicion?"

"Maybe that's too strong a statement. You remember, when he produced his alibi all neat and pat this morning, I sent a man round to the Temple to check on it? His report was phoned through to me while I was at the Mortlakes'. It was so interesting that, when I went to check on Carolyn's alibi in Bloomsbury, I went down and paid a visit to the Temple myself. Now, Sir Andrew stated that he was in his chambers all yesterday afternoon; that, though he was in the inner room and could not actually be seen by his clerk, still the clerk remained in the outer office all the time; and, finally, that there is no way out of the chambers except through the clerk's room. . . . Well, sir, that's a plain, flat, thundering lie. There is another way out. There's a fire-escape at the back of the building and it runs past the window of Travers's study."

"Fire-escapes in the Temple?" inquired the other, with interest. "I didn't know they had 'em."

"They don't; not the iron ones, anyway. But this was a sort of experiment, or something of the kind, tried out by the Benchers a number of years ago. It was put up at the back of the building in Hare Court so as not to be visible. But it's an iron fire-escape in good condition. Sir Andrew Travers could have gone down that. I don't say he *did,* you understand. And it's not the interesting point of the whole thing. The interesting point is this: Travers is a clever man, and one of the shrewdest lawyers practicing. We know that. Why, therefore, does he tell such a whacking and obviously poor lie? Even if he's innocent, why does he tell it? Believing Sir Andrew Travers to be soft-headed is much more difficult than believing him to be a murderer."

"H'm," said Marquis.

He sat down again and eyed the overmantel dreamily.

"There is a hive of offices thereabouts," he added. "Somehow, I can't help feeling that the spectacle of a portly and dignified barrister in a top hat climbing down a fire escape in the middle of the afternoon would be bound to excite some comment, not to say mirth. Damn it, Page, the picture is all wrong. It's comic. Such goings-on are not for the Temple. Do you see the fine shade of difference?"

"I see it all right, sir. But you understand the problem, even if it's an innocent problem. And I'm bound to admit I can't produce anybody who actually did see him sneak down the fire escape. All the same, the fact remains that his alibi is shot to blazes."

"I wonder."

"How do you mean?"

Colonel Marquis was not addicted to gestures, but he made slight gestures with energy. "In this case, Sir Andrew Travers is like Sir Andrew Travers's own pistol: he's an excrescence. How does he fit in? Where is his motive for murdering his friend? Where is his motive for doing anything? How could he have got inside the grounds of the house under Robinson's watchful eye? I see him marching along like a sultan, with drums and panoply; I see him sailing along like an overfed balloon; but I don't see that stately top hat involved in any such business as this."

"I though you had some idea of the truth, sir?" Page suggested. He was not without malice in saying it, and he stung Marquis.

"You are quite right, young man. I know the murderer and I know how the crime was committed. But I need facts and I need proof; in addition to which, I have sufficient humility to think I may be wrong, though the possibility is so slight that it needn't bother us. Hum. Let's have facts. Did you dig up anything more today?"

"No more that concerns alibis. For instance, there's Davies." He looked sharply at the other, but Colonel Marquis was very bland. "His alibi—the story that he was in the kitchen with the cook and the maid between twenty minutes past five and a quarter to six—is more or less substantiated. I say 'more or less' because the cook says he was down in the cellar, fetching beer, for some three minutes round about five-thirty. The question is whether he would have had time to nip down to the pavilion, vanish and nip back again. Besides, where's his motive? He inherits £500, yes. It's a tidy sum, and God knows I'd like to have it to my own account at the bank, but I can't see Davies doing murder for it. Finally, both Robinson and the cook, who have been with the judge for fifteen years, inherit the same amount."

"Like myself, you have tried your hand at character-reading," said his companion rather gloomily. "But go on."

"There's only one other person associated with the case—old Alfred Penney. He hasn't got an alibi, in the sense that it's impossible to check it. He says he left the Guildhall Library at five o'clock and came home by Underground; but, due to missing trains at a couple of changes, and being held up generally, he didn't arrive home until five-forty. The last man in the world whose movements you can ever prove is someone traveling by Underground. Personally, I think he's telling the truth."

Page closed his notebook with a snap.

"And that's the lot, sir," he concluded. "That's *everybody* connected with the case. It's got to be one of those. You say you know who the murderer is, and in good time you'll speak out; but I admit that I haven't got the ghost of an idea. I'm hesitating between several of them. Even if I could definitely pick out a murderer I can't hazard a suggestion as to how the murderer disappeared out of that locked room. I have two pieces of evidence which round out my report, and I'll repeat them if you like; but they only go to show how narrow the circle has become."

"We'd better have everything. I think you said something about shoes a while ago?"

"Yes, sir. I tried to find out who had faked those number ten shoeprints and also the woman's tracks. I had no difficulty getting permission to go through any wardrobe in the house I liked; in fact, Miss Ida Mortlake helped me."

"Oh, she did, did she?" asked the colonel offensively. "And I suppose she offered you tea as well."

"No; she had to go out. But she told me to make myself at home. She was certainly very pleasant, especially considering the fact that y—we dashed out and left her this morning at the Yard without so much as by-your-leave. I had to explain . . ." He caught the other's eye, pulled himself up stiffly, and coughed. "But you'll want to hear about the shoes. That print of a woman's right slipper was a number four. Both Ida and

Carolyn wear number fours. But there was no sign of mud on any of the shoes in the house, aside from the ordinary rain splashes you'd get walking about in the street. That's point number one. Point number two concerns the men's shoes. Only one person in that house wears number tens—"

"Who's that?" demanded Colonel Marquis sharply.

"Penney."

From the other's expression, Page could not tell whether he was stimulated or disappointed; but there was undoubtedly a reaction of some kind. He sat forward in the firelight, snapping his long fingers, and his eyes were shining. But since he did not comment, Page went on:

"Penney owns two pairs of shoes; no more. That's established. There's a brown pair and a black pair. The black pair he wore yesterday, and were wet. But neither pair had any mudstains; and mud is devilish difficult to clear off completely so that you leave *no* traces. And there we are, sir. We're right back where we started from."

He stopped, because he noticed that the waiter who had served them was now poking his head cautiously round the door of the room and looking mysterious. The waiter approached.

"Excuse me," he said, "but are you Colonel Marquis? Yes. I think," he added in the manner of one making a deduction, "you're wanted on the telephone."

The Assistant Commissioner got up sharply and Page observed that for the first time he looked uneasy. "All right," he said, and added to Page: "Look here, this is bad. Only my secretary knows where I am. I told him he wasn't to get in touch with me unless . . . you'd better come along, Inspector."

The telephone was in a narrow hallway, smelling of old wood and beer, at the back of the house. A crooked light hung over it; Page could see the expression on his superior's face and the same uneasiness began to pluck at his own nerves. A heavy voice popped out of the telephone receiver, speaking so loudly and squeakily that Colonel Marquis had to hold the receiver away from his ear. Page heard every word. It was a man's voice, and the man was badly rattled.

"Is that you?" said the voice. "Andrew Travers speaking."

It cleared its throat, wavered, and became loud again. "I'm at Mortlake's place," the voice added.

"Anything wrong?"

"Yes. Do you know anything about a girl—named Sara Samuels, I think—who's just been engaged as a maid here, and who was to come next month to replace Millie Reilly? You do. Well, you know she was in the grounds here yesterday afternoon and was the last of the maid contingent to leave. I think she must have seen or heard something she shouldn't have seen or heard."

"Hold on to yourself," said Marquis sharply, as the voice thickened again. "What's up?"

"She phoned here about an hour ago. She asked to speak to Carolyn; she said she had something vitally important to tell her, and was afraid to tell it to anybody else; Carolyn engaged her, you see, and she doesn't seem to trust anybody else. But Carolyn's out, seeing to the funeral arrangements. I said I was the—legal representative. I asked whether she couldn't tell me. She hemm'd and haw'd, but finally she said she would come round to the house as soon as she could."

"Well?"

Now Page could imagine Sir Andrew Travers's large white face, its chin showing more blue against the pallor, almost shouting to the telephone. "She never got to the house, Marquis," he said. "She's lying out in the driveway here, dead, with the knife out of a carving set run through her back."

Very slowly Colonel Marquis replaced the receiver, contemplated the telephone, and turned away. But Page could see a blue vein twisted and swollen in his temple.

"I might have expected that," he said. "My God, Inspector, I might have foreseen it. But I never saw the explanation of one thing until just that second when Travers spoke. . . . Evidently someone at Mortlake's was listening in on that telephone extension again."

"The murderer," said Page blankly.

"Yes. And a carving knife is used this time. I tell you, Inspector, this murderer is *a* devil or *the* devil. I can almost see that body under the trees. Sara Samuels got past the gates of the lodge—but she didn't get as far as the house."

"You mean she was killed to shut her mouth about something?"

"I do."

Page rubbed his forehead. "But I don't understand what it was she could have seen or heard. Look here, sir: Sara Samuels was in the big batch of applicants who were there yesterday applying for the post as maid. Even if she stayed a bit behind the others and went out after them, she must have gone before four o'clock. At that time the judge was alive and well. And—you're not going to shift the time of the murder, are you?"

"No, no; the judge was killed at half-past five right enough. There was no hocus-pocus before then. I think I may assure you of that."

"Well, then?"

His companion did not seem to hear him. Colonel Marquis had almost reached a point of biting his nails. "But that's not what is bothering me,

Inspector. I might have assumed the murderer would have killed Sara Samuels. But in that way? No, no. That was a bad blunder, a fatal blunder. You can see that I've got my evidence now; one more thing to do and I can make an arrest. Yes, I can't understand why the murderer killed her in that particular way, and inside the grounds of the place; unless it was blind panic, of course, or unless—"

He swept his worry aside; he became brisk.

"You are in charge, Inspector. Hop into a squad car and get out there as fast as you can. Photographs and fingerprints, of course. Carry the usual routine until I get there. I'll follow in a very short time. Let me have that notebook of yours a minute, will you?" He ran through the leaves quickly. "Good, good. I thought so. I am going to bring two people along with me when I follow you. Both are very important witnesses. One is—you will see. But the other is Gabriel White."

Page stared at him. "I suppose you know what you're doing, sir. But are you going to tell me that the changes are rung again, and the double-cross returns? Do you think Gabriel White was guilty after all?"

"No, White didn't kill the judge. And it isn't likely he killed the Samuels girl while he was sitting under our eye at Scotland Yard. But he will be very useful in the reconstruction," said Colonel Marquis, with slow and terrifying pleasantry, "when I demonstrate, in about an hour's time, how the murderer got out of the locked room."

## Chapter 11

The lights of the Scotland Yard car were turned almost diagonally across the drive in the darkness. Ahead the broad gravel driveway curved up a slight incline towards the house; there were elm trees on either side, and due to the ornamental curves of the drive, this point was visible neither from the house nor from the lodge gates. Outlines were still more blurred by a smoky white vapor, not light enough to be called mist or thick enough to be called fog, which clung to the ground like a facecloth and moved in gentle billows—even before a light. Under the elms they seemed in a hollow space where noises were intensified; where there were many breaths, and it was very cold.

In the front of the police car Page stood up and looked over the windshield. The headlights played directly across on a body lying some two or three feet off the drive to the left, near the base of an elm. It was that of a woman, lying partly on her back and partly on her right side. Page could see the soles of the shoes, and a hat crushed tipsily over her ear, and an open mouth.

Then he got out of the car, taking his flashlight. There were other figures, shrinking or motionless, drawn some distance away from the body. Sir Andrew Travers was there; hatless, and with the collar of his blue overcoat drawn up, he looked somewhat less impressive. Ida Mort-lake was there, looking round the edge of a tree. Finally, Robinson the gatekeeper stood guard like a gnome in a sou'wester, holding a lantern.

As Page stepped towards the body, Ida Mortlake skirted round the edge of the trees and approached him from the other side. Even her blue eyes seemed pale with fear, and she had difficulty in speaking while she pressed the mink coat against her breast.

"What is it?" she said. "Oh, *what* is it? Who—?"

"Sorry, miss; you'll have to stand back," said Page in his best Force manner. But under cover of darkness he touched her arm reassuringly. She followed him nevertheless, with that touch of morbid curiosity which even the most shrinking girl can exhibit.

The dead woman lay on a carpet of fallen leaves which, Page realized, would make it impossible to trace any footprints. By the condition of the leaves it was clear that she had been struck down in the driveway and then had been dragged over to where she lay. Without moving the body, he could see by stooping down the handle of the knife protruding from her back just under the left shoulder blade. His light showed that it was an ordinary carving knife, such as may be seen on any dinner table, with a black bone handle of fluted design. There was a good deal of blood.

She was a woman in the late twenties, short, rather plump, and quietly dressed. No good idea could be gained of the face under the tipsy hat, for the face was grimy with mud and cut with gravel. When the murderer took her from behind, she had evidently been flung forward on her face in the drive; and afterwards she had been turned on her back and dragged to where she lay. But it was a bold face under the rather pitiful coating of dirt, and the white-slitted eyes showed horror.

Page's light roamed round the spot, in and out of the trees, and across in the direction of the pavilion. "Damn," he said; and focused the beam. Some three or four feet away from the body there lay in the leaves a heavy hammer.

"Right," said Page, straightening up toward the police car. "Crosby, photographs first. Baine, fingerprints. Cook and Marshall, make a circle round the body, spread out, and cover every inch of the ground for anything you can find.—The rest of you over here a little way, please. Who found the body?"

Robinson, defiantly, held up the lantern so as to illumine his swollen-veined face and telescopic neck. But his teeth were jumping and clacking together in a series of spasms; and he looked chilled.

"Me," he said.

"When and how?"

" 'Bout half an hour ago. Maybe. I dunno. Sir Andrew," he nodded, "phoned down and said to expect a woman name of Samuels, and to let her in. She got here and I did. She went on up the drive here. But I didn't like her ways—"

"What do you mean, you didn't like her ways?"

"I dunno," cried Robinson rather despairingly. "I didn't like the way she acted, that's all. Funny: I can't describe it. When she went up the drive, I stuck my head out the door of the lodge and looked up after her. I couldn't see her, becos the drive turns so much. Like it is here. I was going to shut the door, but I heard a queer sort of noise."

"What sort of noise? A cry? A scream?"

Robinson jumped a little. "I dunno. More like a gurgle. Only loud. I didn't like it, but there wasn't nothing else to do. I got my lantern and started running up the drive. Just as I turned round the corner—right here—I see something like someone dropping something and running away. . . ."

"What do you mean by that?"

"I can't tell you any fairer than that," Robinson declared doggedly. "I didn't *see* much. . . . Kind of a rustle, like, and something like a coat. It run away in the trees. It dropped something. If you want to know what I think it dropped, it was that." He pointed unsteadily towards the hammer lying among the leaves. "I'd got a bit of an idea that someone turned the poor damn woman over on her back and was going to bash in 'er face with that hammer. Only I got here too quick. Then I hopped it up to the house and told Sir Andrew."

Page felt his flesh crawl, for it was a savage vision. He had little doubt that Robinson was correct, and that this was the use meant for the hammer. All his witnesses were trembling, but he was not disposed to let them go anywhere else for the moment. Behind them flashbulbs glared in the dark.

"Did you ever see this woman before?"

"I dunno. Yes, I think so. She was one of that crowd that came yesterday, about the maid's job. I noticed her becos she was good-looking."

"Do you know what time she left?"

"No. No, I don't. But I know they was all outside the grounds by a quarter to four, becos I counted them and I remember. 'Ere, stop a bit! Yes, she went out about quarter to four; she was carrying a parcel."

Page directed his light on the body again. "Come here and look at the knife. Did you ever see it before?"

"No."

"Or the hammer? (Stand over to one side, Crosby)."

"No."

At this point Page became conscious that the group was growing; that other people were silently drawn to the magnet of a dead body and the dull lights. A rich, husky, old-port voice, the voice of Davies, spoke up.

"If you'll let me get a better look, sir," said Davies grimly, "I think I can identify both the knife and the hammer. I think that's the carving knife out of the ordinary set in our dining room. The hammer looks like one that's kept at a workbench in the cellar. I've got a bit of an idea what you're going to ask, too. Well, sir, the last time I saw the knife was yesterday evening after dinner, when I put away the silver. I don't know about the hammer. I haven't seen it for some time."

"Sir Andrew Travers—?" said Page.

Travers, though a trifle hoarse, was master of himself again, as his courtroom manner showed. "At your service, Inspector," he intoned, in a vein of attentive irony. "May I suggest, though, that we adjourn to some more comfortable place? Miss Mortlake must be frozen. Or would you like us all to touch the body in order to see whether blood flows?"

"That won't be necessary," said Page. "When did Robinson bring you the news about this?"

"Something less than half an hour ago, I think. I tried to get in touch with Colonel Marquis immediately, and had some difficulty. He was at a public house."

He spoke humorously, but Page ignored it.

"Were you here at the house all afternoon, Sir Andrew?" Page asked.

"All afternoon, since about three o'clock. I believe I reached here just as you, Inspector, were leaving." He hesitated, and then spread bland wings. "But that's hardly what you want to know, is it? You would like to know my whereabouts when this poor young woman was killed. When Robinson brought the news to the house, I was playing backgammon with Miss Mortlake here. We have been in each other's company all afternoon. That's true, isn't it, Ida?"

Ida Mortlake opened her mouth and shut it again. "Yes, of course," she answered. "Why, certainly it's true. They don't think any differently, do they, Andrew? Oh, this is *horrible!* Mr. Page—?"

"Just a moment, miss," said Page, and swung round as he heard a step on gravel. "Who's there?"

Out of the dimness of flickering lights swam the white, square, pale face of Carolyn Mortlake; and it had a startled expression which vanished instantly. What caused that startled expression Page could not see, but it became again the old cynical mockery which could not quite keep back fear. She cradled her arms in her sleeves and jeered.

"It's only the black sheep," she said. "Only the poor b——— so-and-so, I mean, who runs around with blackmailers, turning up again. Sorry I was off the lot when the newest corpse dropped in. Inspector, this place is turning into a positive morgue." For the first time she got a good view of the body, and turned a trifle sickly, but she went on in the same determined vein: "You know what this scene looks like, with your popping flashlamps and your shadows and your bowler hats? It looks like hell, which is popularly supposed to be cold. See our breath steam. And here am I, turning up like a bad pen—" She stopped. "I say, that reminds me. Where is Penney? When he turns up we shall all be here, and we can all go to hell together."

Ida Mortlake flushed. Page could see her hands clench in the protective shadow of Travers. "Mr. Penney's at the pavilion," she replied. "He went there an hour or so ago to straighten up some of father's papers. Carolyn, you mustn't talk like that! Please don't. It's wicked. It's—"

"*That's* wicked, if you like," said Carolyn, pointing.

Page interposed, and clamored for silence. "You say Mr. Penney is still at the pavilion? Hasn't anyone told him?"

"I'm afraid not," said Ida. "I—I'm afraid I never thought of it. And he probably hasn't heard anything, over there."

"Look out, you chaps!" cried Carolyn Mortlake.

With a roar, a flourish, and a glare of headlamps, another police car had swung through the lodge gates a little way down the slope, and it came bucketing round the curve toward them in a way that made Page jump back. When it was almost on the group, the driver jammed on his brakes as though at a signal. The black bulk ground to a dead stop. Then, behind a faintly luminous windshield in the front seat, a tall figure rose with great politeness and lifted its hat.

"Good evening, ladies and gentlemen," said Colonel Marquis, like a BBC announcer.

There was a silence. Page was well enough acquainted with his chief to be aware of the latter's deplorable fondness for flourish and gesture. In this monkey business Page saw nothing good. In fact, it made him swear, since the wheel of the car grazed his shin. Yet, as Colonel Marquis leaned his elbows on the windshield and peered out over the group with an air of refreshed interest, there was a curious grimness of certainty about him. In the rear of the car Page could see that three persons were sitting, but he could not tell who they were.

"Most of you are here, I notice," Colonel Marquis went on. "Good! I should be obliged if you would all come over to the pavilion with me. Yes, all of you. I have one other guest to increase our number. He calls himself Gabriel White, though some of you know him under another name."

He made a gesture. One of the dark figures in the back of the car stirred and climbed out. In the group before the headlights there was silence; Page could read no expressions. But Gabriel White himself seemed drawn and nervous.

They walked in a sort of Indian file to the pavilion, choosing the path so that they might not interfere with any traces round the body. There was little whispering or comment. All of them were aware that this was the end, although few of them knew what end.

The pavilion was illuminated in all its rooms, the curtains drawn across the windows. When that tramping procession went down to the study a somewhat frightened Mr. Alfred Penney—with a pair of spectacles down his nose—started up from behind the judge's desk. The dragon lamp threw a flood of light on him and on the papers he was examining.

"Join the group, Mr. Penney," said Colonel Marquis. "You will be interested in this. No, Davies; you needn't trouble to bring chairs. We can stand. Our business will not take long."

Again from various pockets he produced his arsenal of three pistols, and arranged them in a line on the writing table, from which Penney had moved back. Page noticed the positions of the various people. Ida Mortlake stood very far back from the table, in shadow, with Travers beside her. Carolyn Mortlake, her arms folded with a swaggering gesture, leaned against the east wall. Davies, imperturbable, but clearly enjoying this, was at Colonel Marquis's elbow as though to anticipate any want. Penney hovered in the background. The defiant Robinson (still refusing to remove his cap) was by the window. Gabriel White—who suddenly seemed on the verge of crumbling to pieces—stood in the middle of the room with his hands in his pockets.

And Colonel Marquis took up a position behind the table under the lamp, smiling at them, with the three pistols ranged before him.

"Is there any necessity for this mummery, my friend?" asked Travers crisply.

"Please be careful of that manuscript," implored Penney, in an agony of good manners. "I really don't see—"

"*I* think we're having fun," said Carolyn.

Only those three voices were raised. Page had almost expected a babble, a characteristic remark from all of them, beating up out of tension or fright; it seemed almost unnatural when the others kept tight-shut lips. The voices wavered, and stopped.

"It is very necessary," said Colonel Marquis, with grave correction. "Inspector Page: will you please stand by these three guns? I hold you responsible for seeing that nobody lays hold of them. When I have said what I have to say, there may be more firing even yet.

"At this moment, ladies and gentlemen, Sergeant Borden is showing the body of Sara Samuels to someone who may make a strange identification. I will not attempt to explain what I mean. They will be here with the report in just a minute, and then you will understand. But in the meantime, in order to round out my evidence, I should like to ask two questions . . . of Miss Ida Mortlake."

Ida took a step forward, more vigorous than Page had ever seen her. Her lovely face had little color; but it looked much less soft.

"Whatever you wish to know," she said.

"Good! At the beginning of this investigation, Miss Mortlake, we heard that there were two keys to the tradesmen's entrance in the wall round these grounds. Robinson had one; you, in your nominal capacity as housekeeper, had the other. These keys were of little value, since nobody ever keeps a tradesman's entrance locked up. They were of value only yesterday afternoon, when you asked for that gate to be locked. Robinson locked the gate with his key. Where was, and is, yours?"

She looked at him calmly. "I know the answer to that, because I thought of it when all the fuss was being made about keys. It was in the drawer of the butler's pantry, along with the other keys. And it's still there."

"But—a corollary to the first question—the key could be taken out, a copy made, and put back again, without anyone being the wiser?"

"Well . . . yes, I should think so. It was never used. But why?"

"Good. My last question, then. Today our friend Robinson told us a significant thing. He said that a short time ago a great fuss and rumpus was being cut up about these west windows in here: the ones with the loose frames, on which the judge kept the shutters closed at all times. He said that you suggested getting new frames put into the windows, so that there could be more light in the room. I want you to think carefully before you answer. Was what Robinson said true?"

Her eyes widened. "Well . . . yes, in a way. That is, I was the one who actually *spoke* about it to father. But he wouldn't hear of it; there was a most awful argument, and I let it drop. But it wasn't my idea, really. I mean, it would never have occurred to me."

"Then who suggested it to you? Can you remember?"

"Yes, of course. It—"

There was a clumping of feet outside in the hall, and the door opened. Sergeant Borden appeared, saluting, his shining face well satisfied.

"All set, sir," he reported. "It took a few minutes longer than we thought, because this Samuels girl's face was dirty and we had to wash it before the lady could be sure. But here she is and she's ready to testify any time you like."

He stood aside, to show a flustered, dumpy little woman, with a glassy eye and gray hair. She wore black; she took protection behind an umbrella; and at first glance Page thought he had never seen her before. Then he realized with a shock who she was. Colonel Marquis nodded to her.

"That's settled, then," he said. "Your name, madam?"

"Clara McCann," replied the woman, getting her breath. "Mrs." she added.

"What is your occupation, Mrs. McCann?"

"*You* know what it is, sir. I keep a newsagent's shop at number 32 Hastings Street, Bloomsbury."

"You have just looked at the body of Sara Samuels, Mrs. McCann. Did you ever see her before?"

Mrs. McCann took a grip of her umbrella and spoke in a rush: "Yes, sir, I did. There's no mistake about it now, like there was when I only saw the photograph. She was the lady who came into my shop yesterday afternoon at twenty minutes past five, and asked if I had a letter for her in the name of Carolyn Baer."

At the end of a dead silence, which sounded in Page's ears like a sort of roar, one face in the room shifted and changed. Colonel Marquis lifted his hand.

"Your warning, Inspector," he said. "It's not my duty to give it. But there's your prisoner."

Page said: "Carolyn Mortlake, I arrest you for the murder of Charles Mortlake and Sara Samuels. I have to warn you that anything you say will be taken down in writing and may be used as evidence."

## Chapter 12

For a space of time in which you might have counted five slowly, no one moved or spoke. Carolyn Mortlake remained leaning against the wall, her arms folded; the only change about her was that her eyes had acquired a steady, hard shine, and her dark-painted mouth stood out against her face. Her breath seemed to come with a jerk.

"Don't—don't be an ass," she said harshly. "You can't prove that." Then she screamed one word at him, and was calm again.

"I can prove it, my young lady," said Colonel Marquis. "I'll show you just how far I can prove it by giving you time to think of an answer and a defense. I'll leave you alone with your thoughts for a few minutes, while I speak of somebody else."

He swung round abruptly, the light making harsh shadows on his face. Someone in the group protested, but it was not the one towards whom his attention was directed. There was a queer sucking sort of noise: the noise of Gabriel White trying to moisten his lips. White was not standing quite so erect. It was his face which had shifted and changed, not Carolyn Mortlake's.

"Yes, I mean you," said Colonel Marquis. "I mean Carolyn Mortlake's lover. I mean Gabriel White, or Lord Edward Whiteford, or whatever you care to call yourself. God's death, you're a pretty pair, you are!"

"You haven't got anything on me," said White. "*I* didn't kill him."

"I know you didn't," agreed the other. "But, all the same, I can send you to the gallows as accessory before and after the fact."

Page says to this day that there was no alteration you could actually define in White's expression or his manner. It was only that whereas before he had stood there longhaired, artistic, and misjudged, now there appeared to be different lines to his face. Briefly something looked out of his eyes, and it was not pleasant. White took a step forward. But Sergeant Borden put a hand on his shoulder.

"Watch him, Borden," ordered Colonel Marquis. "I don't think he's got the nerve for anything now, but he's a dead shot—and he once beat a woman half to death in a tobacconist's shop merely because she had only a pound or two in the till when he needed a little spending money. The old judge was right. There seems to have been some doubt as to whether Friend White is a saint or a well-defined swine; but the old judge knew long before we did."

Marquis looked at the rest of them.

"I owe some of you an explanation, I think," he went on; "and the shortest way will be to show you how I knew that White was lying from the very first—lying through and through—lying about even the things he *admitted* having done. That was (as he believed) the cleverness of his whole plan. Oh, yes: he was going to kill the judge. He would have killed the judge, if his sweetheart hadn't interfered. But he was never going to hang for it.

"Stand back, now, and look at certain bullet holes. There has been one basis in this case, one starting point for all investigation, one solid background which we all believed from the outset. We took it for granted. It concerns the two shots which were fired in here—the shots from the .38 Ivor-Johnson revolver and the .32 Browning automatic—the two shots which did *not* kill the judge. We accepted, on White's word, the statement that the first shot was from the .38 revolver and the second shot from the .32 automatic. We were meant to accept that statement. White's defense was based on it. And that statement was a lie.

"But even at first glance, if you look at the physical evidence, White's story seemed wildly improbable on the very points of guilt that he admitted. Look at this room. Look at your plan of it. What was his story? He said that he rushed into the room, flourishing the .38 revolver; that the judge was then at the open window; that the judge turned round, shouting something; and at this moment, while the judge was still in front of the window, he fired.

"Yes; but what happened to that .38 bullet? That bullet, which White said he fired as soon as he got in here, smashed the tube of the dictaphone and crashed into the wall *more than a full six feet away from the window where the judge was standing.* Now this is incredible. It cannot be believed that even the worst revolver shot, even one who did not know a pistol from a cabbage, could stand only fifteen feet away from the target and yet miss the target by six feet.

"And what follows? Outside the window—on a direct line with the window—there is a tree; and in this tree—also in a direct line with the window—we find embedded a bullet from the .32 Browning automatic. In other words, this Browning bullet is in precisely the position we should have expected if White, coming into the room, had fired his first shot from the Browning .32. He missed the judge, though he came close; the bullet went through the open window and struck the tree.

"It is therefore plain that his first shot must have been fired from the Browning. As a clinching proof, we note that his story about the mysterious shot from the Browning—the second shot, fired from behind him and to the right, over in the corner by the yellow vase—is a manifest lie. The bullet could not have first described a curve, then gone out the window, and then entered the tree in a straight line. More! Not only was it a lie, but obviously he knew it was a lie.

"So the course of events was like this. He entered this room, he fired with the Browning .32, and he missed. (I will presently show you why he missed.) White then ran across the room, dropped the Browning into the vase, ran back, and *then* he fired the second shot with the Ivor-Johnson .38. Do you care for proof? My own officers can supply it. This morning I conducted a little experiment here. I stood over there in the corner by the vase and I myself fired a shot. I was not aiming at anything in particular, except in the direction of the wall between the windows. It struck the wall between the windows, a foot to the right of the open one. Had I been farther out into the room, more on a line with the table, my bullet would have struck exactly the spot where the Ivor-Johnson .38 shot went into the wall. In other words, where White was standing when he pulled a trigger for the second time."

Sir Andrew Travers pushed to the forefront.

"Are you saying, my friend, that White fired both the shots after all? But that's insane! You said so yourself. Why did he do it in a room that was sealed up? What was the sense of it?"

"I will try to show you," said Colonel Marquis, "for it was one of the most ingenious tricks I know of. But it went wrong. . . .

"The next bit of evidence to claim our attention is a set of well-stamped footprints, made by a man's number-ten shoe, crossing a ten-foot flowerbed outside the west windows. All these tracks led away from the window. We were meant to believe that someone in a number-ten shoe (which was larger than White's) had got out of that window and run away. But it was impossible for anybody to have got out there, due to the condition of the window sashes. So the footprints were obviously faked.

Yet, if they were faked, how did the person who made them get *across* that big stretch of flowerbed in order to make a line of tracks coming away from the window? It was even asked whether he flew. And the person must have done just that. In other words, he jumped. He jumped across, and walked back, thus faking his evidence an hour or so before the judge was actually killed. There is only one person in the case who is capable of making a leap like that: Gabriel White, who, as Mr. Penney told us this afternoon, holds an unbeaten record for the broadjump at Oxford. . . .

"And next? Next we hear from Robinson of a sudden and energetic plan, originating in the judge's household not long ago, to open up those windows so that they shall be like ordinary windows. All things—you begin to see—center round a phantom murderer who shall kill the judge and escape from that window, leaving his tracks and his gun behind.

"White's plan was just this. He meant to kill Mr. Justice Mortlake, but he is clever enough—kindly look at him now—to know that, no matter how the judge died, he is bound to be suspected. I do not need to review the case to convince you of that. He cannot possibly commit a murder where *no* suspicion will attach to him. If he tries some subtle trick to keep out of the limelight and the public eye, they will nail him. But he can commit a murder for which there will not be enough evidence to convict him, and of which most people will believe him innocent.

"He can—with the assistance of an accomplice in Mortlake's household—obtain possession of a Browning pistol, any pistol, belonging to some friend of the family. It does not really matter what pistol, so long as it can be shown that *White* could not have stolen it. Very well. He can make wild threats against the judge in the hearing of anyone. He can with blatant swagger and obviousness purchase a .38 caliber gun from a pawnbroker whom he knows to be a copper's nark—and who, he also knows quite well, will immediately report it. He can also procure, from any source you like, a pair of number-ten shoes which are nothing like his own shoes. He can get, from his accomplice, a duplicate key to the tradesmen's entrance which will enable him to enter the grounds when he likes. Finally, he can get his accomplice's word that the rusted windows and shutters are now in ordinary working order.

"Then he is ready. On any given afternoon, when the judge is alone in the pavilion, he can get into the grounds an hour or so before he means to make his attack. He can implant his footprints. He can give the shutters a pull to make sure they are in order. Then he can alarm the household— get them to chase him—get any convenient witnesses on his trail. He can rush into the pavilion, as though wildly, a long distance ahead of them. The shoes in which he made the tracks are now buried somewhere in the grounds; he wears his own shoes. He can lock the door. He can fire two shots; one a miss, one killing his victim. He can fling up one of the west windows and toss the Browning outside. When the pursuers arrive, there he is: a man who has tried to murder—*and failed.* A real murder, instead, has been done by someone who fired from a window, and jumped out; someone who wore shoes that are not White's shoes and carried a gun White could not have carried. In short, White was blackening his character in order to whitewash it. He was admitting he intended murder; at the same time he was showing he could not have done it. He was creating a phantom. He would not get off scot-free; he was in danger; but he could not possibly be convicted, because in any court there would loom large that horned and devilish discomfort known as the Reasonable Doubt. His deliberate walking into the hangman's noose was the only sure way of making certain it never tightened round his neck."

Page turned round toward White; and again there was a subtle alteration on the young man's face. Though the same ugliness still moved behind the eyes, his handsome face had almost a smile of urbanity and charm. He had drawn himself upright.

"There is still a reasonable doubt, my dear old chap," said Lord Edward Whiteford lightly. "I didn't kill him, you know."

For some reason that lightness was more freezing than anything that had gone before. In the silence Penney spoke snuffily:

"I warned you, Mr. Assistant Commissioner. I told you what he was like."

"Look here, Marquis, I am trying to keep my head," thundered Travers. "But I don't see this. Even if this is true, *how did the real murderer get out of the room?* We're as badly off as we were before. And why was White such an ass, or his accomplice such an ass, as to go through with the old scheme when the windows *hadn't* been altered? You say Carolyn is the murderer. I can't believe that—"

"Many thanks, Andrew," interrupted Carolyn mockingly. She shifted her position and walked forward with quick jerky steps. It was clear that she had not got herself completely under control: she could master her intellect, but she could not master her rage, which was a rage at all the world.

"Don't let them force you into admitting anything, Gabriel," she went on almost sweetly. "They are bluffing, you know. They haven't a scrap of real evidence against me. They accuse me of killing father, but they don't seem to realize that in order to do it I must have made myself invisible; and they won't dare go to a jury unless they can show how father really was killed. Besides, they'll make fools of themselves as it is. You spotted it, Andrew. If Gabriel and I were concerned in any such wild scheme, we should have known the windows were sealed up—"

A hoarse voice said:

"Miss Carolyn, I lied to you."

Robinson had taken off his hat at last and he was kneading it in his hands. He continued: "I lied to you. I been on hot bricks all day; I been nearly crazy; but, so help me, I'm glad now I lied to you. You—the tall gent—you, sir: a couple of nights ago she gave me a five-pun note if I would sneak down here and put one of them windows right, so it could be opened, anyhow. And I went. But the judge caught me. And he said he'd skin me. And I went back to you; and I wanted that five-pun note; so I lied and said I'd fixed the window. I know I swore on the Bible to you I'd never mention it to anybody, and you said I wouldn't be believed if I told it, but I ain't going to be hanged for anybody. . . ."

*"Catch her, Page,"* snapped Marquis.

But, though Carolyn Mortlake sprang at him, it was not necessary to restrain her. She turned round to face them with a smiling calmness.

"Go on," she said.

"You and White planned this together, then," said Colonel Marquis. "I think you hated the judge almost as much as he did: his every mannerism, his very mildness. Also, I am inclined to believe you were getting into desperate straits over your earlier affair with Ralph Stratfield the blackmailer. If your father ever heard of that, you would be unlikely to get a penny under the will. And you needed money for your various fancy men like Stratfield—and Gabriel White.

"Of course, it was plain from the start that White had an accomplice here in the house. He could not have known so much, followed so much, got so much, learned so much unless that were so. It was also clear that his accomplice was a woman. The case had what Inspector Page described as a woman's touch in it: and no other possible accomplice in the house had any adequate motive except yourself—and your sister. That, I admit, bothered me. I did not know which of you it was. I was inclined to suspect Ida, until it became obvious that all these apparent attempts to throw suspicion on you were really intended against her and one other. . . . What size shoes do you wear, Travers?"

"Tens," said Sir Andrew grimly. "I'm rather bulky, as you've noticed."

"Yes. And it was your pistol; above all, it was your known afternoon to visit the judge. That was why White delayed so long, hoping you would appear. You are—um—associated with Ida Mortlake. Yes; you were the combination intended to bear the suspicion, you two.

"In the scheme as planned, Carolyn Mortlake was to have no hand in the actual murder. But she must have an alibi. For they were going to create a mystery, you see. Anybody might be suspected in addition to Travers and they must keep their own skirts absolutely clean. Hence the trick: 'Ralph Stratfield' was to be used as a blind, in a brilliant alibi which was all the more strong for being a discreditable alibi. Gabriel White should put through a phone call to the house, saying to go to such-and-such an (imaginary) address and ask for a letter. You, Carolyn Mortlake, *were really intended to go.* It was an ingenious sham plot: there was no such address, and you and White knew it; but it would serve more strikingly to call attention to you later, when you wandered up and down a street for the inspection of later witnesses, and had an alibi for half an hour in any direction, no matter what time White should kill the judge. It would, in other words, give you an excuse for wandering all over the place under the eyes of certain witnesses. Also, you were to refuse to answer any questions about it: knowing quite well that the police would find it and that the invaluable Millie Reilly, the maid, was listening in to all phone conversations. She would report it. You could afford to have the apparent truth, the 'alibi,' dragged out of you. It was exactly like White's plan: you were blackening your character in order to whitewash it.

"But you did not go to Hastings Street after all." Marquis stopped. He looked at her curiously, almost gently; then he nodded toward White. "You are very much in love with him, aren't you?"

"Whether I am or not," she told him, "is none of your damned business and has no connection with this case."

She was pale nevertheless. What puzzled Page throughout this was the gentle, aloof, almost indifferent air of Gabriel White himself, who had none of the bounce or fire which had characterized him in the morning. He stood far away on a polar star.

"Yes," Colonel Marquis said sharply, "it has a great deal of connection with the matter. You were afraid for him. You thought him, and you think him, weak. You were afraid he would lose his nerve; or that he would grow flurried and bungle the business. And above all you were afraid—fiercely afraid—*for* him, because you love him. You wished to remain behind here. Yet you are, I venture to think, a cold-hearted young devil, almost as cold-hearted as that smirking Adonis there. And yet you wanted that alibi. And the opportunity you wanted came along and knocked at your door yesterday afternoon: for you interviewed a batch of applicants for the maid's position—?"

"Well?"

"And one of them looked like you," said the Assistant Commissioner. He glanced at Page. "Surely you noticed it, Inspector, in Sara Samuels? The short, plump figure, the dark good looks? She wasn't by any means a double, but she was near enough for the purpose. Suppose the Samuels girl were sent to Hastings Street? It was a dark, rainy day; the girl could put her coat collar up, as she was instructed; and to a casual witness she would later appear to *be* Carolyn Mortlake. It might be a case of 'Oh, you badly want a job, do you? Then I'll test you. Go to Hastings Street—' and the rest of it—'otherwise you get no job.' The girl would agree. You, Carolyn Mortlake, might even make her a present of some of your own clothes and tell her to wear them. When Sara Samuels left the grounds, didn't Robinson tell us she was carrying a parcel?

"If later the Samuels girl came to suspect something . . . well, you weren't much afraid: you have great faith in the power of blackmail and of saying 'You daren't speak now; they'd arrest you.' But it was unlikely the Samuels girl ever would come into it. She was not to take over her job until next month. There was absolutely no reason why the police should think of her at all.

"And there was your plot, all cooked up in ten minutes. You could remain behind now—and even kill the old man yourself if White wavered.

"That, I think, was why you went down to the pavilion before you ostensibly 'left' the grounds. It wasn't that you wanted money. But you did want the gun in your father's desk. To get it without his knowing might have been difficult. But you yourself, unfortunately, gave a clue as to how you might have stolen it, when you were so eager to throw suspicion toward Sir Andrew Travers by stressing the point of his being expected there. You mentioned to your father that the electric fire wasn't turned on in the living room; and that it would be freezing cold, and that the tea things were not set out. We have heard from others about his extremely finicky nature and how he would not allow others to touch things he manipulated himself. He would, to prevent your doing it, go into the living room, turn on the fire, and set out the kettle. In his absence you, in this room, would steal the Erckmann air pistol out of the drawer.

"I don't know whether it occurred to you to shoot him through the heart then and there, and so prevent White's bungling. But you realized the chances against you and you were wise enough not to do it. In one place you erred: you forgot to look closely at the west window, to make sure Robinson had repaired it as he had sworn: but I suppose you couldn't do it without being seen by your father. Well, you left the grounds after that.

"Meantime, White is talking to your sister at a teashop. He didn't want to see her, really; it was a bad chance meeting; but since it couldn't be avoided, he tried to pile it on thickly by raving out threats against your father so as to strengthen his position. But, unfortunately, he went too far. He scared her. He scared her to such an extent that when she went home, she phoned the police. You two conspirators did not want the police—emphatically not; it was too dangerous. White wanted to run into that pavilion pursued by a servant, or seen by a few servants; no more.

"When Ida had gone home, White followed and let himself in through the tradesmen's entrance with the duplicate key. It was providential foresight to have had that key, for he couldn't have known in the ordinary way that Ida would order the gate locked. By the way, my friend White: you told a foolish lie when you said you got into the grounds in her car. That was not only foolish, it was unnecessary. And I am tolerably sure it was done to direct attention towards her, making us wonder just how innocent she might have been in the rest of it.

"For consider—I am still following you, White—what you did then. Once in the grounds you set about prowling round the pavilion. You made your tracks. When you touched the shutters of the west window they still seemed tolerably solid: which bothered you. You went round and threw a pebble at one of the front windows, so as to draw the judge and Penney (who was with him then) to the front of the pavilion. And then you would be able to get a closer look at the shutters on the west window. Unfortunately, the judge only opened the front window and looked out; you didn't draw him away at all. But you thought, as Carolyn had assured you on Robinson's word, that the west window would open easily from inside.

"Presently you went to the house. In the yarn you told us there was one truth: you did get into the house through a side window, after a long failure to penetrate anywhere else. The purpose was to appear suddenly in the house before the servants; to run out pursued by the redoubtable Davies; to be seen lurking and dashing, and leave a trail to the pavilion. But—when you got through a window at twenty minutes past five—you heard a terrible thing. You heard Ida Mortlake talking to the butler. I say, Davies: in that conversation did Miss Mortlake tell you anything else besides the fact that the judge was taking tea at the pavilion?"

Davies nodded glumly.

"Yes, sir. She said not to be alarmed if I saw any policemen on the grounds. She said she had telephoned for them. I already knew it, as a matter of fact. Millie heard her on the phone extension."

Colonel Marquis snapped his fingers. "Good! Now see White's position. He is up in the air. He is wild. He doesn't want the police or he may lose his nerve. Or will he? He climbs out of the window and stands in the rain wondering like hell. (Yes, I saw you flinch then. You were frightened silly, weren't you?) And White omitted to tell us about that hiatus of ten minutes next day; he placed the conversation at close on half-past five, thereby neatly throwing suspicion on Ida Mortlake when we learned the real time of it. Thus he stands in the rain, and finally he goes to the pavilion, still wild and weak and undecided. But thunder and lightning inspired him and he makes up his mind to be a god. He makes up his mind to kill the damned judge in front of all the police in the world . . . just as lightning shows him two policemen in the path. . . .

"But," snapped Marquis grimly, "let's not forget Miss Carolyn Mortlake, for hers is now the most important part in the story.

"She has come back into the grounds, unknown to White. (She was almost locked out unexpectedly; and, if White hadn't conveniently left the tradesmen's entrance unlocked when *he* went through, she wouldn't have got in at all.) She is watching, and I am inclined to think she is praying a little. And what does she hear? At close on half-past five, near the lodge gates, she hears Robinson arguing with a couple of police officers who have just arrived.

"This must seem like the end. She runs back towards the pavilion before they can get there. There are trees round that pavilion. There is one particular tree, a dozen or more feet out from one of the front windows, and she hides behind that. And she sees two things in the lightning —the policemen running for the pavilion and a distracted Gabriel White running for it ahead of them.

"There is now no question about worrying whether he might lose his nerve; she *knows* he has lost his nerve and will smash all their plans like china, if he goes ahead now. The worst of it is that she cannot stop him. He will be caught and hanged for a certainty. Is there any way she can keep him from being caught for a murder which has now become a foolery? There is none . . . but she is given one.

"She is now in front of the tree, between it and the pavilion, hidden from Page's view by the bole of the tree. But at Sergeant Borden's yell the providential occurs. The curtains are pushed back. Mr. Justice Mortlake opens the window halfway, thrusts out his head, and shouts. There is her stepfather, facing her ten feet away, illuminated like a target in the window. There is one thing, my lads, you have forgotten. If a Browning .32 bullet can fly out of an open window, *an Erckmann air-pistol bullet can fly in!*

"She lifts the Erckmann and fires. There is no flash. There is no noise, nothing which would not be drowned out easily by the storm. The Erckmann bullet was in Mr. Justice Mortlake's chest about one second before Gabriel White threw open the door of the study. She has only to draw to the other side of the tree and the inspector will not see her as he runs past."

Sir Andrew Travers put out his hand like a man signaling a bus.

"You mean that it was the first shot? That both the other two were fired afterward?"

"Of course I do. And now you will understand. Struck in the chest, he barely knows what has happened when White bursts into the room. Re-

member, the doctor told us that death was not instantaneous; that Mortlake could have taken several steps, or spoken, before he collapsed. He
turned round when he heard White enter. And then . . .

"You will be able to see what turned our friend White witless and
inhuman, and why he had on his face an expression of bewilderment
which no actor could produce. White lifted the Browning and fired; but
on the instant he fired or even before, his victim took a few sideways steps
and fell across the writing table. Well, has he shot the judge or hasn't he?
What is more, he has no time. He has forgotten that window. He has
bolted the door, but now they may be in and catch him before he can
make his second-to-second plans. He runs to the window to throw out
the Browning. And the universe collapses, for the window will not budge.
There is only one thing he can do; he simply drops the Browning, and it
goes into the vase. Now all he wants to do is strike back, for he hears
Page's footsteps within ten paces of the window. He swings round with
the .38 revolver and fires blindly again. Was it with the intention of
completing his story and his plan somehow? Yes. For, whatever happens,
he has got to stick to his story. The worst and most devilish point is this:
he does not really know whether he has killed the judge. He does not
know it until this morning.

"But now you will be able to see why Inspector Page, running for that
window, swore no bullet could have been fired past him into the tree, or
he would have heard signs of it. It was because the bullet which struck
the tree was the first of the two fired by White, and was fired when the
Inspector was seventy feet away from the tree. You also see why Page
saw no woman or no footprints. She had already run away. But she came
back, when he had got through the window. She hid behind the tree, and
peered round it, in order to get a direct view into the room. That was
how she slipped—you noticed the blurred toeprint on one shoe—and
planted that smashing heavy footprint (all unknowingly) in the soft soil.
It is a great irony, gentlemen. For that was a perfectly genuine footprint.
We must assume that she remembered it and destroyed the slippers afterwards.

"We must assume many things, I think, until I prove them in the case
of Sara Samuels. When you went out this afternoon, Miss Mortlake, did
you see the Samuels girl on her way here? Did you realize that she knew
the trap alibi she had fallen into and that she was coming here to betray
you? Did you dodge here ahead of her, through that invaluable tradesmen's entrance now unlocked? Did you get into the house unobserved
and find the knife and the hammer? Did you wish to make her un-
recognizable, so that it should never be observed that she looked like you
and thus betray the alibi? Only you had interviewed her, you know, and
Robinson had no good description. It was blind panic. You little devil, it

was murderous panic. But at least you did not err on the side of over-subtlety—as you have done ever since you planted that air pistol in your own bureau drawer, and so conveniently made out that your sister was trying to throw suspicion on you."

Carolyn Mortlake opened and shut her hands. She remained under the brilliant light by the table; but abruptly she flung round toward White. She did not scream, because her voice was very low, but her words had the effect of a scream of panic.

"Aren't you going to do anything?" she cried to White. "Aren't you going to say anything? Deny it? Do something? Are you a man? Don't stand there like a dummy. For God's sake, don't stand there smirking. They haven't got any evidence. They're bluffing. There's not one piece of real evidence in anything he's said. If—"

White spoke in such a cool, detached voice that it was like a physical chill on the rest of them.

"Terribly sorry, old girl," he said, with a grotesque return of the old-school-tie; "but there really isn't much I can say, is there?"

She stared at him.

"After all, you know, that attack on the girl—that was a nasty bit of work," he went on, frowning. "I couldn't be expected to support that. It's like this. Rotten bad luck for you, but I'm afraid I shall have to save my own skin. *Sauve qui peut,* you know. I didn't commit the murder. Under the circumstances I'm afraid I shall have to turn King's evidence. I must tell them I saw you shoot the old boy through the window; it can't hurt you any more than their own evidence, now that the murder's out, and it may do me a bit of good. Sorry, old girl; there it is."

He adjusted his shabby coat, looked at her with great charm, and was agreeable. Page, as well as many another there, was so staggered that he could not speak or even think. Carolyn Mortlake did not speak. She remained looking at him curiously. It was only when they took her away that she began to sob.

"So," said Colonel Marquis formally, "you saw her fire the shot, I take it?"

"I did. No doubt about that."

"You make that statement of your own free will, knowing that it will be taken down in writing and may be used as evidence?"

"I do," said White with the air of a martyr. "Rotten bad luck for her, but what can I do? How does one go about turning King's evidence?"

"I am happy to say," roared Colonel Marquis, suddenly rising to his full height, "that you can't. Making a statement like that will no more save your neck than it saved William Henry Kennedy's in 1928. You'll hang, my lad, you'll hang by the neck until you are dead; and if the hangman kicks your behind all the way to the gallows, I can't say it will ever weigh very heavily on my conscience."

* * *

Colonel Marquis sat at the writing table under the dragon lamp. He looked pale and tired and he smoked a cigarette as though it were taste-less. In the room now there were left only Ida Mortlake, Sir Andrew Travers, and Page busy at his notebook.

"Sir," said Travers in his most formal fashion, "my congratulations."

Marquis gave him a crooked grin. "There is one thing," he said, "on which you can enlighten me. Look here, Travers: why did you tell that idiotic lie about there being no way out of your rooms at the Temple except through the front? No, I'll change the question: what were you really doing at five-thirty yesterday afternoon?"

"At five-thirty yesterday afternoon," Travers replied gravely, "I was talking on the telephone with the Director of Public Prosecutions."

"Telephones!" said Marquis bitterly, striking the desk. Then he looked up with an air of inspiration. "Ha! I see. Yes, of course. You had an absolutely watertight alibi, but you didn't care to use it. You spun out all that cloud of rubbish because—"

"Because I was afraid you suspected Miss Ida Mortlake," said Travers. Page, glancing up, thought that he looked rather a stuffed shirt. "I—hum—there were times when I was afraid she might have been—" He grew honest. "Fair is fair, Marquis. She might have done it, especially as I thought she might have stolen my gun. So I directed your attention towards me. I thought if the hounds kept on my trail for a while, I could devise something for her whether she were guilty or whether she were innocent. I had a quite sound alibi, in case you were in danger of arrest-ing me. You see, I happen to be rather fond of Miss Mortlake."

Ida Mortlake turned up a radiant and lovely face.

*"Oh, Andrew,"* she said—and simpered.

If a hand grenade had come through the window and burst under his chair, Page could not have been more astounded. He could not believe his ears. He looked up from his notebook and stared. In the act of moist-ening his pencil he stared so long that he tasted black lead for an hour afterwards. The sudden gush of those words, no less than the simper, caused a sudden revulsion of feeling to go through him. And it was as though, in his sight, a blurred lens came into focus. He saw Ida Mortlake differently. He compared her with Mary O'Dennistoun of Loughborough Road, Brixton. He thought again. He was glad. He fell to writing busily, and thinking of Mary O'Dennistoun. . . .

"In one way this has been a very remarkable case," said Colonel Mar-quis. "I do not mean that it was exceptionally ingenious in the way of murders, or (heaven knows) that it was exceptionally ingenious in the way of detection. But it has just this point: it upsets a long-established and domineering canon of fiction. Thus. In a story of violence there are two girls. One of these girls seems dark-browed, sour, cold-hearted, and vindictive, with hell in her heart. The other is pink-and-white, golden of hair, innocent of intent, sweet of disposition, and (ahem) vacant of head. Now by the rules of sensational fiction there is only one thing that can happen. At the end of the story it is proved that the sullen brunette, who snarls all the way through, is really a misjudged innocent who wants a lot of children and whose hardboiled worldly airs are a cloak for a modern girl's sweet nature. The baby-faced blonde, on the other hand, will prove to be a raging, spitting demon who has murdered half the community and is only prevented by arrest from murdering the other half. I glorify the high fates, we have here broken that tradition! We have here a dark-browed, sour, cold-hearted girl who really *is* a murderess. We have a rose-leaf, injured, generous innocent who really *is* innocent. Play up, you cads! *Vive le roman policier! Ave Virgo!* Inspector Page, gimme my hat and coat. I want a pint of beer."

# John Dickson Carr

The man many readers think of as the most British of detective story writers was born in Uniontown, Pennsylvania in 1906. After attending Haverford College, Carr went to Paris where, his parents hoped, he would continue his education at the Sorbonne. Instead he became a writer. His first novel, *It Walks By Night*, was published in 1930. Shortly thereafter, Carr married and settled in his wife's native country, England.

The Thirties were a highly prolific period for Carr, who was turning out three to five novels a year. Some of these were published under what became his most famous *nom de plume*, Carter Dickson. He created four of fiction's greatest detectives, Dr. Gideon Fell, Sir Henry Merrivale, Henri Bencolin, and Colonel March.

In 1965 Carr left England and moved to Greenville, South Carolina, where he remained until his death in 1977.

In his lifetime, Carr received the Mystery Writers of America's highest honor, the Grand Master Award, and was one of only two Americans ever admitted into the prestigious Detection Club — among whose other luminaries were Agatha Christie, Dorothy L. Sayers and Margery Allingham. In his famous essay "The Grandest Game in the World," Carr listed the qualities always present in the detective novel at its best: fair play, sound plot construction, and ingenuity. (He added, "Though this quality of ingenuity is not necessary to the detective story as such, you will never find the great masterpiece without it.") That these qualities are prevalent in Carr's work is obvious to his legions of readers. In the words of the great detective novelist-critic Edmund Crispin, "For subtlety, ingenuity, and atmosphere, he was one of the three or four best detective-story writers since Poe that the English language has known."

**Douglas G. Greene** is currently writing the authorized biography of John Dickson Carr. He is a widely recognized expert on crime and mystery fiction, having contributed articles to *The Armchair Detective, The Poisoned Pen, CADS: Crime and Detective Stories, The Baker Street Journal, The Thorndyke File, The Chesterton Review,* and *Critical Survey of Mystery and Detective Fiction.* He graduated from the University of South Florida in 1966, and after earning the degrees of Master of Arts and Doctor of Philosophy from the University of Chicago he joined the faculty of Old Dominion University in Norfolk, Virginia, where he is currently Director of the Institute of Humanities. He has written or edited ten books, ranging from studies of seventeenth-century Britain to bibliographies of L. Frank Baum's Oz books. His most recent work is *The Collected Short Fiction of Ngaio Marsh,* published by International Polygonics.

Dr. Greene is married and has two children (and an uncountable number of books).